THE OFFICER OF DACHAU

A Gripping and Unputdownable WW2 Historical Novel

DORIT JOURNO

Producer & International Distributor
eBookPro Publishing
www.ebook-pro.com

The Officer of Dachau
Dorit Journo
Copyright © 2023 Dorit Journo

All rights reserved; no parts of this book may be reproduced or transmitted in any form or by any means, electronic or mechanical, including photocopying, recording, taping, or by any information retrieval system, without the permission, in writing, of the author.

Translation: Yael Schonfeld Abel
Editing: Elisheva Lahav
Contact: dorit.journo@gmail.com

ISBN 9798867524135

Contents

Author's Note 5

Prologue 7

PART ONE 11

PART TWO 39

PART THREE 81

PART FOUR 189

PART FIVE 281

PART SIX 353

PART SEVEN 375

Author's Note

The 1930s and 1940s were a period that impacted the course of life for humanity as a whole, causing suffering, sickness, loss, disability, ruin, destruction, and—above all—turning people into vicious predators and creating monsters. Was it really possible for humans to eradicate every drop of emotion, even as a result of brainwashing? Was evil innate, acquired, or motivated by self-interest?

I could not be a physical part of that era, as I had not yet been born. I was also precluded from helping in any way in its aftermath, once again due to my young age.

More than six decades later, the only thing I could give of myself was writing about the topic, while identifying, empathizing, and taking a hidden, retroactive part in the annals of the world in general and of Germany in particular during those years—the most horrific, inconceivable years in the history of mankind.

This is a human story in an inhumane period, when rationality ceased to exist and any type of inhumane behavior, even the unimaginable, was possible—a microcosm of the predominant mindset during a truly unique period in time...

Prologue

New York, 1963

John Church strode vigorously down the hospital corridor, a cardboard file containing documents under his arm. He was heading for the office of Dr. Heimann, the oncologist. Church's energetic steps were attempting to camouflage the shiver coursing through his body. He was worried—a lot more worried than he was willing to admit to himself. When he reached the doctor's office, he faced a brown door displaying a sign with a white background and blue lettering:

Dr. Manny Heimann
Oncologist

Church filled his lungs with air and raised his hand to knock on the door.

◆ ◆ ◆

Dr. Heimann sat in his room and waited for the next patient, scheduled for 5:00 p.m. He glanced at the clock on the wall. It was already 5:10. Dr. Heimann did not like tardiness. He himself was naturally punctual—truly pedantic, as people like him were usually described. "You must have inherited that trait from your father," Gertrude would always tell him with a smile.

Suddenly he heard a faint knock on the door.

"Come in," the doctor thundered.

A man of 60 or so, with a striking appearance, walked into the room with tentative steps. He was tall, very handsome, elegantly and meticulously dressed, and enveloped in the fresh scent of cologne.

"Good evening, Dr. Heimann. Sorry I'm late. I apologize," the man said, his voice somewhat hoarse.

"Your apology is accepted, Mr. Church," the doctor said, unable to refrain from glancing at the watch on his left wrist with a somewhat demonstrative gesture. "Come, sit down please."

Church approached the chair pointed to by the doctor and sat down heavily. "I was referred to you by my physician, Dr. Rogers," he said, with no further delay. "He told me that you're the only one who could help me, since you're the best in your field."

"That's very nice to hear," Dr. Heimann replied, "but first of all, of course, I have to understand what we're dealing with."

"Dr. Heimann," Church began to explain, "some time ago, while I was washing my hair, I found an irregular sort of lump behind my right ear. I panicked. That lump hadn't been there previously, or at least I hadn't felt anything until that moment. Since I'd been suffering from frequent headaches, and some nausea as well, I began to suspect that the lump might be related to the pain. The following day, I rushed to see Dr. Rogers and he sent me for all kinds of tests. I've brought all the results with me." Church opened the cardboard folder and extracted a large manila envelope from which he carefully produced some pages secured with a paper clip. "There you are, doctor, please," he said.

Dr. Heimann stared at Church with a look of assessment and then turned to the paperwork before him. He leafed through page after page, his eyes picking up on every detail, until he reached the last one; then he stacked them again, straightened them by vigorously tapping them against the desk, and reattached the paper clip. He placed the tidy pile at the corner of the desk. "Mr. Church," he turned to the patient, "please undress and lie down on the examining table behind the partition. I'd like to examine you, and then we'll discuss your condition."

Church obeyed the doctor, and once he was reclining in his underwear, signaled that he was ready.

Dr. Heimann approached the examining table, shifted the partition behind him, and began the examination. Church's brawny body was full of old scars alongside stiff muscles and prominent veins marking his ankles. The doctor's fingers probed the regions of his body one by one before arriving at his head and then asked the patient to sit up. He moved Church's head, with its golden-silver hair, from side to side, probing for the suspicious lump.

Suddenly, Dr. Heimann spotted a birthmark in the shape of a distorted heart on the nape of the patient's neck, its edges stretching to its left side. His eyes were fixated on the mark and didn't leave it for some time. He continued to probe the lump itself while also examining Church's face from up close.

Dr. Heimann's gaze pierced his patient's eyes, which possessed a distinct, metallic blue-gray hue, and he carefully examined his lips, his prominent cheekbones, the dimple in his chin, and the fine lines marking his face. There was something familiar about that face, and about the man's form as a whole as he sat in his underwear on the pristine examination table. The name John Church meant nothing to Dr. Heimann. He didn't remember ever having known a John Church, unless that wasn't the man's original name. John... Church... John Church... he repeated to himself again and again, still trying to retrieve something from his memory while continuing to palpate Church's head at length.

Suddenly, a shiver ran through Dr. Heimann's body and his throat closed up. He remembered that Church had a slightly odd accent, with an emphatic "R" that wasn't typical in the English language.

It can't be, Heimann thought to himself. *This man named John Church sitting here in front of me can't be the man from back then. It's simply impossible.*

PART ONE

∽ Chapter 1 ∾

Johan was born in Munich in 1903 to Helmut and Beatrice Kirche. Most of his childhood memories were related, in various ways, to sadness and adversity. Beatrice always took on a larger role in providing for the household than Helmut, as Helmut was a sickly, short-tempered, bewildered man who spent most of his days immersed in self-pity. While Beatrice would leave every morning to work as a housekeeper for a wealthy family in the city, spend about eight hours there, and then rush off to a large law office, which she would thoroughly clean, Helmut spent the morning hours wandering the streets. Around noontime, he would return home, curl up in his usual armchair in the parlor, and descend into melancholy rumination born of frustration.

The house had not always been engulfed in gloom. When Johan was about five, his sister was born. The time his mother spent at home after the birth was the most pleasant period he remembered. They were happy. His father helped with childcare while taking on various odd jobs. When the short maternity leave ended, Beatrice was forced to return to her place of employment and Helmut devoted himself completely to taking care of the little girl. Johan experienced the troubling suspicion that his father loved his sister more than he loved him. The father always treated the little one gently, showering her with numerous terms of endearment, while he expected Johan to be a mature boy and respond to his every demand with complete obedience—despite the fact that Johan himself was only a young boy, craving attention of the kind bestowed upon his sister.

When Johan was seven and his sister about two years old, she contracted a severe infection. She had a high fever, her consciousness became hazy, her body limp, and she began to resemble a rag doll. They were told that she had meningitis. In order to try and save her, the parents needed to purchase expensive medication that they couldn't afford. The poor toddler passed away, leaving behind two grief-stricken parents and a confused brother.

From that day on, the situation at home changed beyond recognition. Beatrice and Helmut expressed their terrible sorrow through repeated arguments and mutual accusations. Beatrice had no choice but to calm down over time, while Helmut remained belligerent. He blamed the entire world for the death of his beloved daughter, including himself. If he had been a better provider, he could have saved his baby.

Helmut's health began to suffer, mainly his mental health. He severed his few connections with the people around him, and mostly stayed home, doing nothing. Worst of all, he ignored his son. Life in a household that was filled with bitter tension had an acute effect on the young Johan, whose *joie de vivre* abandoned him almost completely. He had a hard time understanding his father and his irresponsible behavior, since nothing in the world could bring the girl back to life. And what would become of him? Did he—the oldest child—play no part in the life of his alienated, alienating father?

Johan's childhood was characterized by difficulties focused on his marginalized status among his peers. The constantly murky circumstances at home had an effect on him, making him introverted, reticent, and often ill-tempered. It was hard for Johan to connect with other children, although he did his best to succeed at school. He was a lone wolf who seldom spoke, participated, or shared. Ultimately, he managed to forge bonds only with two or three of his classmates. The others found him frightening and preferred to keep their distance.

And yet despite it all, Johan was always meticulous in his attire and with regard to his personal possessions, which were few; due to his diligent, tidy nature, he found it harder and harder to live in his parents' small, packed apartment, which was usually characterized by oppressive disorder. Even when his mother succeeded in tidying up the apartment at night, before going to bed, his messy father would overturn it all in one fell swoop, especially during the outbursts of rage that resulted from his despondent mood. Every day, when Johan returned from school and found his father sitting in the parlor armchair, a lit cigarette in his mouth and the whole apartment reeking of smoke, he was overcome by dejection. The boy nearly stopped communicating with the father once he realized that Helmut had no interest in conversing with him or with anyone other than Beatrice. And when his father talked to his mother, his voice was usually raised in rebuke.

Johan's ears were battered by the endless arguments he heard between his parents, and he would often cover them with his hands and hum a song to himself until the worst was over. The unhealthy relationship forged between them after his sister's death repulsed him immensely. Again and again, he wondered why his mother was so hard on herself, agreeing to continue living in the degrading way she did. It defied all logic for him. Beyond that, he couldn't understand why his father hadn't managed to rehabilitate himself since his sister had died, unlike his mother.

At his young age, Johan couldn't plumb the profound depths of a frustration stemming from guilt, nor understand what took place deep in the hearts of his tormented parents.

Chapter 2

In 1914, when war broke out, pulling more and more countries into its sphere, Johan was 11 years old. Due to his father's fragile health, Helmut wasn't drafted, in contrast to many of the fathers of Johan's classmates and the men in the neighborhood, who were called to report for duty. The streets were filled with men in uniform, their faces reflecting their patriotic pride.

The war years were a time of bitter deprivation for the Kirche family, as they were for many others. Before too long, Beatrice was fired from her job as a cleaner at the law office and her wages as a housekeeper also decreased, along with the reduction of her work hours. Johan had no choice but to come to his mother's aid by offering his services for any task whatsoever. Secretly, Johan despised his father, who was truly mostly useless—both within the household and outside it. Helmut confined himself to the apartment more than ever, as he was ashamed to go out. His head echoed constantly with sounds—some of which were imaginary—of bombing and the thundering of soldiers marching. He was, quite literally, a pathetic creature who was a burden on his wife and son.

It was very difficult for Johan to witness his mother's poverty. He often mused that it would be better if Beatrice left his father, and together mother and son could live a different, more peaceful life, far away from him. But when Johan looked at Helmut—"the head of the family"—who always sat idly in his favorite chair, silent when he was not shouting, Johan also felt some measure of pity for him, beyond his immense contempt. A pathetic, frustrated, helpless creature. Who would take care of him if not his wife? And Beatrice was devoted, with an admirable endurance for suffering. Johan knew she was sacrificing her life for his father, and despite his admiration for her, he found fault with her as well. No one should sacrifice their life for someone else like that, he thought to himself, and certainly not when that other person was a zombie of sorts, hollowly whiling his life away, being a burden on the members of his household, and making their lives miserable.

At this stage in his life, Johan had no idea how many times he would cross paths with people who tended toward sacrifice in general, and particularly those willing to sacrifice their very lives.

And if things weren't tough enough before and during the war, more difficult times awaited Johan and his parents once it was over. But they were already used to adversity. And how was one difficulty worse than another? Apparently, they felt, it was their destiny—to live a life of suffering.

◆◆◆

About a year after the terrible war ended, having sown destruction and brought on great calamity, when Johan was 17, Germany experienced a major financial crisis that primarily and severely harmed the middle and lower classes. Johan quit school, as he had to continue contributing to the household's shaky income, but he was joining the workforce precisely when millions of workers and employees found themselves drowning in massive inflation that surged and peaked in 1921, leaving many unemployed. The value of German currency plummeted in double digits, which resulted in a loss of savings, wage erosion, and unprecedented financial chaos. The main causes for the grave economic situation were the excessive cost of the war and the transition from a wartime economy to one that was pledged to paying compensation to the Allies, in accordance with the Versailles Treaty. Another component of this harsh reality was the thousands of combatants who returned home after the war wanting to join the workforce but finding themselves unemployed, thereby creating plenty of frustration and disappointment, low morale and, of course, exacerbating the country's social problems.

And what did young Johan Kirche have to offer, other than being handsome, impressive, and fashionably dressed? Nothing. After all, he hadn't finished school or managed to acquire a proper profession, and his frustration—like that of many others, including family men and breadwinners—gradually intensified.

As the weeks and months went by, Johan gradually established an autonomous worldview, alongside dreams and desires of his own. He didn't want to resemble his parents in any way, and felt horribly chagrined by what was going on in his country and by the fact that he wasn't given an opportunity to realize his dreams.

By the time he was approaching his nineteenth birthday, the tall, impressively built Johan, a handsome young man with light blond hair and a striking, brawny, masculine appearance, had tried his luck at several odd jobs that were far from being gratifying or profitable. Just as Johan himself had nothing special to offer, the German economy, too, at the time wallowing in a quagmire, had no reasonable jobs to offer someone like Johan. He failed to last for very long at any of the jobs. Despite his elegant appearance, which always left a great impression at prospective places of employment, his employers quickly picked up on his shortcomings. It was soon apparent that the handsome young man with the pleasant demeanor was incapable of building a proper relationship with his colleagues. Wherever he ended up, he would get embroiled in some type of loud argument, and would sometimes even physically threaten a fellow employee who disagreed with his opinions. The extreme discrepancy between his impressive appearance and his unruly behavior would always cause those around him to wonder how a young man with an innocent face, a pleasant expression, and such a sharp, handsome appearance could so quickly turn into a threatening, reckless hooligan. That was Johan's nature and he couldn't control himself, although sometimes he tried. He was contemptuous of junior managers, reacted in an extreme manner to any form of condescension and, most of all, became enraged when he was the subject of gossip, as he knew was often the case.

Due to all this, the employers always preferred to seek out a different employee, someone who was a better fit than Johan Kirche, as the workforce was flooded with job seekers while jobs were few and far between.

∽ Chapter 3 ∾

In 1922, when Johan was 19 years old, his frustration reached unprecedented heights, encompassing immense internal anger at the entire world and its conduct, and mostly at what was taking place in his own country. One fine day, however, was about to provide him with a fitting solution with regard to employment and wages, as well as concerning his complex, multi-layered personality.

Johan happened to run into Herman Sturm, one of his better friends from school, and the two engaged in a genial conversation. Johan was truly happy to see Herman, and in his distress, uncharacteristically revealed his personal problems to his friend, while emphasizing the matter of employment.

"I can't find myself, Herman," he said. "I've been spinning my wheels with no work and with empty pockets for a long time now, and it's driving me crazy. The last thing I need is to ultimately turn out like my father, that crazy bum..." Johan failed to mention that one of the main reasons he could not manage to stay on at the meager positions where he was hired was his own volatile nature.

Herman told Johan that for some time, he had been a part of the National Socialist Party's Sports Division which, about a year ago, had produced a sort of military organization called *Sturmabteilung* (Stormtroopers), or the SA.

"At first," Herman said, "the head of the organization was Emil Moritz. I'm sure you've heard of him, Johan. He's that thug that everyone knows, who's also a watchmaker. You must know him," Herman repeated as he saw Johan's eyes narrowing while he searched his memory. "A short time later, Ulrich Klintzsch was appointed to head the SA, but the top commander is Ernst Röhm," Herman continued elaborating knowledgeably.

At that point, Johan had no connection to politics and was not at all interested in knowing who was running the country and in what manner, or what the main parties were and what their ideological platforms were. All he wanted was for the economic situation to improve, for the great crisis to pass, and to be able to get a good job that would provide him with decent wages and allow him to finally leave his parents' home, which was making him feel increasingly smothered. He was no longer a little boy and now, more than ever, he wanted to build a life of his own. He wouldn't even mind moving to a different city. He would do whatever was required, as long as he could achieve his goal—being independent and able to support himself.

Herman continued to enthusiastically tell Johan about the organization's structure and its worldview. "The main headquarters is in Stuttgart and is in charge of the sub-offices responsible for supplying, funding, and recruiting new members. The organization assists unemployed people like you and like I used to be, to fit into society, and it also recruits army veterans. We undergo military training and become real men. They take care of all our needs. They even gave us uniforms. You'll look great in that brown, ironed uniform, Johan. After all, you like looking nice and neat." He smiled. "I've known you for a while, you know."

Johan didn't try to stop the rush of Herman's speech. He was waiting to hear more. Everything he had heard thus far appealed to him greatly. Herman interpreted Johan's silence as agreement and therefore continued: "Our main role is to protect Adolf Hitler and his National Socialist Party. We get detailed lessons and explanations about our role. Our defense of Hitler includes breaking up demonstrations, rioting in the streets a bit, some violence here and there, all intended to let the public know who's in charge, and the most important part is that we're paid for our services. Believe me, Johan, it doesn't hurt to let the public know who's tidying up all this mess in our country, and as for Hitler, we have to watch over him and protect him from all kind of opponents, snitches, and other criminals, and apparently there's no shortage of those. If you want, I'll make sure to let them know, through my coordinator, that they should take you on. You'd be a great fit, believe me. You'll thank me."

Johan continued staring at Herman. He had taken in everything he was told and was feeling enthusiastic, mostly when he imagined himself in the pressed uniform, imperially imposing order in the streets. "Tell me, Herman, is it like a kind of army? Based on what you said, it really sounds like a sort of internal army, right?"

"Something like that," Herman replied, "but not really. We're more like a militia. We're a group of people that doesn't belong to the country's main army, but we've become our own little army. They wanted us to be a proper military organization, but Hitler objected. He prefers that we continue to focus on what we're doing now. It's more important than being an army, which is what they told us."

"The truth is, Herman, I've never had a real connection to any political matters, but if everything you're saying is true, I'm willing to join, if they'll take me," Johan said. "I actually do think I'm a good fit for roles like that. I'm always being accused of verbal or physical violence anyway, in every job I've had. I'm already desperate, and nothing interests me. Maybe I'll finally find something that suits me, and then I'll also get into politics. Why not? It won't hurt anyone, anyway. How long before I know if I'm in?" he asked, increasingly interested.

"It won't be long," Herman replied. "The organization is constantly taking in more and more members. In a few days, you'll be hearing from me, I promise."

"Herman," Johan persisted, "now that you mention it, why

does Hitler need to be protected all the time? What kind of opponents is he worried about?"

"Believe me, Johan, I really don't know. They're mainly talking about communists, although to this day, I personally haven't encountered any really serious opponents. But it's important to Hitler, and he's certain that there are plenty of people opposing him, with more to come. Our organization, which safeguards him, makes him feel more important. Apparently, if he's concerned, he's got good reasons to be concerned. Who am I to disagree? The important thing is that I belong to a proper organization, that I have an occupation, and that I'm appreciated. I don't really care about the rest. You know what I mean?"

Johan understood Herman's attitude, but didn't quite understand the matter as a whole. He hoped to understand more once he was allowed to join the SA. Unlike Herman, he actually thought it was interesting, and truly wanted to know who Adolf Hitler's potential opponents were, the ones from whom he needed to defend himself by surrounding himself with an organization that served as a kind of personal bodyguard.

The encounter with Herman left Johan with plenty of food for thought. The conversation with his old friend stayed on his mind. Providence had placed Herman in his path precisely now, when he had already lost hope on all fronts. It would be wonderful to be part of a militia like that, with uniforms and roles to fill, while getting paid for it on top of everything. Johan was quite certain he would be invited to join the organization. He would fit in just as well as Herman Sturm or the others whom Herman had told him about.

Several days later, Herman came knocking on Johan's door one evening. Johan, who had not been expecting him, was glad he was still home. He had been on his way out to roam around a bit in order to soothe his unrelenting anger.

"Johan," Herman said, "my coordinator asked that you come

with me. He wants to get to know you in order to see if you would fit in with the organization. Do you think you can come with me now? He's waiting for us at headquarters."

Johan didn't think twice. Herman had come just in time to save him from his feeling of dreariness and from idly and aimlessly walking around in the streets once again.

Johan followed Herman, who led him to an office in the center of the city. Herman said goodbye, claiming he had to rush off to his pursuits. "You'll get along just fine on your own in there," Herman told him. "You're a big boy now, really big," he concluded with a laugh and turned to go.

The coordinator was a serious-looking man whose uniform emphasized his powerful muscles. His rigid face didn't assume even a trace of a smile. He surveyed Johan's frame from head to foot, lingering on his face, then commanded, "Sit down." Johan hurried to obey, out of respect, or fear, or both.

"Sturm asked me to take you in for an interview. He recommended you, and I hope what he said was true. Tell me a little about yourself," the coordinator said brusquely.

Johan told him nearly everything, although he tried to be brief. He wanted to primarily emphasize the matter of wages and his preference for spending his time on important issues. He hoped he would not be asked to answer any political questions or things of that nature, as he had no idea what his reply would be.

Fortunately, he was not asked anything of the sort. The coordinator looked him over again, his gaze lingering and invasive, then told him, "The SA organization was founded out of the Nazi Party, and therefore, if you're allowed to join us, you too will have to adhere to the party's ideological agenda, which supports pan-German nationalism, racism, and mostly antisemitism, anti-liberalism, anti-democracy, and anti-communism."

In the same breath, the coordinator added, "The organization has three clear, main goals.

"First—to protect gatherings of party members from supporters of the republic.

"Second—to disrupt and sabotage the political gatherings of rival parties, while terrorizing these political rivals and even murdering them. And there's no lack of opponents, young man—we stop at nothing to enhance our power." A small shiver ran through Johan's body when he heard this.

"And the third, which is a daily goal and task—to spread fear and terror in the streets while exhibiting military strength. We demand strong discipline and full devotion to the organization while taking care to carry out all orders in the most exacting manner and out of uncompromising loyalty to the party and to the person heading it, our esteemed leader—the one and only Adolf Hitler."

The coordinator caught Johan's gaze, his harsh eyes fixed solemnly on Johan's. He was trying to see past his façade in order to assess the impact of his words on the young man. He then continued, his voice emphatic: "A member of the organization who doesn't follow orders, or violates them in any way, must be punished. If you commit to taking on everything I've explained, you can count yourself among the members of the organization and begin conducting yourself as a soldier starting tomorrow morning."

Johan nodded wordlessly. The coordinator's statements and the way in which they had been conveyed had paralyzed him. It was serious, this whole business, very serious, and he yearned to be a part of such solemn seriousness. He was certain he would no longer find himself scuffling with his superiors, that he would obey instructions and orders, and avoid any sort of violent argument or other unruly behavior outside of the roles with which he would be tasked. He sensed that his days of suffering and frustration were about to come to an end, and he didn't care what his occupation within the organization would be, so long as he himself could belong to an orderly institution. If it was an aggressive and forceful one—even better. That would suit him very well, as for some time he had had enough of the manners and the courtesy he was expected to exhibit within every other framework he had tried to join.

"You're accepted conditionally," the coordinator concluded, invading Johan's volatile thoughts. "We'll watch you and your conduct closely. If you prove yourself, you'll become a permanent member. If you don't—you'll be sent back to where you came from. Report back to me here at headquarters tomorrow morning."

The coordinator rose from his seat and glanced towards the door. He didn't utter a single word of parting. As far as he was concerned, the interview was over, and Johan understood that he must take his leave.

Johan's joy was boundless. All the way home, he hummed a cheerful song. He had finally found a proper occupation. At long last, he would no longer walk around like a man possessed, trying to find another short-term job. From now on he would be among Hitler's informal bodyguards, and he silently thanked his friend Herman again and again.

♦ ♦ ♦

The next morning, Johan reported to the office at headquarters. He was asked to sign several forms that he didn't even bother to read or pore over, and he proudly received an ironed brown uniform. Johan Kirche had become a member—albeit a conditional one for now—of the SA organization. But he was certain that he would pass muster, and that soon his status would be permanent. He felt that his life was about to change completely.

Johan shared his happiness with his mother. Beatrice wasn't really thrilled with this aggressive organization, with its goals and its violent aspect, but she was truly thrilled that the smile she had not seen on her son's face for quite a while had returned to it, and that her Johan was in seventh heaven due to his new occupation and the organization that filled him with confidence. Another thing that greatly eased her mind was that Johan's new occupation would come with some financial compensation. She would no longer be obliged to funnel a portion of the meager wages she had managed to keep bringing home over the years to him as well.

Now that Johan was making a living of sorts, Beatrice could manage the household budget differently. She was lucky to work for an employer who was among the wealthiest people in Munich, and who could still afford to employ a housekeeper despite the financial crisis. It was true that both her working hours and her wages were reduced some time ago, but at least she wasn't unemployed and didn't need to resort to charity. She was grateful for this as well.

Johan did indeed fit in; in fact, he was a very good fit for the organization and soon attained permanent status within it. He fulfilled his assigned tasks as best he could, imposed an iron discipline on himself, and was thrilled every time he was paid for his labor. His connection with Herman deepened, and the two once again became good friends. Johan was assigned to Herman's team, so that whenever they embarked on an assignment, they would do everything together.

The companionship of the SA members satisfied Johan immensely. He put all his faith in Adolf Hitler. For some reason, he felt as if this man—the leader—had a past that resembled his own when it came to the familial aspect. After discovering some important details about Hitler, Johan felt that he could sympathize with him in several regards. Like him, Hitler, too, had not worked at any kind of conventional job other than during his wartime military service, had attained a sense of belonging, and begun to work enthusiastically only after joining the German Workers' Party, whose name he had eventually managed to change to the National Socialist Party, while significantly expanding its membership.

Johan's sympathy for Hitler increased after the first time he witnessed the leader give an assertive, impassioned speech in Munich in September. In this speech, Hitler detailed all the serious problems that the German nation was facing, while pointing an accusatory finger primarily at Judaism and the Jews who were a part of it—the nation's great disaster. This was also the first time Johan had been directly exposed to the concept of "Judaism." And if Hitler was so vociferously negative in his opinion of the Jews, apparently he had good reasons for it, Johan thought to himself. Hitler concluded his fascinating speech with a vitriolic statement: "Extremists must be fought by extremists. In opposing the ills of imperialism, in opposing the plague of the Jews, we must brandish the flame of idealism over our heads. And if others speak of the world and of humanity, we say 'Fatherland'—and only *our* Fatherland."

This somewhat philosophical statement left an intense impression on Johan, as it did on other listeners. Hitler had referred to Judaism as a "plague"—a chilling statement. His mother's employer, Johan knew, was a Jew, and thanks to him, their livelihood had been regularly ensured for years now. Johan had never before considered that the Jewish minority in his country held such crucial influence over various aspects of life, as Hitler had posited in his speech. Now that he had met him face to face, Johan couldn't help but be impressed by Hitler's rhetorical talent and his theatrical, charismatic personality. The occasion moved him greatly, and his admiration for the heroic figure increased. Like many others within the organization and outside it, he foresaw a brilliant future for the man as a leader.

◈ Chapter 4 ◈

It had been almost a year since Johan joined the SA. All in all, life had been good to him, and his activity within the organization also hadn't necessitated too much of a display of force. Everything was flowing along as usual, but the uprising against the government's ineptitude in tackling the crisis and restoring order to the country was gradually expanding. How long was it possible to live in distress, with no end in sight? It was frustrating, and as more and more time elapsed since the end of the war—the initial cause and trigger of the crisis—an increasing number of people began to suffer from emotional problems as well.

Johan did his best to attend Hitler's speeches, which were becoming more frequent, as well as increasingly more exciting, inflammatory, and thrilling, as well as much more convincing. He was aware that most of the people attending these speeches were swept up in the charm of the talented speaker, who promised to bring all manner of miracles to their beloved homeland, alongside actual salvation.

And then whispered rumors began to spread through the organization that Hitler intended to compel the leaders of Bavaria to act against the failing central administration by means of a coup, and that he intended to use the SA's support and help for this purpose. Like the other members, Johan was enthusiastic. Here at last was the worthy action he had been waiting for the entire time, a real operational activity that was sure to have far-reaching consequences. The plan was to take over the Bürgerbräukeller—the large beer hall in Munich—and to declare a coup that would proceed with the support of the Bavarian leadership, and then continue with extensive operational activity.

Johan waited anxiously for the day of the operation, believing that it would prove successful. And indeed, the much-anticipated moment arrived. On the evening of November 8, 1923, in accordance with the plan, Hitler and his SA supporters marched to the assembly space in the beer hall. Hitler stationed himself in the middle of the hall and fired at the ceiling. Chaos broke out among the attendees. Hitler took advantage of the moment of confusion and sharply yelled out, "Silence! The national revolution has begun. No one may leave, and if you don't keep quiet, you'll all be shot. The German government has been removed from office and a new government has been established. We've taken over the police and the army, and the city is now under our control—ruled by the swastika!"[1] The tumult increased, and no one could have known that Hitler's words were a deceptive ploy.

Early the next morning, it was discovered that the Bavarian leaders had reneged on their forced support of the coup, and furthermore had instructed that the party and its Stormtroopers be dismantled.

The disappointed Hitler decided to march through the streets of Munich, hoping this would inspire support for the coup among the public. He began the procession with hundreds of SA members accompanying him, brandishing the party's swastika flag, and calling for an uprising against the central government.

A police battalion blocked the marchers' path and opened fire, creating massive panic and injuring some of the organization's members, including Hitler himself.

The attempted coup ended in humiliating defeat. Johan and his friends, who fled for their lives from the police fire, were shocked and amazed. They had been fiercely anticipating the

---

1   In German, *the hakenkreuz,* or "hooked cross."

mission, pinning their hopes on the belief that as Hitler's prestige increased, so would the organization's value and importance, as when a leader rises to prominence, he usually pulls along everyone else in his wake.

After wandering through the streets of the city in idle frustration, the group dispersed, but not before filling their bellies with ale in order to blunt their disappointment.

"After all the preparations and the faith in our cause and our success, we were really left with our tails between our legs," Johan told Herman. "The last thing I was expecting was for the Bavarians to betray us. Pathetic chickens!"

Johan returned home angry and half-drunk. He found his mother shedding tears. "Mother, what happened? Did you already hear about our failed *putsch* attempt, and that's why you're crying?" he asked with mock innocence.

"I did hear about it," Beatrice replied through her tears. "But that's not why I'm crying. It's not as important to me, this *putsch*, as it is to all of you. I'm much more focused on our livelihood, Johan. Unfortunately, today I encountered inappropriate behavior from my employer."

Johan looked at her, immediately suspicious. "What did that ugly *Jude* do to you? What did he take the liberty of doing to you?" he thundered.

Beatrice was slightly alarmed by her son's tone, but mostly by the way he emphasized the word "Jew," and decided to be sparing in the details she disclosed, once she realized that he wasn't quite sober. His temper was also always more volatile than others,' and therefore it made sense to be cautious in what she said to him.

"He just addressed me in a tone that was different than usual, which included some insinuations that are improper for a relationship between an employer and his employee," she said briefly, swallowing uneasily. She hoped that this would bring the conversation to an end. But Johan, smelling something rotten in the air, continued to interrogate her.

"What do you mean, Mother? Be direct. Was he making a pass at you?" And when Beatrice didn't answer, Johan understood that he was right. "That dirty old man, that despicable Jew. How dare he! After all, you've been working for him for so long. Why would he suddenly remember to humiliate you now? Believe me, Mother! Hitler is right in his negative view of the Jews. He's not the only one—this employer of yours—to behave that way. Lots of Jews think they rule the world and are all-powerful and allow themselves to behave inappropriately. It's truly disgusting."

"Johan, Johan, calm down," Beatrice said. "He didn't try to insult me or humiliate me—quite the contrary. He was very flattering, but it wasn't only about my work. He just got a bit personal." She chuckled in embarrassment.

"And how did the whole thing end?" Johan asked.

"When I continued what I was doing and didn't answer him, he talked a little bit more. Then when I whispered that it was inappropriate and that it would be a shame to ruin the proper relationship between employer and employee, he let it go, and even apologized," Beatrice replied. After witnessing her son's extreme reaction, she didn't dare tell him that her employer had mentioned the fact that she was still employed even during such a turbulent period, and that thanks to him, she continued to make a living, thus implying that she owed him a debt in the personal sphere as well. Their exchange continued for a bit longer and Beatrice said that she would quit her job and was willing to starve rather than compromise her honor. At that point, he did apologize, but the apology wasn't worth much. The damage had already been done, and they came to a wordless agreement to proceed as if nothing had happened. Beatrice was sure that if she told Johan all this, her employer would certainly find himself with a knife in his back. After all, she knew the nature of the organization her son belonged to, and was also well aware of its antisemitic aspect. Now, more than ever, she understood that her son was highly influenced by the views of Hitler's organization when it came to the Jewish issue as well.

Johan was appeased. He didn't feel like continuing this discussion, preferring to think about the glum consequences of the failed coup. As a result, he barricaded himself in his room and didn't emerge until evening. He was deeply distraught that their illustrious leader would now be charged with treason.

Hitler was indeed found guilty, and in April 1924 was sentenced to five years in the fortress-like Landsberg Prison. The sentence was considered political, but he was granted the possibility of early release. Johan was proud to hear that at the trial itself, due to the prevailing support for Hitler's nationalistic ideas and the permission he received to use the court as a stage for political speeches, the leader admitted that he wanted to replace the government. He outlined his ideas while portraying himself as a loyal patriot and depicting the democratic government in Berlin and its founders as traitors. "I alone bear the blame," he declared in court, standing tall before the judges, "but that doesn't make me a criminal. Even if I stand before you today as a revolutionary, it is a revolution against a revolution. There is no such thing as treason against the traitors of 1918."

The next day it was all reported in the newspapers, which publicized Hitler's statements, and to a great extent transformed him from a local rabble-rouser, whose name was largely unknown beyond Munich and its environs, to an esteemed national celebrity. Germany learned to know the man and his ideas, and many grew to admire him. Johan silently thanked the media for doing their leader such a good turn, which also helped his arrest seem less terrible.

In the prison within the fortress to which he was taken, Hitler was assigned a roomy cell and given the right to receive gifts and visitors with no restrictions. Johan and Herman came to visit him. Hitler was happy with each visitor who expressed his sympathy and offered support, and also revealed to his guests that the spacious cell and the relative freedom he enjoyed were inspiring him to write a book of supreme importance. He told them that all his ideas and worldview would be fully detailed in this book, and that anyone who read it would acquire an understanding of all that they had not previously considered.

Johan and Herman were glad to see their esteemed leader in such a good mood. "We're behind you and always will be, since we believe whole-heartedly in your cause and in everything related to your philosophy," they told him, their eyes sparkling.

◆ ◆ ◆

At the end of the year, in December, joy spread throughout the organization and the party when Hitler was released from prison after serving only eight months. The organization's members now knew that their leader would soon be returning to the political scene and would begin rehabilitating everything that had come to a stop on the day he was imprisoned. And the rehabilitation would certainly include the SA, bringing on the arrival of the happy days they had been so patiently awaiting. There were also indications that Germany was emerging from the financial crisis, and the long-suffering citizens dared to heave a sigh of relief.

In contrast to the economic revival, Helmut, Johan's sickly father, appeared to be near death. His condition worsened from day to day, and no one could save him. Helmut Kirche bid farewell to this mortal coil while seated in his usual armchair in the living room, staring out the window, with ashes from his cigarette scattered all over his thighs. Beatrice shed tears aplenty, while Johan could not really understand why she grieved. After all, Helmut had been a burden to her for almost the entire marriage; he was far from being a husband in any sense of the word, and was a constant reminder of the death of their young daughter, for which she silently blamed him in a way of which her son was well aware—if Helmut had been a proper provider, they would have found the money to buy medicine for the poor girl.

"Mother, please tell me why you're crying so much! Don't you think this will bring relief for both you and me? What was the point of Father's pathetic, empty life?"

Beatrice looked at her son with great love and told him, "That's precisely what's grieving me, Johan, because your father sentenced himself to such a meager life, and because I was part of it."

A short time after Hitler was released from prison and returned to the political scene with renewed vigor and open enthusiasm, the Nazi Party held its first gathering since the failed coup. Hitler, who gave an impassioned speech, talked about his future plans. After speaking to the attentive crowd for two hours, the talented orator began to once again level accusations at the government, the Social Democrat Party, the Jews, and the Marxists. This was a *de facto* mantra that characterized all his speeches. The tone of Hitler's speech, and the meaning clearly conveyed by it, caused the government to discipline him and prohibit him from speaking in public for the next two years. For Hitler, this proved to be even more difficult than his period of imprisonment, as most of the party's success stemmed from his ability to deliver speeches and inflame his audience. However, Hitler, who had already begun to reorganize the Nazi Party, was undeterred. He was stronger than ever.

Chapter 5

Johan's life was about to take another turn, one that was much more significant than its predecessor. One day in 1926, he was summoned to a meeting with Joseph Brechtold, one of Hitler's most loyal disciples and the head of the *Schutzstaffel* (Protection Squadron) Unit, or SS, which was currently undergoing reorganization. Johan was familiar with the SS and knew it as the small, elite unit initially formed from within the SA organization and intended to be the personal guard unit protecting Hitler and other senior party members at demonstrations, protests, and other public events, as well as guarding party meetings. Johan respected any leading figure who was close to Hitler in one way or another, and was curious to know what Brechtold wanted from him.

"You're not like most of the SA thugs, who usually perform random acts of violence," Brechtold told him. "You're different. I'm sure you'll be a much better fit for my unit than for the SA. We've been restructuring it for a while, and we're recruiting only the best people. I've conducted several inquiries about you, Kirche. There's a reason I summoned you. Even if the unit isn't too big yet and we have to act discreetly, you'll see that we'll expand in the future and become very important. Our discreet activity is only temporary. After all, we serve as Hitler's personal protection unit and our people are chosen from among the party's elite—the most loyal, talented people, who undergo military-style training and special instruction in maintaining iron discipline. We're strict with regard to tidiness, appearance, absolute loyalty, proper conduct and d-i-s-c-i-p-l-i-n-e," he said in a rigid tone, particularly emphasizing this last word, "and I know that those traits are all very important to you, which is your main distinguishing feature."

Johan looked at Brechtold and did not react. Although he liked his role in the SA, he still strove to make his way up the ranks, and now he was being given an opportunity to do so. If the SA was an organization consisting primarily of unemployed thugs—who were sometimes unnecessarily violent and unruly, as Johan was also aware—and he himself had been chosen to join a more respectable elite unit, why shouldn't he leap aboard the carriage that was racing ahead?

"What do I need to do?" Johan asked, and Brechtold smiled.

"You don't need to do anything. I'll take care of everything. Starting tomorrow, you'll show up here, receive a black cap and tie in addition to the brown uniform, and start your training course. Don't forget, Kirche, we're an elite unit, and our motto is, *"Meine Ehre heißt Treue"* (my honor is loyalty), and I promise you that we'll go far and that all of Germany will know about us and acknowledge our authority."

And so that same day, Johan said goodbye to the SA. Those members who were fond of him were sorry to see him go, while those to whom he posed a threat because he was different were glad to see the last of him. But they were all unanimous in their view that there was something that distinguished Johan Kirche from those around him.

Johan was initiated into the SS unit in a religious-style ceremony that integrated ancient Germanic symbols, pagan myths, and militaristic elements. The ceremony itself was moving, leaving a profound impression on him. Johan soon discerned the difference between the two organizations and now understood what Brechtold had meant. The intellectual and personal level of the handful of members forming this elite unit was incomparable to that of the SA, to which he had belonged only yesterday.

❖ ❖ ❖

Over the next three years, Johan flourished within the ranks of the SS, which had turned into an organization that already consisted of about 280 members, while still not fully meeting Brechtold's aspirations of expansion. During the winter of 1926, Joseph Goebbels was sent to Berlin by Hitler to reorganize the Nazi Party and bring it to the public's awareness. Goebbels organized conventions, gave speeches, and provoked the party's rivals, primarily the Communists. He achieved his aim—party membership was on the rise.

Johan found himself increasingly invested in the party's views, wanting to learn everything about it and its ideology. He studied German politics and exhibited a highly knowledgeable fluency in all its aspects. From a simple man who had not completed his schooling due to family obligations, Johan Kirche became an important figure within the SS. His adherence to the organization's entire code of conduct, accompanied by scrupulous behavior and devotion to the party and its leaders, did not go unnoticed. Both sides benefited from this—Johan garnered recognition and an extreme change of status, while the organization enjoyed the services of an outstanding member who served as a role model to his colleagues.

And if Johan was meticulous, obedient, disciplined, dedicated, and a perfectionist in his work, he sowed his wild oats during his free time. He dated women, partied at every opportunity, and enjoyed every moment. He loved life and life loved him. He didn't become emotionally attached to any of his companions, using the women as playthings and wanting nothing more from them. His activity within the organization was his top priority, while everything else was restricted to his leisure time and intended to sweeten it. The most important woman in his life was his mother, who had grown even more fiercely attached to him since she had been widowed.

❖ ❖ ❖

At the beginning of 1928, Johan was ordered to relocate to Berlin. Munich was no longer the focus of SS activity, mainly after Hitler's speech in Berlin in the summer of 1927. Johan was appointed to join the Berlin-Brandenburg HQ unit and serve as a bodyguard. He welcomed the opportunity to say goodbye to the city of his birth, finally leave his mother's home, and become independent. He loved his mother very much, but since his father's death, although his mother's life had become much easier, she was melancholy. Most of her days were characterized by an oppressive sense of emptiness, and she couldn't determine precisely whether it was caused by her husband's departure from life or because she had sacrificed the best years of her own life for him, although he truly hadn't deserved it.

When Johan told her, with some apprehension, about his plans to leave home, she surprised him by actually encouraging him to go. "This house has never been a source of much joy, Johan. It would be good if you found yourself a happier future elsewhere, and Berlin is a wonderful city, modern and full of life. I'll only be happy if you tell me that your new life there is better and more pleasant."

She helped him pack his possessions and sent him off with a noisy peck on the cheek. "Don't worry about me, Johan. I'll be fine. But don't forget to write to me, you hear? And definitely don't forget me."

Her words caused the tough Johan's blue-gray eyes to well up with tears. No doubt about it—his mother was an admirable woman, even if she had consciously turned herself into a victim.

A small apartment was found for Johan on Wilhelmstrasse, the street where the Reichstag building, an architectural gem, was located. Johan was overjoyed. For a whole year, he maintained his exceptional activity in the organization, all the while continuing to reward himself with various outings and indulgences in his free time.

PART TWO

⁃ Chapter 6 ⁃

It was a particularly cold day in the winter of 1929 when Johan strode down frozen Potsdamer Street after a torrid interlude in a woman's arms. Mentally reliving the wild experience of the previous hour, along with rhythmic walking, he managed to warm his body, but his face remained painfully cold. Suddenly he was assaulted by three brawny men in brown uniforms. They were rivals from the SA; since the SS had risen to power, there was no love lost between the two organizations. One of the SA members, who had recognized Johan, dragged the other two into the violent confrontation. The thugs began to pummel Johan, who single-handedly had to fight off all three of them while sustaining more and more blows. As he tried to fight off his assailants, who were now cursing him as well, he felt a powerful blow to his private parts.

Johan folded where he stood before falling to the sidewalk, hitting his head against it. For a moment he couldn't move, and it was that moment that saved him; his three attackers, apparently frightened by what they had done, decided to flee as fast as they could.

At the time, the street was abandoned. Johan was having a hard time overcoming the pain and remained sprawled over the sidewalk for a while longer. Shivering from the cold and the agony, he made a concerted effort to get up, swaying like a rickety pole when he tried to walk. His clothes were wet and covered in mud, and his privates, which had been in seventh heaven just an hour ago, were now in precisely the opposite condition. Johan looked ahead and realized that, to his great fortune, he was close to Lützow Street, and to Elisabeth Hospital. He began to hobble toward the hospital, battered and bruised, with blood dripping from his forehead.

Johan was led to the surgery department and was asked to wait patiently for the nurse who had been assigned to tend to him. Within several minutes, he was facing a damsel with the face of an angel, all dressed in white, a nurse's cap covering her honey-colored hair. She was holding a medical file in one hand while her emerald eyes surveyed him with smiling empathy. She beckoned him with her finger and led him to the treatment room. Johan followed her with a noticeable limp.

"Yes, sir, and what have we here?" she asked in a serene voice, after helping him sit down.

Johan looked at the immaculately dressed nurse and his heart melted. Her soft gaze and the green of her eyes seemed to caress him and he felt an unfamiliar internal quiver.

"I got hurt during a soccer game," he blurted out with a torturous smile. "I sustained a random, but well-placed kick in the area below my belt," he recounted, somewhat drily, "and because of the terrible pain, I fell onto the grass and my forehead hit a sharp stone." The false details shot out of his mouth one by one. He certainly didn't want to tell this breathtaking beauty in front of him about the actual circumstances that brought him to the hospital.

"An unfortunate sports incident," the nurse said. "That really is some bad luck."

"That's true," Johan said, further elaborating, "Out of that whole grassy field, I had to fall on a stone, apparently to complete the full extent of damage to two strategic places, mostly to a young man's body, *nicht wahr* ("Isn't that so?")?" he concluded in a characteristic tone, his privates still screaming in pain and the wound in his head dripping blood that had already reached the bottom of his cheek.

The nurse gazed at Johan, her eyes full of understanding, and touched his forehead in order to get a better look at the bleeding wound. She managed to ease his grunts and groans, to which he gave free rein—perhaps even excessively so, in her opinion—only after she placed a warm hand on his own. At the time, it was not important to her where and how he had been injured, so long as he received urgent medical treatment. That was what was on her mind, although if she had dedicated another moment of thought to the circumstances of the injury as described by the patient, she would have raised a skeptical eyebrow. Amateur soccer on the grass in the snowy, freezing chill of January?

There was something truly unusual about the suffering young man sitting before her in his grubby clothes. All in all, he seemed handsome, but his features had a certain distinction. His eyes shone with a metallic blue-gray hue, and his pale blond hair stuck out in all directions like a whirlwind, truly disheveled. His cheekbones were prominent and his upper lip was slightly narrow, while the bottom one was fleshier. In the middle of his chin was a small dimple. He had another prominent feature—on the back of his neck was a birthmark in the shape of a distorted heart, its edges stretching to the left side of his neck.

That face was impossible to ignore, and it sank deep into her consciousness. On the one hand, she was impressed by its distinct quality and by the patient's presence in general. On the other hand, something about that distinction left her skeptical, although at the time she couldn't really single out the reason for it. "The doctor will be here soon to assess the nature of the injury and its severity," she said, continuing to comfort him.

The doctor entered the room. He smiled at the nurse and turned to the patient. "Your name, sir?" he asked.

"Johan. Johan Kirche," Johan replied, looking at the nurse.

"I'm Dr. Genscher, and I'll take a look at you now." the doctor said.

Johan implored him to allow the nurse to stay by his side during the examination. He kept hold of her hand and she felt as if she had been grabbed by pincers. It must have been the patient's distress that made him hold on to her so tightly, even somewhat painfully.

Dr. Genscher's medical examination, accompanied by a wink in the nurse's direction, came to an end. "Fräulein Heine," he addressed her, "with regard to the privates, there's nothing to be done. They did sustain a massive blow, but only rest will help there and with the other bruises. As for the head injury, the wound does not require suturing; it's not very deep, although there has been quite a lot of bleeding. Ointment and a bandage will suffice." The doctor gave the nurse precise, detailed orders on how to continue treating the wounded man and quickly left the treatment room.

"Sit here, Herr Kirche. Sit down and relax," she told him in a caressing, confident voice.

"Yes, *Fräulein Schwester* (Sister, Nurse), yes," he replied.

Nurse Heine, who knew her job well, took good care of Johan. Within several minutes, the wound had been cleaned, ointment had been applied, and Johan's forehead had been dressed with a tight, tidy bandage. Fräulein Heine explained what he should do next, when to return to the ward to have the bandage removed, and she started to say goodbye. Johan was not her only patient, of course, and much more work awaited her in the surgery department.

"Herr Kirche, take care of yourself and make sure to keep your forehead clean. Get some proper rest and don't play soccer again for at least a week." She glanced at her medical chart, made some mark in it, and then said, "As I've told you, I'll see you in three days to remove the bandage. That will be on Thursday."

"*Frau Schwester*, what is your first name? Please, I would really like to know. I already heard the doctor address you as 'Fräulein Heine,' but what name precedes the 'Heine?'"

The nurse looked at him and his blue-gray eyes pierced her. His mouth curved in a tiny smile and she felt mesmerized. It was simply impossible to remain indifferent to his smile. She looked down, feeling uneasy, and noticed that Johan had sensed it. After a fraction of a second, she gazed directly at him once more. "My first name is Ilse," she told him softly.

Johan's gaze continued to hold on to her own. After a slight hesitation, he asked, "Perhaps I could invite you for a cup of coffee sometime?"

"First of all, you should recover completely, and then we'll discuss it," she replied, her voice still sounding somewhat faint. She wanted to buy some time, still uncertain whether she wanted a relationship with him beyond that of patient and nurse.

Johan didn't react. His eyes were still boring into hers and she could no longer look at them directly. Once again she looked down.

"You're the nurse," he finally told her. "You determine the rules; you're the knowledgeable one when it comes to injuries. When I come back on Thursday to remove the bandage, we'll go out for coffee at the end of your workday. You're in charge of the medical issue, and I'm in charge of the outing."

He didn't expect an answer, nor did he wait for one. He was simply stating a fact. Next, he blew a kiss at the flustered Ilse and left in an exalted mood, now that his pain had also subsided. His initial limp had also improved and he was walking much more easily.

༴ Chapter 7 ༴

Ilse could not stop thinking about Johan Kirche. Something about him, in addition to his unconventional features, touched her deeply. He was like a child who needed attention. While she tended to his wound, she remembered, he grimaced and she'd been afraid that she'd hurt him. When he maintained the grimace even after she was done, she decided that he simply wanted to evoke her pity. She also felt it when he directed a tentative look at her. *Poor man*, she told herself, *to be injured like that during a silly game of soccer*. Then another thought crossed her mind: *Who plays soccer in the freezing chill of January, when the grass is half-frozen? He must either be a dedicated athlete or an incorrigible lunatic*. And she smiled inwardly, overcome by a wave of affection for her patient.

Ilse continued to arrange the medical instruments and devices in the treatment room, in a supremely orderly manner. She had several more things to do before she went home and could feel her thoughts somewhat interfering with her concentration. She often tended to handsome young patients, but none of them had ever crossed the line between patient and caretaker by asking her out. Johan was really a bold fellow, she chuckled to herself.

Ilse's workday came to an end. It was 4:00 p.m., and outside it was quite dark—a typical winter afternoon. And the winter that year was particularly cold and biting. Ilse took off her white uniform, removed her cap, carefully tidied up her cubby, and got dressed. She looked in the mirror, spruced up her hair, put on some pale lipstick, sprayed herself with a bit of refreshing perfume, and turned to go. She left the hospital grounds and decided to head for her mother's store so they could go home together once the shop closed for the day. Ilse didn't want to return to an empty apartment that afternoon. She sought her mother's company, feeling an inexplicable need to share the events of the day with her. Ilse had treated countless patients over the years, but for some reason tending to Johan Kirche evoked different thoughts within her and she wasn't able to come up with a fitting explanation for it. *A good conversation with Mama is sure to provide me with some answers*, she thought.

Ilse boarded the tram on Lützow Street and after some time arrived at the station on Kurfürstendamm that was close to "Damen" ("Ladies")—Frau Hildegard Heine's clothing store.

"Hello, Mama," Ilse's voice rang out as she entered the store.

"Hello, Ilse," her mother replied from among the hangers that were laden with clothes. Hildegard was busy with a particularly troublesome customer at the time, and knew that Ilse would wait patiently until she was free to talk to her.

"Frau Heine, this feels tight in the bust area," Ilse heard the customer complaining from the depths of the fitting room and watched her mother emerge from between the hangers and rush to take care of the customer.

"There, Frau Stückler, please try on this blouse. I'm sure it will be a better fit," Hildegard said.

Ilse sat next to the counter in the store and looked around. Her eyes spotted her mother's hair, which popped up every time she rose from her kneeling position among the hangers and the shelves.

She adored her mother—an elegant, pretty, hardworking woman who never rested for a moment, her hands always busy. Her mother, who had been widowed at such a young age and successfully raised Ilse, all on her own. Her mother, who gave her so much love and wanted only what was best for her, who saved every penny to provide her with the best life possible, despite the difficult times she had been through.

Above all else, Ilse appreciated her mother's perseverance with regard to her goals, which had allowed her to save a substantial amount of money that was enough to send Ilse to nursing school. Hildegard had made sure that her daughter would have a respectable profession that would provide her with a good, reliable living. It was true that the apparel store was flourishing, but who knew what the future would bring? After all, during the rough periods, customers skimped on buying elegant clothes, especially when the cost of food and other essentials increased and didn't always leave enough for luxuries.

Ilse continued to watch her mother, who was being relentlessly harassed by her problematic, inconsiderate customer, before retreating back into her thoughts. Apparently, the customer knew that Hildegard was infinitely patient when it came to the challenges of finding the proper outfit. It was only after the picky customer had tried on nearly half the items in the store that Hildegard finally managed to find her an article of clothing that both fit her and flattered her.

The satisfied customer's plump face assumed a contented smile. "Frau Heine, you've made me very happy. To tell you the truth, I was beginning to lose hope. I'm very pleased with what you've found for me, and I thank you." She placed several bills in Hildegard's hand, waved goodbye, and left the store. Hildegard turned to look at her daughter. She sighed, then smiled in relief.

"Ilse, it's not always easy for me, you know, mostly when there are customers like Frau Stückler," she said. "How are you, my darling? How was your day at work, and what brought you rushing to the store, unlike your usual habit? Ilse, your cheeks are flushed and you've been sitting in the store long enough to warm up… Ilse?"

Ilse was half-listening to her mother, who had caught her ruminating. "Oh, Mama, I'm sorry, I wasn't quite listening to what you said. I heard you ask how I am. I'm just fine. How was your day?"

Hildegard ignored the question, gazing directly at her daughter. "Ilse, your cheeks are flushed and you don't really seem to be here. Did something happen at work?" she asked once more.

Ilse looked at her, a smile dawning on her face. "Yes, Mama, something happened— something nice, all in all—but you're right. I really am immersed in my thoughts and wasn't focusing on what you were saying."

"And maybe you want to share this nice thing that happened? Maybe both the knight in shining armor and his horse came to be treated at the ward?" She laughed at her own joke, knowing that her daughter would get her intention.

"Mama, you're not far off track. It wasn't actually a horse and not quite a knight who showed up, but I did take care of an injured man who asked me to go out with him."

"Ilse, I'm really glad to hear that. If he's nice and looks good, I hope you didn't turn him down."

"No, Mama, I didn't, but I'm still having some doubts. He simply decided for me, you know what I mean? He didn't even give me the option of responding one way or another."

"Ah, that's a proper man, one who takes the reins. So he actually is a knight in shining armor—riding a horse and holding the reins, too. Come on, Ilse, let's close up here. I'm already tired yet curious to hear the entire story from beginning to end."

Hildegard and Ilse returned the misplaced items to the shelves and surveyed the store to make sure everything was in order; then Hildegard locked the cash register, put on her hat and coat, locked the door, and the two women turned to go. The cold was simply unbearable and Hildegard began to shiver. In contrast, Ilse didn't feel the cold. She was still internally fired up by all the thoughts running through her mind.

Fortunately, the tram came quickly, and after a short ride arrived at Lietzenburger Street, where they lived. Both women decided to postpone Ilse's story until they were at the dinner table.

Together, they prepared a light meal. They didn't like to eat a lot in the evening; cheese or salami sandwiches and some vegetables were quite enough.

As they were appreciating the soothing warmth of home

and savoring dinner and resting after the workday, Ilse told her mother about her experiences that day.

"I don't understand, Ilse, what distinguishes this Johan so much when it comes to his appearance. He sounds like a regular person, despite his coloring, which might be unusual, and his features. A nice fellow who got injured and simply took the initiative to save you from your spinsterhood," Hildegard said with a smile.

"Mama, don't exaggerate. 'Save me from my spinsterhood.' Ha! We haven't even gone out yet and you're already looking for a way to marry me off?" Ilse laughed.

"It wouldn't hurt you to go out a little. All you do is work all day and all you think about is work. It's unfortunate. It really is time to develop a life for yourself outside the hospital. You need friends, boyfriends, outings, some fun. With all due respect to work, there's life beyond it, too. You're too pretty, too wonderful, too talented, and too charming to stay on your own, without anyone but me personally enjoying you. Don't you understand? At long last, you've crossed paths with someone who apparently sees all this beauty in you and wants to enjoy it. I'm sure you'll have a wonderful time with him."

"And what about the fact that something about him makes me slightly uncomfortable, Mama? Doesn't that mean anything?"

"Not at this point. Maybe you're just imagining it because you're nervous, don't you think?"

"Maybe so, and maybe not. I don't know, but I'll give him a chance. He's supposed to come on Thursday to have his bandage removed, and we'll see what happens."

The two women spent the rest of the evening chatting about other topics and then went to bed early. Both were tired, and the warm, clean beds awaiting them were an irresistible temptation.

◆ ◆ ◆

Three days after the incident that resulted in his injuries, Johan returned to the surgery department to have the bandage removed from his forehead. He was no longer limping and his steps were in fact light and energetic as he entered the treatment room. Ilse was glad to see that he was walking more easily, which meant that the pain in his privates was no longer an issue.

"Good afternoon, Herr Kirche," she greeted him. "Please sit down and relax and we'll remove the dressing," she told him.

"Good afternoon to you, too, Fräulein Heine. I'll sit down and relax only if you stop being so formal and call me 'Johan' instead of this 'Herr Kirche.'" Don't you remember? You promised me we'd go out to a café on the day you remove my bandage, *nicht wahr?*"

Ilse looked directly into his blue-gray eyes. She hadn't promised him anything of the sort; he had just decided for her. Did he not remember that, or did he prefer not to remember? She began to handle the bandage and felt Johan's warm breath caressing her face. A shiver ran through her. When the bandage had been removed, Johan shifted restlessly.

"Does it still hurt?" Ilse asked in concern.

"A little," Johan replied, "but I'm a big boy, and can hold it in despite my suffering." He directed a blue-gray wink at her.

Ilse suppressed a smile while placing the dressing she had just removed on a tray, and examining the wound. She cleaned it, checked it again and announced in a pleased, ceremonious voice, "It looks a lot better, Johan. I think you're on your way to a full recovery."

"Johan, you called me Johan—how wonderful!" Johan said with victorious delight. "Now I'll certainly make a swift, complete recovery. And now you should also promise me that you'll come to a café with me today."

"Johan, I only get off work at 4:00."

"I'll wait for you right here. I won't move."

"You can't wait for me here. Come pick me up precisely at

4:00. I'll be ready then." At that moment, Ilse realized that she had consented, and that from that point on, there was no way back.

"Frau Heine, you've made me happy," Johan said, a big grin appearing on his face and warming his metallic eyes. "Happy, that's what you've made me," he reiterated.

"And if I'm calling you Johan, I ask that you call me by first name as well, and not 'Frau Heine,'" Ilse said. "Besides, I'm not a 'Frau' but a 'Fräulein,' right?"

"To me, 'Frau' is the ultimate form of respectful address for a woman," Johan stated with emphatic gallantry. "After all, I understood that you're not married. I also looked at your lovely white hands when you took care of me the first time, and I didn't see a ring on any of your delicate fingers. But due to my great respect for women in the field of medicine, I called you 'Frau,' and from now on I'll call you by your name—Ilse. What a lovely name. Your parents chose a beautiful name for you, and it suits you like an elegant dress on a pretty woman."

Ilse looked down with an embarrassed smile. *He's downright poetic*, she thought to herself. "And now, Johan, you should go. I have a few more things to take care of before the end of the workday. You know, there are a few other patients here who need care. I've devoted far more time to you than is usually allotted to treating a problem like yours."

Offended, Johan grimaced and said, "Don't take care of those others as nicely as you took care of me; I'll get jealous." Immediately he put on a smile, took hold of Ilse's hand, and kissed her fingers. "Thanks to your magic touch, I got better," he whispered to her and hurried off.

Ilse felt a sharp twinge within her. She was excited, and a fierce flush burned in her cheeks. For the first time in her life, she was thrilled by the proximity of a young man, and not only due to what was going on at work. It was a different sensation, full of mystery and very pleasant. It seemed that her mother was right—there was more to life than work, and she was about to get a taste of it this afternoon at the café, alongside the handsome Johan Kirche, with his blue-gray eyes.

◆ ◆ ◆

Johan waited in breathless anticipation for 4:00. He had several more urgent matters to attend to and knew that he would rush to finish everything so that he had time to return home and prepare diligently. He couldn't stop thinking about Ilse. He was bewitched by her charms, amazed by the unique combination of her special, delicate beauty and natural shyness. He had already consorted with quite a few women in the past, but had never before experienced such thrilling excitement. He couldn't even hold back from imagining her in his arms during a wild sexual encounter. She had to be his. He had to have her, whatever it took, and possess her completely. *This time, it will be entirely different*, he thought to himself. *This is the woman I've been waiting for all my life. I feel it. I'm certain of it. It can't be otherwise. Out of the entire nursing staff, she was the one who took on my care. It's the hand of fate that brought her to me.*

And with these sweet thoughts in mind, Johan finished his errands and rushed off to his apartment, where he shaved, showered, dressed carefully, combed his rebellious hair, which always found a way to stick up from his scalp, and massaged his cheeks with a cologne with a woodsy scent, which always appealed to the women with whom he kept company.

Several minutes before 4:00 p.m., Johan stationed himself on the hospital steps, holding a bouquet of flowers. He had decided he would wait for Ilse outside, in some hidden corner, as he was truly eager to observe her, unseen, until she approached him.

At precisely 4:00, Ilse was ready to leave the ward. About 15 minutes earlier, she had spruced up, put on a bit of makeup, sprayed herself lightly with perfume, and glanced at the mirror again and again. She was looking her best. Despite the cold, her cheeks were rosy and her body was ablaze. She wore her warm coat and felt as if she were inside an oven. This was not at all typical of her; she always suffered from the January chill every year. She put the wool hat she so loved over her head. At that moment, the hat felt like a heavy, fire-resistant helmet.

A pleasant internal warmth spread through her. Ilse had to admit to herself that she was a bit too excited. *After all, what's actually happening?* she thought to herself. *I'm simply going to a café with a fellow.* What was with all the noise and the bustle that her body was conveying, and which had subsumed her soul as well? Yet despite these musings, Ilse couldn't control her excitement, which grew exponentially as she descended the hospital steps and her eyes sought out Johan.

Johan saw Ilse from where he stood and a big grin appeared on his face. She was wearing a blue winter coat with a matching hat, her honey-colored hair peeking out beneath its edge. Her eyes, searching for him, made his breath quicken. She looked like a delicate china doll.

Ilse's heart leaped within her when she suddenly spotted the handsome, elegant Johan. He approached her leisurely, holding a colorful bouquet. She stood still and smiled at him. Johan felt his body tense up as he got closer to her. He held himself back from wrapping her in his arms and, beyond that, crushing her in a passionate embrace.

"Good afternoon, Ilse," he greeted her, placing the perfumed flowers in her tentatively extended hands and caressing them at the moment of contact. "I did just what you said and waited for 4:00, when you got off work," he told her tenderly.

"Thank you, Johan. The flowers are really lovely," Ilse said, burying her clear, gentle face in the bouquet and breathing in the wonderful scent emitted by the blossoms. Johan's face assumed a satisfied smile. He took her arm, linked it with his own, and began to walk toward the tram station with her.

"How do you feel?" she asked, in order to camouflage how flustered she felt.

"Couldn't be better, my pretty."

"Where are you taking me?"

"You'll see. And I promise you won't be disappointed."

On the way, Johan treated Ilse with excessive chivalry. He complimented her constantly and she found herself increasingly fired up and thrilled. Beyond this, their conversation was not too lively. Johan, who wanted to maintain a sense of intimacy, didn't want to utter even a single word at the wrong time. He took her to a quiet, cozy café in Potsdamer Platz, led her to a secluded nook, ceremoniously pushed back her chair for her, and helped her take off her coat; only after she sat down and put the bouquet on the far side of the table did he turn to sit down as well. "Here we'll get the most privacy," he told her with a wink.

And until the coffee arrived, along with the *apfelkuchen* (apple cake) he had ordered for both of them, claiming that this café served the best version of this delicacy in the world, they conducted a leisurely conversation.

"Tell me about yourself," Johan said. "You already know enough about me for the time being. Now I want to know everything about you."

Ilse smiled. "I'll tell you everything, Johan," she said, suddenly feeling ready to open up to him. "And if you suddenly get bored while I'm talking, don't hesitate to stop me. Okay?" Before he could respond, she continued, "So, it's like this. I was born in Berlin in 1908 to Hildegard and Manfred Heine. Both of them nurtured me as if I were a princess. My father worked in a large engine factory and my mother was a housewife. They gave me everything, those parents of mine, anything they could afford. When the war broke out, I was only about six years old, and within a short time my father was drafted. Afterwards, my mother and I went through difficult days of suffering and deprivation. My mother made great efforts to protect me from feeling distressed. She had to go out to work, and was hired by a factory that manufactured uniforms. For hours upon hours, she sat there and sewed uniforms. She had never learned to sew, or at least not professionally, but she had a natural affinity for it and got along well with fabrics and needlework."

Ilse smiled and Johan responded with an encouraging smile, waiting for her to continue her story.

"Very fortunately for my mother, I was a considerate and sensitive girl who knew how to make do with little, and I always helped her in any way I could. Most of all, I managed to encourage her during the difficult hours of her loneliness. She has often said that due to the war, I lost nearly all of my childhood and became serious and unusually resilient. My mother would cry a lot during those days, mostly because of my father's absence and her great concern for him, and I always tried to console her."

"An exemplary child—a true *wunderkind* ('wonder kid')," Johan said. "Pretty, and also good and mature—a rare wonder indeed." He smiled once again, and Ilse's cheeks flushed.

"The great crisis arrived," Ilse continued, "when toward the end of the war, we received a telegram that broke the news to my mother that she had been widowed. My father had been killed on the battlefield. It was so sad that for the four years of the war he managed to survive, and it was precisely as the end was near that he lost his life to a horrific war that meant nothing to him, beyond his status as a German who must serve his country. My mother was only 30 when she realized that she and I—who had just turned 10—had been left alone in the world. After a few days of weeping, my mother began to bounce back. She had no choice. She had to be stronger, come to her senses, and be realistic. She had a daughter to raise."

The warm coffee and the cake were served and Ilse paused briefly until the waitress left. Johan stirred sugar into her cup first and then into his own.

"I can understand your mother's sorrow," Johan said, after sipping carefully from his steaming coffee. "It's not easy to be a widow with a young daughter and so much responsibility." He bit into his apple cake with obvious relish.

"My mother decided to open a small clothing store for women with the little money she had," Ilse continued. "She opened 'Damen on Kurfürstendamm,' a tiny, cute store that she runs to this day, and because she wanted to be close to the store, we moved to Lietzenburger Street. Soon she was doing very well and managed to acquire a permanent and quite sizable clientele." Ilse giggled suddenly and Johan looked at her questioningly.

"Johan, you have powdered sugar on your chin," she said, handing him her napkin.

Johan smiled, licked his lips, wiped his chin and said, "Wow, your mother was so brave. She couldn't have chosen a better location for the store. The cake is really excellent, Ilse."

Ilse tasted a tiny morsel of the cake and continued her tale. "My mother really was brave, but before too long things got difficult again. As you remember, following the Versailles Treaty, inflation began to rise steeply, and then came the financial crisis that hurt everyone, including, of course, my mother's livelihood. The public, which was rapidly losing its money and savings, as well as its jobs, mostly lost interest in the clothing she was selling. Bread was obviously much more important. But she didn't despair, hoping the hard days would pass. She took solace in the fact that I continued to go to a good school, that I excelled in my studies, and that she owned the apartment. And then the crisis began to show signs of abating. I was about 17 when life began to smile at everyone again, including us."

"Your mother didn't want to meet a new man who would provide for her?" Johan asked in interest. "Although you didn't mention it, I imagine your mother is a very attractive woman. It's enough to look at her daughter to realize that. Ilse, you're not eating your cake? You've barely tasted it," he said, tucking the last piece into his mouth.

"Yes, yes, I'm eating, although it's a little hard to eat and talk at the same time," she replied jokingly, biting into her cake and immediately wiping the powdered sugar off her lips. "My mother had a few suitors." She smiled with slight embarrassment. "But she rejected them all. She didn't want any sort of relationship with anyone but her customers and me."

"And how did you decide you wanted to be a nurse, in particular?" Johan asked, suddenly grabbing hold of her hand.

"My mother is the one who always directed me toward that profession," she replied, feeling the heat passing from Johan's hand to her own. "She always told me that being a nurse is a good profession, one that only those with a tender, sensitive heart should take on. It's a profession where, every day, you encounter human suffering and do all you can to help, and an occupation that was my calling. You understand, my mother had been truly affected by the war, especially when she saw what happened to the young soldiers, and what the bloody battles had done to them. This damned war left so many disabled people, and people who had been hurt physically and mentally, in its wake."

"I agree with your mother, Ilse. I couldn't imagine you working in a different profession."

Johan's recurring interjections encouraged her to go on with her life story. "And then in 1926," Ilse continued, "I was accepted to the nursing school at Charité Hospital. I excelled in my studies. I really loved learning, and beyond that I loved seeing the gratification it brought my mother. Once I graduated, I started to look for a job. I didn't want to work at Charité. I wanted a change of atmosphere and also to be a little closer to home. So I contacted Elisabeth Hospital, mostly because I knew it had a special policy toward patients who can't afford to pay, who are given medical treatment for free. No one is ever turned away. That tells you something right there, doesn't it?"

"Of course," Johan replied. "Medical care isn't cheap, and, it's very sad to say, but there are quite a few poor people in our city."

"After a short interview, I was hired. I was interviewed by Dr. Genscher, whom you've already met, and who's the deputy director of the hospital, as well as head of the surgery department. Apparently I made a particularly good impression on him."

"Well, Ilse, who wouldn't be impressed by a beautiful young woman, with abundant honey-colored hair, whose green eyes reflect an expression of kindness, who is pleasant, speaks quietly, and probably exhibited a dazzling knowledge and great willingness to take part in the hospital's sacred undertaking, and to do it all professionally, with uncompromising dedication?" Johan said with obvious admiration, causing a ripple of pleasure to shoot through her.

"Thank you, Johan," she whispered, before continuing. "Dr. Genscher assigned me to the surgery department, which is not an easy unit. Everyone who requires surgery, as well as the tough cases, all come to us, and our hands are always full."

"Ilse," Johan smiled again, "if nurses are usually portrayed as angels in immaculate white uniforms, you're a perfect fit for that description."

"Johan, will you stop embarrassing me? I'm nearly done with the story of my life. Soon it will be morning, and I'm still talking and talking."

"Go on, go on," Johan said. "I promise to shut up."

"Within a short time, I knew my mother was right. Being a nurse really does fit me like a glove. I truly love my work and sometimes, Johan, I feel as if I have a calling in this world—the calling of saving the patients from their illnesses and pain. Unfortunately, every day I'm exposed to cases of misery and suffering, and every day I feel myself getting emotionally attached to the patients. I always feel sorry for everyone and want to help them and make them well, and whenever patients don't survive for some reason, I feel as if not enough effort was made on their behalf, and that maybe their lives could still have been extended and they could have been saved."

"Ilse, I did promise to shut up, but I have to tell you something. You have to understand, sweetheart, some things in this world don't depend on you or on the medical staff, however experienced they might be. You can't take on all this responsibility, nor are you expected to. After all, you're doing the best you can, and maybe a lot more than that, too. And ultimately, Ilse, you're not God. Those who are fated to bid farewell to this life must accept the verdict."

"I know, Johan, you're right, but sometimes I have a really hard time with the sights and the awful sounds coming from the throats of those who are suffering, especially when it comes to children. And the hardest part for me is making that emotional distinction between the treatment itself and the patients."

"Ilse, you'll wind up getting hurt if you don't know how to toughen yourself up a bit. You have to tamp down your emotional reactions and your complete devotion to each and every patient."

Ilse remained silent. After all, she was an angel dressed in white, wasn't she? She then decided to wrap things up: "My mother is the most wonderful mother in the world, and I love and appreciate her so much. It's mostly thanks to her that I am where I am. And after her, the most important thing to me, as you already know, is my work at the hospital."

"Ilse, my dear, I truly hope that I'll be the next thing that will be important and precious to you." Johan's metallic blue-gray eyes pierced her own once more, causing a shiver of excitation to run through her.

"Johan," she said, "other than the fact that you like to play soccer in the winter, too, and that you're not careful during the game, letting yourself get hurt easily, and that you live on Wilhelmstrasse, I don't know a thing about you. I still don't know what you do for a living, what you like, what you like less, or who your parents are. Please tell me. And I only found out where you live from filling out your medical form. So to tell the truth, I know next to nothing about you. And here I've gone and told you about everything that's important in my life, including my little history."

Johan's eyes narrowed slightly, his face taking on an inexplicable rigidity. Ilse recoiled somewhat. *Have I hit a nerve here?* she asked herself. She waited patiently for him to reply, but didn't have to wait long. As he spoke, his face softened again.

"Ilse, my pretty, there are things I really don't like to talk about, and there are things I'm not allowed to talk about at the moment, but still, since you're interested in me and my life, I'll tell you only what's essential. I know that with a nature like yours, you'll be understanding."

Ilse nodded, her cheeks flushed. The last thing she wanted was to embarrass this young man or to appear nosy. Maybe he had had a hard life, or undergone unpleasant experiences, and therefore didn't want to discuss them. *It could be anything*, she thought to herself. After all, men, as she had often heard, did not usually talk about themselves openly like women did. They needed to take their time.

"The two of us are like two peas in a pod, Ilse," Johan said now. "My father passed away several years ago from a serious illness. I was born in Munich and moved to Berlin about a year ago. My mother stayed in Munich because of her work. I was very happy to move here. You know, a bit of a change. The atmosphere at home wasn't particularly pleasant and besides, how much longer could I continue living with my mother? For a long time I'd wanted to live on my own and be independent, and my mother was very supportive of that. She is really pleasant and understanding, just the way you described yours." He then switched topics abruptly. "I love… soccer, as you already know. I really like to spend time with my friends. I'm crazy about life in Berlin, I admire the German Army, and, above all, I'm a great believer in Adolf Hitler and his cause. He's the only one who will know how to lead our country to growth and greatness."

Ilse considered the fact that Johan had listed all his hobbies in a single breath, switching from trivial pursuits in the context of his friends and outings to his political and ideological sympathies. There was no connection between the two subjects, and she wondered somewhat about the way he linked two such extremely different topics. So, ultimately, he did know quite well how to talk about himself, being fairly open about it. But amidst all that, she wondered, what couldn't he tell her, as he had noted when he began speaking? After all, he had provided her with information that was quite detailed.

More than anything else, she was confounded by the way he had brought up the army and Hitler. What did they have to do with his passions and his personal preferences? She didn't react. Unlike Johan, she had an aversion to anything related to the military in general, and the German Army in particular, and certainly felt no affinity towards the militant, aggressive Hitler. As far as she was concerned, anything having to do with the army and with Hitler stood for war, while war stood for loss, death, injuries, deprivation, oppression, and, of course, the loss of her father. She had a feeling that if she were to respond callously to Johan's last enthusiastic statements, his reaction wouldn't be a good one, so she changed the subject. She didn't want to be the one pouring cold water on the kind of fiery enthusiasm that his speech had implied.

"You sound like someone who's interested in a wide variety of topics," she said, seemingly supporting his statement. "But I still don't know what you do for a living."

"I work... in the city's Sports Promotion Bureau," he told her and immediately moved on to a different topic. He told her about his school days, chattered about outings in Munich and its environs, and continued on to various current events. Ilse showed great interest in what he had to say. She had no idea that most of what he was telling her was fabricated. Johan had done his homework, and knew exactly what he would tell her—when he would stick to the truth, and when he would not. He was also well aware of why he needed to hide the truth occasionally. He had to make the best possible impression on this wonderful young woman if he wanted their relationship to continue. She was not just some frivolous bit of fluff like the girls he had spent time with until now. She was special and different and therefore he had to treat her differently, with all that that idea implied.

The time flew by quickly and Ilse glanced at her watch. "Johan, I have to go home. It's getting late and my mother will worry," she told him.

"You're not a little girl anymore, Ilse," he replied. "Why should your mother worry about you? I'm sure you told her about our date, right?"

"Yes, I told her, but I never imagined, and I'm sure she didn't either, that we'd be sitting at the café for so long."

"Well, that's a clear indication that we enjoyed ourselves and had a good time, isn't it?"

"Yes, Johan, I really did have a very nice time, but still, it's time to go. This cold winter and the darkness that comes so early make me feel like it's already the middle of the night. Don't you agree?"

"I thought I'd invite you to dinner, too," he told her, "but if you insist on going home, I won't pressure you."

Johan got up and put down some money on the table to pay for the coffee and cake. He helped Ilse put on her coat, unable to hold back from touching her body, seemingly accidentally, and then shrugged on his own coat. Together they left the café, the bouquet encircled in her arm.

"I want to walk you home," he told her.

"There's no need, Johan," she replied. "Just walk me to the tram station. It stops right next to my building. It'll start raining soon, maybe even snowing, and it would be a shame for you to come all the way to my place for no reason, and then have to go back to yours, which is quite nearby." She smiled at him.

Johan didn't argue. He saw that she was determined and didn't want to come off as intimidating. The truth was that the only thing he yearned to do at that moment was engulf her in his arms and not let her go. He did truly want to walk her to her doorstep and say goodbye there, but preferred not to coerce her. *That, too, will come,* he told himself. *In life, you need to be patient.* He waited with Ilse until her tram arrived and then said goodbye to her, but not before venturing to hold her close to his heart and whisper sweet nothings in her ear. Ilse shivered more because of his whispers than because of the fierce chill.

"I'll call you soon," he said. Ilse boarded the tram and waved goodbye. She wanted to be alone. She had a lot to think about after that date. When she arrived home, heavy rain mixed with snowflakes was coming down. She hoped that Johan had managed to make it home as well.

Hildegard was waiting for Ilse in the parlor, eager to hear about her evening.

"Ilse, *liebchen* (sweetheart), you were gone so long!" Hildegard said. "And what a beautiful bouquet. I'm sure you had a good time. Right?"

"Yes, Mama, it was really nice," Ilse said, placing the bouquet in a vase and taking off her coat. She sat down next to her mother and told her about everything she had experienced from the moment she left work at four until the moment she had said goodbye to Johan.

"Mama," Ilse concluded, "he really is nice and I feel that he really likes me, but there's also something, some really small thing about him, that makes me feel uncomfortable. Do you remember when I mentioned it before? Well, spending a long time with him this evening didn't make that feeling go away. On the contrary, it's gotten stronger. I can't explain it, and I can't quite get to the root of it, but still..."

"*Liebchen*, it's only your first date," Hildegard said. "See how it develops and where things go. Be patient. Based on your description, he really does sound like a nice fellow."

Ilse had told her mother everything, but had skipped over the matter of Johan's great admiration for Adolf Hitler. The reason she chose not to mention it was that she had often heard her mother referring to Hitler in a tone that was quite positive, often exhibiting interest in his speeches and their contents.

Ilse remembered clearly that in the winter of 1926, her mother had told her about a political speech she had attended, and how she had listened attentively to a charismatic speaker with black hair, a mustache, and assertive body language, who had spoken with great confidence about the Nazi Party and its goals. *It's not enough for things to get better*, the speaker had said at the time. *We must make sure that a crisis like the major crisis of the Twenties will not recur*, and her mother had thought that it would be absolutely right to do everything possible to bring about a strong, stable economy in Germany. "Even if the major crisis has passed," she said, "who knows what the future holds? And who wants to walk on eggshells, constantly worrying about our livelihood? No one, and certainly not me."

Ilse found Hildegard's interest in politics and strident speeches quite surprising, but she could also understand that it stemmed from the great distress created by the financial crisis—a crisis that had caused many people, including perhaps Johan himself, to cling desperately to hopes and promises, and listen to spirited speeches that offered solutions as well. She also remembered the speech that Hitler had given before 5,000 avid supporters in Berlin in the summer of 1927, because her mother couldn't attend and had expressed her chagrin about it. But the gist of the speech, as later became clear, resembled the previous ones.

As she mulled it over further before she fell asleep, Ilse tended to believe that this was the main source of her uneasy feelings about Johan. Something about his fervent support for

Hitler continued to trouble her. And then, before she fell into sweet slumber, she admitted to herself, in the dark stillness, that all in all Johan had thrilled her, and she had quite fallen in love with him. She then consoled herself—*so what if he loves Hitler? What has that got to do with his relationship with me? Good for him—it's really none of my business.*

∽ Chapter 8 ∾

After the meeting at the café, Johan continued passionately courting Ilse, and she agreed to see him again. Spending time in his company during all these encounters caused her great pleasure. Her life had changed radically. Before each of their dates, she was filled with much excitement. Johan's flattering attention made her see herself in a different—and much more feminine—light, something that she had been missing before the day he first set eyes on her. And since Johan was in no hurry to bring her to his apartment, claiming that it was too run down for the presence of a delicate, elegant woman like her, Ilse invited him to her own home for dinner.

"My mother is really looking forward to getting to know you," she told Johan. "'It's time for your boyfriend to eat a proper home-cooked dinner,' is what she asked me to tell you. Can you come this evening?"

Johan couldn't have been happier. He was curious to meet Hildegard and saw this explicit invitation to dinner as a deepening of his relationship with Ilse, which was becoming more and more serious. "Of course I'll come, *meine liebe* (my love). I'll meet your mother with open arms and a willing stomach." He laughed as he saw an immense smile light up her face.

Hildegard was indeed eager to meet Johan—Ilse's first real, serious boyfriend, with whom her daughter, it appeared, was truly in love.

Johan made a great impression on Hildegard with his smooth elegance, formal manners and demonstrative chivalry. He conducted an open, pleasant conversation with her, complimented her, and, as he had done with Ilse, told her about the deprivations of his early life and about his mother. Hildegard expressed honest sympathy in response, and also truly enjoyed discussing politics with him, a topic he brought up immediately once he had told her the story of his life.

Ilse, who was sitting and merely listening, noticed that Johan had steered the discussion to politics with the same abruptness that had characterized him during their first date at the café. She didn't say a word, of course, her eyes continuing to bounce between him and her mother. Johan exhibited a great deal of knowledge about politics in general and discussed the subject with great passion, something Hildegard found quite odd. What was the source of all his knowledge, and why did he have such an unquenchable need to be so involved in political matters and express his support so avidly? It was true that she could discuss anything at all with Ilse, but this detailed political analysis had nothing to do with her daughter. Hildegard already knew that when Ilse did discuss such matters, it was only in a general way. Her daughter didn't want any further involvement, and she respected this.

◆ ◆ ◆

As time went by, and the meetings with Ilse—some of which took place at her home—increased in number, Johan grew more and more attached to her. He loved her almost madly, and was certain, without a doubt, that she was the woman meant for him. Thoughts of her remained with him throughout the day, and even after all this time he was still gripped by excitement every time they were together. He had never felt this way before, and had never experienced such burning desire for any woman with whom he had spent time.

Unlike his usual strict attitude, which drove him to suppress any display of gratuitous sentimentality, Johan found himself mentioning Ilse to his mother in almost every conversation or letter. He had to share his feelings for Ilse with someone close, and the only close person he knew who would be interested in the subject was his mother. He used words that primarily expressed emotion and much love. Since he had moved to Berlin, he had only been back to see his mother two or three times. He didn't have the time, and when he did, he couldn't find the desire to make the long trip to Munich. And ever since he met Ilse, he wanted to take every opportunity to be with her. At the very least, he appeased his conscience by keeping in touch with his mother continuously, mostly through letters.

Beatrice was happy for him. Her son had reliable employment, he lived in a nice apartment in the pretty, lively, capital city, and now he was also in love with a wonderful girl, as he described her. Beatrice hoped that before too long, Johan would marry Ilse and produce a grandson or granddaughter for her. Secretly, she yearned for a granddaughter—a sweet little girl who would resemble the pretty daughter who was taken from her, leaving a hole in her heart that she knew she would be unable to fill until her last day on earth.

Johan did all he could to appeal to Ilse and cause her love for him to deepen. He was gripped by the feeling that he was more enamored with her than she was with him, which troubled him. He ruthlessly battled the wilder aspect of his nature, and although he often arrived to meet Ilse when he was feeling distraught or angry for some reason or another, he made a major effort to repress it so that she wouldn't notice. Sometimes it was difficult; his demanding occupation caused him quite a bit of stress.

Johan also did his best to hold back when Ilse made him angry in some way or another, such as when she thought about or treated various things in a way that was quite opposed to his own views. It bothered him. He hoped that over time, she would grow closer to him and adopt his opinions. He did believe in uncompromising obedience, as this was the way he had been trained in recent years, but for Ilse's sake—and only for her—he was patient. Once they got married, it would all be different, he thought. She would have to be obedient and adhere to her husband's views. Obedience was above all else—the ultimate value, without which a person was completely worthless.

Johan was mostly put off by their disagreements about political topics. First of all, Ilse didn't like to discuss politics in general, but sometimes he felt the need to discuss the issues that he saw as highly important, mostly due to his work. These conversations would always end with an argument of some sort. Ilse didn't want to compromise when it came to her opinions, and he certainly did not want to relinquish his own. Johan remembered the time when he told Ilse he was among the many people and supporters who attended one of Hitler's incendiary speeches. He mentioned the event with tremendous enthusiasm, his eyes sparkling as he described every detail concerning the speaker and his method of delivery. He had nearly memorized every sentence of the speech, and expressed his full support for every opinion and statement that Hitler had voiced.

"Ilse, what a great, charismatic man he is," he declared repeatedly. "He seems to hypnotize his listeners, and he's right in what he's saying, entirely right. A great many people think so." He saw Ilse shivering again and again in response, and also vividly remembered her reaction: silence. She didn't say a word, and her silence was in fact a full-blown—albeit wordless—admission that she did not agree with a single word he said, which truly frustrated him.

Johan had already gotten to know Ilse's way of keeping quiet when she decided not to continue an argument, or not to start one in the first place. She was very bright and her quiet wisdom also made him inexplicably anxious at times. There was power in Ilse Heine's silence, as he had frequently admitted to himself. At least with Hildegard, he consoled himself, he had uncompromising conversations, which he cherished.

There was one thing that Johan continued to share with neither Ilse nor Hildegard—what exactly it was that he did for a living. His membership in the SS organization and his activity on its behalf remained out of bounds for the Heine women. He had a feeling that it was mostly Ilse who wouldn't really approve—and that was an understatement. He was also very careful not to absent-mindedly appear before them in his uniform. When he was going to see Ilse, he worked out the timing carefully so as not to get caught. Luckily for him, most of his activities were scheduled for times when the two women were at work, or while they were fast asleep at night. He continued to stick to his claim that he worked for the Sports Promotion Bureau. This was the most convenient and reasonable option, as far as he was concerned, and occasionally he would share various small, trivial details about work so as not to ignore the subject completely. After all, Ilse, too, often told him about what was happening at the hospital.

One evening, Johan invited Ilse to his apartment, which he had made sure to clean and tidy up first. Ilse had never been insistent about visiting and was quite understanding, but the time had truly come. "Ilse, we've been together for quite a few weeks now, and it's time you saw where I live, *nicht wahr?*" he said, lobbing the ball to her court.

"I'll be happy to come to your place, Johan," she replied. "It really is time, and I promise you I'm not going to play at being a military inspector while I'm there or, heaven forbid, criticize you in any way. After all, you always claim your apartment is messy and that's why you don't want to have me over. It's such nonsense, really."

And when Ilse entered Johan's apartment and saw that it was in reasonable shape, although rather charmless and obviously ruled by a masculine hand, she realized that Johan had spruced up the apartment for her sake. Her heart smiled within her. As her eyes roamed all around, she felt Johan sticking close behind her. He wrapped his arms around her and brought his mouth to her neck. Her skin prickled. She wanted to turn toward him and felt as if his arms were restraining her. He wouldn't let her move. His grasp became more and more constricting and his gentle kisses suddenly turned into little bites. Ilse asked herself whether this was why he had decided to bring her to his apartment after all this time. But she was not ready for this. Panic began to creep up within her.

"Johan," she whispered, "please, not like this. You're scaring me."

Johan loosened his grip and turned her toward him abruptly. His mouth was on hers, demanding and ravishing, and she felt that he was burning up. His eyes shot out blue-gray sparks and his hair had become more disheveled than ever. "Ilse, I can't hold back anymore," he said, enflamed. "I want you so badly. I have to make you mine. Now." Once again, he grasped her in an aggressive embrace.

"Johan, I'm not ready to go all the way. Please, Johan, understand me. This whole thing is stressful for me. I promise you that very soon we'll get to this, too." She had to buy time. She didn't want him to realize that the way he looked at her, and his reckless behavior, were frightening her.

Johan stopped. He grasped her shoulders and looked directly into her eyes, his breathing heavy. "I'm sorry, my darling. I didn't mean to assault you like that. I simply can't restrain myself anymore. You have to understand. If I frightened you, I'm really sorry. That wasn't my intention. The last thing I want is for you to be afraid of me. I'll wait patiently for the right moment, I promise. All right? Do you forgive me?"

And Ilse nodded and kissed his mouth lightly. The main thing was that, for now, she had managed to prevent him from doing what he so yearned to do. She was no longer truly sure that she was sexually attracted to him.

◆ ◆ ◆

Beyond their disagreements on political topics, which Ilse could choose not to discuss, thus preventing unnecessary arguments, another thing that began to bother her about Johan was his growing obsession with her. After the failed attempt to sleep with her, Ilse felt that Johan was seeking absolute control of her and over her, wanting her to love what he loved, to agree with whatever he said and not to object to anything. She began to feel as if she was losing her identity when she was with him, as well as, much to her chagrin, her personality. She no longer enjoyed his company as she had before. If at first, Johan had done anything he could to ensure that she enjoyed herself by passionately courting her and exhibiting great sensitivity with regard to her and to all her needs, his presence gradually became more dominating and even demanding.

Ilse believed that there was another side to Johan's character that was now being exposed, one that was the opposite of the way he had first portrayed himself. She even began to feel frightened, and, worst of all—threatened. Johan Kirche was increasingly evoking a certain fear within her in his approach to those who didn't think like him, or in a similar manner. She saw this as a red flag that made her want to re-examine their relationship. Until then, she hadn't said a word about it to her mother, but she decided the time had come to tell her about the new feelings that were troubling her.

Hildegard's interpretation of Johan's behavior was actually different than her daughter's. She claimed this was his way of expressing his enormous love for her, by wanting them to fully share everything.

"It's natural, Ilse," Hildegard said, trying to dispel her daughter's apprehensions. "Of course he doesn't want to argue with the woman he loves, and according to what you say, the two of you argue quite a bit. It must create unpleasantness. You have to try and understand him."

"Mama, there's sharing everything out of mutual understanding, and then there's forced sharing," Ilse said. "I expect him to accept the fact that not everyone thinks like he does—including me—and that it's fine. Everyone is entitled to his or her own thoughts. Sometimes he acts like I'm trying to thwart him when I disagree with him, which isn't the case at all. If I respect his opinions, even though I don't agree with all of them, why can't he respect mine?"

Hildegard looked at Ilse softly, stroked her hand and didn't answer. She knew exactly where the root of the problem lay. Unlike her daughter, Hildegard couldn't help but sympathize somewhat with the way Johan had been swept up by the charismatic speaker. After all, she, too, had often listened to some of Hitler's speeches when they were broadcast on the radio, and she certainly understood his listeners' enthusiasm. And she enjoyed her conversations with Johan and their deepening closeness due to the opinions they shared.

As she looked at her silent mother, Ilse's eyes filled with tears, and she couldn't hold back from saying, "Mama, I feel like you agree more and more with Johan's opinions and views. Those views are sometimes so extreme, and I wouldn't want to think that you share them, too."

Hildegard kept her silence and increased her caressing, which had risen to Ilse's face.

Ilse found her mother's silence oppressive. She interpreted it to mean that her beloved mother was conspiring against her with Johan, making Ilse feel both isolated and lonely. It was simply unbearable.

Ilse considered consulting with Dr. Genscher. She saw him as the father figure she had been missing for so long. And since at the time she felt that she could no longer talk to her mother about what was bothering her and leaving her uneasy, she decided to appeal to Dr. Genscher for help.

Ilse briefly described her problem to Dr. Genscher. "My mother's silence was what made me feel worst," she told the doctor, who advised her to try speaking to her mother again.

"She won't be hurt, Ilse. Your mother is a smart, sensitive woman. You're giving both of you short shrift by keeping your true feelings from her. Johan is not the last man on earth, and if he's not your intended, you should say so, rather than repressing it or whitewashing it. Explain it to Frau Heine again, in clear, simple words and without beating around the bush, and you'll see that she'll understand."

At that exact time, suddenly and with no advance notice, Johan came to visit Ilse at the ward. It was around noon and he happened to be in the vicinity of the hospital and wanted to see her. He found her immersed in a conversation with Dr. Genscher and greeted the doctor. Dr. Genscher invited Johan to his office in order to exchange a few words with him, and as he ushered him forward, he glanced swiftly back at Ilse and winked at her.

The conversation flowed in a friendly manner until Johan began, as was his habit, to discuss political matters; as he became more passionate, he suddenly declared emphatically: "Leaders like Hitler are the only ones who can save the world, and should be followed come hell or high water..." He then added ardently, following the same line of thought, "The man is the woman's leader and she should obey him unquestioningly..."

At that, Dr. Genscher appraised Johan, saw the spark in his eyes, nodded noncommittally and realized what had not been explicitly stated. He understood Ilse's concerns more than he had before. Even based on this one initial, brief conversation, his impression of Johan was that he was a disciple of extreme opinions, unwilling to compromise, controlling, and possibly also susceptible to the effects of brainwashing.

After Johan left Dr. Genscher's office—not before shaking his hand—and turned to go, Dr. Genscher returned to Ilse and told her, "He's not for you, Ilse my dear. He's not the one you're intended for," and said no more.

Ilse looked at Dr. Genscher questioningly, and the doctor decided to add a few words after all. "He speaks in elevated language and in words that are not his own, trying to be someone he isn't. Sometimes that can be dangerous."

Ilse didn't need to hear any more. She understood what Dr. Genscher meant. After all, it was exactly the way she felt as well.

∽ Chapter 9 ∾

Ilse was uneasy about talking to her mother and knew exactly why. It was the first time she felt leery of her mother—her own flesh and blood—which only increased her feeling of frustration. The ideological gap between them, which was becoming deeper, made her terribly sad. And then she began to feel as if she were on the precipice of an abyss when Hildegard began to urge her to marry Johan.

"What are you waiting for, *liebchen*? You've been together for a respectable amount of time. He's crazy about you, constantly talks about you and..."

"And about Hitler, right?" Ilse interrupted her mother, deciding at that moment to overcome her fears and follow Dr. Genscher's advice. She lost control of herself and did something she found inexcusable: She raised her voice at her mother. "What does his love for me have to do with his love for Hitler?" she screeched. "What do I have to do with Hitler, that disturbed despot? Can't you see that something's wrong here, Mama? Why is it so important to Johan that I think like him? Why can't he accept the fact that he and I have different views on certain matters? If he really loves me, Mama, he has to show some sensitivity and respect me for my opinions and thoughts, too, without thinking that I'm against him." And when she saw that her mother was looking at her through narrowed eyes and shrugging as if dismissing her statements, Ilse blurted out, with increasing rage, "Mama, I don't want to get married yet, do you understand? And I'm not at all sure that Johan is the right one for me."

Hildegard's mouth opened in amazement.

"Please, Mama." Ilse burst into tears. "You have to understand me. Please! You're my mother. You have to understand that I won't do something that is against my conscience and my views... not... not even for you," she concluded in a hushed voice suffused with tears.

Hildegard was dumbstruck. She felt as if a blade had been thrust deep into her heart. "*Liebchen*, I'm sorry, my darling. I didn't mean to cause you sorrow," she said in a choked-up voice. "After all, you saw how happy I was that you finally found a nice man after being entirely focused on work, the patients, and the staff members for so long. You know how much I worried that you would get accustomed only to life around the hospital, and would be unable to find your place in society outside it. Then Johan came into your life, a young, handsome man who loves you so much and definitely wants to marry you—by the way, he's hinted at it to me quite a few times—and I was truly happy for you. But you will certainly not marry someone who you're not sure is suited to you. I made the mistake of thinking you were happy with him, that you were happy together, despite the arguments and despite the topics on which you don't entirely agree. In any case, that's what he made sure to tell me, again and again. All in all, he's actually a nice, serious fellow, and has promised me repeatedly that he would do anything for your happiness, that you mean everything to him, and that he's never before felt this way about anyone else."

Hildegard was mesmerizing Ilse, who couldn't say a word in light of the outpouring her mother had delivered in such complete honesty and out of true love.

"I want there to be someone who will always take care of you in addition to me, don't you see, *liebchen*?" Hildegard continued in a conciliatory tone. "Life is cruel and no one gets off easily. All I want is the very best for you, that you never suffer deprivation like we did together during the war and the crisis that followed it. Don't be angry with me, please. I love you too much and I can't stand it. And Ilse? I forgive you for raising your voice at me."

Ilse started to sob again and held her mother close. "I'm sorry, I'm so sorry, Mama, if I hurt you. Mama, you're the dearest person to me in the whole world. I want you to be happy too. I know you remained a widow mostly because of me. I know that you've always sacrificed everything just for me, and I appreciate it, but please, my dear Mama, trust me and my judgment and accept things as they are."

◆ ◆ ◆

Following that day of emotional upheaval between Ilse and Hildegard, they didn't discuss the matter of marriage to Johan again. Ilse continued to see him, but felt increasingly reluctant to do so, and Hildegard, in her wisdom, held her tongue. Johan, in turn, did his best to avoid arguing with Ilse. He felt that these arguments, which were, in fact, quite unnecessary, had begun to dull her feelings for him, which he was unwilling to accept. Time would have its inevitable effect, and ultimately she would come to accept him fully, he thought to himself. There were enough other things to dwell on besides politics, or issues on which they disagreed. He even made a concerted effort to keep holding back and not impose himself on Ilse physically. His explorations in that direction led to a firm "Stop" signal from her, most recently based on the claim that Christianity permitted sexual relations only after marriage. As unconvincing as that claim might have sounded to him, he couldn't object to it. *The right time for it will indeed arrive,* he told himself, *and if there is a chance that this will deter her, or even worse, turn her heart against me, it would be best not to pressure her.*

Johan and Ilse's relationship calmed down and fell into a comfortable routine, until the day when they were sitting in a restaurant and suddenly, in mid-meal, Ilse burst into tears.

"Ilse, what's wrong, my sweet? What's making you cry in a

public place, and so copiously?" asked Johan, who was indeed concerned, but was also looking around to make sure they weren't being watched. Displaying excessive emotions in general, and particularly in public, was not condoned by his worldview. He held her hand and handed her his handkerchief, hoping she would bounce back as quickly as possible.

Ilse dabbed at her tears. "Johan, today a young boy passed away in our ward," she whispered. "He had abdominal surgery and apparently there were complications. He died in my arms, Johan. You have no idea how much sorrow it caused me, and then watching his parents' heartbreaking outburst after they heard the news..." And the tears flowed from her eyes once more.

"Ilse," Johan said quietly, but with no tenderness, "this is your work, and you're not supposed to develop feelings toward the patients. It makes no sense that you're sitting here in the restaurant with me, shedding tears because of a patient who died. After all, cases like that happen every day, and not just at Elisabeth Hospital. It's embarrassing to wail like that in front of everyone, don't you think?"

Ilse looked at him and couldn't believe her ears. He was showing a blatant lack of emotion. She wiped her eyes once more, handed the wet handkerchief back to him, and didn't say a word. If he remained unemotional in response to what she'd just told him, explaining or further describing the details of the event would only be a waste of time.

While Ilse pecked at her dinner, Johan ravenously wolfed down the juicy lamb shank and aromatic side dishes and eagerly sipped the wine. Ilse became even sadder in response to Johan's attitude than she did when remembering the poor boy who died. She decided that she would no longer share such occurrences with Johan. He didn't understand, and apparently never would. One more subject on which their worldviews were fundamentally different...

After Johan wiped the remaining sauce off his plate with the last slice of bread left on the table, he looked at Ilse's nearly full plate and suddenly felt sorry for her. *What do I want from her anyway?* he tormented himself. *Why am I always so hard on her when she's at her most vulnerable...?* He then felt his loins grow full and heavy. His face grew flushed and he knew that if they had not been at the restaurant but rather at home, he would no longer have been able to control himself and would have done what he had been yearning to do for some time... and with no further consideration of her feelings.

Ilse noticed that Johan was gazing at her with avid eyes. She also noticed the color his face had assumed, and a shiver ran through her. She found it hard to believe that what had just occurred had the reaction that it did on Johan. She looked down, gripped by nausea.

After their relationship had found a certain stability, the episode in the restaurant and all it entailed had a ruinous effect; Ilse felt that her love for Johan—or what was left of it—was gradually fading away. Everything having to do with him, above all being physically close to him, no longer gave her pleasure, and she began to come up with various excuses to decrease the frequency of their dates. She needed to think quietly and in solitude in order to come to a decision.

Part Three

ઠ Chapter 10 ૐ

Johan was sent to Munich for three days of training. He left Berlin on Saturday and planned to arrive in Munich a day before the training began in order to spend Sunday with his mother. He wanted to devote sufficient time to her after the long period during which they hadn't seen each other. An entire day in her company was supposed to compensate them for all that.

On Sunday morning he knocked on the door of his childhood home. Beatrice was very excited to see him. She had missed him and was glad that her loneliness would be somewhat eased, if only for a brief time.

"Johan, my dear son, it's so good to see you again. You're so handsome and elegant. What kind of training are you here for?"

He hugged her tightly and then replied, appeasing, "First of all, I'm here mainly for you, and the training doesn't matter now." What could he say to her? That he had arrived for some military training accompanied by lectures on behalf of the SS? She had nothing to do with all that. He didn't want to share any of it with her. He was more interested in talking to her about Ilse. He had decided that after he returned to Berlin, he would ask Ilse for her hand in marriage. He had given much thought to the subject, and the long hours he spent on the train to Munich had provided the right time to do so.

He *had* to marry Ilse. He simply had to attain full, legal possession of her, which would grant him the authority to have his way with her. He'd realized some time ago that she wouldn't succumb to him until they were married, although the sanctimonious refuge she found in Christianity made him smirk.

Beatrice quickly fixed her son the best of meals: roast chicken with potatoes and sour cream, his old favorite.

The kitchen was overpowered by the tantalizing aromas of roasting, and mother and son sat at the table. And so, as Johan chewed with gusto and his mother watched him with obvious pleasure, he talked mainly about Ilse. He told his mother again and again about his great love for Ilse, about their relationship, and, yes, also about their frequent arguments.

"Johan, why do you have to upset this girl with unnecessary arguments? Who instigates political arguments with a sweetheart? Why do you even talk to her about issues like that?"

"Because it's important to me, Mother. It's important to me that we're in agreement, and when it comes to this topic, we have nothing in common. It also makes me angry that she won't meet me halfway. And you know what else?" he added, somewhat drily, "She doesn't even want to sleep with me. It's important to her to be a virgin until she gets married."

"A girl after my own heart indeed, Johan, with values and self-discipline. And if she really is so important to you and you want to share your life with her, you have to make some concessions, too. Be flexible. Don't be so stubborn. Focus on what counts and not on trivial things. If I had been stubborn, uncompromising, and inflexible with your father, I might have killed him. But I held back. My whole life, I held back."

And Beatrice felt a sudden need to tell her son about her private life with his father, as she had never really allowed herself to do before. The need to do so arose mostly because he had told her about his desire to marry Ilse.

"Really, Mother, if we're talking about it, why were you so willing to concede when it came to Father? It was like you sacrificed yourself and your life for him. It didn't have to be like that. Don't you think you could have found a different, more suitable husband?"

"No, Johan, I couldn't. It's true, your father didn't really make an effort to make me happy, but I never would have left him. I loved him, and maybe sometimes I felt sorry for him more than I loved him. I want to tell you something, something I've never told anyone. You know, Johan, Father had a stepfather that your grandmother—whom you never got to meet, and neither did I—married. This stepfather, who I think Father often claimed, using derogatory slurs, had been Jewish, abused him when he was a child, for whatever reason, and he grew up in the shadow of violence. His mother didn't always step up to protect him, because she herself was weak and frightened, and was afraid to incur her husband's wrath.

"Your father was a poor boy, Johan, a miserable boy, oppressed and frustrated, and his frustration increased when his mother, too, fell victim to her husband's abuse. She passed away at a relatively young age and then your father ran away from home because he didn't want to stay with the violent stepfather. And so he was tossed out on the street, your father, and over time, his situation worsened. He couldn't find himself. When I met him, he clung to me like a drowning man holding on to a reed, believe me. He loved me and enjoyed my company so much that he never wanted us to be apart. I felt sorry for him and decided I'd make a proper human being out of him, that I would ease his pain, and that together we would have a model family.

"I failed, Johan. That's how it goes sometimes. Despite all my good will, very soon Father sank into a deep depression, and the family we started did not keep him happy over time. After all, you remember how your sister's death wreaked havoc on him, when he blamed himself for her death and knew that I blamed him as well. And you yourself experienced the ultimate result of all that misery.

"So it's true that it seems like I sacrificed my life for him, but I couldn't have done otherwise. If I had left him, he would have died, literally, and I couldn't have taken something like that on myself and on my conscience. Try to understand, my dear Johan, and forgive both him and me. I know that you were often angry with me and I couldn't find the way or the strength to explain it to you. Now you and I are on equal ground, and I can and want to be entirely honest with you."

All the while Beatrice was talking, Johan didn't say a word. He listened to her attentively, appreciating her openness and honesty. He really didn't know much about the mother who had brought him into the world, and knew next to nothing about his father as well. He was truly pleased that after all those years, the moment had arrived—the moment of honesty.

"Mother, it makes me very sad to hear all this," he finally said. "It's true. Now I understand a lot more, but I still think that no one should sacrifice himself for another—such an absolute sacrifice, I mean. Each of us receives life as a gift, and there's no reason in the world for an absolute sacrifice, unless it's for the sake of an exalted national principle."

Beatrice looked at him for some time, but didn't reply. So they didn't agree on this subject. Each could come to his own opinion and maintain it. And as for her sacrifice on behalf of Helmut—it was no longer important. For some time now, Helmut had belonged to the realm of the dead, while she still had some good years to live without him, with the peace of mind resulting from the knowledge that her husband was now at rest.

Johan spent the night in his old room. Sleep did not come to him quickly. He thought about the entire conversation with his mother. She really was right about Ilse. He would have to change if he wanted to have a proper marital life with her. He decided that the moment he got back to Berlin, he would have a long talk with her and promise her that he would change. After all, he knew how to carry out orders in the best possible way, but this time, he would be his own commander. And as for the rest of what Beatrice had told him, if up until now, he had supported Hitler's views as a whole, now he was an even greater proponent of his antisemitic approach. Apparently Jews really were an affliction. And here was the proof—because of a Jewish stepfather, his father had become the wretched mental invalid that he was.

That night, the seeds of antisemitism within Johan sprouted even further after he remembered that his mother's Jewish employer had treated her disrespectfully. *What is it with these Jews?* he asked himself. *After all, they're guests in all the countries where they dwell. Well, then, why can't they respect their hosts? Why do they always try to seize control and take matters into their own hands? Hitler is so right in his attitude toward them and in the way he views them. Hitler is right about everything, absolutely everything.* And with that thought, at last, he fell asleep, with the leader's face flickering in front of his eyes.

The next morning, Beatrice and Johan woke up, had breakfast together, and Johan said goodbye.

"Be patient, Johan," she told him again. "Less tough, and sometimes, think with your heart and not just with your brain."

It was Monday morning, and Johan headed for the SS headquarters in the center of the city, where he began the training to which he had been sent along with several other members of the Berlin branch. As the organization had been gradually expanding over the year, it was currently in a process of bureaucratic restructuring and was now divided into five main centers: Administration, Personnel, Finance, Security, and Race. The current course aimed to further mold its students and teach them an important lesson about forging a tough, uncompromising character, eliminating, to the greatest extent possible, the sort of sentimentality that might bring about insubordination, while enhancing the principles of leadership and total submission to the views of the leader and his cause.

On the second day of training, Johan felt that he wasn't as focused as he should be. He did all that he was asked to do and listened to the lectures and sermons framed as impassioned speeches, but his mind was wandering.

Suddenly, the training instructor approached him and challenged him: "Kirche, you're everywhere but here with us. I noticed that yesterday, too. As far as I'm concerned, you're out. I'm suspending you from the course. You'll have to take it some other time, and I hope for your sake that you don't get kicked out of the organization completely."

Johan swallowed hard. He was so distraught that his eyes filled with tears of rage. This was the last thing he needed. To be ousted from the organization—and for what? Because of a temporary lack of focus? He bowed his head and said nothing.

"Come to my office at the end of the lesson," the commander concluded, signaling to Johan to leave the class.

At the appointed time, Johan showed up at the commander's office, twitchy with nervousness. Even if he had wanted to apologize or express his regret, he would only have compounded his original transgression, as this would be a display of cowardice—the main topic of the training.

"Kirche," the commander growled, "you'll return to Berlin this evening, where you'll learn a lesson about focus and discipline. Since you have a good reputation, it was decided not to oust you from the organization this time. Consider this a warning." He gestured dismissively, signaling to Johan to leave the room.

Johan left the commander's office quietly. Ultimately, he had been forgiven, and next time, if and when it came, he would take great care to stay on task. *How shameful*, he reflected, *to lose control of myself like that. It's all because of you, my dear Ilse*, he thought bitterly. *You're the only one in the world who can cause me to drift into distant thoughts that have nothing to do with my work. You're the only one in the world who can cause me to anger my commanders, and I swear I won't let it happen again.*

Johan boarded the train back to Berlin with a heavy heart. He arrived on Wednesday morning and hurried to his apartment for an internal reckoning. He was livid with himself for bringing about his own suspension from the important course, which had been ill-timed for him. He wanted to propose to Ilse, and the delay caused by taking part in the training felt as if it would not serve him well. Usually, he was highly attentive to what was going on with Ilse, although sometimes he expressed it negatively, and he couldn't ignore her recent chilly attitude toward him, which hurt him and left him in a foul mood.

Johan could hardly wait for the afternoon, when Ilse would return from work. He planned to go see her, talk to her, and try to appease her, and then take advantage of the moment of reconciliation to propose to her. He would go to her at a time when Hildegard would be at home as well, to make the whole matter formal and official. He truly hoped he would not be turned down, as that, he was certain, would be unbearable. He had already made his decision—to do whatever he could to move beyond his personal desires and be more sensitive to Ilse's needs. Now he had to prove to her that he was capable of following through.

Chapter 11

On that Wednesday in early summer, the air was wonderful, permeated with caressing warmth. Ilse was cheerful and upbeat when she got to work. On Saturday, Johan had left for Munich for some work-related training and said he would take the opportunity to visit his mother as well, returning to Berlin around Thursday morning. Ilse was glad to have several whole days to herself, days that she could dedicate solely to her own thoughts. She already felt better just knowing he was out of town, as if she were breathing freely. In fact, since the candid conversation with her mother, Ilse no longer felt much love for Johan, and after their exchange at the restaurant, she knew that her cooling feelings for him would not warm up again, even if they were placed on a fiery stove. But she still hadn't come to the decision to end her relationship with him, as she was afraid of hurting him.

And it was precisely at that time, during the more infrequent meetings that were still taking place between them, with little enthusiasm on her part, that Johan began to apply pressure on her to sleep with him. Not only did this repulse her, it also created tense atmosphere between them.

"Ilse, we've been together for over six months," he told her, "and you won't let me have my way with you. It's strange, isn't it? It's a clear indication that you don't love me," he told her repeatedly, trying to manipulate her conscience. He no longer wanted to accept the excuse to which she clung, that she was a practicing Christian and wanted to remain a virgin until she got married. "That's ridiculous. Really? Come on, Ilse. After all, you're not religious and you're already 21, so what are we waiting for? Or more precisely, what are *you* waiting for?"

Ilse clenched her jaws, stuck to her refusal, and the tension between them gradually escalated. Johan was right. Her refusal indeed did not stem from her Christian values. She was simply not sexually attracted to him. She had no desire to begin an intimate relationship with him when she felt the way she did about him, or, more accurately, when she no longer felt anything for him but mild pity. If, at the beginning of their relationship, she had often imagined, quite enthusiastically, the two of them between the sheets and under the covers with no clothes on, doing as others who were like them probably did under similar circumstances, as time went by, these imaginings were characterized by ever-increasing revulsion, and lately she had simply stopped thinking about it. It was no longer an option. Not at all.

Now that Johan had been away from her for four days, she toyed with the thought that all this might be a passing malaise, and that she would suddenly find herself missing him. But when she gave it further consideration, she knew that what had died could not be revived.

Ilse entered the ward with a light step. Within a short time, she was wearing her white lab coat and tucking two pins into her hair to keep her cap in place. As was the case every morning, she was called to join the doctors on their rounds as they examined the patients currently hospitalized in the surgery ward.

Near the bed of Otto Franz, who had been hospitalized the day before due to a growth in his leg that required immediate excision, stood a young man in his twenties wearing a white lab coat. She found him to be breathtaking. He was particularly tall and very handsome, sporting a dark, thick mane. His brown eyes were radiant, his full lips curved in a slight smile, and his masculine features also projected a sense of gentleness. Ilse's heart leaped within her. *I wonder who this debonair fellow is*, she thought. *A new doctor who joined the staff whom I haven't heard about yet?* She waited with increasing curiosity to find out more about him.

"Good morning, Dr. Liebmann," Dr. Genscher addressed him. "I see that you're here early this morning to visit your patient."

"Good morning to all of you," the young doctor replied, his voice deep and authoritative. "I couldn't help but be early. Herr Franz's family kept begging me to see him early this morning. They're anxious and worried, which is very understandable."

"Well, let's examine our patient," Dr. Genscher said. "But first, I'll introduce you to our staff. Please meet Dr. Abe Liebmann, who recently joined a private clinic that refers patients to us when they need to be hospitalized for treatment and supervision." He proceeded to introduce the three staff members to Dr. Liebmann.

Dr. Liebmann nodded to each of them separately after his smiling eyes had assessed them. It seemed as if his gaze lingered a bit longer on Ilse, causing her to blush and look down. *His eyes and gaze are magnetic, possessing a special sort of magic,* she thought.

The doctors' examination passed without incident. The sutures on the patient's leg looked good, with no evidence of inflammation, and he was exhibiting promising signs of recovery. He was told that within a few days he would be able to return to his family.

"Come visit me tomorrow too, please," Franz said to Dr. Liebmann. "Your visit is helping. It's not that I'm not getting good care here, but I'm used to you and your father. How is your papa doing?"

"Tomorrow morning you'll see me by your bed, Herr Franz, and my father is just fine. Thank you for asking," Dr. Liebmann replied and turned to leave the patient's room. He followed the medical team out and said his goodbyes to all of them, mostly to Dr. Genscher. Before he turned to go, he glanced briefly at Ilse, who didn't fail to notice. She was caught in his gaze but this time didn't look down. He smiled at her, waved goodbye, and turned toward the doors of the hospital.

Once the doctors' rounds were over, Ilse returned to her routine tasks. Something drew her to Otto Franz's room. She decided to go in and ask how he was feeling. Franz was lying in his bed after the examination, leafing through the newspaper.

"Herr Franz," Ilse addressed him, "how do you feel?"

He was surprised to see her again. "You actually just visited me, and nothing has changed, in fact, but thank you for showing interest in me again so quickly."

"Everyone here is very important to me," Ilse said, as she knew she would be unable to explain what had actually drawn her back to his room. She had to say something that would provide her with an excuse to ask what she had meant to ask from the start.

"Herr Franz, why was it that Dr. Liebmann sent you here in particular, and not to Charité?" There, she had just dared to bring up Dr. Liebmann's name.

"Young Dr. Liebmann and Dr. Liebmann Senior, his father, usually refer patients like me here to Elisabeth, and not to Charité. I think it's because Elisabeth Hospital is known for admitting patients with financial difficulties, and helping them in a sympathetic way. I'm sure they offer help at Charité Hospital, too, but it's cozier here, and I think it's just standard procedure for the Liebmanns. I'm not really a big expert. If you want to know more, you'll have to ask Dr. Liebmann himself," he concluded with a wink.

Indeed, the breakthrough had been achieved. They were talking about Dr. Liebmann. Ilse allowed herself to pursue the topic. "Where is the Liebmanns' clinic?" she asked, tucking in Franz's foot, which had popped out from under the covers, as she marveled at her own sudden courage.

"Ah, it's near Alexanderplatz, on Landsberger Street. It's located in their house. The father is an internist and the son is a family doctor. They work as a team."

Ilse became breathless. The patient had supplied her with

additional information before she could even ask him for it. She continued to gently question him while pouring fresh water into Franz's glass. "How long has the son been working with the father?" she asked.

"Oh, he started sometime last year. Until then, he was studying, and also worked at Charité a little. What a brilliant man—so polite, and dedicated to his patients. This isn't the first time he's taken care of us. He's become our whole family's personal physician. I wish I had a son like him," Franz said, staring straight ahead.

"How did you first meet him?" Ilse continued asking once she saw that Franz was as eager for this conversation as she was.

"A few months ago, I felt really awful and my wife brought me to the Liebmanns' clinic. Before that, I'd been treated by Dr. Isadore Liebmann, but when I arrived, he was busy, so the son saw me. The father is tougher than the son, rarely smiles, but he's professional and very serious, and he's seen us many times. But from the moment Dr. Abe saw me, I fell in love with him. Such relaxed smiles, such a soothing tone, compared to his father's cracked voice, and most of all, his professional accuracy is equal to his father's, that's for sure. He'll wind up with a great reputation, I'm certain. From that day on, I only see the son. The father can tend to those who don't really care about smiles and soothing expressions. To me, it's almost as important as the medical treatment itself." A big smile spread across his face.

Ilse sat down next to Franz's bed. "What were you suffering from the first time you came to him?" she asked, increasingly curious, causing Franz to marvel at her ongoing interest in him.

"I had a particularly aggressive cough and my wife couldn't alleviate it. Dr. Liebmann examined me thoroughly and gave me some magic potion that helped within a day. And now, about a month ago, I started getting strong pains in my leg, so that's why I came. I had a tumor and Dr. Liebmann recommended surgery and sent me here. He arranged it all for me, including the paperwork. You know, after that whole story with the cough, Dr. Liebmann came to visit me at home. He just showed up suddenly, knocked on the door and wanted to know if the potion helped. It really surprised me, this personal treatment. I don't know many doctors who would have done that."

Otto began to yawn. He was tired after a night of interrupted sleep and the long conversation had further exhausted him.

Ilse tucked the blanket around him once more and fluffed up his pillows. "Herr Franz, get some rest. You have to get stronger and feel better so you'll be at your best when you go back home, right?" He nodded, smiled at her, and closed his eyes.

Ilse returned to the nurses' room, smiling to herself. She had managed to learn quite a bit about Dr. Liebmann within a short time. The memory of the handsome doctor's attractive face stayed with her, and the entire discussion by Franz's bedside as well as the medical analysis of his condition also remained at the forefront of her thoughts. Above all else, she was struck by the conversation with Franz, which had revolved mostly around Dr. Abe Liebmann. She had never before been as deeply impressed by a stranger as she had been by this doctor. It was true that in the first stages of her acquaintance with Johan, he had dazzled her as well, but her current positive impression and its impact on her were very different from those previous encounters, and she hadn't yet gotten acquainted with the talented, handsome doctor. She remembered that the next day Dr. Liebmann would be coming back to visit Otto Franz again. She suddenly felt a breathless anticipation for his return, just as she remembered that Johan, too, would be returning that same day.

Before her shift ended, Ilse swung by Franz's bed once more to see how he was feeling. He was now her secret connection to Dr. Liebmann—unbeknownst to him, of course.

"*Schwester* Heine, how nice of you to come visit me again," Franz said as she smiled and adjusted the pillows and the blanket.

"Herr Franz, my shift is over, and I have to go home. I'll see you again tomorrow morning during the doctors' rounds, okay?"

"That's perfectly fine. And I thank you again for taking such an interest in me. You remind me of Dr. Liebmann. He also shows great interest in his patients, as if they were family members. Have a good evening, *Schwester*, and see you tomorrow."

ৰ্ড Chapter 12 ক্ষ

Ilse got ready to leave the hospital. When she emerged from the building, she immediately detected the delightful scent of flowers—the blossoms of early summer. The perfumed air soothed her distracted mind a bit, although she couldn't stop thinking about Dr. Liebmann and about her conversation with Otto Franz. Her heart pounded every time she remembered the sound of the charming doctor's voice, his appearance, and the quick glance he directed at her before leaving the unit after visiting Franz. If she had thought Johan's absence would give her time to contemplate their relationship—or what was left of it—as well as providing her an opportunity to be on her own and come to a decision, now her head was full of thoughts of Dr. Liebmann, which were preventing her from delving into any other topics.

Ilse arrived home with her hair somewhat disheveled. This time, uncharacteristically, she hadn't spent much time on her hairdo. One of the hairpins that secured her cap to her head was still tucked in her hair, making her look like a little girl.

Hildegard had closed the shop early that day. She wanted to go out to dinner and to the cinema with Ilse. She knew that Ilse's mood had been quite low over the last few days and that Johan was the main cause of it. Hildegard was extremely perceptive, and had become even more so after her last conversation with Ilse about Johan. Ironically, just like Ilse, she, too, had begun to find fault with Johan for a number of reasons, but she didn't want to interfere any further. She had already done so once before when she tried to urge Ilse to marry him, and she couldn't forget the quarrel that had broken out between them afterwards. The argument had greatly affected her, causing her to think more deeply and try to examine Ilse's impressions more seriously. Perhaps, after all, Ilse had been right. Perhaps her daughter's feminine intuition had signaled to her that marriage to Johan would not be the right decision at the moment—or perhaps ever. Hildegard resolved to be as attentive to her daughter as she could. She had to be her closest companion and confidante. And if she had made a mistake or two with regard to Ilse, or if it seemed as though she hadn't truly understood her, it was only her uncompromising aspiration to ensure that Ilse was happy that had caused her to behave as she did.

Hildegard, who was sitting on the sofa in the parlor reading the newspaper, said hello to Ilse. Her sharp eyes didn't miss her daughter's intense agitation. Her mussed hair was hardly typical of her tidy, meticulous Ilse. Apparently something had distracted her daughter from her appearance that afternoon. She didn't pry, expecting that when the time was right, Ilse would tell her of her own initiative. And, indeed, Ilse's outburst soon arrived.

"Mama, I can't stand Johan anymore," she burst out without even responding to her mother's greeting. "He's become coarse and vulgar. Lately I've even begun to loathe him, and now that he's not here, I feel a lot better." Suddenly, she burst into tears, her sobs gradually increasing.

Hildegard didn't reply. She did what she usually did under such circumstances: take the weeping girl in her arms, stroke her messy hair and wet cheeks, and whisper, "*Liebchen*, nothing can be forced. If you don't love him anymore," she chose to use a tactful phrasing, "just end your relationship with him. There's no point pretending and dragging it out."

"Mama," Ilse said after blowing her nose and calming down somewhat, "today I met a charming man. He's a doctor, he has a private clinic, and sometimes he sends his patients to us for surgery and a longer stay when they need hospital care and supervision." Although she was still sniffling, she was now speaking enthusiastically. "You have no idea what an impressive, charismatic person he is, and I felt, when the doctors and staff were making their rounds, that he was looking at me in a different way than he looked at the others."

Hildegard smiled discreetly. So this was the heart of the matter! It was true that Johan was no longer the man of her daughter's dreams, but this doctor—whom she talked about with unusual passion—had injected her with more of an antidote, helping turn Johan into a bone sticking in her craw.

"Ilse, my pretty, my beloved girl, I want only what's best for you, you know that. Wait and see where all this is going. In the meantime, Johan is far away now, busy with his training. You'll have another day or two of quiet and we'll see what happens. And if we're being truthful, you haven't had any sort of personal exchange with this doctor yet, have you?"

Ilse hugged her mother. "Mama, it's true that I barely know him, and it's true that we haven't had any sort of private conversation yet, but if you saw him, you'd know what I was talking about. You'd understand what attracted me to him in the first place."

That evening, mother and daughter went out to a restaurant and to the movies. They were now closer than ever. *If something were to happen to her, I'd kill myself*, Hildegard thought. *This girl is my whole world and my only real, solid connection to Manfred.*

◆ ◆ ◆

Johan arrived at the Heine residence in the evening hours. He knocked on the door several times and when there was no answer, he realized that there was no one home. He sat down on the steps to wait. When an hour went by, and Ilse and her mother still hadn't returned, he ran out of patience and became enraged. He walked to the nearby pub and poured two pitchers of beer down his throat. He couldn't imagine turning around and going back home. *I have to take care of the matter this evening*, he told himself. *I have to see Ilse, I just have to.* How could it be that she had gone out that night, of all nights? Where had they gone? He forgot that he hadn't eaten a thing for most of the day, and so the beer began to wreak havoc on his gut, which was not the ale's only victim—his head absorbed quite a bit of it as well. The ale completely blurred his already questionable lucidity, due to his disappointment over the two women's absence. Johan managed to realize that this would not be an appropriate night for emotional declarations of love and an official marriage proposal, and turned to walk away. He would have to put it off until tomorrow, which irritated him even more.

Around 11:00 p.m., Johan decided to return to the Heine residence after all. At the end of the street, he spotted Ilse and Hildegard walking arm in arm toward him. They were giggling cheerfully like two teenagers and appeared to be in a wonderful mood.

Ilse and Hildegard approached the entrance to the building and Ilse's heart sank when she saw the figure emerge from the shadows. It was Johan, a hostile expression on his face. That face, always smoothly shaven, was now covered with stubble, and he smelled of ale. He definitely didn't look his best—or to put it more plainly, he looked bad, in every sense of the word.

Johan didn't say hello, but rather proceeded immediately to what was on his mind. "Ilse, the training ended earlier than planned," he said rigidly. "I want us to meet tomorrow evening. I have a lot to say to you."

Unlike her usual habit, Hildegard didn't invite him to come in. It was late and she was tired and beyond that, she knew how her daughter felt about him. She also thought it was somewhat presumptuous of him to show up like this and insist on waiting at the entrance, for who knew how long, until they returned. And what if they had been even later? Would he still have kept on waiting like a fool?

Ilse hadn't been expecting to see Johan that night, and after everything she had been through that day, merely nodded. She agreed to see him the next day, as long as he went away and left her alone. He was scaring her with his appearance and his attitude. When she saw him the next evening, she would tell him that she was not interested in continuing their relationship. Indeed, as her mother had said, there was no point in dragging it out. She was still very wary of him, but determined to muster up all her courage and end the story, once and for all. The tone of Johan's address that evening seemed more "off" than usual to her, cold and alienated, and the threatening undertone made her shiver. The moment Johan saw Ilse nod, he said goodbye to her and Hildegard with a wave of his hand, not even smiling as he always did.

The two women were certain that he had also gone through something. They were glad to quickly disappear up the stairs, and furthermore, to bolt the door behind them and be rid of Johan Kirche's unwanted presence.

"I'll break up with him tomorrow," Ilse said. "There really is no point anymore. Did you see, Mama, what he looked like? Did you hear how he sounded? What's happened to him lately? He should just leave me alone and go somewhere else to find himself."

Hildegard nodded in agreement and didn't say a word. This time, she believed Johan had gone too far.

◆ ◆ ◆

Johan turned to go home, enraged as ever, though mostly at himself. He had been aware of the hostile looks that both Ilse and Hildegard were directing at him, and was deeply offended. It was true that he wasn't looking his best, he was dizzy, still feeling the aftereffects of the beer, and he was certain the two women hadn't been thrilled to see him. And yet he still felt hurt. Something was very wrong about all this. His bad mood increased when he remembered that the following day he was scheduled to take part in a very special activity along with several other SS members.

∽ Chapter 13 ∾

On Thursday morning, Ilse headed for work. Dr. Liebmann, with his appealing, distinctive smile, whom she had thought about before falling asleep, showed up in her dreams. It was true that Johan had also popped up in her mind, but she preferred to push him aside. She would dwell on Johan only as she approached her meeting with him that evening. At the moment, it seemed a shame to waste any unnecessary thoughts on him when she was filled with expectation for Dr. Liebmann's visit with Otto Franz.

Ilse entered the ward, and after putting on her uniform rushed impulsively to Otto Franz's bedside. Franz was happy to see her, hurrying to complain about the restless night he had experienced. She consoled him.

"In about two hours, the doctors and staff will be making their rounds, and you can tell them as well," she said, tucking him in and turning to her other tasks.

A short time before the morning rounds, Ilse spotted Dr. Liebmann's tall, impressive form striding confidently toward Dr. Genscher's office. The blood coursing through her left her flushed; today the doctor looked even more charming than he had yesterday. He nodded to her and disappeared inside Dr. Genscher's office.

And just as he had the day before, Dr. Liebmann once again joined the staff in visiting Otto Franz that morning.

The patient was thoroughly examined. "You can go home in two days," Dr. Liebmann said. "You're recovering nicely from the surgery, your pain is decreasing, and there's no reason you shouldn't go back to your usual routine. We'll be in touch, of course. We're not saying goodbye that quickly, are we?"

Franz grinned happily. He shook Dr. Liebmann's hand and thanked him again and again. Ilse didn't miss this gesture, or the look that the handsome doctor directed at her. She couldn't help but send him a quick smile; she had no other choice, even if she risked divulging the meaning of her smile to others as well.

With some measure of difficulty, Ilse continued to accompany the doctors as they visited the other patients in the ward. From the corner of her eye, she noticed that Dr. Liebmann was still lingering by Franz's bedside and heard them continue to talk.

Their voices gradually faded away as she and the other staff members continued on their way. Her heart was full of Dr. Liebmann, and for the first time since she started working on the ward, she was distracted during rounds. She simply couldn't control it. Much to her relief, the visitations finally ended and each of the staff members returned to his or her own tasks. Ilse went to the nurses' room to organize the instruments, in accordance with her usual routine, while Dr. Liebmann remained constantly on her mind. A slight shiver ran through her hands as they held several glass test tubes, and she heard a tinkling sound. She hurried to put the test tubes down on the tray. Suddenly, she sensed that she was no longer alone in the room. She idly assumed that one of the other nurses had come in. When she turned around, what she saw took her breath away. It was Dr. Liebmann.

"Fräulein Heine," he addressed her. "I would be very interested in getting to know you personally, and not just as a nurse at the hospital. I would be happy if you could join me tonight. We'll go somewhere quiet where we can talk. Will you do me the honor?"

It took Ilse some time to answer him, as she was overcome by great excitement. And then, much to her chagrin, she had to tell him, "I can't this evening. I have a previous commitment." She then hastily and bravely added, "But tomorrow—Friday night—I'm free, and would be happy to join you."

Dr. Liebmann's face assumed an endearing smile. "Well, then, it's a date. I'll come pick you up from home tomorrow evening. What's your address?"

She gave it to him. What a shame it was that she had to wait until tomorrow and couldn,t join him that evening, as this was the evening that she had promised to meet Johan. She had no choice. She had to be patient, smart, and careful.

Dr. Liebmann said goodbye, but not before kissing her hand, reaching out with a gentle finger and caressing her cheek with a touch that was barely there. *Auf Wiedersehen* ("Until we meet again"), Fräulein Heine," he told her. "I'm looking forward to tomorrow evening. I'll come to pick you up at 7:00 on the dot. Don't forget. Enjoy the rest of your day." And he turned to go.

Forget? How could I forget? she thought. *God heard my prayer and provided me with this wonderful fellow.* She was so curious to get to know him and so optimistic—both characteristics that filled her with pleasure tinged with a certain pain. *Is this what's called "love at first sight"?* she thought, the blood rushing through her veins.

◆ ◆ ◆

At the end of her work day, Ilse decided to walk part of the way home. She couldn't shake off her apprehension about the impending meeting with Johan. She really did need to muster up a special sort of strength for it. She still had to plan how she would tell Johan what she meant to say to him. It wouldn't be easy, of that she was certain. She stepped off the tram at the station near Kaiser Wilhelm Memorial Church and began to walk energetically. Strolling in the fresh weather calmed her down. As she approached the church square, she suddenly heard sounds of singing and laughter that were getting closer. They also grew louder, resembling the rowdiness of drunks. *What's going on with these people?* she thought. *Have they totally lost their minds?* The voices suddenly turned into loud shouting and she grew frightened and hurriedly crossed to the other side of the street. When she saw who was responsible for the ruckus, a shudder ran through her: It was a group of SS members, consisting of five brawny, muscular young men. She recognized them by their brown uniforms, the black caps with the skull insignia, and the black tie. They looked rowdy, but not too violent, and Ilse hoped they would pass by quickly.

From where she stood, Ilse quickly glanced at the gleeful group. She froze and her breath was trapped inside her. She covered her mouth with her hand to keep from crying out. At the head of the group, three sheets to the wind, was the one and only Johan Kirche, who was cheerfully trudging along.

Ilse felt as if a boa constrictor was wrapped around her throat and applying pressure. She quickly spun around before he could spot her. Johan was a member of the SS? Since when? And how was it possible that she didn't know anything about it? Or, more accurately, why had he never mentioned it to her? She began to get away with brisk steps and soon broke into a run. The group continued on its mirthful way, singing joyfully and talking loudly, and Ilse rushed home. She no longer had any desire to keep strolling. That was *it*! She had no choice but to tell Johan to go straight to hell. The SS organization and its notorious troops were a refuge for the most extreme, aggressive people who couldn't find any other kind of employment. She knew and believed it. By belonging to the organization, its members accrued false power owing to the uniform they wore and the encouragement they received from the Nazi Party, for whose benefit they had been founded. What was Johan's connection with all this? What about the job at the Sports Promotion Bureau that he'd told her about? It was true, he had talked about his support for Hitler and his party—quite a few times—but how was it that he never said, or even hinted, that he actually *belonged* to Hitler's party? This went far beyond mere admiration or political beliefs—this was everything.

Apparently, Johan knew how she would react and was wary, and therefore chose to hide it.

She so wanted to share all that she had discovered with her mother. But she had to hurry home and had no time to drop by the store.

◆ ◆ ◆

After the successful mission, which left Johan and his four friends in a splendid mood, they decided to celebrate by getting a little drunk. The magic of the triumphant operation made the four of them gulp down not just a glass or two of beer, but much more, and soon the amber-colored beverage that left white foam on their lips was having its effect on them. Johan confined himself to a single glass. He didn't want to repeat yesterday's mistake and stumble into intoxication. All five left the alehouse and resumed walking, cheering and exuberant. After a while they dispersed, and each continued on his own way.

Johan arrived at his apartment in high spirits. Soon he would meet Ilse, as they had agreed on last night. He was still berating himself for treating her so rudely the night before. He had to make it up to her. It had been a mistake on his part to insist on seeing her in his unruly, ugly condition. Now his lips curved in a smile. Everything related to Ilse, from the moment he first laid eyes on her, made him feel differently, as if something beyond him was trying to control his heart and show him the way. And he had to admit it: quite frequently, focusing on his private life—which mostly involved Ilse—rather than on the party and the organization, disrupted his logical thinking.

Johan took a long shower, and the traces of alcohol that still clung to him after the convivial drinking session evaporated. He dressed carefully and looked his best once more. Now he was all set and ready to leave for Ilse's apartment, and to reveal his great love for her as well as his desire to make her his wife.

Then, once they were married, he would tell her the truth about what he did for a living, and she would accept his explanations about transferring from the Sports Promotion Bureau to the SS elite unit. She would have to understand when he explained to her about the organization and its admirable, essential goals.

◆ ◆ ◆

Around 7:00 p.m., Johan knocked on Ilse's door. She rushed to let him in, albeit with a heavy heart. As she looked at him, she saw that he once again looked his best, as opposed to the previous night when he had been almost unrecognizable. Apparently, the traces of alcohol from the afternoon of debauchery in the street had already been entirely absorbed into his system. She felt nauseous when she thought back to the incident, and her fury surged once more. How dare he address her in the state he had been in last night, carouse in the streets today, and come to meet her as if nothing had happened? And how had he lied to her like that, managing to so successfully conceal his actual occupation? Since she knew her designs for this encounter, and had also already planned everything she would say to him, she decided to hold the meeting in the privacy of her home.

Ilse invited Johan to come in, saying, "Johan, this evening we'll stay home. I know we have a lot to talk about, and home is the best place to do it quietly, don't you think?" She thus seemingly gave him the right to decide, in order to create a relaxed mood. She hoped that her mother would come back soon, as she didn't want to be alone with him. She truly felt trapped. No matter how she looked at her current circumstances, and at what would come to pass once she had her talk with him, she was expecting the worst. Unfortunately, precisely that evening, Hildegard seemed to be late. Ilse walked over to the armchair and sat in it and Johan, who was following her, sat down across from her.

"You're right, Ilse," he said. "Home is best, since I also have so much to tell you."

But before he could begin to say what he was so eager to say and to unburden his heart, it was she who actually began.

"Johan, we have to talk about everything... and I really do mean... everything."

Johan swallowed his words. She sounded too serious to him and her tone was somewhat heavy, as if she found it hard to speak. He decided to break through that heaviness with some pointed humor. "Sure, *liebchen*, we'll talk about everything, but what should we start with, our upcoming wedding or the fact that you've finally decided to agree to sleep with me, and today is the day because you missed me while I was away at the training? I see that Frau Heine is late to arrive, too. Is that intentional?"

Ilse nearly choked in response. He was utterly obtuse, truly a pathetic idiot, if he still thought they would ultimately end up as a married couple, not to mention thinking she would agree to sleep with him, which was as far from her actual desires as Berlin was from Munich, from which she knew he had arrived yesterday.

"No, Johan," she replied. "We have to talk about our relationship."

He looked at her with glazed eyes, their metallic blue shade as odd as ever. "In what respect, Ilse? I agree that we have a lot to talk about, but in a way that will lead to resolving all our differences, *nicht wahr?*" he asked, quite passionately.

"Johan," Ilse continued, in a tone that was as quiet as she could make it, so as not to sabotage herself in advance, "today on my way back from work, I ran across a group of SS men on the street, near Kaiser Wilhelm Church."

She saw his face change color and took advantage of the opportune moment to confront him with everything that had weighed heavily upon her from the moment she had seen him at the head of the group.

"You were leading them, Johan. Since when do you belong to the SS? How is it that I didn't know about it until today? After all, you know exactly what I think about that organization. How could you go behind my back like that? How, Johan? How?"

Johan took a few minutes to reply, but his gaze turned as cold as ice and his metallic eyes seemed as piercing as a dagger. A shudder ran through Ilse, followed by a flush of heat. She was very frightened. He seemed like a monster to her. *Oh, Mama, where are you? Why are you delayed, today of all days?* she thought in horror.

And just as apprehension mounted within Ilse, Johan was overtaken by uncontrollable fury. Ilse had so surprised him that he couldn't control himself, and everything he had planned to tell her about emotion, and understanding, and all the rest evaporated without a trace. His loyalty to the party and to the organization seized control of him during those moments. Suddenly he rose, strode toward her, grabbed her shoulders, and lifted her violently from the armchair in which she was sitting. His hands resembled two large pincers, and a dim pain spread through her. "Listen to me, young lady, and listen carefully," he snarled. "The Nazi Party and the SS are the solution to everything that's taking place on the German streets. You don't understand anything. Even your mother understands better than you do. Can't you see what's going on in our country? Can't you see that the current administration is impotent and incompetent, and will bring us to another crisis? Do you live in a different reality? Don't you have even the slightest bit of foresight? You're so caught up in your work at that damned hospital of yours that you're just disconnected from everything."

He felt Ilse recoiling in his arms and then edging away from him, and his rage increased. "If you want to know, my prissy madam," he renewed his attack, "I've been a member of these organizations since long before I met you. In 1922, I started out on the SA, which provided me with a framework and some money. I transferred to the SS in 1926 because I was chosen from among many others as the best suited for the job. Do you know what an honor that is? To belong to an elite group? Do you know how much energy and thought Hitler is investing in creating a Germany that is healthy, functional, and responsible tor its citizens?" When he mentioned Hitler's name, his eyes glittered as they had whenever he had spoken about him.

Ilse noticed that Johan's entire being had transformed in the passionate heat of his speech. He was far from the Johan she had known—or perhaps she had never really known him at all. He went on and on and she remained silent, not understanding where her mother had disappeared to precisely when she needed her most. It was as if she had been sentenced to be alone with Johan in the living room and take in everything he had to say, all on her own. Never before had she feared him as she did now, in light of everything he just told her. SA, SS—she had been with a man who belonged to terrorist organizations and was a member of the Nazi Party for over six months, and she hadn't even known it—which she found horrific. What else didn't she know about Johan? And was what she did know about him really true? The entire image of this well-groomed, handsome man, with his woodsy scent, currently standing before her and thundering at her in a grandiloquent, fervent voice, spouting an impassioned sermon in support of the Nazi organization and party he belonged to, and of Hitler, its leader, was gradually fading away in front of her eyes. Had he now adopted Hitler's brand of rhetoric as well? She simply found it chilling.

And then, after Johan had finally stopped talking and was expecting some reaction from her, Ilse rebounded, gathered all her mental strength, and told him—still completely distraught yet highly restrained—"Johan, we can't be in a relationship anymore. It's not working between us. There are too many disagreements, especially lately."

She watched Johan's face, increasingly frightened, as it grew redder and redder. His eyes were shooting sparks and the corners of his mouth were foaming, He had lost the little that remained of his self-control.

"Damn you! Is this how you want to dump me? After everything I gave you? What do you think? That you're better than other people? You and your sanctimonious mother?" He slapped her with animalistic strength, splitting her lip. A hot, metallic flavor filled her mouth and she reached out to touch her burning cheek with a trembling hand. "Don't do me any favors, Fräulein Heine! There are women who are a thousand times better than you just waiting to be seen with me. I don't need anything from you." His deepening frustration caused him to say what he had thought he would never say. "You didn't even let me sleep with you. It really was a waste of time. Something must be wrong with you, not with me. If you hadn't broken up with me, it certainly wouldn't have taken me long to do it. Believe me, Ilse, you did me a big favor." And he spat in her direction and turned to go.

He had totally forgotten that he was about to discuss marriage with her...

The door slammed after him and Ilse fell back into the armchair, her palm still covering the spot of the slap as well as her split, bleeding lip. She sat there by herself, trembling and staring into space. A part of her was still stunned by the intensity of the battle between her and Johan, while another part was grateful that it was all over.

Hildegard, who had been unexpectedly delayed because of a valued customer who wanted a heart-to-heart talk that went far beyond purchasing a new dress, finally came home. She saw her daughter in her wretched state and could already imagine what had happened. She could accept everything—a heated argument, curses, insults, yelling—but physical harm? That was too much, truly unbearable, and definitely unforgivable. How dare Johan hurt her daughter like that? That violent brute! She ran to her distraught daughter and held her tightly for a long time..

In a barely audible voice, Ilse told her mother everything that had happened from the moment she saw Johan and the group of SS men near Kaiser Wilhelm Church, until the brutal conversation between them that ended with incredibly ugly verbal and physical violence.

Hildegard expressed her amazement that they hadn't known about Johan being a member of the SS, and, like her daughter, realized that if Johan had managed to mislead them in this way for months, they didn't really know much about him. It was one thing to listen to speeches and hope things got better in the country, and quite another to be an agent of terror or to devote oneself to similar activities. As far as Hildegard was concerned, the SA and the SS were one and the same. The last thing she wanted was for her daughter to be married to a member of such an organization, without even having the privilege of knowing about it in advance.

"Ilse," Hildegard said, her voice consoling, "don't cry, my darling. He's not worth your tears. In one moment of fury, he let out his entire true nature. Let's be glad that it's over. I'll take care of your wound and by tomorrow there won't be a trace of it. Apparently your instincts guided you throughout, and now, thank God, this whole affair is behind you."

Ilse didn't reply. She let Hildegard tend to her wound, glad that for once her mother had taken on the role of nurse. Once Hildegard was finished, Ilse smiled faintly. "Thank you, Mama," she said peacefully. "I swear, you could be quite a good nurse yourself."

The thing that gave Ilse solace that evening was her planned date with Dr. Liebmann the next day. The worst was indeed behind her now.

◆ ◆ ◆

Johan rushed down the stairs and stormed into the street. He looked back, toward the Heine residence, and colossal rage churned within him. He had never felt as furious, humiliated, and frustrated as he did at that moment. Ilse, whom he loved more than anyone else, had tossed him out on the street as if he was a worthless piece of garbage. Ilse, who was supposed to have been his one and only, had ended their relationship. And what a pathetic excuse she had used: seeing him with the SS group. So what? After all, the SS was doing blessed work, and it was thanks to the organization that he was where he was. So what if he hadn't told her about it? Everyone had a little something they didn't want to share with certain people. He knew her opinions on the matter were different than his own, and, for that reason he didn't tell her so he could protect her and not upset her. The important thing was that he had treated her with kid gloves, and this was his reward. *It can't be*, he thought to himself. *That can't be the actual reason that she decided to end our relationship. She must have found herself another man. That has to be it. Even if she was angry about the SS, it doesn't justify ending a relationship that was good and satisfying for more than six months.* His rage increased sevenfold at the very thought that Ilse might be seeing someone else. His soul seethed inside him, and he couldn't bear the thought. *That has to be it—otherwise she wouldn't have refused to sleep with me. Well, then, was she being duplicitous as well? Does she have secrets too? Apparently, everyone has some kind of secret. That's life.*

He decided to follow her. He had to uncover the truth. For some reason, he had the feeling that it would turn out to be exactly as he suspected, and this whole matter of political arguments and everything surrounding them was just one big excuse. He believed that his membership in the SS, with all that it entailed, did not make him a better person or a worse one. What truly made him a good person was the way he felt about Ilse, and despite his violent behavior toward her during their conversation, he knew that his love for her had not faded. He was crazy about her—now more than ever—if only because he knew she didn't want him anymore.

Chapter 14

On Friday evening, precisely at 7:00, Dr. Liebmann arrived in his gleaming white Maybach W5 car to pick Ilse up. Hildegard didn't want to miss meeting the charming doctor of whom her daughter spoke with open admiration, so she was the one who opened the door for him. And indeed, the moment her eyes met the doctor's, she understood Ilse's sentiments. There was something extraordinary about this man—of that she had no doubt. Dr. Liebmann laid a beautiful bouquet of flowers in Hildegard's arms and kissed her hand gallantly.

"Good evening, Frau Heine," he greeted her. "It's a pleasure and an honor to make your acquaintance."

"An excellent evening to you, too," she replied. "And thank you so much for the beautiful bouquet."

At that moment Ilse emerged from her room. She had spent quite a while preparing for the date, managing to use makeup to practically obscure the traces of yesterday's slap, which still lingered on her cheek. Only the small cut on her lip remained swollen. Even her mother's devoted treatment could not make it disappear completely. She wore a light blue dress made of a delicate, summery material, her feet encased in high-heeled white sandals. Her elegant hairstyle emphasized the honeyed hue of her hair.

"Good evening, Fräulein Heine," Dr. Liebmann said with an enchanting smile, kissing her cheek. He lightly touched the little cut on her lip but said nothing.

"Shall we go?" he asked and Ilse nodded, linking her arm with the arm he offered her as they turned to go, but not before saying goodbye to Hildegard, of course. Hildegard kissed her daughter's cheek, using the opportunity to whisper, "He really *is* charming," and then waved goodbye to the two of them.

And what was the most fitting destination on a fragrant, early-summer evening? The pastoral Tiergarten Park, which was some distance from where Ilse lived. Dr. Liebmann chivalrously opened the car door for Ilse and she sat down, leaning back in the luxurious velvety seat.

"What a beautiful car," she said, "and so comfortable."

The doctor sat down behind the wheel, started the engine, and they set out, arriving at the sprawling park a short time later. He parked the car and led Ilse to a small, intimate café with a particularly pastoral atmosphere. Ilse shivered briefly, remembering her first date with Johan, which had also taken place at a cozy café, although… not in the park. It was a kind of *déjà vu*, but the male lead was different, completely different. At the moment, she was sitting across from Dr. Abe Liebmann, who didn't resemble Johan at all—not in appearance, and certainly not in his behavior.

"What happened to your pretty lips? What's this cut adorning them?" he asked her, the doctor in him reawakening at the sight of the injury. "I don't remember seeing anything like that yesterday at the ward."

Ilse was embarrassed. She didn't want to lie and make up some flimsy excuse, but Johan was not an appropriate opening topic for a conversation on their first date.

"I'll tell you later," she deflected elegantly, thereby also sparing herself the need to come up with an excuse.

Dr. Liebmann respected her wish and didn't persist. He ordered cool, refreshing drinks for them. Later, if they wanted it, he would order coffee as well, he said. In fact, Ilse didn't want anything. All she wanted was to gaze at the captivating man sitting opposite her and to dive into his soul, but the only way to do so without embarrassment—and perhaps embarrassing him as well—was through conversation. He insisted that she tell him about herself and her life first, and she complied, sticking to generalities, as she wanted to move beyond her own tale and hear his. After all, he had stirred her curiosity right from the start.

Once she was finished speaking, the doctor began to share the story of his life in a chronological manner. "I was born in 1903 here in Berlin to my parents, Anna and Isadore. I'm an only child and a third-generation doctor. My late grandfather was also a physician," he said with a smile. "My mother, may she rest in peace, was a professor of literature at the University of Berlin. I live with my father on Landsberger Street, near Alexanderplatz, where our clinic is also located."

"How nice and easy to get up in the morning and go to work in the other room, without having to drive to work," Ilse said. "What a wonderful arrangement."

"Yes, it's very convenient that our clinic is part of the house, no doubt about it, but my father and I drive around quite a bit, as we sometimes make house calls or visit our patients at the hospital, as you've already seen," he responded, before continuing: "I was a very obedient boy, a good student and very calm, unlike many of my peers. About two years after the war ended, when I was 16, my mother passed away. She had a malignant tumor in her stomach that had spread, and she couldn't be saved."

"That's so sad," Ilse said, emotional. "Unlike you, I lost a parent at age 10 when my father was killed in the war. And the ironic part," she said, somewhat contemplatively, "is that my father hated the army and wasn't in favor of fighting. He was a man of peace who appreciated a quiet life."

Dr. Liebmann took her hand and brought it to his lips. "It's not easy growing up without a father, but growing up without a mother, alongside a grief-stricken father, is even harder," he said quietly. "And when the financial crisis broke out and everyone was suffering, including you and your mother, I'm sure, we might have suffered a little less. The medical profession is always lucrative, you know. There wasn't a single day when more and more patients and other wretched people weren't knocking on our door. In my free time, I helped my father a lot, and gradually began to feel myself getting attached to medicine. After graduating at the top of my class, I was accepted—like my father before me—to study medicine at Charité University Hospital."

"That's interesting," Ilse said. "We both attended Charité around the same time and never met. Now that I think about it, it's a little strange, isn't it? On the other hand, the medical campus is not really close to the nursing campus."

"It really is strange," he replied. "But apparently, those days weren't the right time for us to meet. We were in the frenzy of studying, while now each of us has a proper job, and we have all the time in the world to get to know each other. So what made you decide to work at Elisabeth in particular, rather than continuing on at Charité?" he asked.

"Elisabeth Hospital is less busy, closer to where I live, and the medical staff members are simply wonderful, just like family. In any case, I liked Elisabeth a lot more than Charité in terms of work, and trying out a different environment once I was done with school was quite appealing to me."

"We share something very essential," Abe said. "We have a lot in common—we both lost a parent at a young age, we're both grateful to our parents for raising us on good values and funding our training in a proper profession, and we were both were attracted to a profession that allows us to care for those who are sick and suffering. That really is an interesting coincidence. I truly enjoyed studying medicine and my love for the profession increases from day to day. I graduated in 1928, worked at Charité for a while in order to specialize in family medicine, and then transitioned to working in my father's clinic, where I remain, as you know, to this day. I'll be honest with you. The decision to become a doctor was the result of two main factors: the first is that from the day I was born, I've been living in the company of doctors, but mostly because of my mother's illness, which took her at such a young age and left me motherless."

"You were fortunate that your mother lived to see you as a young man before passing away. My poor father did not, but I have many happy, loving memories of him," Ilse said, her eyes becoming teary.

Dr. Liebmann caressed Ilse's cheek with a gentle finger that sent currents of pleasure coursing through her body. As he continued to share all that he saw as proper and desirable about himself, Ilse found herself increasingly mesmerized by him, unable to look away, and unwilling to miss even a single word.

"You know, my parents were the most precious thing in the world to me, and I was very close to my mother. I always admired that wonderful woman, energetic and multi-talented, and her quiet nature and inner peace always held a special sort of magic for me. Both my father and I were devastated when she passed away. I'll never forget the last thing she said before her eyes closed forever: 'Abe, take good care of Papa. It will probably be a lot harder for him than it will be for you. He—the great doctor—couldn't help me the way he always helped and will continue to help others.' And she was right. For a whole year after her death, I took devoted care of him until he began to smile again. You'll get to know him at some point—he's a very tough, rigid person, but deep inside, he's the most tenderhearted, kind, and sensitive person on earth."

Ilse found this so nice to hear. She savored his every word, completely empathizing with him and appreciating him for his great honesty, even though it was only their first date. She didn't want the time to go by, preferring to ground herself forever in these moments. But the time flew by and Dr. Liebmann still hadn't found the right moment to order coffee for them. When at last he offered to do so, she refused.

"The cold beverage filled me up," she told him. "Anyway, I don't really like to have coffee in the evening—it gives me insomnia."

"Well, then, I'll skip it too. Let's go for a walk in the park. It's so pleasant outside at night."

He paid for their drinks and they turned to go. Then he took her hand again and kissed it. As she had before, Ilse felt a ripple of heat traveling from the tips of her toes to the roots of her hair.

After a short stroll, during which they chatted constantly, Dr. Liebmann sat her down in a well-lit corner on one of the benches among the blooming shrubs, which were emitting intoxicating scents.

"Ilse," he addressed her by name for the first time, "there's one essential thing I haven't told you yet. It's something that's very important to me, so I'm sure you'll feel the same."

Ilse looked at him solemnly. After the long, honest talk they had just had, what else could he possibly find so important that he was now emphasizing and isolating it from all their previous topics of conversation?

"Ilse, I'm Jewish—both my parents are Jewish, as were my ancestors. It's important to me that you're aware of this. I still don't know you well enough to have a sense of your views on the matter. In the past, I've encountered people who have reacted in a variety of ways—from blatant extremism to complete acceptance and even admiration, which I usually attribute to the fact that I'm a doctor. In light of the honest and quite promising relationship we've just started to develop, I don't want anything to come between us or raise any doubts."

Abe saw Ilse's pretty face change color and, at that moment did not know how to interpret it. He continued to talk, somewhat flustered, hoping that the meaning of her reaction would become clear while he spoke.

"Just so you understand, we've never really been observant, but I always, always knew that I was Jewish. It was mostly my mother who took an active part in Jewish public life and maintained traditions at home, noting the Jewish holidays and celebrating the more important ones. My father gave her all the freedom in the world and followed her lead like a disciplined child, as long as she didn't interfere in his work and his private pursuits. I've been to the synagogue maybe a handful of times in my life, and even then I was mostly accompanying my parents to a wedding or a circumcision ceremony, which didn't happen too frequently. The only occasion related to the synagogue that I'll always remember is my Bar Mitzvah celebration, which my mother very capably arranged for me. Unfortunately, since her death, my father no longer makes an effort in that regard. It's true, he's still involved in the Jewish community's public life, but not like before. It was my mother who led him in all those matters, and she took the reins with her. The truth, Ilse, is that today, the most prominent aspect of my Judaism is, of course, the fact that I was circumcised. I'm also always greatly interested in the histories of nations in general, and in that of the Jewish people in particular."

Ilse's face became flushed once more, and she remained silent, but suddenly her fingertips reached out to touch Abe's, and he covered her hand with his free one and decided to wrap up the subject.

"Ilse, for most of my life, my family was as involved in the lives of Christians as much as it was in the lives of Jews. We always categorized ourselves as German Jews—Germans first and foremost, after five generations in Germany—and only then Jewish; maybe that's why our religious traditions were so important to my mother, so that we would always remember our original religious heritage. Most of my father's patients, and now mine as well, were and are Christian, and we've always gotten along well with everyone."

Now Ilse's face lit up with a smile. Her eyes were shining and her complexion returned to its natural peach hue.

"Abe, dear Abe, I'm not indifferent to what's going on around me, and I'm also not oblivious to people's names. Right from the start, when you were introduced to the hospital staff by name, it occurred to me that you were Jewish, but it really didn't register much, or, more accurately, that is the last thing

I'd pay attention to in my attitude towards you. You see, I was always raised to accept all people as human beings, without classifying them by religion, color, race, and so on. Since I've been working at Elisabeth Hospital, I've encountered all kinds of types and characters in every possible shade of the rainbow and from all over, and it never mattered to me what their religious affiliation or origin was. I always gave each of them, with no exception, devoted care."

Ilse watched Abe's face assume a calm that it hadn't possessed while he was disclosing his Judaism. *Poor man*, she thought. *He must have worried that I'd take it badly and maybe like him less.* It had never been easy being Jewish at any time, of that she was sure, and considering the atmosphere in Germany in recent years, especially after Hitler had begun to try to raise his profile and influence and had been maligning Judaism and all Jews, it had become much harder, perhaps even somewhat frightening.

"Abe," she addressed him again, "I enjoy your company more than I can express in words at the moment. Based on our brief acquaintance, my impression is that you're an honest, open, and earnest person, so I'll be honest too, and say that it's been a long time, if ever, since I've felt so good in someone's company." She couldn't help but think back to Johan, who was Abe's complete opposite in almost every regard... especially when it came to honesty.

This time Abe did heave a sigh of relief, albeit a quiet one. He didn't want Ilse to know how important the issue of Judaism had suddenly become to him. At that exact moment, he felt a wave of warm, sweet emotion toward her rising within him. He found her absolutely perfect. And then, after examining her face, his eyes once again fell on the small cut on her lip.

"Ilse, I really don't want to pry, but the doctor in me won't be put off. The cut on your lip is the kind that might leave a scar if it's not treated properly. You're surely aware of that, Madam Nurse, aren't you?" He smiled at her tenderly. "At the beginning of the evening, you said you'd tell me about it. Maybe you should..."

Ilse was silent, bowing her head, and Abe regretted asking, but he really was worried about her and her split lip, and, if he was being honest, was also quite curious as well.

"Abe, it's hard for me to talk about it, but since we've already shared quite a few things and were open with each other, I'll tell you, although I'll be brief, since it's something that is really weighing on me."

Ilse took a deep breath, looking directly into Abe's eyes, and he almost swept her up in his arms, moved by the warmth he felt toward her. He had a premonition that he wouldn't like what he was about to hear.

"Abe, for a few months, I'd been romantically involved with a young man named Johan Kirche. We met at the beginning of the year, and at first everything was pleasant and fun. Over time, I discovered some aspects of him that were not so nice. Most of all, I became very troubled by his political views and his fanaticism about them, and when I didn't agree with him and his opinions, he reacted harshly, making me fear further confrontations with him.

"About a month ago, I came to the decision to end the relationship that had suddenly become overbearing, and for some reason, threatening as well. Meanwhile, Johan became increasingly determined that we get married. I found it hard to tell him what I was thinking. He just scared me. He's a somewhat unpredictable person, who would occasionally lash out for no particular reason. When you and I first met, something happened later on that day that made me come to a final decision on the matter. In addition to the initial connection the two of us formed, which was very apparent to me, when I was walking home after work, I saw Johan in an SS uniform among a group of hooligans. He was drunk, singing loudly, and cursing. It shocked me, Abe; my jaw literally dropped and I couldn't close my mouth again. The SS—how long had he belonged to the organization, and why hadn't he told me during the time we were a couple?

"That same evening," she continued, while also lightly touching the cut on her lip, "Johan came to my home and we got into a terrible argument that was loud as well as violent. It resulted in this cut on my lip. Luckily, my mother was on her way home and Johan knew it, so he rushed off. Obviously he didn't want to run into her because she would have killed him with her bare hands if she had seen what he did to me. I haven't seen him since and I hope our paths never again cross. In fact, I made it clear to him that I don't want to continue our relationship. My initial feelings for him, which faded over time, have simply turned into terrible loathing."

Abe looked at her and then couldn't keep himself from putting his arms around her. He didn't say a word, but he was fuming inside. He wanted to protect her, take care of her, and watch over her.

"I said I'd be brief," she whispered, her cheek clinging to his shoulder, "and look how, all at once, I told you everything..."

Abe shifted her away slightly, saying, as he held on to both her arms, "No one has the right to raise a hand against another. You can argue, you can disagree, people can have disputes —even very serious ones—but all that is completely different from displays of physical violence, Ilse. I'm so sorry that you experienced that."

"It really is a shame," she replied, "but apparently it was inevitable. Otherwise, I would still be afraid to say what I thought and end that relationship, which had become so ugly."

"You might be right, but I still thoroughly denounce violence," Abe said, tightening his grip on her. Then his gaze pierced her eyes and he leaned in closer, bringing his lips to hers— one of which was still wounded—in a kiss that was long and particularly sensuous, yet careful as well. Ilse responded in kind, reciprocating his desire. It was simply the right thing to do.

Johan watched the kissing couple from his hiding spot. Although it was summer, a winter storm raged inside him. *That traitorous bitch!* She had just dumped him, and already she was in the arms of another man. Or perhaps she had been seeing the man for a while and had only been toying with Johan recently until she cut him loose? After all, he had already decided last night to reconsider the whole matter, and that morning after he woke up, had made up his mind to come over again, apologize, and do all he could so that Ilse would forgive him. And then when evening came, he had gone to her home and Hildegard had told him that Ilse was out. Hildegard hadn't even smiled at him; on the contrary, she scowled at him as though he were a stranger, even after the close relationship they'd shared. The way she treated him might as well have been a door slammed in his face. He felt so humiliated that he began to roam the streets like an abused dog, his legs carrying him toward the park. Suddenly, he saw Ilse and the man she was with as they sat in his fancy Maybach, which he'd parked in the café's adjacent parking lot. He followed them discreetly, hiding in a corner near the café they went into, with the patience of a detective. And after that, he saw them sitting on the bench, ensconced in the intimacy and sweetness of lovers. Johan feared that he was losing his mind, his fury igniting a fire within him that threatened to consume him.

Your day will come, Ilse Heine. I'll pay you back. I don't forget and I certainly don't forgive, Johan whispered to himself soundlessly, taking off. He decided to track down the handsome man in whose arms his detested beloved was snuggling like a cat in heat.

Johan went into the first bar he saw and drank himself under the table. He was lucky. One of his fellow SS members showed up and, seeing him in his inebriated state, helped him get to his apartment, which, on that fragrant early-summer night, appeared more neglected and pathetic than ever.

Chapter 15

Ilse and Abe's first date quickly led to a loving, caring relationship of mutual understanding. Ilse looked forward to their meetings like a sentimental teenager, and Abe provided her with all that she needed, primarily emotionally. She was completely in love with him, and had developed a deep, immense regard for his soul. If she had ever thought she loved Johan, she now realized how different that sentiment was from what she felt for Abe.

Her admiration for Abe increased every time she witnessed, however briefly, the devoted way he cared for the patients at the clinic. Abe's unique personality shone brightly; apparently he had never managed to suppress his great sensitivity toward the world he lived in. Ilse thanked her lucky stars for bringing her to this wonderful man and making him want her.

Abe also couldn't ignore all that was happening inside him, and was sometimes frightened by the intensity of his feelings for Ilse. Like her, he, too, was living from one date with her to the next, and as time went by, he realized that she was the woman with whom he wanted to spend the rest of his life, and that she, and only she, would be the mother of his children. He had had been in relationships with several women before but had never experienced such passion and such emotions.

Abe thought back to the first time he introduced Ilse to his father. He had invited her to the clinic one afternoon when he and his father were less busy. Ilse was as lovely as ever, returning Dr. Isadore Liebmann's strong, confident handshake with a trembling hand. Ilse didn't stay long, not wanting to inconvenience them, but even their brief encounter made Isadore relive the sweetness of his youth, somewhat peeling off his tough veneer and softening the gruffness of his voice. He then spoke highly of her, mostly due to his son's previous accounts of her.

Hildegard, too, was completely in thrall to the handsome, gallant, talented young doctor who was her daughter's current companion. From one day to the next, Hildegard further realized what had been missing in Johan and what Ilse had found so completely in Dr. Liebmann. He was physically appealing and had an impressive personality, and the respect and affection with which he showered her were also unique. Only an essentially good person, raised on solid values and respect for others, could behave that way. And if at first, and it was quite a while ago, she had tried to encourage Ilse to marry Johan Kirche, now, more than ever, she could admit both to herself and to her daughter that she had been wrong. She also admitted that Ilse's feminine intuition was much more on target than she had thought; while she did indeed have only her best interests at heart, her wonderful daughter knew what was best for her better than anyone else, including, as it turned out, her own mother.

Only one thing cast a shadow on this romantic perfection, in Hildegard's eyes. Unlike her daughter, she was not so cavalier about Abe's Judaism. It was not that she minded personally, as she had never had any problems with anyone who wasn't of her own religion. However, like her fellow Germans, she knew precisely what kind of names the Jews were called wherever they were, and in Germany in particular. It was true that the Jews had always been the subject of talk, but recently they were being maligned more than ever. Special emphasis was put on their negative contribution to Germany's current state, while no one wanted to highlight or even mention their many positive contributions.

And since Hildegard was just a tiny cog within the German nation and its traditions, a minor citizen with hardly any influence at all, she was afraid that one day evil would gain power and treat the Jews harshly. And then what would happen to Dr. Liebmann and the others of his religion? And what if her daughter was married to a Jew? Would harm come to her, too? Starting with the first evening on which Ilse and Abe's relationship began, Hildegard was more attentive to the ricochets spewed by Hitler and his devotees. She was aware of the nation's general state of mind and of the growing public opinion supporting and elevating Hitler. And she was truly frightened.

Hildegard could never forget the terrors of the war of 1914, in which she had lost her beloved husband. And Adolf Hitler's speeches frequently referenced that war. After all, about six years ago, in 1923, when Ilse was only 15 or so, Hitler had tried to carry out a coup, as well as to storm Berlin with his supporters, while heading a military parade. His attempt had failed, it was true, but the seeds of destruction had already been sown, and who knew when it would occur to him to try more extreme measures? Hildegard reminded herself that she had often been swept along in Hitler's charisma as a speaker. He had won over many of his listeners, herself included. But this charisma was not specifically connected to his attitude toward other nations and minorities, but rather to his general manner of speaking, and mostly to the way he portrayed the nation's problems and the burning need to solve them. His proposed solution was still debatable, but the deep concern Hitler displayed in his speeches was undeniable. It now made her shiver. Such powerful charisma—and what if the charismatic speaker ultimately turned into a monster?

At that time, Hildegard had no idea how justified her fears were and how prescient she was being.

◆ ◆ ◆

Johan tracked down the man he had seen with Ilse. He couldn't stop thinking about it, and the image of Ilse in the handsome young man's arms on the park bench continued to taunt him and awaken a sharp rage within him. The memory of their long, erotic kiss tormented him most of all. He found the time to follow Ilse's suitor between his various assignments, and after trailing him several times, followed him to the house on Landsberger Street. Johan was appalled when he saw the man enter a house with a door whose sign stating:

Clinic
Dr. Isadore Liebmann, Internist
Dr. Abe Liebmann, Family Doctor

His eyes narrowed, shooting sparks. Of all the men in Germany, it was precisely a Jew—Abe Liebmann—whom Ilse had chosen as a romantic partner. Johan felt as if by doing this, Ilse had betrayed him again, perhaps even intentionally. As a disciple of Hitler, he had developed a long-standing loathing of the Semitic race to which the Jews were born, and he believed whole-heartedly that the Jews were a pestilence. He had never forgotten the day that his mother's Jewish employer tried to seduce her, and that she had considered leaving her job, although she was ultimately forced not to do so and to continue working for him due to the failing economy. He also remembered that his mother had told him about Helmut's stepfather, a Jew who had been cruel both in his treatment of his wife—the grandmother he never knew, and his stepson—Johan's father.

When Johan's eyes resumed staring at the clinic's prominent sign, an immense wave of fury crested inside him. He walked over to the sign, clenched his hand into a fist and punched it as hard as he could. The sign, affixed to a stone post beside a small iron gate, was unharmed, but Johan's knuckles sustained a fierce blow, enflaming his rage even more. He associated the pain that gripped his fingers, which he alternately relaxed and flexed, trying to seek some relief, with the power of the sign representing the two Jewish doctors, the younger of whom had taken control of his Ilse's heart.

Johan let out a curse and brought his fist to his mouth. The more he thought back to his relationship with Ilse, the more resentful he became, and as he repeatedly imagined her in the Jewish doctor's arms, his frustration deepened and his hatred for the handsome young man's Jewish nature soared sky-high. He wondered contemptuously whether Ilse had also refused to give herself to the damn Jew because of her sacred Christian values. These thoughts consumed him. After all, from the day he had first met Ilse, he had dreamed of the moment when he would envelop her with his body and have his way with her, and her firm refusal humiliated him—mostly owing to the way she clung to Christianity in order to excuse her behavior.

In his heart of hearts, Johan knew that any other man with whom Ilse became romantically involved would have evoked terrible anger within him, but the fact that Liebmann was Jewish, along with the thought that Ilse might have succumbed to his charms, contributed to his bad feeling and to fueling his rage, until he felt that he was simply losing any ability to think rationally.

Your day will come, both of you, Johan snarled between his clenched teeth, *and you, Ilse—you will pay dearly. No one betrays Johan Kirche like that, insulting him and hurting him, and certainly not you and your vile Jewish doctor.* He then turned to go, but not before using his truncheon on the door of the shiny Maybach and leaving an ugly dent in it.

∽ Chapter 16 ∾

About two months after they met, Abe came to have dinner with Hildegard and Ilse. Hildegard cooked some of the finest delicacies the German cuisine had to offer, and the evening passed pleasantly. Hildegard sensed that before too long, Abe would be proposing to her daughter. After the meal, she and Ilse cleared the table and Hildegard decided to retire. She felt that the couple wanted to be alone, and therefore wished them both good night and withdrew to her room.

Abe moved to sit next to Ilse on the sofa. His desire for her was burning in every vein and capillary in his body, thrumming in each and every one of his nerves. His hands roamed over her body and his mouth latched on to her own. Ilse responded to his caresses and kisses, feeling more fired up than ever. She wanted him as much as he wanted her, but the presence of her mother in the next room didn't allow her to shake off her inhibitions. She didn't want to squander the unique beauty of total surrender, and it was important to her that the sweet moment of their union would be perfect. That evening in her mother's house was not the right moment for this, and she was certain that Abe understood that as well.

Suddenly, Abe stopped his caresses and gazed at her with eyes that were full of love. "When the time and place are right, it will happen, and in the most perfect way," he whispered in her ear and hugged her so tightly that for a moment he took her breath away. He certainly did understand.

"Ilse, I want you to marry me," Abe said. "In the days to come, I'll officially ask your mother for your hand in marriage, according to custom. I've already talked about it with my father and he's given me his blessing." Abe didn't want to tell her that his father had also had quite a few things to say about mixed marriages.

"It would make me the happiest woman on earth to be your wife," Ilse replied passionately. "And it's right to do it the formal way. My mother believes in these conventions. They're very important to her."

Around midnight, Abe said goodbye to Ilse, but not before covering her face with kisses. He was reluctant to leave, but it was late and he had no choice. On his way home, he amused himself by thinking about her pretty face, the caressing touch of her skin, and her intoxicating scent. Even as he dwelled on these tangible thoughts, specific sentences from the conversation with his father regarding his intention to marry Ilse were flitting through his mind.

"Abe, there'll be problems," Isadore had said. "She's a lovely girl, a woman after my own heart—talented, with a wonderful personality—but she's not really one of us and never will be. Just as we, because we're Jewish, will never fully belong to her kind." Amidst these statements, Isadore also talked about some philosophical and cultural-religious topics concerning Judaism, and Abe, who didn't want to consider all of them at that moment, felt unable to banish these thoughts. The issue was more acute than ever. After all, he had stated his intentions to Ilse, thus forsaking all of his father's reasoning. Although he had listened attentively to everything his father told him and even agreed with most of his points, he knew that there was no kind of reasoning that could diminish his feelings for Ilse. Ultimately, they were all people, human beings—so what did Christianity, Judaism, or German origin have to do with personality and character? Not a thing! Ilse could just as easily have been an unsuitable Jew, while he could have been a shallow, reckless Christian, and then they certainly would not have been a good match. And why did the world always emphasize differences of origin and religion when it came to couples? Why should anyone care? He loved Ilse in a way he never imagined it was possible to love a woman, and both she and he knew that she felt the exact same way about him. They were a perfect match, a match made in heaven. Both the Jewish and the Christian gods—if such a distinction was even possible—had set it in motion.

Matches made in heaven were something Abe had always believed in. Matches, fates, the course of events—they were all determined in the Kingdom of Heaven, and people's role was to carry them out. Despite coming from families that had been Jewish for many generations, his parents were also well integrated into the German-Christian society in which they lived. Abe had a feeling that if his mother were still alive, she would have a harder time with Ilse's religion, at least from a moral perspective, than his father did, although she would certainly have loved her as well. The last thing Abe wanted was to hurt either of his parents, although he understood that the sincere concern about the future that his father had expressed was not necessarily connected to the religious aspect of assimilation, but rather to the current ideological climate in Germany and his familiarity with Jewish history over time.

Abe was already a 26-year-old adult who was responsible for his own opinions and actions, and he was certain that this was the right thing to do, despite all claims to the contrary. After all, ultimately, he was not supposed to marry the religion or the nationality, but the human being herself. And he didn't want to mull it over anymore. He preferred to focus solely on the moment that he would approach Hildegard and ask her for Ilse's hand in marriage.

◆ ◆ ◆

Abe entered the Heine residence with a bouquet of flowers that filled both his arms and concealed part of his face. Hildegard, as was her custom at this hour, was setting the table in preparation for dinner, while Ilse was in her room, getting dressed for a planned outing to the cinema. Abe was particularly elegant. He looked more handsome than ever, his eyes sparkling brightly.

"Abe, what a beautiful bouquet! Ilse, come see," Hildegard called out.

"This one is especially for you, Frau Heine," Abe said.

Hildegard was far from being naïve. For some time now, her instincts had been signaling her that Abe was about to ask something truly important of her. Apparently, he intended to do so that night.

Ilse entered the parlor wearing a tailored suit. The moment she saw the bouquet in her mother's hands, she knew what it meant. It seemed that he had managed to surprise them both. They hadn't decided on the date that he would ask for her hand; instead, he had come to a decision on his own, and the element of surprise was romantic in itself.

Ilse approached Abe and he kissed her on both cheeks, sealing the greeting with another kiss on the lips. He then turned to Hildegard and, standing across from her, said, "Dear Frau Heine, I am hereby officially asking you for your daughter's hand in marriage. I want to make her the happiest woman in the world. Your daughter is the most beautiful and best thing that has happened to me, and by consenting to my proposal, you'll help me make my dream come true."

Hildegard never could have asked for a more gallant address. At that exact moment, her love for her son-in-law-to-be increased, and she chose to put aside all her apprehensions and the less-pleasant thoughts that had often been running through her mind.

"I hereby grant your request, my dear Abe," she told him, adopting his courtly, formal style. "I congratulate both of you, and wish you a long, happy life. I hope that before too long, you'll be turning me into a proud grandmother." She embraced

Abe warmly, then hugged her daughter, unable to hold back from shedding several bright, transparent tears of excitement.

Ilse felt as if her heart were about to burst with happiness. She felt such immense love for this man, the one who had just asked for her hand and who would soon be her husband, and knew that she was willing to die for him. She would never experience a love that was stronger or more perfect than this one, of that she was sure.

"And when are we planning to hold the joyous event?" Hildegard asked, derailing Ilse's train of thought. "We have to prepare everything properly, you know."

"We'll have the wedding in early January," Ilse said.

Abe added, "We have almost two whole months to prepare. My apartment on Leipziger Street will be available at the end of the year, in mid-December, and we'll still have enough time to get it ready so we can move in."

"That's great, Abe," Hildegard said. "That really is enough time to make Ilse into a beautiful bride and prepare everything she needs. Does your father already know?"

"Yes, he knows I came here today to ask for Ilse's hand. He'll be happy if the four of us meet so he can get to know you and then we'll have the chance to decide on a few things. Let me know when you want to do it, and we'll set up the meeting."

"That sounds just fine, Abe. I think that some evening next week, we'll hold that official meeting. I'm looking forward to getting to know your father."

The wedding date was set for the first week of January 1930.

After Isadore and Abe left the Heine residence, Isadore whispered to his son, "Since our dear Anna died, I have not seen a woman as charming and alluring as Frau Heine. You're lucky, Abe, to be marrying a girl with a mother like that."

Abe smiled in the dark, briefly raising his eyes to the sky.

◆ ◆ ◆

Abe and Ilse began the preparations for the wedding, and as they delved into the arrangements for the ceremony itself, chose new furniture for their apartment, and tended to all they would need in order to begin their life together, the newspapers came out with blaring headlines regarding the crashing of the stock market in the United States, news that left many people shocked.

∽ Chapter 17 ∾

"Ilse," Abe said, "I want you to keep your last name, and register your married name as Ilse Heine-Liebmann. It's important for various reasons, as I'm sure you'll agree."

"I know exactly what's bothering you, Abe," Ilse said. "It's because of what's happening in Germany regarding the attitude toward Jews. What's more, regardless of all that, my mother will be very pleased if I keep our last name. You know, everything concerning my father is a very sensitive subject for her."

The Heine and Liebmann families' personal joy was marred by the effects of the financial crisis sweeping the United States, which soon became a global crisis as it spread to other parts of the world. It was a perfect example of the "domino effect." Germany was among the first to be affected, as it was still in the process of dealing with the repercussions from the war that had ended in 1918 and with the consequences of the financial crisis of the 1920s, from which it was gradually emerging. The high unemployment rates were only expected to increase. The German economy, which was highly dependent on the American economy, suffered a severe blow, as the United States was cutting back on commerce with European countries, and had specifically discontinued the bequests and loans it had provided to Germany. Morale on the streets was going from bad to worse.

◆ ◆ ◆

In early January, as planned, on a cold but particularly pretty day, around noon, Ilse Heine and Abe Liebmann were officially married in Rotes Rathaus, Berlin's town hall. Hildegard managed to provide her daughter with the loveliest gown she could get her hands on, a white dress made of a silky, fluid material that was an exquisite fit for Ilse's slender frame, covering her arms and cascading to her knees. She wrapped a white knitted scarf around her shoulders and wore a small hat fitted with delicate lace that shaded half of her face. Ilse clutched a bouquet combining several types of flowers, with a strand of white silk at its center. She was as delicate and lovely as a fragile porcelain doll, and her great happiness only enhanced her beauty. When Hildegard saw her, all dressed up and utterly radiant in her immaculate white clothes, she burst into tears. She didn't know what made her cry more: the fact that her daughter was about to leave home and move to her new apartment as a married woman, her fears regarding the future and her fierce desire to keep her daughter and her beloved safe from harm, or her sorrow that Manfred was not by her side to witness the beauty of his daughter's nuptials. Or maybe the tears were only the result of her sheer excitement?

When the ceremony was over, all of the guests headed toward the exit from the town hall. Rice was thrown at the young couple's heads to wish them success and happiness, and a photographer who had been invited documented the moving moments with his camera.

And while Ilse and Abe stood at the doorway of the town hall, hugging and kissing and shaking their guests' hands, a man wearing a brown uniform with a black tie and a black cap sporting skull insignia was striding on the other side of the street. Johan, who happened to be passing by at the time, stood and stared at the elegant young couple that had apparently just gotten married, and was suddenly flushed with heat. He recognized that happy couple. He stared at them from where he stood, unable to tear his eyes away. A mighty maelstrom raged in his heart. He hadn't seen Ilse since the day he'd followed her and found her in the park, in the Jewish arms of Dr. Abe Liebmann, who was now embracing her possessively. Throughout the months since he and Ilse had gone their separate ways, he hadn't stopped thinking about her. He knew he could never get her back—that was a lost cause. But to see her radiant, lovely, and dressed in white on her wedding day brought up strong emotions of hatred infused with immeasurably frustrating fury.

◆ ◆ ◆

After the ceremony, Abe and Ilse drove to the apartment on Leipziger Street, near Potsdamer Platz—their new residence. They both turned to take off their elegant clothes—Ilse shedding her dress, and Abe removing his suit. They filled up the bathtub, after pouring in fragrant foaming soap, and dipped in it together. Abe poured them both some of the champagne left in the bottle from which they had drunk after the wedding ceremony. The warm, aromatic water, and the bubbly champagne, filled them with sweet bliss. Their bodies, clinging to each other, seemed to come together as one.

 Abe's gaze caressed Ilse and she felt her heart fluttering in all her limbs. She loved him so much. There was something intoxicating, sweet, and thrilling in this anticipation—something special that she knew she would never have wanted to miss, something that belonged solely to them, which justified every second they lingered there. Although they had had the option of consummating their relationship while working on the apartment and furnishing it, they hadn't done so. "Only when you are my lawfully wedded wife," Abe said, consciously choosing to avoid bringing the issue of religion into the matter, "will I allow myself to have my way with you. That's the decree under Jewish law, and I insist on upholding it." He then winked at her. Canoodling with him often nearly caused her to reach an irreversible state of full surrender, but she held back her passion. And it was precisely because Abe so desired her, finding himself in a near-haze of his own lust, yet sticking to his principles, that she considered him to be unique. No other man would have acted as he did, showing such immense, reasoned restraint after being exposed to her charms and kissing nearly every part of her body.

Abe's blood was churning, and his heart, which had been pounding for some time, delivered the turbulent blood to every organ in his body, including the member that played a major part in this erotic pursuit. In the past, this same member had often come close to betraying its owner and having its say. But Abe knew how to control every aspect of his life, including his rebellious manhood. *Your time will come soon*, he told it soundlessly.

They stepped out of the tub, and while they were still quite wet, Abe turned to Ilse, picked her up, and carried her to the bedroom. He put her on the bed, plucked a few petals from the wedding bouquet, silently apologizing to the fresh flowers, and scattered the colorful petals on Ilse's nude body. She was perfect. It was the first time she was laid out before him, fully and alluringly undressed, her sculpted breasts erect, her thighs barely concealing the honeyed triangle between them, and her body glistening with bright droplets of water that had yet to dry.

"This is an evening you will never forget," he whispered to her as he lay down beside her, and she shivered with excitement and felt her entire body fill with a moist sweetness.

Abe removed the petals from her body with his mouth and kissed every part of her, and once she had been stripped of all the petals, which surrounded her like the frame of a picture in which she was the center, his lips clamped onto her own and his hands roamed all over her clear, perfumed skin. Finally he was unable and unwilling to keep restraining the urges he had been suppressing and pushing aside from the day he first laid eyes on her. He enveloped her with his body and melded with her, and she, who had so anticipated this union and so yearned for it herself, did not feel any pain or discomfort, as if the interior of her body had been expecting it as well, flowing along with her rather than resisting her conquest.

Abe was right. She knew she would never forget the special evening that had brought them together. And since their love was already touching the edge of heaven, they couldn't imagine that any greater love existed.

After a week-long vacation, during which Abe and Ilse joyously roamed the streets of Berlin and its environs to the extent that the wintery weather allowed, they returned to their daily routines. Every day after work, Ilse would hurry home to get everything ready for Abe's return from the clinic. When they were far from each other, they ached with anticipation for the evening hours when they would reunite. And every night, they were subsumed by each other's bodies with immense, insatiable passion.

❧ Chapter 18 ❧

After about two months of marriage, Ilse's period was late. She was certain that she was pregnant. How could her womb remain indifferent to Abe's repeated romantic forays? Before she said anything to him, she decided to look into the matter properly. Dr. Gormann, the gynecologist she contacted, easily confirmed what she already sensed and knew. She was approximately six weeks pregnant. She couldn't have been happier and decided to share the news with her mother first. Hildegard was more accessible, as Ilse never wanted to bother Abe while he was working—not even with such joyous tidings. Tending to his patients remained top priority, unless something was really and truly urgent; in this case, the news could certainly wait until evening while remaining equally blissful.

Ilse arrived at the store and was thrilled to find it empty. She saw only her mother's head, popping up here and there as she arranged the clothes on the shelves and the hangers.

"Hello, Mama. How are you?" Ilse asked.

"Ilse, *liebchen*, what brings you here so early? You're usually rushing to get home after work," Hildegard said, hurrying toward her with an empty clothes hanger in her hand.

"Mama, I have something very important to tell you."

Hildegard abandoned her current task and turned to Ilse, all of her attention focused on her.

"What happened, Ilse? Is everything all right with you and Abe?" she quickly asked.

"Yes, Mama, everything is fine, and everything will be even better once your grandchild is born," Ilse said excitedly.

Hildegard looked at her daughter, took in what she had

heard, and then heaved a sigh of relief and smiled brightly. "Ilse, *liebchen*, I was afraid you had bad news for me, I don't know why. I'm so happy that the news is entirely different. Congratulations—this is wonderful! I'm so happy for you two, and for me and Isadore, too. The next generation is on its way. What did Abe say?"

"He doesn't know yet, Mama. I only found out for sure today after Dr. Gormann examined me and confirmed it. I decided to tell you first, since I didn't want to bother Abe at work."

Hildegard hugged her daughter and kissed her again and again. "You need to take care of yourself now more than ever, Ilse. Eat well, rest, and don't work too hard," she said.

"Don't worry, Mama. I'm sure that the moment Abe knows, he won't let me lift a finger. He pampers me even now, as much as his schedule allows. You know how busy he always is, sometimes even after the clinic's regular business hours, too. Besides, I'm in good hands—the hands of two doctors at home, as well as the entire hospital staff. And more than that, pregnancy is a beautiful period, and I don't want to treat it as something oppressive or difficult."

That evening Ilse prepared a romantic dinner by candlelight for Abe, and as they were savoring it, she said, "Abe, I have something very important to tell you." She paused, enjoying watching Abe's eyes pierce her, as if trying to guess her next words.

"I'm pregnant, Abe. Today I found out for sure. My due date is in mid-October."

Abe's face lit up with a smile and within seconds his eyes were tearing up. He jumped up, rushed to her, picked her up and held her close. "Ilse, this baby will be the complete product of our union, the fruit of our love, and our hearts' desire. You couldn't have given me better news. My father will be so happy too. I'm sure of it."

And in addition to the romantic meal and the joyous news, their shared night was as sweet as always, as well as more gentle and considerate than ever. In Ilse's new condition, Abe didn't think it would be a good idea to shock her body too much before the end of her first trimester of pregnancy.

◆ ◆ ◆

And while Germany struggled to rehabilitate its economy through the special low-interest loans it received from the United States, those loans could no longer sustain it, and the Weimar Republic slowly began to collapse.

Johan was aware of the fact that ever since the world had found out about the financial crisis in the United States, which had also begun to affect the German economy, the crisis had become the main topic of conversation within the party. Hitler's outlook had been pessimistic for some time, and he began to invest all his rhetorical powers in explaining the catastrophic situation that was gradually drowning the country. The picture was indeed bleak. According to Hitler, Germany was on the verge of its own new financial crisis, which would apparently be much more dire than its predecessor. Johan was grateful for one thing—that he was a member of the party and of the organization, and that his place within them was secure.

Owing to this difficult period, the citizens were willing to listen to anything from anyone, and this was certainly the case when the speaker was a talented demagogue like Adolf Hitler. The Nazi Party initiated a propaganda campaign that was unprecedented in Germany: Joseph Goebbels, who was in charge of the propaganda, brilliantly arranged many meetings, torchlight parades and conferences; he also hung attention-grabbing posters, and published the Nazi newspaper and distributed it throughout Germany.

For Hitler—the master of speeches—the opportunity to unleash his talent had finally arrived. He traveled all over Germany, giving speeches everywhere, attending conventions, shaking hands, signing photographs, and even hugging babies.

In his speeches, he offered the Germans what they were yearning for—encouragement. He made promises that remained hazy, but were still sufficiently convincing, while repeating short, catchy phrases. His appearances were carefully planned out. The audience was always required to wait in order to allow the tension to mount, only to be broken when the brownshirts, with their black hats bearing the skull insignia, strode in to the sound of a military march, carrying golden flags; finally, Hitler himself marched into the hall, with the roar of "*Heil Hitler*" thundering in the background. Johan was amazed anew every time by the powerful, mesmerizing effect of the closed-off assembly hall on the audience, with all its flags, music, and decorations. It was certainly impossible to stay indifferent to such extravagant displays, which swept along and enflamed everyone in attendance.

◆ ◆ ◆

As Ilse's pregnancy progressed, the financial recession worsened, its oppressive influence apparent everywhere. Widespread employee layoffs had a ripple effect. Banks throughout the country were becoming insolvent as they lost clients' savings. Inflation was sky-high once more, making it difficult for citizens to buy food. Middle-class citizens' lifestyles thus changed gradually while they lost all control over the course of events. For some time, the Great Depression had been obliterating all boundaries, casting people into poverty and deprivation and causing them to seek out a solution—any solution—to the situation.

Hildegard, too, felt the effects of the crisis. Some of her regular clients stayed away from the store. Her gradually dwindling income forced her to make every effort to reduce her expenses. Some days she was so anxious about her livelihood that she believed that at some point it might no longer be profitable to keep the store open—but then how would she make a living?

She was glad she had been wise enough to put aside some savings for a rainy day, as that day had indeed arrived.

Elisabeth Hospital was also suffering the impact of the hard times and initiated some changes to its business practices. Several employees were laid off and others had their work hours reduced. Ilse was among those to have her hours reduced, and had to switch to a four-day work week. She was an outstanding nurse and no one considered letting her go.

There were changes at the Liebmanns' clinic as well, as some of the patients stopped showing up. They could no longer afford to pay for private medical services. Sometimes, Abe would come home earlier than usual, overjoyed that he could spend more time with Ilse, whose belly was gradually swelling. Every day, Abe's admiration for her grew and his love for her soared beyond the altitudes it had already reached.

"I'm very concerned about the immense influence the Nazi Party has on the citizens," Isadore said solemnly. "This is precisely the crucial time to spoon-feed the suffering and the fearful with heaping servings of promises and the vision of a better future. Therefore Hitler is able to accrue more and more power and, over time, use it in radical ways. After all, that's what he's been aiming for, for years now."

"And if we're all suffering, the Jews have worse awaiting them in the days to come," Hildegard said, her voice radiating worry. "Times like these are the perfect breeding ground for laying the blame on others' shoulders, and those others include 'the Jews.'"

"The hatred of foreigners didn't start today," Abe said, "and we—the Jews of Germany—who don't consider ourselves foreigners but rather Germans in all regards, are now forced to change our self-definition due to the emerging circumstances."

Ilse was silent. She knew that if she spoke, she would disclose her true fears. She was already more sensitive than ever since her pregnancy had been revealed, and lately she felt as if she could burst into tears at any given moment. She bit her lip and looked at Abe with open adoration.

Chapter 19

As Ilse entered her seventh month of pregnancy, Gertrude and Sigmund Sontag—a delightful couple around her and Abe's age—moved into an apartment on the floor below them. Gertrude, a sweet, dark-haired, clear-skinned, brown-eyed young woman, was also expecting; she was in her sixth month of pregnancy, and was very happy to meet her new, personable neighbor, and mainly her husband the doctor, who was always available to provide medical aid in a time of need.

Gertrude didn't work. She had been let go in the early stages of her pregnancy during a wave of layoffs at her place of employment. Sigmund, her husband, a handsome, fair-haired, blue-eyed man, held a senior position with the Ministry of the Interior.

Almost immediately, a warm bond formed between the two couples. It was nice to know that in their entire apartment building there was at least one couple with whom they had formed a relationship that transcended merely being neighborly, and as the days went by, their friendship gradually deepened, mostly between the two expectant women, who shared many matters concerning their pregnancies as well as other topics.

One morning, Gertrude showed up at the Liebmanns' apartment and found Ilse on her own. After discussing their gestating bodies and the state of the embryos—which of them was kicking more and when—as was their habit, Gertrude suddenly said, "Ilse, I apologize in advance if I sound nosy, but I wanted to ask you what's it like being married to… a Jew? How did you end up marrying a Jew, in spite of all the social difficulties involved?"

Despite Gertrude's apology, Ilse found herself somewhat

taken aback by this very personal question, and considered how to phrase her answer. Finally she decided to reply briefly and succinctly, but in a way that would be meaningful and, in fact, as honest and real as possible. "Gertrude, I've never given much thought to a person's nationality or religion, as long as he's a decent human being. And as you've had the time to see for yourself, Abe is the most wonderful person I ever met. I love him with all my heart, and to me, his Judaism is not something that should be treated as negative in any way, although these days it is indeed proving to be somewhat problematic."

Gertrude looked at her, nodded, and then concluded, "Ilse, you're right, and thank you for illuminating a point for me in that context that might have been a bit dark."

Ilse could not have asked for a more fitting reaction. The two continued to chat idly until the time came for the husbands' return. Alongside the pleasant closeness that had formed between them as neighbors and as friends, all four also fiercely guarded their privacy and their daily routines, making sure their amiable relationship would always be within the boundaries of good taste.

◆ ◆ ◆

It was at the height of summer when Sigmund felt unwell in the middle of the night. His temperature spiked and he began to hallucinate. Gertrude panicked, and in her distress, her belly weighing her down more than usual, knocked on the Liebmanns' door. At first, her rapping was faint and when no reply came and her fear increased, she began to pound on the door,

Abe opened the door in his pajamas, his eyes half-closed. When he saw Gertrude, looking disheveled and terrified, he asked in concern, "Gertrude, what's wrong, dear? Come in. What happened?"

Ilse, also awakened by the voices coming from the parlor, hurried to find them. "Gertrude, are you sick?" she asked.

"It's Sigmund. He's burning up with fever and not making any sense," Gertrude wailed. "I don't know what to do."

"Come in, come in, and calm down," Abe said. "I'll go take a look at him immediately." He picked up his doctor's bag, with all the equipment in it, and hurried downstairs to see Sigmund.

After a thorough examination, Abe determined that Sigmund had pneumonia and should be hospitalized so he could be properly treated and monitored. "Gertrude, you don't play around with pneumonia, and what's more, you might catch it, which would be highly undesirable in your condition. Sigmund has to be admitted to the hospital. We'll send him to Elisabeth, where Ilse can also be in touch with the doctors taking care of him."

Gertrude burst into worried tears, but she trusted Abe and Ilse to help her.

The next morning, Abe sent Sigmund to the hospital, where he was admitted. Abe came to visit him every day and was also involved in his treatment, along with the unit's doctors.

Within a few days, Sigmund's condition improved considerably and he began to smile again. "Thank you, Abe, for all the devoted treatment from you and Ilse," he said, his voice still somewhat weak.

"Oh, come on, Sigmund. After all, you're my patient—and also our friend, right?" Abe replied, grinning. "And your Gertrude is in good hands. We're taking care of her and she's at our place most of the time, knowing you'll be back home soon, safe and sound."

And, indeed, Gertrude drew encouragement from spending time with the Liebmanns, and her love for them grew from day to day.

On the last day of Sigmund's stay at the hospital, Gertrude spent the evening in the Liebmanns' company. She was in far better spirits and the color had returned to her cheeks.

"Gertrude, Sigmund will be coming home tomorrow," Abe

said, "but I want you to take care of yourself. Don't start babying him, since the real baby is in your uterus, right?" And all three began to laugh.

"I'll never forget everything you did for us," Gertrude said, tears in her eyes. "As you already know, Sigmund and I don't have any close family members here. My only brother immigrated to America a long time ago, back in the days of the previous financial crisis, when he realized he could live a better life elsewhere. After Sigmund and I got married, he often tried to convince us to come to him once his business began to thrive, but we didn't want to. Sigmund holds a senior position, and all in all, we're doing quite well here—besides which, it's always hard to start again in a new, different place. But of course we stay in touch with my brother. Maybe someday, once things are stabilized here, we'll go visit him. Since the crisis broke out, his concern for us has grown, mostly due to my pregnancy, although things are equally bad in the United States these days."

"We have a very small family too," Ilse said, "and mostly we have each other. The last war and the grim circumstances that followed it have hurt a lot of families, and I think that's one reason many of us don't have large families."

"I sympathize with you, Gertrude," Abe said. "On the one hand, majestic America is tempting, but on the other, nowhere in the world is ever really easy, certainly not during a crisis. Germany is our country and, just like everyone else, we need to know how to cope and to hope that this bad period will soon pass. Then we'll all go back to normal life. However, I'd actually like to visit America. I'm sure it's very different there than it is here, and it would be interesting to get to know New York, the big city everyone's always raving about."

The next day, Sigmund returned home. He was thinner and pale but healthy, and grateful to the Liebmanns. "You're more than family to us," he told them. "You're here nearby, while our few family members are scattered all over Germany and outside it. We'll never forget your great help and the devoted care you gave to both of us."

"You're also like family to us," Abe said warmly. "And I've often heard it said that a good neighbor is better than a... distant relative. Isn't that how it goes?" and the four of them smiled in pleasure, mostly due to Abe's improvised proverb.

Gertrude found the right moment when she was alone in the kitchen with Ilse, who was preparing warm beverages for the four of them, and whispered in her ear, "Do you remember your answer to my question about Abe's Judaism? This incident with Sigmund and everything surrounding it only reinforced my understanding of how right you were about a person's humanity. Your husband is a wonderful person by virtue of being a decent human being, and national origin or religion has nothing to do with it."

◆ ◆ ◆

In the elections that took place in September 1930, the Nazi Party increased its number of voters, becoming the second-largest party in the Reichstag, the national parliament. Other parties were on the ascent as well, while the main losers were the Social-Democratic Party—Weimar's ruling force—which lost votes to the communists and the German National People's Party, which ceded some of its influence to the Nazis. But most of the Nazi Party's new supporters came from among the ranks of those experiencing distress and great confusion—the 5,000,000 citizens who chose not to vote in 1928, but who hurried to cast their ballots following the financial crisis that was gradually and avidly eating away at their way of life and consuming every aspect of it.

∽ Chapter 20 ∾

Ilse's due date was approaching. She was heavy and awkward, and the late-summer heat wasn't doing her any favors. Abe did all he could to help her, although she tried to remain energetic and stick to her usual routine. "I'm not the first or the last to be in this condition," she said, "and quite soon, it'll all be over and then we'll both be in the permanent condition of parenting a child," she said as she smiled wearily.

Hildegard also spent many hours with her daughter and came almost daily to help her out. Ilse felt that her mother was more excited by the prospect of the upcoming birth than she was, and that her claims of visiting in order to assist her were only an excuse. Her mother simply wanted to be by her side as much as possible. Ilse sympathized. After all, Hildegard didn't have another living soul beside her, and now she—her daughter—was about to become a mother and make her a grandmother, which was a major event. Life went on, even after her father's death.

When she begged her mother not to tire herself out so much on her behalf, Hildegard chuckled and said, "I can already count the clients coming into the shop on one finger, you know. I don't think my absence has much of an effect on anyone during these crazy times." Her heart went out to Ilse and she hoped she would have an easy birth and not suffer too much. Hildegard knew her daughter would be under the care of the best doctors in the hospital, but she worried nevertheless. She remembered giving birth to Ilse, which had not been easy, and how much Manfred had helped her afterwards. Her eyes filled with tears every time she thought of Manfred in connection with Ilse. He had died so young, and hadn't had time to really enjoy almost anything. How proud he would have been of his daughter, and how he certainly would have rejoiced over his grandson or granddaughter.

Hildegard wiped away her tears. This was fate, and she had no way of changing it, as much as she would have liked to have the ability to do so.

In mid-October, Ilse started experiencing contractions. It was late at night, but she didn't need to wake up Abe, whose open eyes were already staring at her tensely. "Your restlessness and constant shifting woke me up," he told her. "So let me help you get ready and we'll drive to the hospital."

Ilse merely nodded, and holding on to her belly, she stood in place like a little girl and let Abe dress her. He imbued her with calm, and his fluttering touch on her body filled her eyes with tears of love.

Abe didn't leave her bedside even for a minute. He assisted the experienced midwife and his excitement knew no bounds when the baby began to emerge and was pulled out. It was a handsome, healthy boy weighing 3.5 kilograms, and the sweaty, groaning Ilse lit up with a smile of relief and satisfaction. "Show him to me. I have to see him," she whispered.

The baby had already been wrapped in a receiving blanket and placed in Abe's arms. He bent over Ilse and showed her the boy—their first son—the fruit of their great love. Ilse rested her lips on the tiny, somewhat wrinkled face, wanting to kiss his forehead.

"What a lovely, perfect thing, Abe. What an adorable baby we have," she said.

The baby was whisked off for routine tests and treatment and Ilse was taken to the recovery room. Abe stepped out and delivered the news to Isadore and Hildegard. Hildegard could not hold back and a quiet stream of tears flowed from her eyes. Isadore, whose eyes were shiny as well, hugged her shoulder and said in an emotional voice, "Congratulations."

When Ilse was lying in her hospital bed, all cleaned up, her hair brushed, and wearing a white nightgown, her mother, shortly followed by Isadore, came over to give her a huge hug.

"They showed us the baby," they told her. "He's simply enchanting."

"I want to call him Manfred," Ilse said, looking at her mother. "After Papa." She then turned to Abe. "And if you really want… we can have him circumcised."

Abe looked at her and his heart melted. "No, there's no need for that, my darling," he told her. "After all, according to the Jewish religion, he's Christian, based on his mother's religion, and there's no need—especially these days—to create an irreversible situation… Enough said on that. And as for the name: Your wish is my command." He then declared to Hildegard and Isadore, "Your grandson will be named Manfred Liebmann-Heine."

Abe had no idea how the two decisions he had just made—regarding the circumcision and the two last names—would prove to be a wise choice for everyone involved, especially for the child.

The next day the Sontags came to visit, bringing with them a giant bouquet. Gertrude embraced Ilse, hoping to soon be in her good friend's situation.

◆ ◆ ◆

Johan dropped by Elisabeth Hospital to visit a fellow member of the SS who was sick. He had no choice; he didn't want to set himself apart from the others who had already been sent to pay their ailing colleague a courtesy visit. The last thing Johan wanted was to arrive at the surgery ward, where his colleague was hospitalized and where Ilse worked. He knew he would be unable to bear the lovely sight of the golden-haired Ilse in her clean white uniform, that familiar, alluring smile on her face—the smile she generously bestowed on everyone in the hospital.

On the one hand, he so yearned to see her again, while on the other, just thinking about her flooded him with great anger—anger that she wasn't his wife, and even worse, that she was that damned Jewish doctor's wife.

After spending about half an hour with his sick colleague, speaking to him encouragingly and sharing various anecdotes about what was going on in the organization, Johan decided that the time had come to leave. "Feel well, Norman, and come back to us soon. We all miss you," he told the man, bidding him farewell. He turned to go and then, as if gripped and pulled along by imaginary hands, he dragged his feet to the nurses' room on the ward. The room was empty. He turned to trudge down the corridor when he came across Dr. Genscher.

Johan had a brief urge to keep walking, ignoring the very familiar doctor, but once he realized that Dr. Genscher had recognized him, he changed his mind. "Hello, *Herr Doktor*," Johan said. "How are you?"

"I'm well, thank you," Dr. Genscher replied. "And what brings you to us?" he asked in a critical sort of tone that Johan's sharp ears noted.

"Oh, I came to visit my friend Norman, who is hospitalized in this unit."

Dr. Genscher nodded slightly, his gaze piercing Johan's eyes. He was already raising his hand, signaling that he was in a hurry, when Johan, whose head felt as if it were splitting apart from the flurry of thoughts assailing it, could not stop himself from asking, mock-casual, "Dr. Genscher, how is Ilse Heine?"

The doctor looked at him after some time and then cynically replied, "Ilse *Liebmann* is doing very well. She's on maternity leave after the birth of her son, and she and her husband couldn't be happier." He then nodded in parting and disappeared down the corridor.

Johan's eyes tracked the doctor's receding form until he could no longer see him. He was rooted in place and having a hard time recovering. The intentional taunt in every one of

Dr. Genscher's words made his skin prickle, most of all when he had emphasized Ilse's new last name. Only an idiot would fail to pick up on the blatant hint in the doctor's words, and Johan swallowed hard and hurriedly left the hospital. Once again, he felt his yearning turn into insane rage.

◆ ◆ ◆

A short time after Manfred's birth, Gertrude gave birth as well. It was also a boy, whom they named Richard. The two neighbors and friends were overjoyed to raise their children together, and the bond between them grew stronger than ever. As Ilse's time to return to work drew closer, and before she could even consider the question of who would take care of Manfred, Gertrude offered her help. "Ilse, I just love babies," she said, "and I'll simply pretend I had twins. The boys resemble each other a little, too, don't you think? They both have fair hair like you and Sigmund, and darker eyes like Abe and me. Maybe all our closeness had a genetic effect on them." She began to laugh and Ilse joined in. She was greatly relieved that such a motherly, devoted caretaker had been found for Manfred.

Manfred and Richard grew up together and were just like brothers. Sometimes Manfred called Gertrude "Mama," which thrilled her. Abe and Ilse were overjoyed with their son and with the care he received from Gertrude.

Chapter 21

During the second half of 1931, unemployment continued to surge until it reached alarming rates. Industry in Germany collapsed completely, countless banks declared bankruptcy, and inflation was sky-high. A mood of despair and a lack of faith in the democratic government spread throughout the country, along with increasing homelessness and, worst of all—hunger. People fought on the streets about anything at all, resorting even to murder, but there was no response from the longtime political leaders. In their distress, more and more people turned to the only politician who remained consistent and continued to offer a solution—Adolf Hitler, the head of the Nazi Party, who promised to save the nation from the crisis and bring about a better future.

Hildegard tried her utmost to hang on to her store by sheer force of will. She couldn't order much new merchandise, as her cash flow was low, and even if she could have done so, she knew there wouldn't be much demand. There were hours when she stood in the store, rearranging the shelves by shifting around the items that still remained, while bleak thoughts overtook her. Ilse and her grandson were indeed her whole world, but this store was her other entire world. She had opened it after her husband left her forever, and this occupation had given her the strength to survive and the money to support herself and her daughter. Now her fortitude was dwindling, and it had been a while since she'd earned any significant income. Everyone was badmouthing everything. Everyone was having a hard time. Everyone was frustrated and disgruntled, and everyone, with no exceptions, was looking for a scapegoat on whom they could hang their despair.

And soon enough, a scapegoat was found to provide some solace for the German people's distress—the Jews, on whom blame was arbitrarily heaped. Now more than ever, Hildegard found it hard to hear the Jews being maligned and accused of taking an active role in turning Germany into a country suffering from crisis, deprivation, and decline. After all, her son-in-law was a Jew, and he was actually significantly better than many of the Germans she had met during her lifetime. And there were many other fine Jews like him; what part had they actually played in this malaise plaguing Germany, as well as many other countries that were in crisis? Especially since the Jews themselves were suffering under the current circumstances, and were an integral part of the affected victims. After all, she herself had never been indifferent to Hitler's speeches, which proliferated during these difficult times, focusing on the financial depression, its impact on Germany, and the means needed to fix and improve the situation. There was some justice to his claims, but his repeated attempts to place most of the blame on the Jews, of all people, seemed excessive to her, driven by an agenda and sometimes even pathetic in their unfairness and illogic. How was it the Jews' fault that the stock market in New York had crashed, impacting the rest of the world? She had Jewish customers who complained about their difficulties as well. One of them told her in tears that her son had committed suicide after losing his job, and she wasn't the only one to suffer such misfortune. If Hitler was so desperate to find reasons for the current state of affairs, as well as creative solutions, he needed to do so in a much less biased, manipulative way.

She often discussed it with Isadore. He, too, was highly attuned to the public's state of mind and was frequently extremely pessimistic. With growing concern, he tracked the Nazi ideological agenda, which was becoming increasingly influential, and was put off by Hitler's shrill, theatrical speeches. Like many others, he fervently hoped that once the recession ended and the crisis was resolved, sanity would return to the suffering nation, and figures like Hitler and his associates would find something else to focus on other than radical politics and dangerous leadership.

The number of patients needing some sort of medical help was constantly growing and many of them came knocking on the Liebmann Clinic's door. The severe economic depression that had affected all classes of society and countless families triggered a wave of emotional problems, which resulted in physical illnesses as well. It was precisely during this difficult period that Isadore and Abe exhibited much patience, treating everyone who showed up with greater devotion than ever. Their reputation spread by word of mouth and they acquired more and more admirers who preferred the care they provided over that of any other doctor. Alongside the Liebmanns' professionalism and attentiveness to their patients, they often offered medical aid without charging any fee.

◆ ◆ ◆

Johan already knew that Ilse and Abe had had a boy, and kept up with everything that was going on with the young couple. He had his own methods of obtaining this information whenever he wanted. His whole world consisted of his membership in the SS and the events of Ilse's life, which had long ago become an obsession. He hadn't managed to rebound since she broke up with him, or even to mitigate, to any extent, the impact of the severe blow she had inflicted on him. From the day they parted ways, he had dedicated his life—whether consciously or subconsciously—to his need to see her new relationship collapse. She had to be punished, and he hoped to be the one to execute the punishment with his own two hands. It wasn't fair that he felt miserable and battered, while she—who could light up his life—chose to bestow this light and happiness on a despicable Jew, of all people. Perhaps he might have been able to be more forgiving if Ilse had chosen a mate who belonged to her own people and religion, but he would never forgive her for the fact that her marriage to Dr. Liebmann had also resulted in a half-Jewish boy. To him, this was the wretched consequence of a mixed marriage.

Johan was also furious with Hildegard. How had Hildegard, who had always seemed like his ally, turned her back on him as well, allowing her daughter to marry a Jew? Where had her previous views on Jews disappeared to? After all, they had discussed political matters numerous times, and had often mentioned Hitler, with Johan himself bringing up the subject of the Jews' global negative influence and their contribution to the world's ills, and Hildegard had never objected. Was she being hypocritical, merely trying to appease him when she had agreed with him? Apparently so, as it was impossible to think that her opinions had changed so drastically in the blink of an eye. And now she was actually part of a Jewish family! When he came to this conclusion regarding Hildegard's hypocrisy, he became livid.

Johan always managed to fuel his old rage when he thought about Ilse and Hildegard. If the two of them had linked their lives to Jews, as far as he was concerned, they had become Jews as well, which nauseated him while also awakening an unhealthy need to seek revenge on them.

The next thing that pained Johan was the day that his team was sent to suppress a small uprising by the SA, which continued to be a thorn in the party's side. During the skirmish, his old friend Herman Sturm was killed. Johan realized that the entire ideology drilled into them by the organization, about totally dulling their emotions, was not always successful. His emotions had indeed been dulled, but when it came to certain matters, they would awaken, come alive, become sharper, and inspire difficult sensations within him.

In July 1932, as several other parties on the extreme right disappeared, the Nazi Party enjoyed a significant increase in power, managing to exceed 40% of all the ballots cast. The color of the SS uniforms was changed to black, endowing the organization's members with the nickname "black shirts." These shirts sported the insignia of the Nazi eagle, and now, the insignia of the SS as well—a pair of parallel vertical lightning bolts. Towards the end of the year, the SS comprised about 50,000 members, organized in a hierarchical structure whose smallest units were squads, followed by platoons, companies, and battalions. The party had new headquarters in Munich—"The Brown House"—and was rolling in funds that came from all directions. The owners of Germany's major industrial factories viewed the Nazis as the wave of the future and contributed huge amounts of money to Hitler, hoping he would rise to power. The party used these funds to pay the salaries of its increasing number of employees, as well as to fuel the Nazi propaganda machine.

Johan looked wonderful in the new uniform. His silvery-blond hair and his blue metallic eyes—a sharp contrast to the black uniform—endowed his appearance with toughness and created an even more imposing and elegant look. He was promoted to the role of company commander, thereby greatly elevating his self-confidence and imbuing him with an affirming sense of pride.

◆ ◆ ◆

Ilse's fears relating to Abe's Judaism were constantly growing. She had never paid much attention to politics, but now, in these bleak times, she was riveted to it. She avidly consumed the stories in the daily newspapers and listened to the radio, but didn't discuss any of it with him. His own silence on the subject indicated that he was as troubled by it as she was. The Sontags, too, discussed anything but the Jewish issue, which had long become "The Jewish Problem" to the German people.

Hildegard was the one to break the conspiracy of silence when she said to her daughter, "Ilse, I've occasionally considered the difficulty of being a Jew in our country. Nowadays I think about it often, and these thoughts are causing me insomnia. It's true, there are many mixed couples in our country, but all my worry is focused on you, on your son, and of course on Abe. I have a feeling that things will only get worse. The Nazi Party has been ruthlessly attacking the Jews for some time now, casting most of the responsibility and the blame for our current situation on them. Anyone with half a brain knows that there isn't an iota of truth to these claims, but today so many are brainwashed and biased, closing their eyes and flocking after Hitler and the party. Ilse, my intuition is telling me that soon Hitler will not only be the head of the party but also the head of the country."

"Mama, I'm really worried too, but what can we do? We've lived here our whole lives, and so has Abe's family. Abe and Isadore are esteemed, popular doctors, so maybe their situation isn't as bad as it seems. What part do Jewish doctors play in this whole crisis? To this day, Abe and Isadore have helped so many people, both Jews and Germans, so why would they be considered to have a negative influence? Everything that's going on is simply inconceivable. I agree with you that our Germany is really in grave danger—the danger of a regime that's tyrannical, authoritative, militant, and maybe even cruel."

◆ ◆ ◆

And indeed, Ilse and Hildegard's great fears proved to be justified. At the end of January 1933, things came to a head when President Hindenburg declared Hitler to be the country's leader, appointing him Chancellor of Germany. Shortly afterward, Hitler scheduled new elections at the beginning of March and began to enforce various restrictions on the activities of rival parties.

One evening at the end of February, Abe, Ilse, and Manfred had finished eating dinner and Ilse was getting the boy ready for bed. It was 9:00 p.m., and she was reading him a bedtime story when they heard increasing noise coming from the street. Abe peered through the window and saw people gathering downstairs, talking loudly. He couldn't hold back and told her, "Ilse, I'm going downstairs for a minute to see what all the fuss is about. I'll be right back." He didn't wait for her answer and quickly disappeared down the stairs. Soon he blended in with the crowd and with other neighbors who huddled on the sidewalk; he spotted Sigmund among them. There was a strange smell in the air—the smell of burning.

"Sigmund, what's going on? It seems like something to the north of us is burning. Do you know anything?" Abe asked.

"No, Abe. No one here knows anything. One thing's for sure—something serious is going on over there. Look, you can see something in the distance. The sky is gradually changing color. Do you see?" Sigmund asked, pointing at a distant point in the sky. The crowd's ruckus increased, but nobody could figure out, for the time being, the fire's scope or its location. Suddenly they heard the shrill sirens of fire trucks. Abe and Sigmund returned home to wait for further developments.

The next day they heard that the Reichstag building had burned down, and that the intense explosion triggered by the flames caused the stately building's debating hall to collapse.

"Abe, I have a feeling that this was arson, and that it was politically motivated," Sigmund said. "After all, Hitler's already managed to declare a state of emergency. Today we heard that he's already convinced the president to sign "The Reichstag Fire Decree," in order to "protect the nation and the state," which cancels seven articles of the Weimar Constitution and gives the government the right to restrict personal liberties, freedom of expression, freedom of the press, freedom of association, and the right to privacy, and also allows them to conduct searches, confiscate property, and sentence people to death for a long list of crimes."

Abe's heart was heavy. *This is just the beginning*, he thought to himself. If the economic depression facilitated the spread of the Nazis' tyranny and evil, it seemed likely that from the moment the Reichstag was torched and the decree to protect the German nation and people was signed, it wouldn't take long to pave the way to further tyranny and evil.

"Sigmund, the burning of the Reichstag is tremendously significant in so many regards, mainly symbolically. Look at what it led to—the signing of this decree, and an extreme, crucial change in policy. Hitler and the Nazis have left their mark on a central building, leaving behind only smoking embers. It's as if the Nazis are trying to completely erase the existing administration and shape a new reality."

"The worst part, Abe," Sigmund said, "is that it's not 'as if'—it's truly so, and maliciously planned, of that I'm sure. Deep inside, I also believe that the Nazi Party is responsible for the arson, and they're trying to conceal it in various ways, including blaming the communists and their other opponents. This doesn't bode well, and that's an understatement. To phrase it more accurately, it's very ominous. Anyone who can issue a command to burn down the Reichstag will be able to issue other heinous commands. This is outright rebellion against the entire structure of the German government and its rules, its views and its conduct. It's exactly like burning down a central church full of believers to cause religious harm, and this incident of arson was explicitly intended to cause political harm."

"There's plenty of public sympathy for Hitler, which is only growing, and his negative charisma is rapidly infecting many more. It's undeniable," Abe concluded.

The elections held in early March 1933 awarded the Nazi Party 44% of the votes. At the end of the month, after a campaign of intense pressure, the Reichstag approved the Enabling Act by a large majority, with only the Social-Democrats objecting. The Act was intended to ensure that the Nazis retain absolute control and was enacted for a period of four years.

◆ ◆ ◆

"Abe, I'm worried about you, Manfred, and Ilse more that I'm willing to admit," Isadore said, a slight tremor in his voice. "I'm already elderly, but the three of you are just starting out and I don't know where these recent developments will lead. I'm still very pessimistic in that regard, unfortunately."

Abe looked at his father and felt his love for him surge. No one could ever have asked for a more wonderful, admirable father.

"Papa, it's really hard to admit it, but I agree with every word you're saying. What can we do? We don't have anywhere else to go. All our property is here. The apartment with the clinic, my apartment, Mama and several other family members are buried here; Ilse's mother is here, along with all the loyal patients we've retained and our good friends. What can we do other than bow our heads and pray to the Lord above that this horror will pass somehow, or at least won't get any worse?"

Isadore didn't take his eyes off his son. Along with his grandson, they were his entire world, and he was terribly worried about them, especially since the child was born and the financial depression had had an impact on the public attitude toward Jews. Isadore was knowledgeable regarding the Jewish people's history and well aware of their status as a scapegoat to the other nations among whom they dwelled. As a whole, the Jews made positive contributions to every place they inhabited, yet how easy and convenient it was to ignore this and emphasize precisely what was negative about them by greatly exaggerating it.

❖ ❖ ❖

With millions unemployed and industry grinding to a halt, the finance minister resorted to several economic tactics, but the main change consisted of banishing all women from the work force, establishing an extensive system of workfare and enforced public-service jobs, a significant decrease in wages, and a prohibition on workers' unions. Most importantly, Germany made a rapid transition to "war economy"—expanding the army and massively increasing manufacturing that focused on military needs. The Nazi ideology demanded enforcing totalitarian rule in Germany.

The two families living on Leipziger Street were in complete agreement in their disdain for Hitler, the new leader, and his actions. Unlike his many fans, they viewed his latest extreme political moves as a harbinger of disaster, mainly when it came to his attempts to control all areas of life and the massive efforts to manifest the theory of the Aryan race's superiority by physically eliminating those races defined as "inferior," including the Jews. It was true that the Weimar Republic had failed to restore order to Germany and was unable to deal with the severe financial crisis, but this was a far cry from justifying the German people's decision to replace it with a tyrant establishing a totalitarian regime along with the radical party he headed.

Despair often induced thoughts of self-destruction, which might ultimately lead to self-destructive actions as well, both couples found themselves thinking, or even a desire to inflict destruction on others, through a conscious intention to eliminate those viewed as inferior.

If Ilse and Abe had once considered having another child at some point, the latest, greatly troubling developments made them conclude that this wasn't the right time to think about it, and certainly not even to discuss it.

Indeed, one consequence of the sense of loss was preventing a large sector of the German people from truly understanding the scope of the disaster embodied by the aggressive, radical regime that many of them had played a part in bringing to power. At that point, no one could really conceive of the extent to which the yearning for change had blinded them, obscuring their healthy intellect. None of them imagined that the new policies, and all they entailed, would devolve into actual terrorism that would soon be directed against the German nation itself.

☙ Chapter 22 ❧

The worst came to pass when the Nazi regime initiated a policy of persecuting the Jews. Hildegard was utterly shocked when at the beginning of April, as part of the general Nazi boycott against Jewish-owned businesses, the SS raided the street where her clothing store was located and marked the Jewish-owned businesses with a Star of David in order to prevent customers from entering them. Pandemonium prevailed in the street as the men in the black uniforms perpetrated violence all around. The horrified Hildegard locked the door to her store and did her best to recover from the shock. A short time earlier, her Jewish customer had managed to flee the chaotic scene as fast as she could. From between the mannequins in her store's window, Hildegard peeked out at the unfolding events. Her breathing quickened once again when among the SS men she suddenly recognized a familiar figure who was issuing orders and waving around an intimidating truncheon. If the man in front of her hadn't been wearing black, with a matching cap bearing a familiar insignia, he might have been considered handsome. It was none other than Johan Kirche. Hildegard looked at him for another second and then retreated. The last thing she wanted was any kind of contact with this particular SS member.

Johan, who was perfectly familiar with "Damen"—Hildegard's shop—fought an overwhelming temptation to go inside and terrorize the store's owner, but he refrained from doing so. This wasn't the right time to settle the score with her.

During that month, the organized public activities targeting Jews continued, and antisemitic legislation was initiated. At this point, the Nazis were striving to systematically remove the Jews from all hubs of influence in German society, and to segregate them from members of the "Aryan race." They managed to gather widespread support, or at least silent acceptance of these actions among the German public.

Johan's status soared along with the rise of the Nazi Party. He so admired the aggressive nature of the party's activities, and so worshipped Hitler—the leader who was now truly all-powerful. He seemed god-like to Johan, especially when he waved his hands with authoritative vigor during his speeches. There was such potency embodied in this man who had achieved his aims, one by one, elbowing his opponents out of the way or making them disappear, one way or another. And from the moment systematic actions targeting the Jews began, Johan knew that the day of vengeance had arrived. Although he was not personally involved in it at the moment, he viewed the entire antisemitic movement as his personal revenge as well. He imagined that Ilse was going through hard times; the same was certainly true of her husband and his father, and this caused him great pleasure.

◆ ◆ ◆

"If we think back to *Mein Kampf*, the 'illustrious' book Hitler wrote while he was in prison, which mostly focuses on the class struggle and in fact leads in to the conflict between the various races—which goes beyond Hitler's personal struggle—we can see that the Jews were frequently referenced in the book, mostly in a negative context," Isadore said. "I remember the expressions Hitler used to attack the Jews: 'sub-humans' with capitalistic tendencies aiming to enslave the German worker, communist sympathizers capable of committing genocide on the Germans, and imperialist sympathizers wishing to expand their areas of residence. It's true that many of our fellow Germans believed that antisemitism was merely a propaganda tool that served the Nazis to win the public's support, and that once they rose to power they would mitigate their attitude toward the Jews. But now we realize that this hope has been dashed."

"That book is the foundation of everything that's happening now," Abe said. "Even back then, Hitler was already planning his brilliant future as a supreme leader, as well as the actions he wanted to carry out once he achieved that status."

Johan mulled over the issue of mixed marriages, which were perceived as an essential part of the Jews' integration into German society. It was vehemently claimed that such marriages were gradually, yet determinedly, sapping the Aryan race's strength. His thoughts circled back to Ilse. By marrying a Jew, she had contributed to the weakening of her German nature and abetted the destructive mechanism inherent in the Jews. *How could she do that?* he thought. *After all, her German dignity will be trampled along with the Jewish indignity.* Oh, how she would suffer when the marginalization of the Jews from all aspects of life came to include her husband, and indirectly, herself as well. On the one hand, Johan felt malicious joy, but at the edges of his glee, a tiny ripple of pity for Ilse fluttered as well.

◆ ◆ ◆

Hitler's doubts regarding the SA and his increasing suspicion that some of the organization's leaders and members had turned against him, were becoming common knowledge within the ranks of the SS as well. Johan, who was attentive to the prevailing mindset within the organization, had the feeling that something extreme was about to take place as a consequence. He tended to believe that the fear of the SA's growing power would prove justified.

And indeed, one night toward the end of June 1934, the entire leadership of the SA was arrested and Hitler ordered a spate of executions. One by one, the leaders were lined up against the wall of the Lichterfelde Barracks on the outskirts of Berlin and were shot by a firing squad of SS and Gestapo officers.

It was hard for Johan to suppress his exaltation at this killing spree. The power involved in using weapons to kill those threatening Hitler's safety and status was significant. How easy it was to pull the trigger and produce murderous volleys from the weapons! And how much blood was splashed on that wall where those sentenced to death were lined up. There was something thrilling about the sight; it was impossible to look away from the bodies soaking in their own blood, laid out side by side and one on top of the other, with the limpness of death.

Johan was relaxing in his armchair at home, a bottle of beer in his hand. He was reliving the events of the bloody night while sipping his cold beer in pleasure, a smile flickering on his lips. Suddenly, he was overcome by a fierce bout of nausea. He did his best to fight it, but it proved to be stronger than his efforts, forcing him to get up and rush to the bathroom. Crouching down on his knees, his hands gripping the walls of the toilet bowl, his guts relinquished their contents in a fierce stream. In a haze caused by the effort and the contraction of his throat muscles, the vomited contents of his stomach appeared scarlet-colored to him.

Chapter 23

Manfred was growing from day to day and was about to turn five in October 1935. He was still under Gertrude's care, an arrangement that continued to be highly convenient for everyone. At least once a week, Hildegard and Isadore would regularly meet at Abe and Ilse's apartment in order to spend time with their children and grandson. Hildegard herself felt a great need to spend as much time as possible with Manfred, and she treasured every moment in his company.

Sigmund knew that the Reichstag was about to issue new laws, mostly targeting the Jewish population, which were scheduled to be discussed at the Nazi Party's annual rally in Nuremburg in mid-September. These laws were carefully worded, based on the revised definition of the superior Aryan race, and the purity of its blood compared to the inferior Semitic race. Sigmund had already seen a draft of the laws, which shook him to his core. He liked his work in the Ministry of the Interior, but recoiled from the Nazi regime forced upon him. He was aware of all the groundbreaking changes enacted in every state agency since Hitler rose to power, and was appalled by them.

Sigmund understood that other than emerging from the financial crisis—which he viewed as the regime's foremost positive goal—all other steps and actions would be far less positive, to put it mildly. The Nazi ideology was well known. Its integration was gradually expanding, and now a major part of it had also been embedded in laws that were about to be enacted and enforced on the population in general and the Jews in particular. This was truly worrying, as the actual purpose of these laws was revoking human rights from anyone who did not fit the new definition of a German citizen. Sigmund himself had never had anything against the Jews, and Abe was one of his best friends, if not his very best friend; and Abe was Jewish. Sigmund now feared more than ever for Abe's fate as a Jew, as well as for the fates of Ilse and Manfred. Dark days awaited them, of that he was sure, and he was already wondering how he could act on their behalf and how he might be able to help them when push came to shove.

When Sigmund pored over the article defining "Who Is a Jew" again and again, he realized that Manfred would be defined as a first-degree *mischling*, or person of mixed race, as he was the son of a Jewish father. This meant that Manfred would be considered a Jew. The "Law for the Protection of German Blood and German Honor," prohibiting marriage between Jews and Germans, which would also annul existing marriages, shocked him as well, as he believed that Abe and Ilse's marriage was in danger. The scope of these new rules was extensive enough to invade the entirety of every Jew's soul...

◆ ◆ ◆

Johan was well aware of the fact that the new laws would provide legal reinforcement for the Germans' attitude toward the Jews. These laws were aimed against the Jews as a people—as a public separated and segregated by race. They also signaled the beginning of the process of isolating the Jews from other citizens of the country. Johan knew the laws would also badly harm the Liebmanns, including Abe, the pure Jew, and the son who was the product of a mixed marriage and considered a Jew for all intents and purposes. But Ilse, too, would be harmed—first of all because of Abe and the child, but also individually, since as long as she remained married to a Jew, she would also be considered Jewish. The entire Liebmann family was about to find itself in dire straits.

Johan was particularly fond of the sub-article that dealt with the fate of those who were part of a mixed marriage: their marriages would be annulled, and once that happened, Ilse would no longer be considered to be married. The new laws seemed to have arrived just in time to play into his hands, helping him further advance his plans with regard to Ilse. The truth was that the fate of the Jews in general did not interest him much, and the impact on their lives didn't keep him up at night. He had been drawn into the sphere of antisemitism because he supported the Nazi ideology and because he was an avid fan of Hitler's. The only thing he cared about was the fate of the Liebmann family, which was tied up with larger matters concerning the Jewish population.

And indeed, precisely two months later, in mid-November, the initial law that specifically targeted the Jews was issued in a more detailed version. Racism became a state law preventing Jews from legally defending themselves against antisemitism by turning them into second-class subjects. The constitution revoked the Jews' citizenship, defining them as subjects lacking any civil or human rights, including the right to legal defense. What struck Johan as cynical was Hitler's declaration that these new laws were not anti-Jewish, but rather pro-German.

◆ ◆ ◆

In January 1936, the laws began to be actively enforced. The Jews of Germany, most of whom had until that point considered themselves to be an integral part of the framework of German life, experienced an existential crisis as well as an identity crisis.

Ilse and Abe's lives became difficult, frightening, and exhausting, in addition to the ongoing attrition caused by the impact of antisemitism on all aspects of life since Hitler first came to power, and the assimilation of the Nazi ideology within Germany. What kind of life could they expect if they needed to watch their step on a constant basis? The worst part, as far as Abe was concerned, was the cancellation of any contract work for Jewish doctors in the city's hospitals. They were also forced to quit their jobs, and, even worse—their professional credentials were revoked.

Abe's concern for Ilse and his son was escalating, especially because the perplexing new laws were also subject to personal interpretation. As an Aryan Christian based on the Nazi definition, Ilse was guilty of a grave sin. Her initial crime was marrying a Jew in a mixed marriage, which was compounded by the fact that this marriage had produced offspring—defined by law as Jewish—and furthermore, by continuing to have sexual relations with her Jewish husband, which was now, according to his own understanding, prohibited by the new laws. And since they had already heard whispers of heavy penalties issued to those who broke various laws, Abe was afraid that soon they might be caught red-handed in the act of love.

"Abe, if you weren't married to me, maybe you and your father would consider emigrating. It seems like your fate is sealed because of me," Ilse said, as big tears flowed down her cheeks.

"I'd never emigrate, Ilse. Even if I weren't married to you, I wouldn't consider it. I'm too attached to this city and this country," he said in order to comfort her, although privately he thought there was an element of truth to what she was saying.

"But you can't even be a proper doctor with all these new restrictions, prohibitions, and cancellations. It's just inconceivable. What is this evil cruelty toward all Jews, with no exceptions? After all, we've always been perceived as an intelligent, well-educated, and bookish nation. So how is it that we ourselves are so quickly transforming into sub-humans with all our actions as Germans?"

"Ilse, I'm thinking of Manfred first and foremost. He's the one I'm most worried about. I'm so afraid that he, born out of such great love, will pay the greatest price because he was born to a Jewish father. And beyond that, as long as our relationship continues, you yourself will be considered Jewish, and will be severely punished for it."

◆ ◆ ◆

Johan toyed with the idea of expediting the procedure for annulling Ilse and Abe's marriage. He even thought of a convincing excuse, so as not to be perceived as petty for settling any private accounts—he wanted to fully maintain his own pride and dignity. He could claim that Dr. Abe Liebmann was a danger to the public mainly because he was a doctor who habitually treated quite a few German nationals, and would always manage to find a way to exert his influence on them the way he probably did on his wife—the German Aryan frau. The most dangerous part, he would claim, was the possibility that they would have more children, thus continuing the contamination of the German bloodline. He wasn't at all certain that he wouldn't proceed with this plan.

Johan had never stopped hoping that one day he would have Ilse back in his arms again, at which point—considering what was going on in the country with regard to antisemitism—she would, after all, see the light when it came to the great danger inherent in the Jews and in any relationship with them. He would find a way to sway her, even if he chose to do it at the expense of the Jewish boy whom she would certainly do anything to protect.

Now, with the possibility of annulling Abe and Ilse's marriage—an annulment that would probably lead to the mixed couple's separation—there was a chance of Johan's greatest dream coming true. He didn't even consider the fate of the couple's son. He only wanted to imagine reuniting with the woman whom he sometimes hated so fiercely, but in fact, loved so deeply, with the one whom he had chosen, out of all women, to be his own, with the one who inspired such an intense desire for revenge within him.

◈ Chapter 24 ◈

About three months after the new laws were enacted, and following an incessant internal struggle, Abe had no choice but to come to a crucial decision.

"Ilse, I'm going to move in with my father again. You and Manfred will stay here on Leipziger, close to the Sontags. Your mother will live with you part of the time and, of course, I'll find the safest way to see you all."

He saw Ilse's face grow pale, and her breathing get heavy. She cried for a long time and he stroked her shiny, honey-colored hair and constantly kissed her face and her tears, but she didn't say a word; her heartbreaking sobs expressed her feelings. Abe was greatly relieved that not even the trace of an argument took place between them; otherwise, he might have begun to cry.

"Abe, I've been expecting this subject to come up," Ilse said when she calmed down. "I knew it would be inevitable. My mother has talked about it to me many times, and I believe that you and your father have discussed it as well. But with each day that we somehow survived, I hoped that we might be able to keep going as we have been. But you're right. We can't risk it, if only for our son. The new reality imposed on us, and on many others, is terrible and truly inhumane, but we don't have a choice. Abe," she continued, her voice starting to shake, "I want to tell you something I've been keeping to myself for a while now. I simply didn't want to cause you sorrow... But if we're doomed to be apart, even if it is only for appearance's sake..." She exhaled heavily. "I want you to know about it. I can't go on hiding it from you."

Abe looked at her questioningly as concern began to gnaw at

him. "I'm prepared to hear anything you have to say. I promise you that we'll get through everything together, as we've done thus far. Life sometimes forces you to endure hard, wretched times, and we have to be strong enough to fight them."

Ilse took a long breath and then gripped both her husband's hands. "Abe... a short time after the new laws were issued, Sigmund came to see me, all distraught. He was relieved to find me alone at home because he felt uncomfortable saying what he needed to say directly in your presence. 'This is an extremely sensitive subject,' he told me. Abe... Sigmund asked me to discuss it with you first. You know he has a senior position in the Ministry of the Interior, and since he has no other choice, he carries out the instructions he receives obediently and carefully, although he abhors the Führer's views. He knows and understands many things that we might not be aware of." She looked down briefly, then continued softly. "Abe, he asked me, very respectfully, to convince you to have a new birth certificate made for Manfred." She saw Abe tense up as he stared at her intently, and her heart went out to him.

"In his current situation," she went on, "the boy is considered a Jew, subject to all the laws that apply to every Jew. If he had been a second-degree *mischling*, he might have been in a better position with regard to the authorities. Sigmund wanted you to allow him to completely erase your last name from his birth certificate, and to change your first name to some German name, so that our son is considered a German in every regard. In other words, the new name that appears in the birth certificate would be 'Manfred Heine' only, and the father's name would be listed as 'Ulrich.' Sigmund said his conscience would not allow him to do it without your consent. However, based on his close familiarity with the way things are going, to which he's exposed daily at the Ministry, the situation is not becoming any less difficult; quite the contrary."

The words flowed out of her. "After all, from the day the new laws were first enforced, those who violate them are punished in ways that are much more severe than what the laws currently demand. That's what he told me, Abe, and I fear for you—and mostly, I fear for our little boy, who has nothing to do with this whole hell raging around us. I didn't know how to tell you, and now that you're planning to leave, it was exactly the right moment. Abe," Ilse whispered, her voice choked, "I let Sigmund do it without talking to you first. You have to understand. I only did it out of terrible distress and great anxiety about our son's welfare, because I didn't know how you would react—everything's so horrible for you already. I'm asking you to forgive me, Abe, and to try to understand, to understand me as a mother..."

Abe looked at her and felt a lump in his throat. He pitied her so much for the brutal moments with which she had to deal when she took on such a crucial decision on her own.

"Ilse, my darling," he said, "how could I be angry with you? You did the right thing to protect our son. It's true, logically, that it's hard for me to accept that suddenly, officially speaking, it's as if I have no connection to my own son, but in such crazy times there's no room for logic. It's a good thing that you wasted no time and let Sigmund do it. I'll go and thank him for it personally."

Abe believed whole-heartedly that he could trust Sigmund. He didn't envy his neighbor and good friend at all for working for a government office that was prominently positioned in the Nazi regime's hierarchy, and being forced to play a duplicitous and truly dangerous role. It was certainly very difficult to carry out his job meticulously and precisely when Sigmund's own worldview couldn't have been more different from that of his supervisors.

"Abe," Ilse said, "that's not all. I have some more terrible news. Our marriage has been annulled as well. Sigmund discovered it a short time ago, after the official in charge came to consult him on some administrative matters. Our marriage, Abe, like those of many others in our position, has been annulled! From what I understand, according to Hitler, we're no longer married, and apparently he doesn't really care how we'll deal with it as a couple and as parents."

Abe looked at her silently. He had already found himself frequently wondering about it, yet it was still hard for him to believe that it had indeed happened.

"Ilse, you and I will always be married," he said. "No Hitler or Schmitler can take that away from us. After all, we're married in our souls as well. All the rest is just stupid paperwork." He turned away from her, a strangled sob escaping from the depths of his throat. Ilse hurried toward him, embracing him with all her might.

"Abe, my beloved, my darling husband, my one and only, nothing and no one will ever come between us." And she burst into tears again. She had been crying a lot lately. Everything was so bleak, unfair, cruel, and a million other descriptions for which she could not find the right words. One man heading a party he had founded ruled everything, and was the one responsible for the entire cruel reality in which they lived. One man sat on his throne and, with a cheerful ease resulting from blatant tyranny, played with people's fates, with their lives, with their emotions, and with everything about them. It was beyond what any human being could rationally grasp.

"Till death do us part," Abe whispered silently.

Late that night, Abe went over to see Sigmund and thanked him for, in effect, forging Manfred's birth certificate. At that same, almost embarrassing encounter, he told him that he was about to move out. As a subordinate of the regime and an executor of its administrative decrees, Sigmund couldn't help but feel some guilt for what was going on, although he was sure that Abe didn't blame him in any way. He couldn't say goodbye to Abe without commenting on it.

"Abe, my dear friend, even years ago I'd heard it said that antisemitism is largely a result of the fact that society needs a scapegoat. I tend to believe that it's not the majority, but those who control the majority—and we all know who they are—who need this scapegoat as a means to divert attention from the real problems, and it's not as if we lack such problems. You Jews need to understand that the way the majority treats you has little to do with your behavior, for better or for worse. I think one mistake many Jews are making is their certainty that if they had behaved differently, antisemitism wouldn't exist at all. The opposite is true, Abe. You could say that the Jews' 'good behavior'—expressed in their industriousness and perseverance, in their success in areas such as commerce, medicine, and law—is precisely what has contributed and continues to contribute to the emergence of antisemitic views. Antisemitism cannot be stopped with good behavior by every individual Jew, since it's not an individual problem, but a social, collective problem."

"I agree, Sigmund," Abe replied. "Throughout the ages, we Jews have been persecuted for religious reasons, but these days, the basis for the persecution is racial differences. The Aryan race is superior and the Semitic race, to which I also belong, is inferior."

"In response to the accusations leveled at you, you Jews have to understand that you're only the façade under which the depth of the social issues is concealed. I believe that the majority's need for a scapegoat develops as a result of social tension—for example, in this period of economic depression," Sigmund said.

"Sigmund, you and I could continue to idly philosophize for many more hours, but even if our way of thinking is correct, we can't change what is actually happening—not me as a Jew, and not even you, as a senior official in the German Ministry of the Interior."

That week Abe left the apartment on Leipziger Street and moved back in with his father. Ilse was left alone with Manfred and with eyes that constantly asked her, *Why did Papa leave?*

She didn't know how to answer the question, and ultimately decided on a reply that was quite meaningless, but would be acceptable to a young boy: "It's hard for Opa (Grandpa) to be alone all the time, Manfred, and Papa has to help him out a little. Papa will be back. Don't worry—and you also don't need to talk about it to anyone, all right? You see, Oma (Grandma) has a hard time being alone too, and she comes to visit us a lot." And indeed, Hildegard had begun to sleep over at least twice a week—both due to her daughter's new circumstances and because of her own loneliness.

The family was overcome by deep sadness as a result of the new way of life thrust upon its members.

The new laws soon took over all of Germany and were carried out to the letter by both Jews and Germans, as laws enforced upon the Jews necessarily also became laws enforced upon the Germans. If Jewish doctors were forbidden to treat Aryan patients, then those same Aryan patients who had grown accustomed to the treatment of a specific Jewish doctor suffered as well. And if Jews were prohibited from entering certain shops or entertainment venues, then the German business owners suffered as well when their clientele was reduced. Not to mention contact between the two populations—Jewish and Aryan—when many excellent bonds had developed over the years between Jews and Germans, which were now strictly forbidden. The Germans too, somewhat reluctantly, accepted the new restrictions and the disruption of the daily routines to which they had been accustomed. They had been talked into believing that this was for their own good since, as Aryans, they deserved the best, and any kind of association with the Jews was the worst and most dangerous thing for them.

It was very hard for Ilse to deal with her colleagues at work—the ones who maligned the Jews even though they knew she was married to a Jew. She tried to do her job to the best of her ability, but her morale was low. She managed to muster up a faint smile only when she was in the company of her son.

Even when she and Abe risked a brief meeting, she would spend most of the time in tears. Her heart was torn to shreds when Abe would hurry off or urge her to get going. She was living a terrible life—one overshadowed by fear and concern for her husband's life, for her son's life, for her father-in-law's life, for her mother's life, and for her own life.

Hildegard was sad as well. She had been uneasy about Ilse and Abe's relationship for quite a while, but even in her worst, bleakest nightmare, she had never imagined that things would go so far. It was the epitome of insanity.

◆ ◆ ◆

In September 1936, a month before Manfred Heine turned six, he and Richard began to attend school. This was no longer school as it had once been, before the Nazis rose to power. All school and sports organizations were a part of the Reich's Culture Bureau, headed and supervised by Goebbels. All educators were forced to swear allegiance to Hitler, and there were no longer any Jews to be found among the teachers and lecturers. Lessons were based on a set, uniform curriculum that emphasized German history, Nazi ideology, biology, and physical education. The ultimate values highlighted were obedience to the Führer and to the Fatherland.

Every day Manfred would come back from school and share his latest experiences with his mother and grandmother. As his Judaism had never actually been mentioned to him, like several other controversial issues, Manfred expressed his enthusiasm for the lively quality of his schooling. Only one thing caused him great sorrow—that, for some reason that was unclear to him, his father no longer lived with them. It was true that Papa visited them occasionally, and they visited him and Opa as well, but it wasn't the same. To Ilse's relief, he didn't ask any unnecessary questions, and didn't comment in any way on the fact that he was now asked to use only his mother's last name.

He knew that his mother was having a hard time and continued to obey her request not to talk about their private affairs with anyone, including the matter of his last name, which was not the same as his father's.

Her daily contact with the Sontags was a source of solace and encouragement for Ilse. There wasn't a day in which they did not say some kind word to her, or share their lives with her, and the two boys continued to grow up as brothers for all intents and purposes.

Throughout 1937, new, rigid laws were enforced, and the process of isolating the Jews from pure Aryan Germans continued to expand. The Jews were particularly burdened with economic sanctions, but felt no less punished in other spheres as well.

One day Manfred returned from school looking puzzled. "Mama," he said, "today in science class, the teacher brought a boy our age to school. The teacher said that today we would learn about the differences between Aryan boys and Jewish boys."

Ilse looked at her son and a chill ran through her.

"The teacher," Manfred continued, "made him stand next to him and started telling us to look at the shape of his face and head and a few other things, and he held the boy's head and twisted it in all directions so that all of us could see."

Ilse had still not said a word and Manfred looked at her and then blurted out, "Mama, I looked at Richard and he looked at me and then I looked at the Jewish boy again. I couldn't see any difference. That boy even looked a little like me. After all, my hair's not really blond but brown and my eyes aren't really blue and my nose is a bit not really little—so what? You should have seen that poor boy, who was all embarrassed. Other than feeling sorry for him, I wasn't really impressed by that whole big presentation, and Richard agreed with me too."

Ilse's mind was racing wildly. What should she tell him? And then Manfred spared her by simply turning away and going to his room, as if he wasn't even asking her to respond.

Her heart continued to pound. *This is how it starts*, she thought, *and it won't be long before more delicate, complex subjects come up. And then what?* Ilse realized that at some point, Manfred would have to be told. And what would happen to him then? How would he react? She knew that she would postpone the revelation for as long as she could.

The next time Ilse met Abe, she found out his and his father's new names—Abe Israel Liebmann and Isadore Israel Liebmann, as the new laws enacted in mid-August dictated in order to make their Jewish identity more easily apparent.

◆ ◆ ◆

Johan had known for some time about the annulment of Ilse and Abe's marriage. As far as he was concerned, Ilse was now single again. He thought about Abe and his father—the two Jewish doctors whose medical licenses had been revoked. So Ilse's ex-husband was also an ex-doctor. *What a loss of status*, Johan thought to himself with satisfaction. In addition, Dr. Liebmann no longer lived at home with Ilse, but with his elderly father, who probably made his life a living hell. Johan was filled with acute hatred for the two men; he didn't bother, even for a moment, to consider Ilse's feelings on the matter. There was no room for any sort of sentimentality; this was what he had been taught, with the message being constantly repeated. The only emotion he experienced, and which he could not deny, was his obsessive love for Ilse, and he was willing to keep on waiting for as long as it took until he could get her back.

Chapter 25

In September 1938, a month before Manfred's eighth birthday, Ilse and Abe faced another major dilemma—the need to send the boy to the Hitler Youth movement, which had been established shortly after Hitler rose to power, and which all of Manfred's peers were required to join. They knew the youth movement emphasized training its young members to be Aryans efficiently serving the Führer and Germany by teaching them to admire the figure of the uninhibited Aryan warrior, who was all about blind obedience to the Führer. The youth movement also focused on imparting the Nazi ideology—including race theory and the superiority of the Aryan race—and on sports. Most of all, the parents were horrified by the counselors' use of a kind of psychological brainwashing intended to create model Nazi citizens who believed in race theory and were willing to die for Germany. Equally bad was knowing that the boys and girls emerging from the youth movement often became horribly violent, turning into particularly cruel bullies.

Ilse and Abe soon realized that they did not really have a choice in the matter, and their helplessness pained them greatly. *Maybe changing the boy's birth certificate was a bad idea after all*, they thought to themselves silently.

"Papa, I'm going crazy, simply crazy," Abe said in a strained voice. "Especially because of the way the Hitler Youth movement operates—taking innocent young boys and girls, intensively brainwashing them, putting insane ideas into their heads every day, and turning them into indoctrinated dolls with no personalities of their own. Psychologically speaking, it's a crime committed against the entire next generation."

"Is that the only crime, Abe?" Isadore asked. "And what about all the other crimes? The entire way this regime conducts itself is one big crime and we're the last ones who can object to it. We have no choice but to take part—even if it's against our will—in this whole monstrous game raging around us."

The increasingly worsening treatment of Jews reached new heights at the end of that month, in the form of a law permitting Aryan doctors to treat only Aryan patients. Jews were thus denied medical treatment, as the law prohibited Jews from working as doctors.

Abe Israel Liebmann and Isadore Israel Liebmann's passports were stamped with the letter "J" in the beginning of October. The only patients they could treat now, albeit in secret, were Jewish ones. They could no longer be affiliated with Elisabeth Hospital, as they were forbidden to treat Aryans, while Jews could not be admitted to the hospital.

◆ ◆ ◆

Like most other kids their age, Manfred and Richard joined the Hitler Youth movement. Their days were now divided between school and youth movement meetings. Even after the first few days, the boys came back eager to share and describe their experiences at the youth movement.

"Listen to this," they told Ilse and Gertrude, speaking as one, "in every class there's a big picture of Hitler hanging on the wall. It's like he's looking at every one of us and expecting us to really listen to the counselors. If it wasn't bad enough that we have to study history every day at school, now we have to study it at the youth movement, too. What a pain... so much history and lessons about race struggles and leadership. It's a good thing there's a lot of sports, too."

Ilse found herself tasked with an almost unbearable role—to try and disprove to her son what he was learning at youth movement meetings, enacting a sort of counter-brainwashing, but in a very controlled and cautious way so that, heaven forbid, he wouldn't mindlessly accept its messages, primarily everything that was said about the inferior Jews and the misdeeds of which they were falsely accused. She often feared she might be undermining the boy's sanity.

"He's too young for all this," she told her mother repeatedly. "What do they want from him, or from the rest of them? And what do we want from him? The last thing I want is to cause him some kind of split personality with these talks I have with him. How can I explain to him, at his young age, all the things that even we adults mostly can't understand and can't grasp?"

"I agree with you," Hildegard said, "but there's no other choice. Duty is duty, and let's admit that our counter-talks are the ones leaving him confused, since I don't really see that he's suffering much during those meetings. He comes home quite pleased and cheerful, mostly because of the athletic activities."

"Those activities worry me too, Mama. Manfred tells me they play a game called 'Trapper and Indian,' which is a variation on Hide and Seek, as well as war games that involve displays of force. These games often end in fistfights, and weaker children have had their shirts torn and gotten hurt. The counselors explain that it's like army training—and look how enthusiastic the kids are. How can I condemn games? After all, it's well known that children, and especially boys around that age, really love war games. My hands are tied, Mama. That's how I feel."

"It really does sound awful based on your descriptions, and it's truly hard to find an appropriate excuse to restrain that childish enthusiasm, but you and I will do all we can to preserve the boy's kind spirit, and provide him with tools to separate what's going on at school and at the youth movement from what goes on at home—the place where our opinions and views are what counts."

"And the thing that worries me most," Ilse said, "is that over time, once he's older and has been indoctrinated long enough by the spirit of the youth movement, they'll want him to join the SS. That's the last thing I need—Johan No. 2," she sighed heavily.

Hildegard, too, decided to take on the campaign of educating her grandson, just as, when Ilse was a child, she had explained to her about the war and all the problems associated with it. But the current state of affairs was very different from the previous one, and much more complicated. As the days went by, and Manfred grew increasingly integrated into the educational framework to which he belonged, it became harder for him to maintain a rational separation between what he was taught, told, and presented with at the youth movement, and the views and explanations conveyed to him at home. And on the day he turned to Hildegard and asked, "Oma, are those Jews that they keep talking about and saying terrible things about really that bad? Did they really cause us that much harm that now we're harming them?" the grandmother knew that they were quickly approaching the moment at which Manfred would have to find out about his father's origins.

Part Four

⋞ Chapter 26 ⋟

In November of 1938, it rained constantly. Manfred was sick. His whole body ached and he was alternately beset by fever, chills, and uncontrollable shaking. The teacher allowed him to leave school and go home, but not before scolding him for being unable to wait until the end of the day and lacking the endurance of "real" men. Manfred felt too ill to have the energy to be offended. Once he came home, his fever rose even higher, his eyes became glassy, and he felt as if his whole body was being beaten.

"Manfred, you're very sick." Ilse said with concern, her hand constantly cupping his heated forehead. "Where am I going to take you now, in this freezing weather?"

"Take me to Papa and Opa," he whispered. "I want only them to take care of me. I don't want any other doctor!" His eyes closed in fatigue. Ilse had no choice but to comply with his request. Despite all the danger involved, she knew that her son was right. What doctor could she trust if not her husband and her father-in-law? She wrapped him up in a warm blanket, called a taxi and rushed to the clinic. Unfortunately, Hildegard could not accompany them that evening.

Abe and Isadore took them in. They had been expecting them ever since Ilse informed them by phone that they were on their way. Manfred was so happy to see his father. In a gravelly voice, he explained what was hurting, and Abe began his examination.

"He seems to have caught an unusually bad cold," he decreed after examining every part of his body at length. "I don't see any other irregular findings. Come rest a little, Manfred, and I'll give you something to bring down the fever and ease the pain."

Manfred nodded heavily. He didn't say anything to his mother and father about what he had been through the day before. As part of a special training day conducted outdoors, the children had been soaked to the bone in a heavy downpour. They weren't allowed to change and had to stay in their water-soaked clothing. Once Manfred finally put on fresh clothes, he felt that he was coming down with something, but kept his silence. He was afraid. Afraid of not being considered enough of a hero. Afraid of being chastised in front of all his friends, and, more than anything else, afraid of being severely punished. He was certain that he had gotten sick because of all the cold, wet, athletic activity. Now he felt his grandfather's large, warm hand stroking his head. Isadore brought his finger to his lips, instructing him not to say a word when Abe gestured to Ilse and they ensconced themselves in the next room.

Abe descended on Ilse with hugs and kisses. "I've missed you so much, my lovely, my darling," he told her. He didn't want to say too much by telling her that his life had become an ongoing hell since he had been forced to leave their home two years ago. He didn't want to tell her how hard it was for him knowing that she had to deal with day-to-day life on her own. As time went by, things became increasingly difficult for him, and he knew the same was true of her as well. He made himself smile at her while she, typically, couldn't control her emotions and flooded his shoulder with tears. She, too, was suffering—suffering in silence. What could she do? They seemed to have an unspoken agreement not to discuss the difficulties they were both experiencing due to the separation and the distance, as well as their fears of the punishment awaiting anyone who broke the law. No good would come of discussing their mutual torment. After all, they tried to console themselves, the geographical distance between them was still not so great, and they managed to see each other under various circumstances, despite the risk involved. They would not give up entirely.

Time flew by, and Abe was concerned about how Ilse would get home with the sick boy, who in the meantime had fallen asleep. "Tonight you'll sleep here. This is an emergency involving a sick child. No one will come to check who we're treating on such a rainy night. You can only take all of this so far, don't you think?" Abe said. And Ilse, of course, agreed immediately. She yearned to snuggle up in Abe's arms and find the solace of his embrace once more, craving his touch and every aspect of his physical presence.

Isadore sympathized. He himself was experiencing intense frustration when it came to his son and daughter-in-law's relationship. But he considered himself the last person entitled to say anything on the matter. After all, anything he would say would be redundant. Every passing day during which he knew that his three loved ones were suffering seemed to last an eternity. Ultimately, the main victims of the whole situation were the Jews, including his son and himself, and all mixed couples took part in their suffering. So many times he had tried to comfort himself as did many others who, like them, had chosen not to leave the country, thinking that the situation would change and that Hitler would ease off from all this tyranny directed at the Jews, perhaps because of global pressure, which had yet to manifest. Hitler would have to get off his high horse and realize that a great many Jews had contributed significantly to Germany. After all, every nation consisted of all kinds of people—some were benevolent and productive, while others were negative troublemakers. After a positive relationship and good bonds between Jews and Christians that had lasted centuries, how could such a sweeping generalization suddenly be made, causing all Jews, with no exceptions, to be considered the scum of the earth—literally? It really was inconceivable, and there was no solace to be found in the similar attitude directed toward other minorities and nations, which were also viewed as sub-human.

***

Johan prepared for the planned assault on the Jews that was being organized by Minister of Propaganda Joseph Goebbels. It was to be portrayed as a spontaneous outburst by the German people although, in fact, it had been meticulously orchestrated in advance. "The time has come to act against the Jews," Goebbels said in an impassioned speech. That same night, the necessary directives were sent out all over the country, while SS members were ordered to encourage the crowd to take part in the attacks according to the guidelines. The rioters departed from various destinations all over the country. Throughout the day, the Nazis went from door to door, using lists prepared in advance, in order to find Jewish men and arrest them.

Evening had turned into night a while ago,, and as Ilse and Abe snuggled together, refusing to part, Manfred was fast asleep and Isadore was caught up in contemplation, the violent pogrom that had broken out some time earlier came knocking on sleepy Berlin's doors. Isadore didn't take his eyes off his grandson, who was deep in feverish slumber, looking like an angel. As his heart flooded with emotions toward the couple in the next room, loud voices were heard from the street below, accompanied by the sounds of breaking glass, a strange, unusual occurrence. Abe and Ilse, who had awoken from their light sleep, came into the parlor together, looking at Isadore with querying eyes.

"What's going on out there? What are all these harsh sounds and voices?" they asked as one. Isadore shrugged, although he had grown uneasy some time ago. Something was going on out there and it seemed ominous. Despite the natural curiosity they all felt, they decided not to go out and see what was happening. The times were already chaotic, and if those sounds were indeed the result of some anti-Jewish incident, it was smarter not to risk even a furtive peek.

After a while, as the voices continued to sound volatile and the loud booms were reminiscent of actual explosions, a burning smell spread through the air. Suddenly they heard the sound of breaking glass right next to them, immediately followed by the rapid stamping of boots and violent banging on the door.

"Open up immediately!" came a loud call and the pounding on the door increased.

Isadore looked at Abe and Ilse and they at him. They had no choice but to comply as, based on the rate and intensity of the pounding, the door would soon be broken down anyway. Ilse hurried off to the sleeping Manfred, who had been woken up by the loud noise, and quickly dragged him to the other room. Isadore began to open the door, which was almost torn off its hinges as two SS officers holding long truncheons burst into the room.

"You're both under arrest," called out one of them, who had an impressive frame, light-colored hair, metallic blue-gray eyes, and a steely expression on his face. "You are accused of conspiring against the Führer and grave sedition."

Isadore and Abe glanced at each other, increasingly incredulous.

"There's some kind of mistake here," Isadore said. "We have no idea what this is about. We have no dealings with politics or public affairs, and our only connection to the public is the one between doctors and patients, as well as..."

"Shut up, you dirty Jew, and don't you dare talk back to me!" the other officer said, cutting Isadore off in mid-sentence. "You're both coming with us now." He raised his truncheon and waved it at them threateningly.

The voice of the first person who had spoken was familiar to Ilse. The tone, thundering and somewhat shrill, brought back forgotten memories she had no desire to relive. *It can't be*, she whispered to herself. *It can't be!* And before leaving the room in which she was shielding Manfred, she signaled to him to stay quiet by bringing her finger to her lips.

The pale-haired officer's steely demeanor slackened briefly when his eyes fell on Ilse. She was standing face to face with Johan Kirche. He stared at her with restrained chill, the faint spark of a smirk creeping into the corners of his mouth. He fixed his metallic-colored eyes on her and said, before she had time to say anything, "We're arresting these two. We've received information indicating that they have opposed the Führer and violated several articles of the law. They are a danger to the government and to the German people, and they've also had the temerity to come in contact with Aryans, which puts you too, madam, in the category of lawbreakers." His expression was smug as he made this last statement.

Ilse looked at him and didn't want to believe her ears. Despite the fear she felt, she stationed herself between him and Isadore and Abe, who were far from pleased that she had decided to show up precisely during this difficult moment. None of them were aware of the fact that Manfred was peering out at them and witnessing the entire scene from the corner of the room in which his mother had asked him to stay.

"Johan, please don't take them! They're not guilty of anything. They're not seditionists, not conspirators, and not anything of the sort that might endanger the Führer or the government. This is completely baseless. They're just two doctors who have always helped everyone and..."

"Shut up—and I mean right *now!*" he barked at her. "I know very well who and what they are, as well as who and what you are. You have no right to interfere in matters that have nothing to do with you. You never showed any interest in politics and the government, remember?" His mouth spewing venom, he added, "One of your husband's grave offenses is that despite the fact that his marriage to you was annulled some time ago, he continues to see you—otherwise you wouldn't be here in his house. You, too," he repeated his previous accusation, "are guilty of breaking the law and I certainly have the authority to arrest you as well. But for now, we'll make do with arresting the two main instigators."

Ilse looked at Johan with tears in her eyes, feeling frightened. How did he know so many personal details about her? She truly wanted to know, but this was not the time to consider it— nor was it the time to wonder whether this visit resulted from a malicious intention to seek personal revenge against them.

During those critical minutes, Isadore and Abe looked at Ilse before their eyes moved on to Johan, and Abe realized who this Johan was. It was *that* Johan—he, out of all the soldiers in the SS, was the one who showed up at their home—and Abe sensed that this was far from a coincidence. He also brought backup with him, while armed with nothing but false accusations. They hadn't presented any sort of identifying document, or other legal paperwork because, in fact, they didn't *need* to present any documentation whatsoever. The SS could arrest anyone, as it saw fit, without providing any explanation to any person who was detained, or to anyone else other than the Führer and his cronies. Since the anti-Jewish laws were enacted and the Jews' civic rights were revoked, no one had to explain anything to them or treat them as equals before the law—since they were no longer equals.

Ilse began to beg once more, when suddenly, she lost her temper. She raised her voice, beginning to shout, "Johan Kirche, stop this behavior. You know they didn't do anything wrong. What's the matter with you? Why did you come here? Don't tell me," she added sarcastically, "that personal grudges brought you all the way over here."

And when she saw his face turn scarlet and his mouth twitch

with anger, her need to get back at him only increased as she added, "Go back to that cruel gang of hooligans you belong to, and leave us alone." These words proved crucial in escalating the ugly, terrifying incident.

Johan turned to her abruptly and slapped her cheek so hard that her lip split in precisely the same spot it had split back then, over eight years ago, the last time they had met. Blood streamed down her chin and she began to tremble. Abe, who, up until then had been rooted in place while countless thoughts rushed through his mind, leaped at Johan, intending to pummel him, while Isadore rushed toward Ilse to help her.

Johan did not hesitate even for a second. He was as fast as a hawk after all the military and physical training he had undergone during his years of membership in various militant organizations, and he raised his truncheon and brutally brought it down on Abe's shoulder. Abe fell back and hit the floor. He moaned in pain and Ilse, who had broken free of Isadore's hold, approached Johan and slapped his face as hard as she could. The stunned Johan bounced back quickly, propelling the hand that had just touched his burning cheek toward Ilse and pushing her back violently. Ilse landed on her back.

Johan and the other officer handcuffed the wounded Abe, who was still lying on the floor, and they didn't forget Isadore, either. They dragged Abe from his prone position, forcibly bringing him to his feet.

"Now you'll come with us, nice and quiet, or else we'll have to get violent with you again, or even beat you to death," Johan said, his voice as hard as stone. He looked around and suddenly spotted Manfred peering out at everything that was going on, terrified and paralyzed with shock.

"And you," he addressed the boy loudly, pointing at him with his truncheon, "take care of your shameless mother, your traitorous mother who dared marry your despicable Jewish father and continued to sin when she brought you, *mischling* that you are, into this world."

Manfred ran toward Johan as if possessed and sunk his teeth deep into the back of his hand. Johan shouted in pain and tossed the boy from him as if he were a mad dog. Manfred landed next to his mother, who couldn't move from the spot where she lay. He shook with pain and fear. From where he was sprawled out, he looked at Johan and noticed something reddish on the left side of his neck. *He's injured*, Manfred thought to himself with great terror. *Now he'll kill all of us.* And as he stared at the violent officer's metallic blue eyes and his threatening, tyrannical, powerful figure, the child experienced overwhelming panic. *This officer is really capable of killing*, he thought to himself, and he clung to his mother with all his might.

Johan communicated a brief, succinct order to his companion, and the other man went into the clinic with his heavy truncheon and shattered everything in sight. Once the room's contents were all irreversibly destroyed, the two men left the house along with Abe and Isadore, and Johan slammed the door after him as hard as he could. All four disappeared, leaving the stunned Ilse and Manfred on the floor. Manfred had forgotten all about his illness and his aches and pains and was able to focus on his mother and on the new pain in his body from being brutally shoved and falling.

Ilse's tears and moaning made him want to cry too, and he burst into tears. Ilse held him close while still groaning. She heard her son sniffling, and suddenly he asked, "Mama, is my father Jewish?"

At last, the moment Ilse had feared every day—the moment of inevitability—had arrived. "Yes, Manfred. Papa is Jewish." Her sobbing ceased abruptly. "That's the real reason he left us, because he was so worried that you and I would be punished as well. I didn't want to talk about it at all, because I was afraid you'd be very confused, especially after everything you've learned in school, and mostly at the youth movement. You have to understand me, Manfred, you just have to." She looked at him pleadingly.

"But, Mama," he couldn't help but respond, "that means I'm Jewish, too. That's what they taught us, that someone who's the son of a Jewish parent is considered Jewish, too. Is that why I'm not allowed to say Papa's last name?"

"Manfred, it's pretty complicated, this whole thing. According to the Jewish religion, you're Christian—like your mother, while according to the Nazi race laws, you're Jewish—because your father is Jewish. It's all so insane that it's really hard to take it in, and it's all invented by people. Do you understand?"

Manfred adored his father, but it was very hard for him to accept what he had just discovered—that his father was Jewish. After all, they were constantly taught and told how the Jews had harmed and were harming Germany and the world. Every single day they heard how the Jews were inferior and different from others, primarily from the superior Aryan race. It sounded terrible to him.

"But, Mama," he challenged, "Papa and Opa, and a few other Jews I know, are really good people. As doctors, Papa and Opa have helped so many people, and often even saved them. They're wonderful people and I love them very much. How could anyone say that because they're Jews, they're all those horrible things I learned about? What does their being Jewish have to do with anything? Now I really don't understand anything at all!" he concluded in frustration.

"Neither do I, Manfred," Ilse whispered tearfully. "But we're not the ones making the decisions and definitely not the ones in charge. We're nothing, simply nothing. Did you see how easily Papa and Opa were taken away?" She began sobbing bitterly once more.

"Mama, but where did they take them? Who is this Johan? How do you know him? Did you see that his neck got injured? How do you know an SS officer, anyway?" he asked, terror in his eyes.

"Manfred, my boy," she replied faintly as she continued to cry, "God only knows where they took Papa and Opa. They arrested them based on all kinds of false accusations. You must understand that. Unfortunately, it doesn't bode well. It actually looks very, very bad." She stared ahead, saying nothing more.

Manfred knew exactly what SS officers were and what the organization did. He had been taught about it in youth movement meetings. He simply didn't understand what crime his father and grandfather had committed to cause them to be taken away so cruelly. And as he contemplated these difficult thoughts while stroking his mother's hair and mentally reconstructing everything that had happened a short time before, he recalled that she had never told him how she came to know the cruel officer whose neck had been injured and who had whisked Papa and Opa away from them.

Ilse held her son tightly and silently said to herself, *and I was supposed to marry that monstrous thing.* Then she looked at Manfred, whose face was so serious, her love for him filling her entire being, and whispered to him in a strangled voice, "Johan was a patient who was once admitted to my ward, and I treated him very well. And he wasn't injured—it's a birthmark," and she said no more. For now, she was unwilling to expose her son to the bitter truth.

Manfred knew that that face—the face of Johan, the Nazi officer—was one he would never forget. The image of Johan Kirche and his evil face was indelibly etched in his consciousness, along with the terrible incident.

The shocking event, soon followed by groundbreaking revelations, aged Manfred beyond his years. Apparently, however, he was gifted with immense willpower, clear thought, healthy logic, and comprehension that transcended his age, so he somehow managed to overcome the upheaval and the confusion.

Chapter 27

The chaos on the streets continued. The marauders' shouts, interweaving with the victims' cries of pain and mingling with the sounds of shattering glass as the windows of Jewish businesses and synagogues were smashed, alongside the heavy smell of smoke rising from the fires set in Jewish buildings, had already reached every ear and nostril throughout the city and the country. Those were horrendous hours of rioting, looting, vandalism, cruelty, brutality, carnage, and arrests. Obeying instructions from their higher-ups, the police avoided obstructing the marauders or reinstating order. The raging fires were put out only in areas where they threatened to spread to the homes and property of non-Jews. Hundreds of Jews and other political suspects were arrested based on lists prepared in advance, and taken to several assembly points.

Johan found himself somewhat distracted. He and his partner walked the two stumbling detainees toward the assembly spot. The last thing Johan had expected was to meet Ilse on this occasion and act the way he had in front of her. It was now certain that this would be the last image she would retain from their encounter, which did not play out in his favor, and definitely would not help his future plans. *It's ironic*, he thought. *We came to arrest the husband and his father, and it all took place before the eyes of the wife and the child.* A terrible rage suddenly surged within Johan. Because of that despicable Jew, he had humiliated himself in front of Ilse, and not only humiliated himself, but was portrayed as a downright monster which, if he was being honest with himself, he was often forced to be.

Abe walked alongside his father, with the two SS officers behind them. His whole body was in pain. The pounding from

Johan's truncheon had wreaked havoc on him. He glanced at his father, who tried to direct a consoling look at him. They reached a street where many other people had been forcibly assembled. Most of them had been arrested on similar charges. They couldn't talk to each other; the guards patrolling among them didn't allow it. All the detainees—"government dissidents," as they were called—were then ordered to march in line toward an abandoned structure, where they were randomly divided into three groups.

After waiting for many hours, Abe and Isadore's group was loaded onto a truck and driven to the Berlin-Charlottenburg train station. They were roughly crammed into one of the cars, and the train took off. Hours went by and no one knew where the train was headed. The car was crowded, humid, and cold. Everyone was tired, thirsty, and hungry, and some were also bruised and wounded, but most of all they were terrified. They were quite sure their grueling conditions were of no interest to their captors. The detainees felt like cattle that could be endlessly abused, as if they were no longer flesh-and-blood human beings.

After being jostled in the musty train car for what seemed like an eternity, when most of the detainees had lost any sense of time or connection with it, the train came to a stop. They were all forced to disembark amidst shouting, pushing, and the waving of clubs and guns. It was early evening, and a light drizzle was falling in the dimness surrounding them. They had arrived in Munich—or at least that was what the sign at the station stated.

Abe was limping, and Isadore tried to support him, but his own limbs were also stiff from the rough journey, the chill in the train, and his uncomfortable sitting position, so he could barely shuffle along. He was hit with a truncheon and fell to the ground. Abe rushed to him, trying to pick him up, and was struck down as well. Consequently, both men found themselves on the ground. Abe knew that if he didn't get up immediately and find a way to do it at any price, his life would be in immediate danger. He had already seen how the guards treated those who tripped or fell, or who didn't strictly obey orders. He had witnessed the shameful, violent behavior toward those wretched souls.

Abe didn't want to be one of those abused men. After all, at some point he was supposed to be released and return home, and he wanted to do so while alive, rather than as a corpse. He managed to get up, but had a hard time helping his father. Blood was dripping from Isadore's head. *Abe knew that both his father's open wound and the blow to the head that he had sustained posed an immediate danger.*

Abe gathered the last of his remaining strength and managed to pull his father to his feet. "I'll take care of you when we get to wherever they're taking us," he whispered to him. "You have to keep going; otherwise, they'll kill you like a stray dog. No one cares how we feel. We've already seen what's going on here. Make sure to keep that in mind." And Isadore did his best. He wiped away some of the blood with his sleeve and managed to totter alongside his son amidst all the others.

They were loaded onto another truck for another lengthy ride. Once the truck stopped, they were loudly ordered to disembark, and all of the truck's passengers were expelled one by one. They were greeted by tall spotlights, their pale, oppressive beams illuminating a large stone wall, with an intimidating iron gate at its center, flanked by tangled barbed wire fences. At the top of the gate, iron letters spelled out the message "Arbeit Macht Frei."[2]

It was an extremely depressing sight. They had arrived at the Dachau concentration camp, near the city of Dachau. The stone wall was studded with terrifying watchtowers.

Abe and Isadore had heard about the camp some time before. It had been established in March 1933, immediately

---

2   German, "Work shall set you free."

after Hitler rose to power, and was intended to imprison rivals and political dissidents, real or imaginary, as well as social groups labeled as undesirable: criminal prisoners, homosexuals, the homeless, and others. The camp was also intended to break the spirits of those confined within it, and sometimes to eliminate them as well—beatings and death penalties were routinely employed, serving as an effective deterrent to the local populace. The camp was part of the SS's infrastructure and also served as a training base. Abe and Isadore had found out about the camp's horrific nature from one of their patients, who had been released from it by the skin of his teeth several months earlier.

They could already imagine what was in store for them, although they couldn't truly conceive of the fact that the worst was yet to come; some, mostly Jews, were about to be treated somewhat differently than the other prisoners. The Jews were intended to become the next victims of their captors' brutal cruelty.

A thundering order instructed them to pass through the gate and go into the camp. All of the prisoners, down to the last of them, began to scan the new terrain in which they stood, and some of them cried out in dismay. Despite the dim lighting, the sights around them were still clearly visible. Everything was utterly terrifying, and the increasing rain only intensified their fear and distress. Within the stone wall stretched an electric fence, bordered by a wide stretch of grass.

The prisoners were assembled in the drill field in front of one of the buildings and received a brief, factual and monotonous explanation about the structure of the camp, their new place of residence. "Here before you is the most important building: the housekeeping center, which serves as a kitchen, clothing storehouse, laundry, craft workshop, and administrative office." Abe and Isadore saw that the façade of this important building by which they stood bore the inscription, *"There is a way to freedom. Its milestones are obedience, honesty, cleanliness, sobriety, industriousness, order, willpower, sacrifice, openness, and patriotism."* They looked at each other, not daring to say a word.

"You'll be assigned to the rectangular cabins in order," the officer continued to roar. "You'll undergo an intake process and tomorrow morning you'll start working."

It soon became clear that the detainees no longer had any sort of legal status and that they had become prisoners. The meager possessions of those who had managed to bring anything with them were confiscated, along with the clothes they were wearing when they arrived. Their heads were shaved; then they were dressed in striped clothing resembling pajamas and classified according to various criteria. Each prisoner was assigned a number and a colored cloth triangle pinned to his shirt, indicating the category to which he belonged.

The Jews among them were told that they would be released if they could prove that they intended to leave Germany. Abe and Isadore looked at each other helplessly—they didn't have any such proof, as they were not planning to emigrate anywhere. Abe ran his hand over his bald head. It was repulsive and he was glad that he wasn't facing a mirror. His father looked much older than he actually was, now that his thick silver mane no longer adorned his head. Abe saw that his father's wound was still bleeding and was now more apparent. He looked around him and felt nauseous—in their current state, all of the prisoners truly resembled one another.

The prisoners' barracks were arranged in two columns, each consisting of 17 cabins. The first cabins, close to the housekeeping center, served as an SS museum, a library for the German soldiers, a mess hall, and a writing room, rooms in which the prisoners were instructed in various skills, an arms manufacturing workshop, and a hut for the dead.

Abe was sent to Cabin #2, while Isadore was assigned to a different cabin. Now Abe couldn't possibly tend to his wounded father. He hoped that someone else could help him, not wanting to believe that such cruelty would be applied even to the wounded and the sick. Concentration camp or work camp—the Nazis could call it what they liked; if they wanted the prisoners to be fit for work, they had to offer basic medical treatment to the wounded and the sick, of whom there would certainly be many. This was what Abe's logic told him; at the time, he could never have imagined that in the place where he was now confined, regular logic did not apply. The logic to which the camp's commanders, managers, and ultimate rulers subscribed was totally different from his own logic.

◆ ◆ ◆

Hildegard was home alone that night, and the intensity of the rioting sweeping through the streets made her shiver. Her heart went out to her daughter and her sick grandson, and she regretted not being by their side, after deciding to stay home that evening, of all days. But how could she have imagined what would take place? She knew that Ilse and Manfred had gone to see Abe and Isadore, and assumed they had decided to stay the night under the circumstances.

Hildegard didn't sleep a wink that night—who did?—awaiting the morning with bated breath and open eyes. She decided not to open the store, but rather to rush off to see Ilse. She never considered the possibility that there would be nothing for her to open, even if she had wanted to do so.

◆ ◆ ◆

After a brief, nightmarish night on hard, crowded cots, all of the camp's prisoners were woken up and instructed to stand up next to their cots. The cold was paralyzing—it was still dark outside. When the order came, they all marched out in single file to the drill field. The wet chill invaded their bones through the light clothes that had served as pajamas and were now their work uniforms as well. Abe shivered, and a sharp pain shot up his shoulder and back, which had sustained the truncheon blows the day before.

The prisoners were divided into work groups, each headed by a supervisor. They stood with frozen feet, their hands rigid and aching from the cold, waiting for the daily, military-style headcount. Abe's ears and nose were threatening to freeze and fall off. It was simply horrible. Being forced to stand motionless in the bitter chill was unbearable, when any physical motion could have brought relief, albeit minor. The first rays of light began to reflect in the mounds of snow. Everyone's eyes began to blink in the cold, piercing light. And the wait for the greatly anticipated prisoner headcount that would rescue them from this cruel standing went on and on. One of the prisoners, who let out an anguished moan, immediately sustained two blows to the flesh of his back and collapsed where he stood.

At last, the longed-for headcount arrived, and afterward the prisoners were rushed off to their workplaces. Their bodies were in motion, defrosting a bit. When they reached the worksites, they were handed tools and ordered to start digging. Abe's hands held the shovel, finding it hard to heft it up. And the day had just begun—the first day of torture, suffering, and a horrific feeling of oppression.

∽ Chapter 28 ∾

The destruction in the city streets, the abuse of innocents, and the murders accompanied by cheering from the masses continued all night, uninterrupted, and came to a stop the following morning, also due to an explicit instruction from above.

The terrifying pogrom left behind sidewalks full of shattered glass in every shade and every shape. The piles of glass giving the streets a mockingly glittering visage sparked the imagination of Joseph Goebbels, the riot's initiator and planner, who gave it a name with a chilling meaning—*Kristallnacht*, or Crystal Night.

As she rode the tram that passed through Kurfürstendamm Avenue, Hildegard's hands flew to her chest in amazement. The display window of Damen, her beloved store, was shattered, like other shop windows on the avenue. The riots had extended to her store as well, even though she wasn't Jewish. Apparently, vandalism was running amok, and sometimes it didn't make any sort of unnecessary distinctions; in the chaos of looting, destruction, and debauchery, Damen had been harmed as well. Hildegard's heart was pounding wildly, and she didn't know what to do—get off at the next stop and head for the store, or rush to Ilse. Overcome by confusion, she alighted from the tram at the next stop and made a mad dash for the shop. At the time, the owners of the affected stores were already busy assessing the damage and picking up the pieces. A bleak atmosphere had spread through the scenic street in the Wilmersdorf borough's shopping district.

Hildegard needed Abe and Isadore's help urgently. She was

facing a difficult dilemma. If she left, the contents of the store, or whatever was left of it, might be whisked away. If she stayed, she couldn't call her family to help her.

The shoe store next door had been under Jewish ownership for many years. The shop owner witnessed the distress of his neighbor, who had continued to treat him with great courtesy despite the anti-Semitic propaganda, the restrictions, and the severe prohibitions, and he offered to help her.

"Go, Frau Heine. I'm here cleaning up, and I'll keep an eye on your store. Look at this horror! Look what they've done to us. It's unbelievable, what's going on here. The people have gone crazy if it's come to this. My wife was a witness to everything that happened. She saw with her own eyes how a raging mob broke into the Jews' stores and houses, greedily looting whatever they could, and destroying the rest—just for the sake of destruction. The synagogues went up in flames while the fire department turned its water hoses toward the Christian houses, so that, heaven forbid, they wouldn't be harmed by the flames as well. Jews were killed, she told me, and others were injured. And the police—whose job is to uphold the law and protect the citizens—arrested the Jews and left the thugs behind to celebrate as they saw fit." And he burst into tears.

Hildegard placed a consoling hand on the sobbing man's shoulder, overcome by grief. She didn't know what to say. No words of consolation could comfort him, and certainly not those unlucky souls who had been fatally injured by the horrifying events.

The despondent Jewish shop owner looked at Hildegard through eyes wet with tears and, noting that she was focused on him and what he had to say, felt the need to tell her more. "You know, Frau Heine, I've heard that quite a few of our young people risked their lives and stepped in through the flames to save the Torah scrolls, and these rescue attempts did not proceed smoothly. One of them went into the synagogue and took out three Torahs wrapped in a blanket so that they wouldn't go up in flames as well. As he stepped out through the door, a Nazi hooligan kicked him and knocked him down the stairs. *Oy vey vey!* It's horrible." He wiped away his tears again and again. "But you go now, Frau Heine. Go bring your family," he concluded in a strangled voice.

◆ ◆ ◆

Ilse greeted the morning after a night spent sitting on the floor with Manfred, who had been dozing in her arms. She was full of anxiety; her concern for Abe and Isadore, and for her mother, threatened to drive her insane. Her entire body was in pain, her split lip was swollen, and Manfred's fever had spiked again. She could still hear voices outside, but they were different than the ones that had thundered through the night. These were the anguished cries of the people who had been hurt, and the ones who had witnessed the destruction of their houses, stores, and synagogues. The whole city was in turmoil.

Ilse knew that she would have to go back home. Isadore's house was no longer a safe place for her. Who knew what the SS's next steps would be with regard to the property? And as she tried to come to her senses, to bounce back and somehow get ready to leave, while also assisting Manfred, who was doing no better than she was both physically and emotionally, Hildegard stormed into the house, breathing heavily, her body trembling uncontrollably. "Ilse, Ilse, what's going on with you?" And when she saw the state that her daughter and grandson were in, she broke down. "Ilse, *liebchen*, what's going on here? Where are Abe and Isadore?" And as her eyes took in the ransacked clinic, she said again, nearly silently, "*Mein Gott*, what's going on here?"

Ilse was no longer able to control even a single tear. She had tried all night to suppress her need to cry uncontrollably, for the sake of her son, who was already frightened, but she gave free rein to the tears that flowed down her cheeks.

"Mama, the SS took Abe and Isadore. Two SS officers burst in here last night and accused Abe and his father of all kinds of crazy charges, treason, sedition—who knows what else? And when we tried to object, they beat up all of us. Look at the clinic. There's nothing left of what was inside. They broke and destroyed it all, and with great pleasure, I'm sure." She choked up again, weeping bitterly, not daring to tell her mother who one of those officers had been. She wanted to tell her quietly, when Manfred wasn't within earshot.

Manfred clung to his grandmother and refused to let go of her. He couldn't talk. Hildegard hugged him and showered his head and face with kisses and caresses, but she, too, couldn't make a sound. The shock that spread through her in response to what she had just seen and heard prevented her, at that moment, from telling Ilse about the store.

Suddenly, Manfred turned to her and said, his voice, cracking, "Oma do you know that one of the officers used to be a patient of my mother's, and she took care of him at the hospital? How could he have been so cruel to my mother, and so violent with her? How?"

Hildegard looked at him and then at Ilse, a massive question in her eyes.

"His name is Johan," Manfred said. "Mama told me he was a patient of hers," he repeated.

Hildegard's heart sank and she looked at the frozen Ilse in disbelief, but didn't say anything. She closed her eyes and opened them three times, thus signaling to Ilse, *we'll talk about it later*.

The three of them sat hugging for a while longer, and then Hildegard realized she would have to find some unknown reserves of inner strength in order to start tackling the chaos that had devastated her store.

"Ilse, I want the two of you to come live with me for a while. I don't want to leave you alone even for a minute. We'll spend some time at my place and some at yours, and we'll stay together until Abe and Isadore are released. Then we'll decide what to do next. And Ilse, I haven't had time to tell you yet, because you and Manfred seemed to be doing a lot worse than what I had to say, but during that night of vandalism, the store's window was broken and a lot of the merchandise was damaged. The Jewish owner of the shoe store next to me, whose store was destroyed as well, is watching over the shop for me, but I'll have to go back there to take care of everything. Believe me, I don't even know where to start, but first of all we have to get out of here," she said, experiencing a surge of resourcefulness.

Ilse no longer had the strength to keep crying. She looked at her mother, her eyes reflecting her deep pain. Damen—her mother's lovely store, the source of her livelihood for years—had been vandalized by the rioters, even though its owner was not Jewish. Or had it maybe happened because of her connection to Jews? These days it was no longer possible to distinguish friend from foe, to figure out who was a snitch, who knew whom, who was collaborating with the Nazis, and who was a true ally. It was a time of confusion and great tumult.

The three of them turned to go. Ilse's whole body was still in pain. Hobbling after her mother, she kept hold of Manfred's hand. She locked the door after her, knowing that in the next few days, she would have to come back in order to try to straighten up the mess.

On their way to Hildegard's apartment they saw what had taken place throughout the city during the catastrophic night. The heavy smell of the fires still lingered, and the air was suffused with smoke. The streets with Jewish-owned stores were full of broken glass. Ruin and destruction reflected back from every corner, and many people were running around in despair. It was an unbearable sight.

Ilse thought of the Sontags. They, too, were probably worried about them—their good neighbors, their loyal friends who had not abandoned them even for a single day. She remembered the saying "There are a few righteous men in Sodom," which

Abe often used. Isadore had explained to her the meaning and the source of the saying. Ilse knew that from the moment she got home, she would have to start making inquiries and taking action with regard to Abe and Isadore. The one and only person who could truly try to help her with this was Sigmund, through his work for the Ministry of the Interior. He could surely look into what was happening with them, even if he would have to use various ruses to do so.

The moment they came to the apartment, and Hildegard was assured that her daughter and grandson were safe, she turned to leave for the store. "Ilse, I'll come back as soon as I can," she said. "And then we'll talk about everything. All right, *liebchen*?" Ilse nodded silently.

Hildegard didn't want to leave them alone, but she also had to think about the store, her only source of livelihood. She had no other choice, so she took off again with a heavy heart.

When she arrived at the store, the glass spread out before her had already been swept into a pile by the side of the road. She had to restore order to the store as soon as possible, and indeed, within an hour, the glazier showed up to begin installing a new display window. He couldn't help expressing his amazement at what had occurred. "Why would they destroy your store, Frau Heine? What do you have to do with all this *Kristallnacht*?" he asked her.

"*Kristallnacht*?" she replied. "So they've already managed to come up with a name for it? It's horrible, isn't it?"

"Look, Frau Heine, the fact that they destroyed your store by mistake, too—that's the horrible part. The fact that they destroyed the Jews' property, that's perfectly fine. They destroyed almost all the synagogues in Germany, vandalized their cemeteries, and damaged and looted thousands of their shops and department stores. And just wait and see, Frau Heine—I tend to believe that the Jews will probably still be required to pay a fine for all the damages caused to the cities because of this riot."

◈ Chapter 29 ◈

Ilse took care of Manfred, who, like her, could find no peace. He flooded her with more and more questions for which she had no answers. After all, she, too, was experiencing a profound confusion that bordered on despair, and didn't know how she would conduct herself even at the next moment. Millions of thoughts and thought fragments were rushing through her mind, and she tried to sew them all together into one whole picture—but it was hard, so hard.

Ilse called Gertrude, who heaved a sigh of relief after receiving a sign of life from her adored friend. Ilse hinted at what had happened, including the worst of it—Abe and Isadore's arrest. Gertrude was appalled, expressing great shock at what she just heard.

"I'll talk to Sigmund immediately and ask him to make all the necessary inquiries," she said encouragingly. "Don't worry, Ilse, we're both here and we'll help you in any way we can. Richard constantly asks about you. After all, he hasn't seen Manfred since he got sick, and he's worried about him. How is he, Ilse?"

"He's not doing well, Gertrude. How could he be? The illness has become a trivial matter after the events of last night."

At the end of the painful conversation with Ilse, Gertrude found herself in a state of emotional turmoil. She was impatient for Sigmund to return from work, since she didn't want to tell him anything over the phone. They both often felt some unease about their connection to Jews and hoped they would not come under suspicion.

Sigmund had stopped any communication with Jews immediately after the laws were enacted, but he did keep surreptitiously in touch with Abe whenever he could. Even when he knew it was dangerous, mostly due to his position, he preferred to take the risk rather than sever his ties with this wonderful person who was his loyal friend. And if there was indeed a grain of truth to the Nazi propaganda targeting Jews, Abe was certainly not one of those to whom all that applied. In Sigmund's eyes, Abe was at least as worthy as any Aryan.

◆ ◆ ◆

By the afternoon, Hildegard's store had been restored to its previous state. She locked it up and hurried home, as she couldn't bear even one more moment away from her daughter and grandson. She couldn't stop thinking about the very partial information she'd received from Manfred regarding the identity of one of the SS officers who had arrested Abe and Isadore. If this was the same Johan she knew, then the horror had just increased exponentially, and she wanted to hear the rest of the details from her daughter.

Ilse and Manfred were happy to see her. The state of the boy's health had improved somewhat, but his mood was very dejected. Hildegard hugged him and he suddenly told her, "Oma, that Nazi Johan's disgusting face is stuck in my head. That face of his, a hard, mean face—you never saw anything like it! If you did, you'd know what I mean. Do you know that Mama took care of him once? Oh, actually, I already told you that before. How could I forget?" Tears appeared in his eyes.

Hildegard was silent. She was certain that Ilse had not told Manfred the whole truth about Johan. That was the last thing they needed—causing her son more confusion and distress beyond what he had already experienced from the time he turned six and until that moment. What a strange, evil world he had been born into.

"Ilse," she turned to her daughter, "my Damen is up and running again, but the truth is that it doesn't really interest me at the moment. What does interest me is Abe and Isadore's arrest. Have you started to look into it?"

"I contacted Gertrude. She promised to talk to Sigmund. He's the only one who might be able to help us with this. Who else can I turn to, Mama? Who would even be interested?" Ilse raised her eyes to the ceiling in a silent plea.

Several minutes later, when Manfred left the parlor, she whispered to her mother, "Mama, it was Johan Kirche. Can you believe it? Out of everyone—it had to be him, that brute! And it's obvious there was also an aspect of personal revenge here. I'm sure it was all intentional. Johan knew exactly where to go and took advantage of the night's events everywhere to do what he did. I've heard that many other Jews were arrested. Did you hear that too?"

"Yes, Ilse, the whole street was talking about it. It's just terrible. How could he have treated you like that? And you're right—it must have also been out of a desire for revenge. After all, our two men have never harmed anyone. We have no other choice, Ilse. We have to wait patiently for Sigmund. Poor Sigmund. What he'll have to go through to look into it. He's really been in a tough position since the antisemitic laws were passed. After all, he objects to everything that's going on and it's not easy to be a double agent—not easy and also very dangerous—and I don't envy him at all."

"Mama, I want to go back to my apartment. I might suddenly hear from Abe, and he won't know where we are! And most important, I have to talk to Sigmund beyond what Gertrude will tell him. I have a million questions to ask him, and I see him as my salvation. Come home with me. Manfred also has to go back to school somehow, or else they'll come looking for him. You know what the discipline is like at his school., Oh, Mama, it's all become so complicated. Everything's become so hard and full of question marks. I don't know how I'll go back to work. I don't have the patience for anything." And she burst into tears, unable to control herself, especially once her brain was flooded with horrific images of what might be happening to Abe and Isadore.

If she had only known how close her fears were to reality, she would have lost her mind.

◆ ◆ ◆

At the end of the day, all the prisoners were assembled in the drill field. They were counted once again, a process that took much longer this time. The evening chill was even worse than the morning one. The frozen moisture, gradually descending upon them, threatened to transform them all into human blocks of ice. Only when the moon came up were they ordered to go into the musty cabins. After Abe ravenously tore into his slice of bread and quickly consumed it, he curled up on his cot and tried to get warm under the thin woolen blanket covering him. He thought about Ilse and Manfred, and his eyes filled with tears. And when he thought of his father, his heart contracted with worry.

Chapter 30

After the *Kristallnacht* riot, Johan was ordered to report to duty at the Dachau concentration camp. He was chosen to command a wing of prisoners, whose overall number at the camp was growing from day to day. Johan was scheduled to leave for Dachau within a week, after vacating the apartment on Wilhelmstrasse.

◆ ◆ ◆

It was hard for Hildegard to see Ilse in her current state. Her restlessness had infected Hildegard as well. They had to go back to Leipziger Street. Hildegard packed a few things and they took hold of Manfred's hands and set out. It was evening by the time they arrived home, and Gertrude, who had been waiting expectantly for Ilse, came out to meet them. She hugged the three of them, drying her eyes.

"Ilse, my dear, you have no idea how sorry I am that this happened." She then looked at her, examining her face and touching her split lip. "Ilse, you don't deserve this injustice, and Abe and your father-in-law certainly don't, either. Sigmund's already home and I gave him a brief version of what happened. He wants to talk to you. Come in, please, and once you've gotten settled, come see us. Richard is very worried about Manfred. He'll come over to your place to be with him. Richard doesn't know anything about what happened, and I believe Manfred will want to share it with him. Isn't that right, Manfred?" She turned to the boy, who nodded vigorously. She then leaned into Ilse's ear and whispered to her, "After all, we don't want them to catch even the smallest bit of the conversation we're going to have."

Ilse nodded in agreement and they headed for the apartment. "Mama, I know you want to be present during this conversation too, but it'll be better if you stay with the boys."

"Of course, Ilse, and don't worry. I'm sure you'll update me later."

Ilse then turned to Manfred and managed to whisper, "Make sure not to mention the name 'Johan,' and not a word to Richard about Papa, especially not about his being Jewish, okay?"

Manfred looked at her and promptly replied, "You don't even have to ask, Mama."

Ilse changed out of the clothes she had been wearing since the events of the night before. She hadn't had the energy to change earlier. Other than washing her hands and face, she hadn't done a thing for herself, focusing completely on Manfred and Abe. She looked in the mirror and didn't really recognize her own reflection. After washing up and putting on fresh clothes, she went downstairs to the Sontags' apartment as if she were sleepwalking. Sigmund and Gertrude were waiting for her. The second that Richard saw her, he leaped up, hugged her, and then ran upstairs to Manfred. Sigmund stood up, silently walked over to her, and held her tight.

"Ilse, I'm so sorry about what happened to you all. It's a catastrophe, a real catastrophe. So many Jews were arrested during the vandalism, and almost all of them were sent to concentration camps. People were talking about it all day at our office. The Jews were arrested under all kinds of charges and they were led to trucks that transported them to three camps: Dachau, Buchenwald, and Sachsenhausen. 'Enemies of the Reich'—that's what they called them."

Ilse looked at him in fright. "To concentration camps? So they're not just being held at one of the jails in town? When will they be released? Will they be put on trial?" She blurted out one question after another, uncertain which of them Sigmund could answer.

"What trial, Ilse, *liebchen*?" he told her, his heart breaking. "Have you forgotten that the Jews' citizenship was revoked a long time ago? Have you forgotten that as a result, the administration can do whatever it wants to them? And now, as prisoners, they lack any rights whatsoever. This is unbelievably serious. What a state our nation has come to! How have we allowed ourselves to sink so low?"

At that moment, Ilse didn't really care how Germany and its people had gotten to where they were, from a moral-political-administrative-human/subhuman perspective. She cared about getting as much information as possible about Abe and Isadore, as quickly as possible, and, of course, about what she would have to do to secure their release. She quickly made this clear to Sigmund.

"You have to help me, Sigmund. There's no other sane person that I can turn to. Please, guide me; I'll do anything possible to get them released. Please. I believe you're the only friend who really cares about us."

Sigmund looked at her, sadness reflecting in his eyes. He didn't want to add to her despair so soon. "Ilse, tomorrow I'll do what I can about this. I promise you that even with the restrictions I'm facing, I won't come home until I find out as much as I can." He couldn't help but offer her some hope, even though in his heart of hearts, he knew that it was false hope, and therefore said, "I'll help you in any way I can, and together we'll try to find a way to battle this injustice."

"Sigmund," Ilse whispered, "Johan Kirche is the one who arrested them. Johan Kirche, who was my boyfriend before I met Abe."

Ilse went back home, and for the rest of that night, she and Hildegard talked. Manfred rallied, too, without having been told a thing. He was certain that Sigmund would try to help them. He did tell Richard that his father and grandfather were arrested, but didn't mention the issue of their Judaism.

He said they were arrested, apparently by mistake, because of some political matter. Manfred knew that there were certain details Richard was not allowed to know if he wanted to maintain their friendship.

Richard had very firm ideas about the difference between the Aryan race and other nations, and the only thing his parents tried to do was to somewhat reduce the rigidity of his perceptions. Beyond that, they couldn't influence him so as not to create too much of a conflict in views between them and their son, who was integrated into Aryan society to the same extent that they were. This was nearly unbearable, particularly the constant games and pretenses to which they needed to resort as the parents of a child who had been raised on the Nazi ideology, belonged to Hitler Youth, and was exposed to all the antisemitic propaganda just as they were, while also being a couple and parents who were truly revolted by all this.

The next day Ilse returned to work. She had no other choice. Life didn't stop, and she didn't want to share her personal problem with anyone other than the Sontags. She tried to focus on her work, and when her colleagues asked about Manfred's health, she replied briefly and with mere civility. Beyond that, she didn't say a word to anyone.

Manfred, who was feeling better physically, returned to school, but did so with a heavy heart. He, too, had no choice, and at least Richard, who stayed by his side, tried to cheer him up.

In the afternoon, Ilse returned home, eagerly anticipating Sigmund's arrival. She was truly hoping he would have encouraging news for her.

Sigmund didn't have an easy day, either—to put it mildly—as he tried to keep his promise to Ilse and return home with useful information. He did all he could to extract the information from the classified materials in the Economy and Administration Bureau, which was under the authority of the Ministry of the Interior, headed by Heinrich Himmler. In addition to supervising the concentration camps for government dissidents, the Economy and Administration Bureau was also in charge of matters of administration, finance, and maintenance within the SS organization.

Sigmund returned home in the early evening, under a dark cloud. Before going into his own apartment, he knocked on Ilse's door. Manfred was visiting Richard, for which Sigmund was grateful. What he had to say was far from appropriate for the child's ears.

"Ilse, let's sit down and talk," he told her as he came in. He tried to project calm, although it was very difficult in view of what he had to say. Ilse sat down wordlessly, her chin beginning to tremble uncontrollably as she crushed the material of her dress between her fingers.

"Ilse, I spent most of my day secretly and laboriously trying to track down Abe and Isadore. I have to admit, it wasn't an easy task at all. Finally, the list of detainees whose names begin with 'L' was placed on my desk, and I saw Abe and Isadore's names on it, one after the other."

"Where were they taken?" Ilse interjected. She was afraid to ask more than that.

"They were taken to Dachau, along with many other detainees. It's the concentration camp near Munich for political prisoners and other dangerous individuals. Abe and Isadore are at Dachau." He repeated their whereabouts again because he didn't want to say anything more about the terrible place to which his friend's two loved ones had been sent.

"I also looked into their term of imprisonment, and whether they're expected to be released at some point. There was nothing about that, other than that for those Jews who could prove that they intend to leave Germany, release would be considered. Do you think they can prove something like that? As far as I know, you weren't planning to leave, even when the topic came up."

Ilse didn't reply. Sigmund was right. They had no concrete

plans to leave or emigrate, and even if they had talked about it, there was no proof of their intention to leave the country.

"At the moment, in any case," Sigmund continued in response to her silence, "they're prisoners at the camp, with everything that implies, and I'm very sorry to have to tell you that there's no possibility of visiting them there, or finding out much information about them. I'm sorry, Ilse, but for now, I've done the best I can without, I hope, raising any suspicions regarding my interest in these specific people. I also don't think I could find out any more than that, since that would mean finding the right person on the inside—within the camp itself—who would agree to cooperate, and I don't know anyone like that whom I could trust. My own work isn't really related to these camps or to daily life there. The camps are under the authority of a different office, which is also subordinate to the Ministry of the Interior. You know, precision with regard to the chain of command and the people in charge of each subject is a high priority for the Nazi administration. Each of them handles the topics under his supervision, and has no particular interest in handling matters that they aren't qualified to handle."

His heart was breaking as he watched Ilse's face seem to collapse and shatter in front of his eyes. "Ilse, I'm so, so sorry. The only thing Gertrude and I can do is help you and Manfred get through this. You have to understand that we're also facing a serious problem in connection with your own. If something were to happen to us due to our past relationship with Abe and Isadore—after all, you can never tell who will say what, or how it will be interpreted—you and the child might be harmed as well. We can't let that happen—not at any price. We have to pray, to both the Jewish and Christian God, that Abe and Isadore will ultimately be released, and in the meantime, that they remain safe and are treated in a reasonable manner." It was particularly hard for Sigmund to utter this last sentence. He was well aware of the deplorable, brutal way that prisoners in the camps were treated, particularly the Jews among them.

Ilse did not shed any tears, because she no longer had any tears to shed, and felt they wouldn't help in any way other than increasing the terrible pressure in her head and creating an excess of moisture in her nose.

"Sigmund, I want to thank you for everything you've done for me. I know that you've done, and always will do, the best you can. Please don't take any additional risks, and don't endanger Gertrude and Richard either. Thank you for your offer to help us. We'll get through this, Sigmund, because I've made a vow—I won't break down so easily," she concluded, suddenly surging with new energy. She didn't know the source of this new strength, which was imbuing her with some hope. But what she did promise herself was that she would not rest until she had done all she could to find out more about Abe and Isadore.

She also knew whom she would try to contact, although just thinking about it appalled her and filled her with extreme dread.

◆ ◆ ◆

Ilse headed for Wilhelmstrasse around 5:00 p.m., hoping to find Johan at home. She knocked on his door several times and when no response came, resolved to wait for him a while. Even when a whole hour had gone by, Johan was nowhere to be seen. The cold nipped at her flesh and she wrapped her coat around her as best she could. Her teeth were chattering and her lips had already turned blue. She decided she would go see Johan again early the next morning, before he left home and before she had to be at work. She had to catch him. She had spent a restless night mentally rehearsing what she would tell him, again and again, not sharing her plans with anyone.

Ilse didn't know where she had found the fortitude to even contemplate the possibility of going to Johan and appealing to him for help—if that was indeed the right term. She was devastated to find the door on which she knocked to be locked. She had arrived armed with courage, but as the minutes went by, her confidence eroded and she came to question her decision, which now appeared quite extreme to her. *Tomorrow it won't be the same anymore*, she thought. *Now is when I have to talk to him. Right now!* In distress and anxiety, she pounded on Johan's door again, waited a moment or two, and began to walk away. Suddenly, much to her surprise, the door opened. Her heart began to pound wildly

Johan stood in the doorway, half asleep, his hair disheveled, his cheeks unshaven and his attire sloppy. Ilse found it hard to start talking and needed a fair amount of air. Her body was suddenly flushed with heat, which briefly displaced the chill.

"Ilse, what are you doing here at this hour and in this cold? What do you want? I hope you're here for an important reason, and not just to harass me, *nicht wahr*?"

Johan did have a callous, rigid nature, and was subject to uncontrollable whims and a consuming jealousy, but he was no fool. He knew exactly why Ilse had come to him and what she wanted from him. A ripple of pity for her distress did bubble through him, but he also knew that what had already taken place could not be undone, nor did he regret it in the slightest.

"Johan," Ilse said, once she regained the ability to speak, "please, please, Johan, tell me what's happening with my husband and his father. I know that they were taken to a concentration camp, like many others. We heard about it. But please, Johan, I beg you, if only for the sake of those happy days we shared. Tell me exactly where they are and what will happen to them. Please." Although she knew they had been taken to the Dachau camp, she preferred not to mention it.

Johan deliberated briefly and then told her, "I have no idea, Ilse. I really have no idea. You've contacted the wrong person by coming here. I was just following orders; beyond that, I don't know anything."

There was an odd glint in his eyes, one that Ilse had seen

before. His lips were also quivering slightly and Ilse knew that he was lying. She directed a piercing look at him, which said more than the words she chose not to say. She didn't want to keep begging, as her intuition told her that Johan knew quite a lot about Abe and Isadore but chose not to share it with her. Apparently his need for vengeance was stronger than anything else. She wanted to strangle him at that moment, certain that he was the one who was mostly to blame for her husband's and father-in-law's arrest.

She felt the urge to end with a reproach. "Johan," she told him, quietly yet determinedly, "you'll come to regret your behavior and your actions. I thought that despite everything, there would still be a bit of humanity left in you—at least when it came to me—but it turns out I was wrong. It's too bad, Johan, too bad that your desire for revenge is so strong and uncontrollable that it overtakes you and brings you to where you are now." And she turned to go. As she walked away, adjusting her hat and coat, she turned briefly and gave Johan a frigid stare that left him rooted in his place.

Johan felt his limbs growing rigid. He continued tracking Ilse as she walked away, until she disappeared from sight. He loved her so much, but was so furious with her. He knew there was merit to what she'd said about his vindictiveness, and that he would never win her love naturally. But he was willing to make do with keeping her close by unnatural means, and he would do whatever it took. For years he had been in a state of emotional turmoil when it came to her. He loved and hated her at the same time. When he hit her on the night of the arrests, he felt pleasure and gratification, followed by pity toward her, which caused him torment. His feelings were so extreme, so unclear, and so uncontrollable, and the great rage he directed at himself resulted from Ilse's success in awakening all this within him. And indeed, Ilse was the only person who had ever evoked such emotions in him. How had he not managed to eliminate his conflicting feelings toward her? Why couldn't he totally expunge her from his mind, his memories, and his hopes? After all, this excessive sentimentality was the exact opposite of what the Nazi Party's militant ideological education dictated.

This inner fury often turned into self-pity, which frightened him. Johan couldn't go back to perceiving himself as pitiful, as he had been during his entire childhood and adolescence. He was a powerful person, with excellent skills and capabilities—how, then, had he been so won over by a woman, feeling like a doormat at her feet? What was so special about Ilse?

The hours ticked by after Ilse's departure, and as they did, Johan's anguish gradually increased. The memory of his visit to Landsberger Street yesterday, in order to seize Dr. Isadore Liebmann's house, seemed to toy with him. It was not the only house to be seized. Many other houses belonging to Jews had been blacklisted as well, and would soon be commandeered.

᪥ Chapter 31 ᪥

Johan left Berlin and made the long drive to Munich. Before reporting to headquarters at the Dachau concentration camp, he went to visit his mother, whom he hadn't seen for quite a while.

"Johan," Beatrice said excitedly, "it's so wonderful to see you. You look so handsome and elegant in your uniform. And what brings you to Munich this time?" she asked in interest

"Mother, as of today, I begin my role as a commander at the Dachau camp. Lately the camp has been receiving more and more prisoners—political dissidents—and the command force has been enhanced accordingly. It's an important position, very prestigious," he concluded with pride.

Beatrice scrutinized him closely, narrowing her eyes. For a moment, she said nothing, then sighed and blurted out, "Johan, are you sure that it's a good idea for you to work in a concentration camp? I've heard people whispering that it's not really a very pleasant place to be..."

"Oh, Mother, come on," Johan laughed, seemingly jovial, "what do you mean, 'unpleasant'? Orders have to be carried out, and we have to be ready for any assignment or position. More pleasant, less pleasant, who cares? The prisoners at the camp are treated like prisoners. They're not locked in there because they did good deeds; they were arrested under serious charges. Don't you understand? There's nothing worse than government dissidents, who are also seditionists, sowing confusion among the rest of the population. There's only one safe place for people like that—within a compound, surrounded by walls, bars, and an electric fence. You also have to understand," he continued passionately, "that the prisoners' work is highly effective. After all, they're building and maintaining the camp and serving as a deterrent for others. They're also an important economic component for the SS, the state, and weapons efforts. It's a tremendous work force, and it doesn't cost a thing. Do you see now?"

Beatrice decided not to respond. Her opinion on the matter—one that was totally opposed to Johan's views—was of no consequence anyway.

Johan arrived at the camp and reported to headquarters. The standards of conduct and discipline applied to SS personnel carrying out security and administrative roles were very strict. "You have to know and understand unequivocally that those who hold different opinions are inferior creatures who must be treated accordingly. If you have to kill when necessary, you will not shirk that obligation," he was told. "You have to thoroughly memorize the procedures that deal with discipline, punishment, and prisoner classification, and familiarize yourself with every one of the obligations applying to the prisoners—who are, of course, devoid of any rights."

Johan had no problem adjusting to his new role as a commander of prisoners, in charge of the SS administrators overseeing the hospital, subordinate camps, and jail units. The registration officer conducting the barracks headcounts and the officer supervising the work brigades were also under his command. The need to kill when necessary didn't cause him any compunction, either—after all, he had already killed several people in his life, particularly when he took part in the mass murder of SA personnel during the Night of the Long Knives.

◆ ◆ ◆

Abe counted seven days since he had first arrived at the camp. From day to day, he got to know the place better, and gained a deeper understanding of the human tragedy personified by the prisoners detained there. One evening he was sent to the administration building in order to receive equipment for the following workday. As he arrived, he heard bloodcurdling screams. His skin prickled, and he realized that he was hearing someone who was in pain, extreme pain. The heavy darkness around him concealed him, providing him with the opportunity to approach the place from which the horrific sounds were originating.

Behind the administration building, near the southern wall of the camp, he spotted a small sign with the word "Bunker" written on it. He had gotten very close to the source of the screaming, which had increased in volume, making his heart race wildly. He recalled what he had heard two days before regarding the site called "The Bunker." It was an enclosure dedicated to brutal interrogations, ruthless discipline, torture, and isolation. Executions, whippings, and torture sessions in which prisoners were hung out on poles were all carried out in the bunker. Some of the Bunker's cells were "standing rooms," in which prisoners were forced to stand in the dark for hours at a time. The prisoner who had been talking about it had already been personally whipped and punished, for a different reason every time. Hearing his account was enough to paralyze the listener with fear and terror. No one wanted to be taken to this bunker, and the panic it evoked caused them all to be as obedient as frightened mice.

Abe walked away. He had happened upon the entrance to the bunker and hoped with all his heart that he would never see it from the inside. He brought the tools from the storage room and quickly returned to Barrack #2. He didn't tell anyone what he had heard that evening, and throughout the night, the horrific screams of the man whose body was being abused in the notorious bunker continued to ring in his ears.

The next morning, as they did every day, the prisoners lined up for the morning headcount and roll call. Abe noted the appalling fact that the headcount was also an opportunity for gratuitous abuse. If one of the prisoners didn't show up on time, or managed to escape, the headcount could last for hours—hours of standing motionless, hours of torture for torture's sake. It was a means of collective punishment. And indeed, that morning one of the prisoners did not show up for roll call. The missing prisoner's number was thundered out again and again, then screamed out, but he didn't reply. All the prisoners stood in the freezing cold, praying that the problematic prisoner would show up. Faint whispers were heard, and after some time, the prisoners were ordered to disband to their work assignments.

The prisoner who hadn't shown up was found lifeless in his barrack. It was the prisoner whose screams Abe had heard the night before.

There were two types of general work duties: work cohorts tasked with carrying out jobs within the camp, and those tasked with carrying out jobs outside it. The external work cohorts labored to build roads, dig up gravel, and tend to swampy areas. Luckily for Abe, he was assigned to the work cohorts within the camp. These assignments were also far from easy, but the mitigating factor was their proximity to the barracks. The external work cohorts had to make their way to their work sites through the cold and snow, carrying their equipment and dressed in clothes that were far from appropriate for the freezing wintery weather. Abe's work group focused on general maintenance of the camp's grounds, as well as other tasks related to the kitchen, the laundry, and providing personal services to the guards and other camp executives.

An experience shared by both types of cohorts was being subjected to exhausting labor that stretched from the early morning until the late evening, under horrific conditions and while suffering constant hunger due to the scarcity of the food that was allotted in quantities that did not align with their true needs as physical laborers. Their exhaustion was constant, due to the brief hours of restless sleep, the harassment, the drills and the punishment, and, worst of all—the gnawing fear of the brutality exhibited by the sadistic guards, all SS men.

Abe was deeply immersed in this daily ritual, which he experienced along with all the other prisoners from the moment they had first arrived at the camp. He admitted that it was a practice meted out with impressive precision. The timeline was meticulously coordinated, and everything was perfectly planned out—just like a mechanized factory. Every morning, precisely at 5:00 a.m., all 250 exhausted prisoners in Barrack #2 were shocked out of their prone positions by commands and loud voices and led to the bathhouse, wearing their striped pajamas, in order to drizzle a little water, usually ice cold, on their bodies. They ate a meager breakfast that consisted of a little black coffee; "morning drink" would have been a more appropriate term, as no actual food was included. "Dirty Jews, come get your food and eat like pigs," the Jews among them were told. They then received their work clothes and equipment in preparation for the workday.

The actual workday began at 6:00 a.m. and ended at 6:00 p.m.—12 full hours of torture. Most of the work groups were mixed, with Jews, Ukrainians, Poles, Czechs, and Germans, but the Jews always, always fell victim to all the others, even when their "sins" were the most minor. The daily course of the work assignments was overseen by the SS guards who belonged to the "Death's Head" unit, the cruelest of the units, and they were indeed as violent and brutal as the terrifying, teeth-baring German Shepherds that were their loyal companions.

When the prisoners returned from work in the evening, another headcount took place. The guards were as sharp-eyed as hawks—if one of the prisoners was found to have brought in some vegetable he had come across while working, he was sentenced to a public beating. Every time someone was caught violating any of the rigid camp rules, however minor, all of the barracks' residents would be called out for another headcount. The terrible, constant fear of being punished eroded what little energy the prisoners still retained after so many hours of hard labor. The main sustenance they were routinely given consisted of one loaf of bread for several men, stale, moldy soup, spotty potato peels, and sometimes another unidentifiable vegetable, which tasted as bad as it looked.

Abe knew that constant hunger, alongside physical and mental exhaustion, acted as a corrosive acid of sorts, as it was impossible to imagine how long a person could continue to survive under such conditions.

Chapter 32

The next member of her social circle to whom Ilse decided to appeal for help was Dr. Genscher. She knew he had always felt great affection for her, was certain that he wouldn't turn her down, and, if he could, would try to help her. Until that day, she had not shared her personal affairs with any of the staff, her acquaintances, or even her closest friends. She didn't want them to feel sorry for her, and also feared some people's reactions. These were already delicate matters, and sometimes, unfortunately, they might prove dangerous as well. Dr. Genscher had asked her several times how they were faring, especially since the riot. She chose not to say much in reply, merely briefly mentioning the damage caused, apparently by mistake, to her mother's store. She didn't say a word about Abe and Isadore.

Dr. Genscher had always shown interest in her and her family. His attitude toward Dr. Liebmann was one of true admiration, and when he asked about him, Ilse always replied, "We're getting by, Dr. Genscher. What other choice do we have?" Beyond this, she wouldn't say anything else.

Although nearly a month had passed since Abe and Isadore had been arrested, and Ilse hadn't heard a word from either of them, she was still having a hard time taking in what had happened. The absurdity of it was glaringly clear. She was horrified by the fact that they had been dispatched to suffer an unknown fate by none other than the man she had once loved. And the knowledge that there was no one to whom she could appeal in order to amend this travesty, challenge the injustice, and seek its restitution, gnawed at her constantly.

"Dr. Genscher," she addressed him softly, "I would like to

ask for a few minutes of your time, for which I'd be grateful. There's something I have to discuss with you in private."

Dr. Genscher looked at her, and his face took on a kindly smile. "For you, Ilse, I'll find all the time in the world. Come to my office during the lunch break. I promise you that we'll be alone, and that I'll listen attentively to anything you would like to tell me."

"Thank you so much, Dr. Genscher. I'll be at your office at 12:30 on the dot," she said with a faint smile.

While carrying out her routine tasks, Ilse also took advantage of the remaining time until her meeting with Dr. Genscher to carefully plan out what she would tell him. She didn't want to pile on tedious detail, or burden him with sentimentality. She only wanted to be succinct and pragmatic, and receive answers that were as practical as possible.

Ilse's heart began to race as she entered Genscher's office precisely at 12:30 and found him waiting for her, sitting behind his desk, going over paperwork. He raised his head and smiled at her.

"Come in, Ilse. Please sit down. Sit down," he told her, and she complied, feeling a tightening in her chest.

"How can I help you?" he asked.

"Dr. Genscher, I cherish and appreciate the wonderful way you've treated me since the day I was hired here, about a decade ago. I really debated before deciding to talk to you, but believe me—I'm doing so because I truly believe you will offer me a sympathetic ear."

"I'm ready to listen," he said laconically.

"I'll never forget how you opened my eyes when it came to Herr Johan Kirche, some years ago, when you gave me your honest opinion of him. It helped me make up my mind, and you were right. You had a very clear opinion of him, as if you knew him personally." She paused to consider her next words once more.

"Dr. Genscher, I'm going to share something with you that

I've never told any of the staff at the clinic before." She let out a heavy sigh. "Dr. Genscher, during that terrible pogrom... in the Kristallnacht riot, my husband and father-in-law were arrested and sent to a concentration camp, along with thousands of other Jews. My husband and his father were sent to Dachau." She saw the doctor's gaze sharpen and his expression, which had been relaxed until that point, altered. He didn't say a word, allowing her to continue talking.

"The SS officers who arrested them completely destroyed their clinic, and apparently, a little while later, commandeered the entire house." Ilse paused once more as she tried to overcome her agitation. "Dr. Genscher, ever since, I've had no contact with my husband and father-in-law. Nothing at all. I don't know how they're doing. I don't even know whether they're alive or not." She wiped away a rebellious tear she could no longer control, although she had promised herself she would do anything she could to avoid exhibiting excessive emotion. Her terrible despair had still managed to surface. Genscher kept silent and only his eyes remained fixed on her own.

"Dr. Genscher," she continued, approaching the crucial moment, "I know that as deputy director of the hospital, you have all sorts of connections with a wide variety of people. I was just thinking that maybe, as a fellow doctor, you could find out from the doctors at Dachau what has become of my husband and father-in-law. And if not with the doctors, maybe you know someone else who can help, even if it's only by providing the most basic information." She didn't want to go on to tell him that her existence had become a living hell ever since the moment her husband was taken. She didn't want to tell him about the kind of suffering she and her son were going through. That was not the goal. She didn't intend to turn into a pest. She was simply seeking help, any sort of help, if only in the form of some information.

Dr. Genscher was dumbstruck and needed a few minutes before he felt capable of responding. "Ilse, dear Ilse, the grave things you just told me have truly shocked me. Like many others, I, too, heard about what took place during the horrifying pogrom and after it, but I didn't know about Dr. Liebmann and his father. I have to admit, this really doesn't sit well with me. I don't believe in violence, or in anything like what happened and is happening in this country in general since the Nazis rose to power. I want you to understand that this policy and the totalitarian mode the government has adopted are harming some of the German population as well. I don't believe that everyone, with no exception, agrees with everything that's going on, but I do believe that many of them are simply swept up in the leadership's actions.

"And now, to the matter of your husband and father-in-law," he continued. "I do know these camps and I'm aware of what's going on there. And there is indeed one particular physician who once worked here, in the research lab, who, as far as I know, chose to transfer to Dachau, of all places, to work as a doctor to both commanders and prisoners. To tell you the truth, I find it hard to understand how he chose to trade in a proper role at a hospital like ours for a difficult position in an improvised hospital in a concentration camp or prison camp—they can call it what they will, but to me it's all the same. Ilse, I promise you I'll do my best to inquire about Dr. Liebmann Senior and Dr. Liebmann Junior. Give me a few days, and I'll try to get back to you with an answer, whatever it might be."

Ilse's eyes suddenly lit up. "Thank you, thank you so much, *Herr Doktor*. I'm so grateful to you. Any sort of information would be immensely helpful. Of course I'll wait patiently. You have no idea how this meeting with you has also given me some hope." Once again, she dabbed at her eyes with a handkerchief.

"Ilse, I wish I could do more than just inquire about them. I wish I could bring about their release. And I'm asking you not to thank me until I actually have something to tell you."

Ilse rose from her seat and shook Dr. Genscher's hand. She turned to leave the room and then heard him tell her, "Ilse, keep on holding up as you've done thus far. If you hadn't come here and told me, none of us here would have any idea what you're going through."

She looked at him, flashed a fleeting smile that swiftly disappeared, and blurted out, "Johan Kirche was the one who arrested them," then hurriedly left the room.

Dr. Genscher continued to stare in horror at the space left in her wake.

♦ ♦ ♦

From the day Manfred found out about his father's Judaism as well as his own, he experienced a major change, mostly with regard to his perception of what he was learning at school and at the youth movement. He no longer enjoyed the warlike sports games, either. Suddenly he understood things that he hadn't thought about before. He knew he had no other choice—he had to continue attending youth movement meetings and striving for excellence, which would now be considerably harder, as his efforts were always maintained only for appearance's sake, while he fought to manage his internal contempt for what he was being taught.

He also felt that his relationship with Richard had become somewhat artificial, as while Richard continued to behave as usual, having no idea of the mental turmoil his friend was enduring, Manfred was struggling every night, as he lay in bed, with the crucial questions to which he could not find a single, fitting answer. He desperately missed his father and grandfather. Worry for them also ate away at him, but he didn't ever mention it to his mother or grandmother.

Chapter 33

Winter that year brought with it long days of hazy chill. Heavy snow fell often, covering the ground with an endless white carpet. The terrible frost always claimed its own victims, and during that winter, which had begun relatively early, the casualties of the cold were constantly increasing. When the temperatures outside dropped below freezing, reaching −18 Celsius,[3] the prisoners were not sent out to work. *Such consideration*, Abe thought sarcastically, while contemplating the fact that the ritual torture had become worse as well.

Almost every day the prisoners were forced to undress in the barracks and then run naked to a different cabin, where they faced guards and a doctor who assessed their physical condition. Those whose bodies were deemed to be more or less healthy were directed by the doctor to go to the right, while those whose bodies were emaciated and weak were sent to the left. It was a well-known fact that those sent to the left would no longer be seen within the camp grounds—they had been sentenced to death. It was devastating to watch the left column, whose members knew where they were headed, but didn't utter a peep as they were marched to their deaths in horrific silence.

Abe was already thoroughly familiar with the grounds of the camp, its rules of conduct and its dreadful significance. During the entire month, with its endless days that resembled a single unified mass of suffering, Abe found out for certain what he had not entirely managed to acknowledge to himself previously; during that month, he learned something new every day, saw more, and tried to find some light at the end of the tunnel.

---

[3] Minus-one Fahrenheit.

When he realized that no light would emerge in that terrible camp, he lay on his cot at night and, despite his severe fatigue, sleep would not claim him. The many thoughts racing wildly through his mind brought him to the harshest conclusions, leaving him in a state of bleakness and profound sadness.

To Abe, the camp resembled a factory of torture and murder, striving to take maximal advantage of the helpless inhabitants who had been deprived of all rights. It was a machine of terror, ruin, and destruction by means of hard labor performed under unbearable conditions, in which the victims—most of whom lived short lives full of distress, sorrow, and brutality—were ground down to dust. The basic terms of existence, characterized by a constant lack of supplies, poor hygiene, and inhumane crowding in the barracks, accelerated outbreaks of disease—resulting in yet more victims. And the unbearable pressures created hostility between the camp workers and the prisoners, forging a hierarchy within the prisoners' society—the workers appointed as supervisors over everyone else formed an elite faction that treated their fellow prisoners with extreme violence. Sometimes Abe felt as if he were living in a wild jungle inhabited by vicious animals seeking prey, where he had to be on guard at every single moment of every endless day.

He had to survive. Had to hang on, not lose hope, and yearn passionately for the moment he would be released, whenever it might come. He remembered that the last few days he'd heard whispering about a new commander who'd arrived at the camp a short time ago. "A cruel, unbelievably horrible man," the rumors claimed. What could be worse than what they'd experienced thus far? How many more calamities could the prisoners be forced to endure? Were there no ultimate boundaries? He hoped with all his heart that Ilse would find a way to do something. He missed her and Manfred so much, and was deeply worried about his father; with every day that went by in which he didn't see him, his fears for his life increased. Abe had already seen quite a few prisoners die around him. Their legs would suddenly collapse under them, and they would say goodbye to their wretched lives—including prisoners who were younger and healthier than his father. But maybe his father was still in the hospital, or in some other place where he couldn't be reached, he thought, in a state of desperation, while knowing in his heart of hearts that his hope had no basis in reality.

The next morning, at precisely 6:00 a.m., the roll call was held as it was every day. The numbers of the prisoners from Abe's group were called out one by one in order to make certain that they were all present and ready to leave for work. And, as was the case every day, the headcount served as a ruse for violence as the day began. Anyone who didn't respond to his number being read out within a reasonable amount of time was roughly prodded with a truncheon after being counted. Suddenly, Abe's number was read out again, this time along with his name—which he had not heard from the officials conducting the roll call since the day he first arrived at the camp. "Prisoner #180960, Dr. Abe Liebmann, take three steps forward."

Abe immediately stepped toward a tough-looking guard, fearing the worst. Even if he had not done anything, one could never tell. Perhaps an accidental sniffle had enraged one of the guards, which, in itself, was cause for punishment. "Follow me," the guard commanded. Abe obeyed in terror. He didn't understand what the summons meant and fervently hoped he was being called in for some sort of inquiry, and not in order to be punished. He was led to the administration building and shoved into one of the rooms.

As he stood rooted to his spot, motionless, he looked around. The room was pleasant and tidy, furnished with gleaming elegance. The walls displayed photos of Nazi "saints" and top leaders, with a giant portrait of Hitler towering above all of them. If he hadn't been at the concentration camp, he might have thought he had entered a portrait gallery. On the floor, he noticed a luxurious carpet. At the polished wood desk, a man in uniform was sitting in a padded swivel chair, his back to the front door. He was talking on the phone, or, more precisely, spitting out a series of decisive, terse commands in a firm voice. Abe stood where he was, not making a sound, and trying to suppress his breath. The man at the desk had thick, somewhat spiky, light blond hair. When he shifted slightly to the left in his chair, Abe's heart skipped a beat. He saw a blood-red birthmark in the shape of a distorted heart on his neck.

Abe remembered someone who had a birthmark like that, with pale blond hair and a similar voice, and a shiver ran through him. The man returned the receiver to its cradle with a metallic clang, then slowly turned around in his chair and was revealed in his full glory.

Abe's mouth dried out instantly as he saw that he hadn't been wrong. Sitting before him, puffed up with self-importance, and radiating elegant dignity, was none other than Johan Kirche—his captor on Kristallnacht.

Abe had never imagined that Johan might be at the camp. He had never seen him before and had heard no mention of him. And then he remembered the whispering about the arrival of a new commander. It never would have occurred to him that Johan, of all people, had been chosen to serve as a commander at the camp to which he himself had been sent. Like Ilse, Abe was also certain that Johan had been the one to bring about his arrest, out of the SS officer's indirect yet personal acquaintance with him, and his desire to seek revenge and maliciously incriminate him. *If this is the man who now plays a part in managing the camp, I'm in for more brutal days*, Abe thought in horror. If things had been difficult thus far, this encounter alone would surely bring about much more terrible developments. If this man had not exhibited any trace of humaneness on the night he and his partner had burst into the house and clinic, abusing its residents and plundering their belongings, and worst of all, not sparing the sick child who had witnessed the whole horror show and even physically hurting him, then here at the camp, where he held a senior position of authority, what chance was there that he would behave any differently?

Abe looked at Johan, who was half-swiveling from side to side in his chair. Johan had yet to say a word, but his metallic blue-gray eyes pierced Abe's own. His gaze was cold and invasive, exuding no humanity whatsoever. Simply nothing. More precisely, he was horrifying, in the most literal sense of the word. Abe wondered how Johan had managed to develop such hostility toward the human race. After all, Ilse had once felt some sort of affection toward him. He couldn't have always been like this. Some essential change had obviously occurred within him; Abe was certain of this, without ever having known him personally.

"Abe Liebmann, Dr. Abe Liebmann," Johan said after the long, tense silence. "We meet again, and quite quickly. It's only been a month since your arrest, *nicht wahr*?"

Abe didn't answer. He preferred to keep silent and wait for what Johan had to say next. After all, Johan had summoned him for a reason, hadn't he? Johan then smiled and let out a giggle: "The striped work clothes don't really suit you, Doctor, and the hair shaved down to your scalp makes you look sickly. From a clean, tidy person, a physician who maintains hygiene and is highly knowledgeable about it, look what you've become here. Look at yourself," he declared with a thunderous laugh.

Abe didn't really know what his face looked like. He hadn't looked in any mirror since he arrived at the camp, as there was no mirror to be found, and he had stopped inspecting his achy body as well. The cruel, insulting things that Johan was saying to him left their impression on him. Johan had managed to effectively hit a nerve.

Once Johan saw that his insults had achieved their intended purpose, he went on. "Since I've come to the conclusion that you can be of much more use to us here at the camp as someone who understands illness than as a pathetic forced laborer,

I've decided to transfer you to work at the clinic. Make no mistake," he continued. "You will still have to carry out the duties that all other prisoners are tasked with, and you will divide your time between the clinic and other jobs, but you'll no longer go out with the work brigade on the assignments you've been accustomed to thus far. You'll continue to live in Barrack #2 with the rest of the prisoners and you'll have your own special schedule, which will shortly be given to you by your barrack supervisor."

Once again, Abe did not reply. After all, what could he have said? His role had already been dictated and determined in advance, and, of course, he couldn't challenge the decision or express his opinion. And maybe this was the light at the end of the tunnel of which he had been thinking constantly? Working at the hospital, or at the clinic, as Johan called it, even for a few hours a day, would certainly be better than any other kind of work. At least he would be practicing the profession he so loved. He didn't know exactly what he would be required to do, but a hospital was a hospital and patients were patients, and he was well equipped to find the best, most dedicated way to treat them.

Abe decided to make use of the meeting to try and seek news of his father. "Herr Kirche," he addressed Johan for the first time since the conversation began, "as you know, my father is a doctor as well, a good doctor, and maybe it would be possible to have him work as a physician as well. He could contribute a lot to the patients that way." Unable to control himself, he added, his voice becoming more emotional, "My father is quite elderly and is no good at hard manual labor. Maybe he could be given the position at the clinic instead of me?" Abe silently prayed that he would manage to evoke some trace of understanding, stemming from self-interest, in the tough, monstrous man sitting across from him. What did he have to lose? Any attempt, in and of itself, was always worthwhile.

"Dr. Abe Liebmann," Johan said, his words shooting like

poison arrows from his mouth, "you are unbelievably impudent. First you addressed me as 'Herr' rather than 'Kommandant,' which is a grave offense. And secondly, how dare you try to interfere in camp procedures and prisoner assignments? What do you think, that I had to wait for you to tell me what you just told me? Do you think I don't know that Dr. Isadore knows how to take care of patients? I decided to send *you* to work at the clinic, and not him. If I had wanted him, I would have informed him."

Abe's heart sank. He was now even more fearful about his father's fate than he had been before. If his father hadn't been treated on the day he arrived at the camp, there wasn't much hope that he had survived. "My father was injured when he arrived here, and needed treatment."

Johan's face took on a malicious smile. "Your father received appropriate treatment. Don't worry, Dr. Liebmann; everyone here receives appropriate treatment, as needed." He paused.

Abe felt his throat closing up. After all, he had been exposed to the "appropriate" treatment to which the prisoners were daily subjected.

Johan's gaze pierced through Abe and he concluded, "Go back to your cabin. Tomorrow morning, show up at the hospital. You'll receive the rest of your tasks and duties then."

Johan swiveled in his chair, turning his back to Abe again. Abe wanted to speak up once more, but kept silent. Anything he could say would only cause him trouble—of that he was certain. For now, it was better to say nothing and return to the barracks. He began to walk toward the door, and as he was at the threshold, he heard Johan's rigid, mocking voice once more: "Dr. Isadore Liebmann has not been with us for quite a while. He's dead."

◆ ◆ ◆

Outside, it was snowing heavily. The ground was muddy, and when Abe reached the barracks, he found them empty. All of the prisoners who shared the cabin with him had already been sent out to their various tasks immediately after the morning headcount. He waited for the barracks supervisor to come and give him instructions, as Johan had said. In the meantime, he sat on the item allocated to him—the one called a "bed." He bowed his head, gripped it with his hands and succumbed to his melancholy reflections. His father was indeed dead. This was, after all, what he had feared from the moment they entered the camp, and once he had not seen him for a while, his doubts increasingly consumed him. Isadore had probably died of his wounds a short time after they arrived.

Abe felt a sense of anguish that spread through all his limbs. His thoughts wandered to Berlin, to Ilse and Manfred. His heart was bitter and heavy. He remembered the night of his arrest and the brutal violence directed against his wife and son. He was terrified that their physical injuries had been serious as well, and perhaps had left scars or, even worse, fractures. After all, he hadn't had the opportunity to examine them that night. He fervently hoped that Hildegard had managed to take care of them. What a cruel world it was! And when would he be released from this sickening, horrifying place, if ever? He wasn't at all optimistic, although he yearned to feel some hope, as he had before. The little bit of optimism left within him, and his fierce desire to survive—a desire whose intensity even he hadn't been aware of until that moment—had sustained a harsh blow after his encounter with Johan Kirche.

Abe knew that Johan would do anything to prevent his release. He had realized some time ago that the desire for revenge was one of Johan's dominant traits. Even if Abe could somehow prove that he would leave Germany, he had a feeling his fate had already been sealed, thanks to Johan.

Abe believed that Johan blamed him first and foremost for losing Ilse's affections. Abe was aware of this and, if he was truthful, he now felt deep despair. If it were possible to assign degrees to despair, he had reached the utmost degree.

♦ ♦ ♦

Johan remained alone in his room. He couldn't think of a more enjoyable sight than Abe's pathetic appearance. The handsome, glamorous man, with his thick mane and impressive frame, with whom Ilse had fallen helplessly in love to the extent of preferring him over Johan himself, was now a shuffling, dim-eyed, grimy, sickly creature. Without his thick hair, elegant clothing and gleaming cleanliness, Dr. Liebmann no longer resembled his former self. He looked exactly like all the other prisoners, who were sometimes indistinguishable—a large herd of bald men wearing stripes and exuding a constant stench. The noble Jewish doctor who had bestowed his good services upon dozens of patients was now himself bruised and blistered due to exhausting physical labor. If Ilse could see him in his current state, she might well have vomited at his feet. And the worst part for the doctor with the humane approach who was always attuned to others' pain would be to join the staff of the camp's hospital, which had its own procedures, rules, approaches, and methods of treatment.

♦ ♦ ♦

Luck was on Abe's side that day. He wasn't summoned for any work, as everyone was already outside. Even the barracks supervisor didn't arrive to give him instructions. That was strange. He could continue resting and thinking. Perhaps Johan had suddenly managed to discover a trace of compassion within himself and was allowing him to process his father's death? He found it hard to believe, but was grateful for the quiet hours he had been granted, mistakenly or not. The foremost topic on his mind was wondering why he had actually been assigned to work at the hospital.

Late in the evening, the other prisoners returned to the cabin. They were filthy with mud and wet from the snow and the rain, and some of them were sneezing and coughing constantly. Worst of all, though, was the glazed look in their eyes. They all resembled the walking dead. The power struggles among the prisoners, over every trivial matter, were gradually diminishing. No one had any energy to spare. They were all trying to conserve their strength, and if they still initiated such battles, they tended to restrict them to essential reasons, such as food—the cornerstone of survival.

The end of December marked the second month of the Kristallnacht detainees' stay at the camp, and if they hadn't yet managed to adapt to the cruel, wretched, threatening, exhausting way of life imposed upon them, there was no longer any chance that they would learn to do so. There was now no room for unnecessary thinking. Anyone who had not figured out how his life would look from the moment he first stepped into the camp and became a prisoner was already in a state of trauma from which it would be hard to emerge. And indeed, after a month or so, those who were still alive had gotten used to the situation, having no other choice, but their bodies and souls were crying out to the heavens. Apparently, the will to survive was stronger than any form of suffering, as was the hope of being released one day.

Abe was having a hard time falling asleep, as was the case every night. The new job he was scheduled to start the next day evoked mixed feelings in him, and the tormented voices coming from the mouths of the tortured and the suffering threatened to overwhelm him.

After the morning headcount, Abe arrived at the hospital at precisely 6:00 a.m. Several assistants and orderlies were standing next to the camp's chief SS doctor. Abe was assigned the role of head "prisoner-doctor" after his predecessor had passed away. He was glad that he hadn't been appointed as a barracks doctor, which would have tasked him with ensuring cleanliness, arranging patient inspections, providing work and illness authorizations and, worst of all, clearing out dead bodies. Practical management of the hospital was handed over to prisoner inspectors who didn't necessarily have a background in medicine, but were granted the authority to decide on medical issues such as surgeries, which they often personally carried out.

Abe realized that the hospital lacked many crucial resources: beds for hospitalized patients, personnel, equipment for treatment and diagnosis, sterile conditions, and anesthesia. The facility was overcrowded, and several patients were laid out on each cot, regardless of their condition. Abe thought that under the circumstances, no life-saving procedures could take place, not to mention surgeries, which, when unavoidable, would certainly be carried out—to the great shame of the science of medicine—without anesthesia. It was already well known that the mortality rate among those admitted was high, and the hospital was generally perceived by the prisoners not as a place where healing took place, but as a place to die. Abe soon found out that his fears regarding his new position—despite being granted the opportunity to work within his profession—had indeed been justified. As a doctor who had always striven to help his patients, he considered this slaughterhouse called a "clinic," or, even more ridiculously, a "hospital," to be the epitome of horror.

Abe was summoned to assist the SS doctor in carrying out the prisoner inspection several days after beginning his new job. Before he had time to think about it, he had assumed that the inspection was intended to determine who was still sick and who was fit to return to work; however, he soon realized that the main goal of the inspection was the "selection" process. It was chilling to witness those who were severely ill and stood no chance of returning to work simply sent off to their deaths, with a single hand gesture, while others, whose exhaustion was deemed to be reasonable, were sent off to work, despite their condition.

Abe knew that during the next selection, he would do all he could to keep as many prisoners as possible from being sentenced to death. To the extent that it was up to him, he would act in accordance with the Hippocratic Oath and with the standards on which he had been raised and educated at home and at Charité Hospital.

Chapter 34

Within several days of their conversation, Dr. Genscher approached Ilse as she arrived at the ward and asked her to come to his office. She assumed he had something to tell her and felt great excitement.

As she said a prayer, Ilse hurried to the doctor's office, and he signaled her to lock the door behind her. He promptly commenced speaking: "Ilse, *liebchen*, Abe was assigned to work as a prisoner-doctor at the camp's clinic about a month after he arrived at Dachau. Without going into too much detail, I can tell you that his living conditions are not as bad as the other prisoners'—which should encourage you." He didn't say anything about Isadore. He simply couldn't tell her that her father-in-law had been left to die some time ago, due to lack of proper medical treatment.

Ilse didn''t want to ask any more questions and decided to make do with these fragments of information. Her curiosity, fueled by worry, was gnawing at her, but she was also afraid to expose herself to more information. Abe was alive and had even been permitted to practice his profession, in some manner. She didn't need to know anything else at the moment and hoped that his occupation would give him the strength to survive until he was freed. She couldn't give up the hope that he would be released at some point; otherwise, she would have broken down completely, and she had Manfred to live for—the fruit of her enormous love for Abe.

Ilse simply could not conceive of what it was that Abe actually did at the hospital. She couldn't imagine how the medical profession was interpreted at the camp, and the form it took in the prisoners' day-to-day lives. And she kept the new information Dr. Genscher had just given her to herself.

The days went by, and every time Ilse crossed paths with Dr. Genscher, she still hoped he would tell her something new. But Genscher had many other matters keeping him busy, and other than sending her his best encouraging smile, he could no longer help her in any way.

Ilse understood that. After all, many other good men like Abe and his father had disappeared within the camps, maintaining very little, if any, contact with their loved ones. There were multiple factors at play, and for the most part, no one wanted to make waves in a sea that didn't belong to them. Anything and everything could prove dangerous at the time. In addition, no one knew who would be the next in the line to be suspected of plotting against the regime and opposing it, ending up a prisoner in one of the notorious camps. The people had chosen Nazism and Hitler in a majority vote; as a result, the administration had risen against the people, turning them into a corps of brainwashed dolls, restricted and confined to an enforced ideology, and in constant danger of severe punishment for any violation of the law.

♦ ♦ ♦

One evening, Sigmund came in to see Ilse, his face pale. He looked at her with compassion. "Ilse, today I found out, simply by chance, something that I believe will be very important to you. I debated whether to share it with you, but Gertrude helped me decide by saying that you had to know."

Ilse's pulse began to race madly. She clutched her hand to her chest, waiting for Sigmund to continue.

"Ilse, I found out that Johan Kirche has been appointed to be one of the prisoner commanders at Dachau."

A heartbreaking cry escaped from Ilse's lips, and she knew exactly why. She now feared for Abe's fate much more than she had before. Even thinking about his occupation as a doctor at the camp hospital could no longer encourage her in any way.

◆ ◆ ◆

More than three months had passed since Abe and Isadore were arrested. Ilse's growing despair prompted her to take one more step in order to discover the fate of her husband and father-in-law. The more she thought about it, the more she realized that it was her great love for her Abe, and her constant concern for him, that had provided her with the courage to make such a decision. Crazy as it might be, she decided to travel to Dachau and knock at the camp's gates, hoping someone there might help her. She didn't dismiss the possibility that she might meet Johan himself. *I really am insane*, she constantly told herself, *but if I don't do it, I'll never forgive myself.*

It was an overcast day in early March 1939. Ilse asked Dr. Genscher if she could take the following day off. She didn't disclose her real plan to anyone, telling her mother she was being sent to Munich for a two-day nursing conference. "We're taking the night train in order to arrive in Munich early in the morning," she said. "I hope you won't mind taking care of Manfred." Luckily, Hildegard asked no questions in response.

Around 10:00 that night, Ilse arrived at the station and boarded a Munich-bound train. She didn't sleep a wink the entire way, although the monotonous jostling of the journey was conducive to dozing off. Every time she thought about the purpose of the trip, her heart skipped a beat. She was terrified of what was about to happen, and even more so of what she might find out.

It was early in the morning when the train reached its destination. After arriving, Ilse took the bus to the town of Dachau, getting off at the station closest to the concentration camp. It took a while before she reached the camp itself.

She slipped into a state of shock as she slowly approached the camp's intimidating front gate. There was no one in sight. She was on her own. The snow that still covered the roofs of the buildings, forming icicles on the barbed-wire fences, evoked trepidation and distress in her. Everything was so dreary, cold, alienating, and terrifying. In the distance she saw a group of prisoners working in construction. Her eyes flitted around madly, tracking what was going on within the tall, barbed-wire fences.

Ilse stood next to the massive front gate, where she expected to see a guard of some kind. The iron gate in its stone framework, with a barred door at its center displaying metalwork letters that spelled out *"Arbeit Macht Frei"* was securely locked, but surprisingly abandoned. Seeing no one in the vicinity, she was bewildered. Where was everyone so early in the morning? She couldn't imagine that the prisoners' morning had begun at 5:00 a.m., and that it was now nearly mid-day for them.

Ilse's innards fluttered in agitation. She refused to have made her way to Dachau in vain, and was determined to return home with some sort of information. Tears flooded her eyes and she wiped them away. Suddenly, she saw an armed, uniformed man marching toward the gate. He looked at her from head to foot, and in a metallic, terse voice, asked, "What are you doing here?" He didn't even address her with the formal "Frau."

"Good morning, Herr Guard," she replied politely. "There's a prisoner at this camp I would like to inquire about." She did her best to speak clearly and emotionlessly, so as not to sabotage herself straight away.

"I'm not authorized to provide information about any of the prisoners. Who sent you here?" he asked firmly. "Do you have the proper documents?"

"No one sent me, sir. I came here on my own and I don't have any sort of paperwork."

The guard scrutinized her once more, finding it hard to ignore her feminine beauty and her piercing eyes. Meeting women at the camp was not a routine matter for staff members, and the guard was far more impressed with the woman standing on the other side of the gate than he was willing to admit.

"Look, madam," he addressed her in a tone that was slightly more polite and a bit calmer, "I'm not allowed to disclose any sort of information; it's not my job. I'm just a guard. It's not customary to come here like you did and just ask for any information about some prisoner or another. Everyone here has a job to do, and they all carry them out obediently. Sticking to the rules is of ultimate importance here. I'm sure you can understand that. Isn't that right?" he concluded with a formality that was tinged with a bit of empathy for her distress.

Ilse gathered her courage. "All the same, who could I talk to whose job includes conveying some kind of information? Do you have a commander named... Johan Kirche?" she asked, her voice shaking. "Maybe I could speak to him?"

"I'm sorry, madam, but are you insane? Do you think someone can come here and ask to talk to the commanders? You haven't even scheduled anything in advance, and you don't have any documents. That's not how things are done here," he repeated. "You'll have to come another day, and with the required documentation. Otherwise there's no chance that anyone here will even look at you."

Ilse was beginning to lose hope. She hadn't even considered trying to obtain any paperwork, as she had not shared her impulsive plan with anyone. The tall black fence surrounding the camp, the intimidating steel gate, and what little she could see beyond them began to oppress her. She decided to make one more small attempt.

"Maybe you know a prisoner named Liebmann?" she asked faintly, her chin trembling. "He's a prisoner-doctor. Just answer that, please, and then I'll leave." She barely managed to control the tears threatening to fall from her eyes.

The guard looked at her, her image managing to touch his heart. He glanced swiftly to the right and then to the left and behind him. There was no one anywhere near them at the moment.

"I know him," he told her in a low voice. "Now go back where you came from and next time, make sure to bring the right papers." Gazing at her firmly once more, he signaled to her to go and turned to leave the gate.

Ilse's fingers gripped the bars of the gate and before turning to go, her eyes scanned the area of the large camp once more—the chilling ghost town covered with a hostile layer of whiteness. She said a silent prayer for the welfare of her husband and father-in-law and began to trudge away. *The guard said he knows him, in the present tense*, she told herself. *That means he's alive!* She remembered she had only managed to ask after Abe, hoping with all her heart that her father-in-law was all right as well.

◆ ◆ ◆

Johan witnessed the brief encounter between the guard at the gate and the woman bundled up in a coat standing behind it. He had been on his way to the administration building when he spotted the woman's form behind the metal gate. He felt his breathing quicken when the figure's general outline, the color of her hair and her hairdo reminded him of Ilse. *She couldn't have come all this way*, he thought as a light shiver ran through him. But you never knew with Ilse. When she wanted something, she would do anything to get it, especially when it came to her family; of that he had no doubt.

That afternoon Johan found the time to interrogate the guard about the woman who had visited the site in the morning. The frightened guard couldn't say who she was or provide her name, but he did say that she had tried to ask about a prisoner-doctor named Liebmann. The guard quickly added that he hadn't disclosed any information, emphasizing that he had performed his duty by the book. He didn't dare tell him that the woman had also mentioned the commander's name. He was frightened—truly frightened—of Kommandant Kirche.

Johan's face glowed with a malicious smile. So it had indeed been Ilse, and he hadn't thought of her at random after sighting the distant figure on the other side of the gate. He had now discovered another means of abusing Liebmann that day, which pleased him greatly.

Johan hurried to the clinic. He saw Abe treating a prisoner who was screaming with pain. He didn't really care whether Abe had finished the treatment or not. Approaching the head physician, he told him, "Send Liebmann to me in half an hour."

Johan sat in his office, eagerly anticipating Abe's arrival. And indeed, exactly half an hour later, he heard a knock on the door. "Come in," Johan roared, and Abe tentatively stepped into the room, red stains on his lab coat. With no preliminaries, Johan said, "You'll never believe who showed up here this morning!" He was expecting Abe to ask, "Who?" but Abe, who had no idea why he had been called to Johan's office in the middle of work in the first place, stayed silent. What could Johan want from him?

"Do you know a beautiful woman named Ilse?" Johan taunted him.

Abe stared at him in disbelief. *What does the monster want now?* he asked himself.

When he still hadn't said anything, Johan ran out of patience. The mouse was refusing to fall into the trap set for it by the lion.

"You must have lost your wits if you still haven't shown any sign of understanding. Ilse, your beloved ex-wife, was here this morning. She was asking about you."

Abe's heart sank. What did Johan expect him to say? How did he think he would respond to this folly? After all, it was impossible that Johan was telling the truth, he thought, a shudder snaking down his spine.

"It seems you don't really believe me, *Herr Doktor*," Johan said with blatant mockery. "But she was here this morning and apparently, in her great stupidity, was hoping she would be let into the camp, allowed to see you, and maybe," and he let out a grotesque laugh, "permitted to meet you for a conjugal visit. Tell me, has she lost her mind completely, that woman? Where does she think she is? A spa that's open to visitors?" He exhaled contemptuously. "Ahh... what a stupid, irresponsible woman."

Abe could no longer control himself. He still wasn't sure whether Johan was making it up or not. Ilse couldn't have actually come to the camp; it was impossible. What did she think she would achieve by doing so? How could he know for certain? As far as he was concerned, Johan was the last person he could trust. An unbelievably cruel man who gleefully toyed with others' lives. And even if she had come here, who would have allowed her to see him? It was truly admirable courage, if it really had been her.

"Herr Kirche," Abe said, the "Herr" sticking in his throat and making him want to vomit, "if it was Ilse who came all the way here, she wasn't exhibiting stupidity, but exceptional courage. I don't see anything stupid about it."

Johan couldn't believe that once he finally opened his mouth, Abe had contradicted his own statements so brazenly. He was certain that the doctor in the filthy lab coat would react with an outburst of rage, or shed tears of frustration, but had never anticipated such a response. What outraged him even more about the whole matter was his suspicion that Abe didn't believe him, thus tainting all the pleasure of this game of cat-and-mouse.

Johan didn"t give up, deciding to produce his most potent ammunition by saying, "It's one thing that she didn't see you, but what a shame that she missed me too—or, more precisely, that I missed her."

He enjoyed seeing the torment on Abe's face and was certain that under different circumstances, Abe would have said a lot more than he dared to say here. He was therefore surprised when Abe blurted out, "A great shame indeed."

"Get out of here," Johan barked out. "Get back to the bloody clinic immediately, to take care of the pathetic, stinking prisoners."

Abe turned to go wordlessly, greatly relieved that the encounter with Johan was over. The more he thought about him, the more he despised the man's monstrous character. He saw him as the epitome of all the evil in the world. Greater evil could not exist, Abe thought to himself. He once again came to the conclusion that Johan was unworthy of being called a human being. Kommandant Johan Kirche was simply a monster in human form. A vicious, despicable, malicious monster who abused human beings.

The subject of Ilse troubled Abe constantly. Had she really come to the camp, or did Johan just want to drive him mad and make his already miserable life even more miserable? He preferred to think that Johan was merely misleading him. He didn't want to believe that Ilse had really arrived and he hadn't seen her; if he believed it, he would surely lose his mind.

◆ ◆ ◆

Johan was in a foul mood. He hadn't managed to make Abe bend, or break his spirit. Apparently Abe had unique mental resources, he thought; he seemed to be made of particularly fine Jewish stuff.

Johan truly regretted not having seen Ilse. On the one hand, he intently missed her sweet face, and on the other, he could have been granted the opportunity to stand before her again in all his glory, and tell her himself that she had made the long trip from Berlin in vain.

∽ Chapter 35 ∾

Ilse spent the hours after leaving the camp and before the train back to Berlin was due to depart idly strolling through the streets of Munich in the vicinity of the train station. When she felt the cold piercing her bones, she decided to seek shelter from it. She went into a café, sat down at one of the tables, and ordered a cup of coffee. The hot drink infused her frozen body with warmth. She didn't want anything else, as intense nausea gripped her stomach. She hadn't eaten a thing since the day before. For some time, she'd had no appetite and ate only the minimum required to survive. Her thoughts were relentless.

The sight of the terrible camp continued to flicker in front of her eyes. Despite what the guard had told her, she was fraught with worry about Abe. Perhaps the man had said he knew him just to get rid of her? And if Abe was indeed alive, what kind of life was it? Throughout the entire time since Abe and Isadore were arrested, she'd tried to obtain information—any information—about what was going on in these camps, and what she discovered, much to her horror, was always appalling. It was so hard to associate Abe with the terrible world to which the camp's inmates were subjected. Her gentle, meticulously groomed Abe, that wonderful Renaissance man whose entire world had been plucked away from him...

Ilse suddenly recalled, with much horror, a day at the hospital some time ago, when she had overheard one of the hospital's physicians, Dr. Walder, describing his impression of concentration camps and the world of the prisoners there to a colleague.

"The metamorphosis within the prisoner takes place the moment he first encounters the camp," he had said. "The poor soul is robbed of literally everything: his identity, his name—which is replaced by a tattooed number, his social status, his profession, his habits, his family, his home, his property, really everything. I've seen a picture of some prisoners with shaved heads, looking completely bald, forced to wear striped pajamas as clothes. They become the property of the camp's managers and their commanders, left to their mercy..." And he laughed sarcastically. "Some mercy!"

He'd continued, "Life at the camp transforms the prisoner into a different being—an anonymous person with no ability to do anything other than be a prisoner waiting for orders at all hours of the day. I gather that under such conditions, all of the prisoner's mental resources are dedicated solely to survival, while the camp provides them with countless obstacles in this constant race."

Back then, Ilse had no idea of the real meaning of Dr. Walder's chilling words. Now, after having seen a bit of the camp with her own two eyes, she couldn't help but apply Dr. Walder's description to what her husband had also surely been forced to become, under the circumstances; apparently he, too, had turned into the sort of "different being" the doctor had described, even if he was working within his profession. She didn't want to think too deeply about what he did at the clinic, as she imagined that the treatment of sick prisoners was very far from the spirit of the Hippocratic Oath.

The hours went by and she drank another cup of coffee and even bit into a slice of cake she forced herself to order, just so she wouldn't be suspected of being a vagrant due to her lengthy stay at the café.

As evening began to fall, Ilse left the warm café, stepped out into the chilly darkness, and headed for the train station. At the very least, her visit had resulted in one item of information that she was desperate to believe—that Abe was alive. In the early morning hours, she returned to Berlin and hurried to the hospital. She had asked for one day off and no more. She would tell her mother that the conference had been cut short, and they had returned home immediately after the first day.

As she had slept very little that night as well, resulting in two whole sleepless nights, Ilse was exhausted and wrung out, but she didn't want this to interfere with her workday. During her lunch hour, she sat in the nurses' room and sipped a steaming cup of soup, which she then pushed aside, staring ahead blankly.

Suddenly, she felt a gentle hand softly shaking her. "Ilse, wake up, dear. What happened to you, falling asleep like that?" It was one of the other nurses. Ilse shook herself awake in a panic. How had she dozed off like that, unaware? "You took a day off, didn't you? What happened—didn't you get enough rest?" the nurse asked with a smile.

"I did get some rest, but apparently not enough," Ilse replied. "I'm really sorry. That's never happened to me before. I apologize."

"Don't worry. It could happen to anyone once in a decade, right?" the nurse told her with honest sympathy. "Now come with me. There's an urgent case of an injured boy who needs an ugly wound sutured. And no one knows how to calm them down quite like you do. It's your specialty."

Ilse stood up, tidied her hair, and adjusted her white cap. She was ready and willing to help the suffering boy.

◆ ◆ ◆

About nine months had gone by since Abe and Isadore were arrested. It was mid-August and the heat was unbearable. Since that wintery visit to Dachau, Ilse had received no sign of life from them. What she considered to be a sign of life was receiving no notice of their deaths. But could she conclude from this that they were indeed alive? And if they had died or been killed, or tortured to death, or starved to death, or passed away due to an illness, would anyone have bothered to inform her? During those chaotic days, nothing took place in an orderly or rational manner. Everything was different, strange and alienated, cruel and unfair, particularly to that part of the population, small though it might be, that was not won over by the Nazi propaganda and managed to understand that things were not as they should be. Six whole years of terror, of brainwashing, of social oppression, of cruel decrees and humiliations, all justified in the Reich's "sacred" name and in that of its leader, who wanted the population's absolute support and knew he would attain it only through an ongoing campaign of intimidation. And when the state, under the Nazi ideology, viewed its citizens as mere tools serving its function, rather than human beings with individual needs, it became impossible to hope for any sort of humane approach.

Gertrude and Sigmund kept their promise. They helped Ilse, Manfred, and Hildegard, too, whenever they were asked to do so, although such occasions were rare. Ilse and Hildegard knew how to get by on their own and didn't want to become a burden to anyone. Together, they had survived the war of 1914 and the life that followed it, without the family's husband and father; they'd also survived the financial crisis of the 1920s, the drama with Johan, and everything that had happened after Ilse's marriage to Abe. It was true that things were currently difficult, but the adversity wasn't expressed in their day-to-day life financially, or in the routine course of life. The main challenge was their constant concern for Abe and Isadore's welfare, their increasing fear for their lives, the sadness that Ilse could not dislodge from her expression, which no longer displayed even a shadow of a smile, and in dealing with raising Manfred, who was voicing more and more qualms about belonging to the Hitler Youth movement.

Their anxiety was further fueled by growing rumors about an impending war. Hitler had been brewing plans for years, long before he rose to power, and was finally about to execute them one by one, from his perspective in a supremely logical order, and in an uncompromisingly organized manner. And if Hildegard had at one point claimed to Ilse that there was something special about Hitler, something mesmerizing, years ago her opinion of him changed radically. Hildegard's breaking point in that regard had occurred after the Nuremburg Laws were first enforced, and after finding out that Abe and Ilse's marriage had been annulled. These were the events that had caused her point of view to completely turn around once and for all. If the administration's actions had come to this, she thought at the time, they would all still have to deal with further decrees and acts that would prove to be as significant as this one. Reality soon proved her right. Another crisis of faith arrived when Abe and Isadore were arrested through no fault of their own, and their home and property were seized—after which no sign of life, or any other information about them, was forthcoming.

Ilse and Hildegard talked about anything and everything, but tried to avoid that particular subject. What else was left to say? Nothing. Even the Sontags didn't mention it anymore. It was hard for Sigmund and Gertrude, mainly because they were Aryan Germans. Sigmund had relinquished the idea of further inquiries some time ago. He had encountered difficulties even during his first attempts, and despite his honest desire to help, he had no choice but to give up.

◆ ◆ ◆

Johan was thriving in his role at the camp and derived great satisfaction from it. First of all, he controlled a large number of subordinates who were subject to his authority, and therefore could do as he saw fit as long as he maintained the order dictated by his own supervisors. Order was indeed meticulously maintained, but the methods of doing so varied in accordance with his moods. Most of all, he was quite gratified that most of the Jewish prisoners were under his control. He believed it was an opportune time to ensure that they were paying for their sins, in accordance with Hitler's spirit, and so he did his best to make certain that this was the case.

The only thing that displeased Johan was the significant geographical distance between him and Ilse, which didn't make it easy to promote his personal agenda. He continued planning, in great detail, what he had wanted to achieve right from the start, when he brought about Abe's arrest, having no intention of releasing him from the camp.

Johan intended to realize his greatest dream—returning Ilse to his arms by any means necessary. He was even willing to kill in order to achieve this goal, as he had often done before.

⁓ Chapter 36 ⁓

By the first of September 1939, the winds of war that had been blowing for some time led to the German Army's invasion of Poland. Hitler had begun to execute the plans he had apparently been weaving, one by one, for many years.

Ilse and Hildegard reacted to the news with shock. "It's clear that this is a declaration of war," Hildegard said with concern. "And here I had thought that Hitler would make do with merely returning the army to the Rhineland—contrary to the Versailles Treaty—back in 1936, and with the Anschluss of the previous year, which united Germany and Austria, with annexing the Sudetenland, and then with taking over Czechoslovakia.[4] Oh, *liebchen*, it turns out we were entirely wrong, and all this has only further whetted the Führer's appetite."

"War again? And more damages suffered on the home front?" Ilse moaned. "After all, any war always entails some form of harm to those who aren't directly involved in the fighting."

Both women closely followed the publications, the news, and the public's general outlook with regard to the latest developments. Once a state of combat was declared in Germany shortly after the invasion of Poland, they realized that the war could no longer be reduced to mere plans, as it had already begun.

---

[4] Germany's acts of territorial aggression included annexing the neighboring country of Austria in March 1938, an act known as "the Anschluss" (meaning "connection" or "joining" in German), and manufacturing a crisis in the Sudetenland, a region of Czechoslovakia, which led to the region being ceded to Nazi Germany in September 1938 on the condition that the rest of Czechoslovakia remain off limits. In March 1939, Germany violated this agreement and invaded Czechoslovakia, including Prague, followed by the invasion of Poland in September 1939.

They still vividly remembered the terrible suffering caused by the previous war.

As one of Hitler's main aspirations was to eliminate the Jews and the global problem he believed they caused, Ilse's concern for Abe escalated to new heights. Most of all, however, she wanted to protect Manfred. She was appalled by the thought that her son would suffer in any way, yet there was nothing she could do about it. She was merely a tiny, and perhaps non-existent, cog in this entire war chariot, as well as in the country's general conduct. No one cared how she felt, or what her thoughts and opinions were. What was of great concern to the leadership was having no opponents, seditionists, or various threats that might sabotage its plans. Ilse imagined that now, during wartime, Elisabeth Hospital would transition to a different mode of operation. She would certainly be required to work more hours or be on call in some way, but she didn't have the energy to do so. She admitted to herself that she had become a melancholy, depleted, and extremely anxious woman who often nourished her fears into horrific phantasms.

As the days went by and the war progressed, characterized by victories chalked up by the German Army, Ilse's fears regarding the future ate away at her more intensely. They were facing a long war, the media told them. What did they mean by "long"? Weeks? Months? Years? A tremor ran through her. She still missed Abe constantly. With the passing of time, she missed him more and yearned for him more. She couldn't get accustomed to life without him. Some of her nights featured romantic dreams about him, full of love and vivid eroticism, but there were also nights when she had nightmares that filled her with anguish and sadness. She dreamt that he was wounded, bruised, emaciated, and filthy, and his eyes, once brimming with joy and laughter, reflected terrible despair. During these horrifying dreams, he was always trying to tell her something, but she couldn't make it out, although she made a great effort to hear him. She would almost always wake up from these nightmares covered with sweat, her heart heavy and bitter.

Ilse was simply miserable. She had understood this some time ago and acknowledged it daily, yet even her concern and her colossal love for Manfred couldn't provide her with even the slightest *joie de vivre*. Sometimes she thought that she and her mother had suffered a similar fate. Both women had been forced to live without a husband only a short time after getting married. The one great difference was that her father's death was a *fait accompli*, while Abe's life or death was still shrouded in mystery. And her uncertainty regarding his fate was what was driving her crazy.

◆ ◆ ◆

About a month after the war broke out, Ilse and Manfred were sitting in the kitchen and eating dinner. As was her habit, Ilse pecked at the meager contents of her plate. They talked about what was going on at school and about the prevailing atmosphere of war. Once they had finished eating, Manfred wanted to go see Richard, and Ilse allowed it. She wanted to get into bed early, as a busy day awaited her tomorrow. As she washed the dishes, she heard a pounding on the door. A shiver ran through her. Who could it be at this hour? Maybe it was Sigmund, wanting to tell her something. Ilse could not deny the fact that every time she saw Sigmund, the hope that he might have some news for her was awakened within her, but she wasn't overly disappointed when that didn't prove to be the case. After all, as time went by, her expectations had gradually diminished. And yet…

Ilse wiped her wet hands on her apron and headed for the door. As she opened it, her heart stopped beating briefly and her fingers began to tug nervously at the hem of her apron. At the doorstep stood none other than Kommandant Johan Kirche. He was in uniform and looked as smart and elegant as ever. Her dry throat made it hard for her to swallow. The fresh scent of cologne engulfed her. She found herself recalling the evening about a year ago when she had knocked on his door and asked for his help, as well as the terrible night when he arrested Abe and Isadore and taken them with him, and she hadn't heard a word from them since.

"Good evening, Ilse," he said in a calm voice, his eyes studying her closely. She looked so fragile and depleted, her expression sad. "How are you?" His eyes then roamed over the apartment, turning to those places he could see from where he stood at the front door.

"Johan," she said once she caught her breath again, "what do you want now? Who have you come to arrest today?" Despite her anxiety, it was hard for her to hide her contempt for him.

"Where's the boy?" he asked, ignoring her cynicism as he stepped into the apartment.

Ilse suddenly paled. He couldn't have come here to take her child—anything but that.

Johan closed the door behind him.

Ilse felt as if she was about to faint, and Johan, who noticed it, said in a soothing tone, "I just want to talk to you quietly, Ilse, without him around, or anyone else. Just you and me, privately."

Ilse released her trapped breath and hoped he was telling the truth. "My son isn't here," she said, "and I don't think we have anything to talk about privately. It would be better if you hadn't bothered to come and ask how I am, and by the way, I'm doing very badly." She was annoyed with herself for talking to him as she had. After all, he was dangerous—how could she allow herself to taunt him like that?

Johan once again ignored her barbs and said, "Ilse, my dear, your life is about to change. Listen to me and listen carefully, and don't interrupt me, because that would make me very angry."

Ilse looked at Johan with an expression of confusion, but kept her mouth shut.

"At the beginning of next week," Johan said, "I'm coming to take you away from here. You'll be mine again and we'll live together like a married couple for all intents and purposes."

Ilse's face grew even paler, but she didn't respond. She was now more afraid of him than ever. Afraid of angering him in any way and setting him off. She still didn't quite understand what he was saying, and tended to think he was merely toying with her. Suddenly, she recalled that back when he first met her, he had also simply determined that they would go out to a café. He hadn't bothered with any unnecessary preliminaries.

"I know," he continued, "that your son is a first-degree *mischling* according to the criteria of the race laws, since he's the son of a Jewish father. I also know that he's living here with you as if he were fully Aryan, but if the appropriate parties were to find out about his Jewish part, he would be taken from you and you would be charged with withholding information and be severely punished."

Johan saw that Ilse's face was changing colors once again and that she was having a hard time swallowing, but he felt no pity for her. During those moments, the cruel, inhuman part of him, the part that always tried to fight his obsessive love for her, was raging within him. He had to sound frightening and threatening; otherwise his plot would fail. He had to have his way, although he realized that he was about to tear her life apart and cause her great anguish, an anguish that he knew would torment her and probably prevent her from ever truly being his. But nothing would interfere with his plans. Ilse would be his, come what may, even if she would never smile at him, and worse—would utterly hate him. Separating a husband and wife was one thing, but separating a mother from her child, and in the terrifying way he had chosen to do so, was something else entirely... Even he realized it.

Ilse still hadn't said a word, but they could both hear her heart pounding. Johan then decided to deliver the final blow, the immense lie that would help him achieve his intent.

"Your doctor died a few days ago. He simply couldn't survive life at the camp. That means that your status is now that of a widow, even if you still believed in the existence of your marriage despite the fact that it was legally annulled." He saw her break down and collapse onto the sofa, but not a tear escaped from her eyes. "You'll find an arrangement for this child of yours. I'm counting on you to do that, and in five days, I'll come pick you up along with a suitcase in which you'll have packed your clothes. You'll say goodbye to the life you've led until today, and start a new life with me elsewhere."

Johan waited for Ilse to finally react, but she had yet to say a word. He began to lose his patience, admitting to himself that the monologue wasn't easy, to put it mildly. He wanted her to nod and obey his orders like his other subordinates did; it was the reaction to which he was accustomed. He then decided to extract a nod or some other confirmation out of her—even if it was just a single word—by any means necessary, and so he added, in a threatening tone, "Ilse, if you don't do what I say, things won't end well. Your son will suffer along with the rest of the Jews he belongs to. I'm giving you an extension of five days and no more to take care of everything necessary. Do you understand?"

Ilse looked at him from her seat. The woodsy scent of his cologne nauseated her. In a voice as cold as ice, she said, "Where are you going to take me, Johan? To the camp at Dachau? That's the new life you have in mind for me? You've already taken Abe—my only, beloved husband—away from me, and now you're separating me from my son, too? How low will you go in your cruelty, Johan Kirche? How low? If I hadn't believed that you really would carry out this scheme of yours, and that the fact of my son's Judaism would reach the wrong ears, I would laugh in your face."

A tiny muscle twitched in Johan's face, but he didn't react. His eyes penetrated her own, and the blue-gray chill almost froze her to death. *You've got considerable daring and courage, Ilse Heine*, he thought to himself.

"I'll come with you, Johan, but only because I have no other choice, of course—for the sake of my child and for him only," she added, "but if you don't fulfill your part of the deal, and something bad does happen to my son, that will be the end of you as well," she concluded, her tone as threatening as his. At the moment, she didn't know where she had found the courage and the strength to say what she had, and to truly mean it.

Johan decided not to respond in any way. The drama that had taken place between them—one created by both of them—persuaded him to make do with the assent she had finally provided. She would come with him. Apparently she had resigned herself to what he had told her, and apparently he had managed to con her as well. The mother in her was playing in his favor. Her complete devotion to her son, and the terrible fear for his fate and his life, would make her comply with anything he told her. He stroked her cheek with his fingers, savoring the softness of her skin. His loins were calling out to him. He could have wholly devoured her at that moment, but he held back. There would be plenty of opportunities to cherish her touch. He turned to go.

"Ilse, I'll see you in five days. That works out to October 10. I'll come in the morning," he said as he left.

Ilse dropped heavily into the armchair. She felt dizzy and suddenly found herself shivering intensely. *Abe is dead*, she whispered to herself. *My darling Abe is dead, and I'm sure Johan had a hand in it.* She couldn't cry. Her main concern was Manfred. What would she do with him? Who would take care of him? Her mother would certainly be eager and willing to help out, but could she take on a burden of such magnitude? And what if something bad happened to her, too? Who would take care of the child?

These thoughts raced madly through her mind.

Manfred startled her when he came home. "Mama, you still haven't gone to bed?" he asked. "But you said you wanted to go to sleep early since you have a busy day tomorrow, didn't you?" he asked.

She looked at him, her heart flooded with love. Of course she would tell him nothing. After all, she still didn't even know what she would do. There was a long night awaiting her and she was certain that once again she wouldn't sleep a wink.

"I haven't gone to bed yet because I wanted to tidy up a few things," she replied. "But now we'll both go to bed, okay?" And she hugged him and wished him a good night.

Ilse's night was indeed sleepless. She lay in her bed and tried to impose order on the unmanageable thoughts that were nearly drowning her. *So Abe is not alive anymore*, she told herself repeatedly. *I wonder when he passed on to the realm of the dead. Either he died from natural causes, which were not natural at all considering the conditions in which he was living, or else someone made sure to kill him, in the usual sense of the word, and that someone definitely had some connection to Johan.* Ilse really didn't want to believe that Johan had carried out the deed himself, if this was indeed how Abe had died. Although Johan had not mentioned Isadore at all, she supposed that he, too, was no longer alive. Once again, she had no tears in her, having already shed so many for Abe since he was first taken from her.

Her fate had become completely identical to that of her mother. She currently had to worry only about Manfred. How could she part from him? How could she do that to him? After all, they were intensely bonded by mutual dependency and endless love. How could she tear herself away from him? And for whom? And for what? She would have to convince the child that she would only be leaving him for a limited time. He would have to understand, and show patience, restraint, and maturity, although he was only nine years old and still so young.

After spending some time with Johan—the only way in which she could save her son—she would seek an escape route from her captor. It would only be a temporary separation. She would do everything she could to shorten her stay. Sigmund would help her somehow. He would have to help her find a way out.

For now, her mother could help her. Hildegard would take care of her grandson until Ilse figured out how to reunite with him. Ilse knew Johan would keep her close and not allow her to visit her son; after all, he was unwilling to hear about the child— "the *mischling*," as he repeatedly referred to him. The more she thought about it, the more she came to one clear conclusion—Johan was the epitome of inhumanity on earth. He was simply a monster. And this was not the first time she had thought of him in those terms.

Ilse decided to talk to her mother and to the Sontags immediately when she returned from work that day. The last thing she wanted was to go to work, but she had no choice. If her employment had depended on her changeable moods, she would have stayed home at least twice a week. Work did provide her with a routine that allowed her to control a certain aspect of her schedule, but she also found it oppressive, as she was always required to be pleasant and devoted, and during the last year this had required an enormous effort on her part.

Ilse had to constantly deal with patients' suffering and pain while being unable to share her own with anyone. She didn't blame the people around her for this, but she did direct blame aplenty at the administration, and anyone who was connected to it, for making life in Germany the way it was. The war hadn't made things any more pleasant, to put it mildly. Furthermore, Johan hadn't left her much time to put her affairs in order, since if she was doomed to go with him, she would be unable to work. She would have to request a long leave of absence, and didn''t really know what her excuse would be. Although she was unsure exactly where Johan was taking her, she had a feeling he intended to keep her away from Berlin as much as possible.

The first rays of sunshine were seeping through the blinds. Morning was dawning and Ilse was awake and alert as she had never been before after a sleepless night. In the time left until she had to wake Manfred up, she continued to lie in her bed with a heavy heart, until she began to fear that she would not find the emotional strength to drag herself out of it. Once again, her thoughts raced, surveying an entire lifetime: her life from the moment she first met Abe. She was grateful for one thing—that she had met him and that they had had time to live together for close to a decade. He had been a gift bestowed upon her—a gift that proved to be heartbreakingly temporary—back in mid-winter of 1930, when they had gotten married. And he had been taken from her for good in the winter of 1938.

At 6:00 a.m., Ilse placed her feet on the small mat beside her bed, preparing to wake up Manfred and then go to work. She knew that the moment she returned home, she would have to find a way to tell her mother and the Sontags. In less than five days' time, Johan would be coming to take her away. She would have been overjoyed if something were to happen and he didn't arrive, but based on the way life had been abusing her, there was no hope for such a miracle. She resolved to share her news with Sigmund and Gertrude first, since she was truly nervous about her mother's response. Then she sent Manfred on his way and headed for the hospital.

Ilse endured a nearly unbearable day at work. She dropped two glass beakers, which promptly shattered. When anyone addressed her, she nodded mechanically, with no significant involvement in what was being said. Her eyes were glazed and her body was coated with cold sweat that made her skin prickle. The worst part of all was the tears that threatened to flood her, and instead stuck in her throat, making it hard for her to swallow.

Ilse returned home trembling uncontrollably. The moment she had so dreaded—the moment of revelation—had arrived. There was no one there, which allowed her to rein in her mental turmoil somewhat. Manfred was at Richard's, as was often the case, having no idea that soon his life would become even more closely intertwined with that of his friend.

Around 7:00 in the evening, Ilse knocked on the Sontags' door. After greeting Manfred and Richard in a strained voice, she headed for the parlor and whispered to her two friends to get their attention. "Sigmund, Gertrude, I have something important to tell you. I'm asking you not to interrupt me. Everything is hard enough already and to tell you the truth, the only thing that's still giving me any will to live is Manfred. If it weren't for him—I would have already ended my life."

Sigmund and Gertrude were deeply disturbed by what they had just heard, but agreed not to interrupt.

"In less than five days' time, I'll have to leave." She saw the shock spreading across their faces. "You remember me telling you that before I met Abe, Johan Kirche was my boyfriend?" They both nodded. "Johan Kirche is the one coming to take me away." They stared at her, their eyes wide open and their lips mumbling incoherently. Ilse managed to gather her strength and reconstruct her terrible meeting with Johan for them. "He came here last night. He gave me his solemn word that if I don't come with him and obey him, he'll make sure the authorities find out that Manfred is Jewish, and that he would be treated the way all Jews are treated. I know he's capable of following through on everything he said, and I'm terrified for Manfred. If Abe and Isadore were arrested under false charges, then it will also be possible to harm Manfred in any way and for any reason, especially since he's considered Jewish under the race laws."

Unable to keep still any longer, Sigmund broke his silence. "Ilse, this is impossible, simply impossible. After all, Manfred has a birth certificate that says he's German. Johan can't do a thing. That certificate is the proof. He was just trying to frighten you with his threat and manipulate you. We won't let this happen."

"Sigmund, Sigmund, Johan knows that Manfred is half-Jewish. Johan has always known everything about us. After all, he's part of a society that makes a daily habit of spying on people and finding out all kinds of details about them. If he knows that my marriage to Abe was legally annulled, he could always claim that the child's birth certificate was forged, and then you, too, might be in danger, since you played a part in the forgery, although you said no one knew about it. You never can tell, Sigmund. If anyone knows this first-hand, it's you. You have to understand that I can't take that chance and put my son, and you as well, in danger. Even if I try to run away with Manfred, Johan will surely find me. You two have no idea who Johan is. He's an incredibly dangerous man, cruel and entirely inhumane, and this is the creature I'll have to live with for a while. I have to make that sacrifice for my son." And she burst into tears, trying to suppress her sobs as she was afraid the children would hear. "And there's... there's one more important thing you should know." Her weeping increased. "Johan, he... informed me that Abe... that Abe is dead. He said it in one brief sentence, and didn't elaborate. He didn't say a thing about Isadore and I tend to believe that he's not among the living anymore, either."

A stream of tears burst from Gertrude's eyes as well. "Ilse, our dear Ilse, how horrific. How sad. How awful. Sigmund and I so hoped that they would be released at some point, when it was discovered that they had been arrested for no reason, despite being innocent." She couldn't stop crying, and Sigmund's attempts to console her failed.

And now, Ilse knew, the time had come to make the request that was the reason for this conversation.

"Now you know everything, and before my mother does. I'm just so afraid of her reaction that I decided to tell you first. You have to understand—for me, this life is over. I don't have a life anymore, mostly now that I'll have to say goodbye to Manfred, too. I really hope it won't be for long, but after all, there's no way of knowing. The war is still raging and I'm sure Johan has a bright future awaiting him, considering the way he excels at his despicable occupation." Her words were dripping with venom. She was full of loathing for the man she was about to join in several days.

"I'm asking you to help my mother take care of my son for me. You're the only ones who can help me other than her. Please take good care of him until I get back. I'm counting on both of you to make sure he continues to be happy here, or as happy as that poor boy can be. I didn't tell him that his father was dead, of course, because I fear for him and his young mind, which has become so vulnerable. I also don't intend to tell him that I have to leave him. I wouldn't be able to stand it. There's only so much I can take, and making him cry and break down is just something I can't do, I can't do it." She began to sob once more. "I'm leaving it up to you to explain things, rather than asking my mother. Tell him anything you see fit, but promise him one thing unequivocally—that I love him more than anything else in the world and that I'll come back to him, to the extent that it's up to me, as quickly as possible. He'll have to understand that. He won't have any other choice. Please, will you do that for me? You're the only family we have left."

Gertrude hugged her and cried along with her. Sigmund avoided excessive sentimentality, but that was only for appearance's sake. Deep down, he felt himself on the verge of sobbing as well. "Ilse, we'll do everything we can for you and your mother, and for Manfred," he said. "He'll grow up with us exactly as if he were our own son. We'll take care of him along with your mother just like we take care of Richard. He will lack nothing, and we'll do our best to keep him in good spirits. That poor child. What a terrible world he was born into. He was robbed of his loved ones, and now of his mother, too. If you want anything else, just ask us." And he turned to her and hugged her.

Ilse looked at both of them and her face assumed the shadow of a smile. "I'm grateful to both of you. Thanks to you and to your nobility of spirit, your kindness, and your great humanity, I'll have some tiny measure of peace of mind. Now all I have left to do is to tell my mother."

She signaled them to wait and hurried back home. When she returned, she was holding an elegant wooden jewelry box. "In this box are all of Manfred's documents. It also contains his childhood photos, a diary documenting his life and development from the moment he was born, and a few other important mementos related to him and his family. If something happens to my mother or, if for some reason, I don't come back, when Manfred is old enough, please give him this box. Our apartment is registered in my name; Abe gave it to me free and clear some time before he left and moved back in with his father. It will be Manfred's if the worst comes to pass. At least he'll have a home of his own. And here's the other important thing: at the bottom of the box there's a wrapped package that contains a little money. It's for his future."

Gertrude clutched the box and stroked its pretty woodwork. "Ilse, we'll respect your wishes, and I hope you'll be the one to give it to him —not us. We'll keep it safe and sound until you come back to us. And you'll come back quickly. I know you will. I'm sure you'll find a way to return."

"In the next few days, I'll make some more arrangements with regard to my work, and next week, Johan will come to take me away. Manfred will be at school, and when he comes home, a letter from me will be waiting for him. I ask that you be with him when he reads it. I'll try to explain things to him as best I can. Nothing can really explain what's happening to us, but at least he'll have some idea, and maybe it will make up, even slightly, for the fact that I left without saying goodbye to him face to face. And now that I've given it some thought, I don't think I can confront my mother with such terrible news, either. I think I'll let you do that for me as well."

◆ ◆ ◆

In the days left until Johan's arrival, Ilse spent plenty of time in Manfred's company. She informed his school that he was sick. She wanted to be with him exclusively. He didn't understand. "Mama, why are you lying? It's not right," he said, but secretly he was overjoyed. For some time, he had hated school, but was afraid to tell her directly. He was afraid that if he said anything, it would make his mother sad, mostly because there was nothing she could do about it. After all, he had to go to school—otherwise, his mother would face punishment.

Ilse didn't give Manfred even the slightest hint of what was about to take place. She avidly cherished every minute in his company, gazing at him constantly with endless love, particularly when he wasn't really paying attention, so as not to embarrass him, while trying to etch his image deep in her heart and memory. Only at night would her pillow become wet with tears. Luckily, her mother didn't visit them much during those days.

Part Five

⁓ Chapter 37 ⁓

Five days after his first visit, in the morning, exactly as he had promised, Johan Kirche showed up on Leipziger Street to take Ilse with him. Before he could knock on the door, it swung open to reveal Ilse standing in front of him. A suitcase stood beside the door. Ilse, bundled in a brown fur coat, with a hat on her head, stared at him with a frozen expression. Johan's eyes roamed intently beyond her.

"Don't worry, Johan," Ilse said cynically. "My son has already left for school." *And if you were so worried about him,* she added silently, *you wouldn't be coming here to tear me away from him…*

Johan's gaze returned to her. He smiled, and then could not hold back and hugged her. Ilse didn't resist. She had no power to resist at that moment. She found him quite pathetic in his yearning for her, which had overpowered his tough, rigid, consistently cruel demeanor. Johan released her from his grasp and picked up the suitcase. She closed the apartment door and followed him wordlessly. He put the suitcase in the trunk of a gleaming black car parked by the side of the road. A shiver ran through Ilse when she saw two red flags displaying swastikas flanking the car's front end. Johan helped her settle in the passenger's seat with showy gallantry and then joined her in the car. He started the engine. Once the car was in motion, Ilse looked back. Her eyes were dry and in her heart was a prayer for Manfred's wellbeing and for their quick reunion.

The drive went on and on until noontime. Johan stopped along the way and offered Ilse a bite to eat. She refused. He still hadn't told her where he was taking her. He hadn't said much since they'd gotten into the car, merely promising her again and again that she would be fine. He would do anything to make her happy, he told her. Johan was simply an idiot if he thought that he—of all people—could make her happy. Happy—ha... What an inappropriate word for this whole cruel, bizarre situation.

Ilse thanked the Lord for giving her the strength to suppress her all-consuming hatred for the man sitting beside her; otherwise she might have strangled him with her own two hands, especially when he was talking about happiness. She also thanked the Almighty for allowing her to exist beyond her feelings. She was, she felt, something of a dead woman walking, a marionette that would dance to the sound of the music—any music—while her operator pulled the strings, as long as it would allow her to save her son. Nothing mattered to her other than this boy—Abe's offspring. She then closed her eyes and pretended to doze off, which allowed her an interval in which she could seek some sort of peace for herself.

♦ ♦ ♦

Manfred returned from school with a heavy heart. It had been a hard day. He had less than a year left to be a cadet in the Hitler Youth movement, after which he would be promoted to full member. He hated the movement and had a hard time understanding what was still keeping Richard so enthused, when the educational courses were becoming increasingly oppressive from one meeting to the next. It was the only subject on which they disagreed. It was true that Richard sometimes had some reservations of his own, but all in all, he was pleased with the educational framework and was looking forward to becoming an official member of the movement when he turned 10.

On that day, they had been taken to watch a special training session for the boys who were 10 and older, and were already full-blown members. As cadets, they were constantly required to be aware of what awaited them in the future. This special training included actual military maneuvers, which was less awful, but the truly terrible thing was watching a movie that made his hair stand on end, about enforcing discipline on the prisoners of some concentration camp whose name was never mentioned—or maybe it was, and he had merely forgotten. The movie nauseated him. It was horrifying to watch those creatures, who were prisoners dressed in stripes, and how they were so cruelly abused. As he watched, Manfred had to bow his head carefully, so as not to be caught looking away. That was the last thing he needed—for everyone to see that the film wasn't having the desired effect on him. He might even be scolded for it, or even worse—publicly denounced, the worst punishment as far as he was concerned.

Manfred was looking forward to the moment when he would get home in order to share his distress with his mother. As he was walking home, his mind swirling with various thoughts, he had a sudden revelation. He felt as if he understood the reason for his emotional reaction to the film. After all, his own father was a prisoner at one of those camps. And perhaps his father had also become a pitiful creature like the ones in the movie? His eyes filled with tears. He missed his father so much after not having seen him for over a year; he also missed his habitual scent, which sometimes mingled with a sort of medicinal smell. Like his mother, he, too, sometimes tended to believe that his father and grandfather had died some time ago. It was hard for him to accept the possibility that they were alive but still didn't get in touch with them in any way. There was a lot that he chose to share with his mother, as well as with his grandmother, but there were also some personal issues that he preferred not to share with anyone, and these bleak thoughts about his father and grandfather were among them.

On that day, Richard didn't walk home with him, going to visit a friend instead. Manfred reached the entrance to his apartment and found Gertrude there.

"Hello, Gertrude. How are you? Richard will be on his way soon. You know, he went to visit a friend and asked me to tell you that he'll be late."

Manfred had no idea that Gertrude had been the one to ask Richard to come home a bit later that day. Gertrude knew she needed to be alone with Manfred when he read the letter that Ilse had left for him. She'd explained to Richard that something had happened that required her to be alone with Manfred, about which she would tell him later, and Richard hadn't argued. He was unusually obedient, both at school and especially with his parents.

"Hello, Manfred, sweetheart," she replied. "I know that Richard's going to be late. It's all right. Come to our place for a little while and then you'll go home, okay? I want to tell you something."

Manfred nodded silently. Like Richard, he, too, took special care to be obedient. An entire year of education based on the Nazi ideology was enough to enhance his compliance and discipline, as was the case with many others.

"Come here, Manfred, come sit across from me. You'll soon understand everything. I only ask that you allow me to finish talking without interrupting me, okay?"

Manfred didn't understand the reason for all this formality, but he sensed that Gertrude had something really important to tell him. He simply could not have imagined, even in his worst nightmares, what she was about to say. He nodded obediently once more, his curiosity already piqued.

"Manfred, my dear boy, what I'm about to tell you won't be easy for you to hear, just as it's not easy for me to say. But we'll get through it together, and Sigmund and Richard and I will be with you throughout it all, okay?"

Fear began to stir within Manfred. Maybe something bad had happened? Lately things were happening all the time, and they were usually very bad things. *Maybe she's heard something about my father?* he thought silently before nodding at her again. He had yet to say a word.

"Manfred, do you remember the officer who arrested Papa and Opa more than a year ago? The one who Mama told you was a patient she had taken care of in the hospital?"

Manfred nodded. "Johan Kirche," he blurted out. *I wish she would just tell me what happened*, he thought. The tension threatened to suffocate him, along with the anxiety that was still paralyzing him.

"A few days ago," Gertrude continued in a quiet voice, "Johan Kirche paid a visit to Mama." Manfred's eyes narrowed. "He told her she had to come with him, and if she didn't, he threatened, he would make sure to inform the proper authorities that you're Jewish, and then you would be treated the way all Jews are treated."

She saw Manfred's face change color and felt endlessly sorry for him. It was so sad that she, of all people, had to be the one to tell him. When it came to things like this, Sigmund was even more sensitive than she was. "Only a mother can tell a child something like that," he had told her. "And once you've finished, I'll take over from that point on."

"Your mother was very frightened," Gertrude continued. "She knew that she would not have any choice. The last thing she wanted was for something to happen to you, too. And the matter of your Judaism, as you know, is nothing to flaunt during these terrible times, especially with regard to someone whose birth certificate was forged, and..."

"Just a minute. Hold on, Gertrude. What are you talking about? Mama never said anything to me about that. Who forged it, and why?" Manfred's panic was increasing from one moment to the next.

"There was no other choice, Manfred. Sigmund helped get it done, so that no one would know you were Jewish. Mama agreed. Your father's name was erased and his first name was changed to some German name. I thought you'd been told about it."

Manfred was silent. He knew he had to call himself only by his mother's last name, but he had never imagined that this had been documented. Gertrude took advantage of his silence to continue, "And Mama, she promised Johan she would go with him. What else could she do at that moment, the poor woman? She only wanted to buy some time, for him to leave, so she could find some way out of this whole mess." Gertrude saw that the Manfred's bottom lip had started to tremble. She got up and sat down beside him. He clung to her and she embraced him, her heart bleeding inside. "The next evening, Mama shared everything that had happened with Sigmund and me...."

"So that's why she was crying?" he interjected. "I heard her blowing her nose and I thought she was crying for Papa again, or something like that..."

"Mama decided to tell us before she told Oma, because she was worried about her. Oma still doesn't know. Mama asked us to tell her," Gertrude said, ignoring the child's question.

Manfred disengaged from Gertrude and looked into her eyes. "Please don't tell me she went with him. Please!" And he burst into tears.

"She had to, my darling, she simply had to. This morning, after the two of you went to school, Johan came and took her. She left a letter for you and Oma, since she said she couldn't say goodbye to you and see even a single tear from you or from Oma. Manfred, based on what I know of your heroic mother, she will do everything she can to come back to you as quickly as possible. She also told us that. You'll see," she added encouragingly, "she'll be back soon. She only went with Johan to keep him quiet, but she'll do anything—anything," she repeated, "to come back very, very soon."

"Gertrude," he said in a strained voice, "so now Papa and Opa are gone, and Mama is, too. What does this Johan want from us? If he was once a patient of Mama's, and she took such good care of him, like you all said, why is he being so cruel to her? What did she do to him? Do you know? Maybe Mama told you? I'll never forget his scary face, with those strange, pale blue eyes and the hole in his chin and the birthmark on his neck. Never."

Gertrude swallowed hard. *Poor boy, oh, my poor boy*, she thought. She knew that she couldn't, at that moment, break the news to him that his father had passed away. She then said, "My sweet Manfred, sometimes things happen for which there's no explanation. Maybe something or other that Mama did hurt him and he decided to get even with her. Maybe something else happened, something we don't really know about, which caused him to behave that way. We can think and think and never find an answer. What I want to tell you, my dear boy, is that Sigmund and I gave Mama our word—from now until she comes back, you are fully under our care, as well as that of your grandma, who is on her way here. You're just like Richard, as far as we're concerned. We'll make sure that you lack nothing and that you're happy. You'll see, it'll all work out in the end. Just be patient and give your mother some time. Okay?" Gertrude herself truly wanted to believe in what she was saying, but her ultimate priority was providing the child with some hope. It would be terrible if the poor lad grew depressed. No good would come of it. "And I believe," she concluded, "that over time, Johan's face will be gradually erased from your memory."

Manfred looked at her and wiped his eyes. "I know you'll take care of me and watch over me. You always have, and I love you very much, but it won't be like having Mama here. It'll be different. Oma can't replace Mama, either." His eyes filled with tears once more. Gertrude held him tight, showering his head and face with dozens of kisses. "And you can't erase a face like Johan's," he whispered into her dress.

Suddenly, Manfred eased his head away from Gertrude's hands. "I want to read the letter Mama left me," he said. It had been some time since he thought about what he had gone through at school that day, or of wanting to tell his mother about the terrible film he had seen. In light of what he had found out during the last hour, all he wanted was to read his mother's letter.

"Come with me, Manfred. Let me give it to you," Gertrude said, heading for the bedroom.

October 9, 1939

Manfred, my beloved child,

To my great sorrow, I'm forced to say goodbye to you in a letter, rather than with a big hug and kisses, as would have been expected of me. I will tell you the truth, my boy—I've never been able to see you sad or shedding a tear, regardless of the cause, much less when it's because we must be apart. This is harder for me than you can ever imagine. It's always hard for a mother to part from her children—you have to understand that—especially a separation like this, when I was forced to leave you behind.

Gertrude and Sigmund will explain everything to you, as well as to Oma, about whom I'm very, very worried. There is only one thing I want you to know: I'm saying goodbye to you for a while—until things blow over, as they say—and not, heaven forbid, forever. I will do everything I can to get back to you quickly. And until then, my dear son, please be patient and listen to our neighbors and good friends; thanks to them, I can spend time away without losing my mind with worry for you. And, of course, take care of Oma.

Have courage, my dear, beloved boy, my son, whom I've been so proud of since the day you were born.

Love you more than anything in the world,
Mama

Manfred continued staring at the letter, and read its last two lines again and again. The missive touched his heart with gripping intensity, but his tears did not resume. He exhibited impressive maturity in that regard as well, and Gertrude was grateful for this, on his behalf as well as her own; if he had behaved differently, she would have simply broken down. She loathed everything that she had to go through because of one evil man who played with other people's lives and fates that way—other people who happened to be close to her as well, and whom she loved more than anything.

~ Chapter 38 ~

"Johan, where are we going?" Ilse could no longer refrain from asking. She saw that they were still on the road, and that Berlin had disappeared behind them some time ago. She suspected they were heading for Munich, which would not make it easy for her to see her son, even briefly.

At last, Johan allowed himself to share their destination with her. "Ilse, for about a year now, I've been a commander at Dachau. I prepared a nice apartment for you in Munich, and I'm taking you there. You'll be happy there, I promise you. You'll see," he told her in a soft voice.

Her suspicions about the destination of their journey had indeed proved correct. "What happened, Johan, that you're suddenly speaking to me so gently and care about my well-being?" she taunted him. "If you had really cared about my happiness, you wouldn't have taken me away from my son, don't you think?" Of course, she didn't say a word about knowing exactly where he was stationed, what his position at the camp was, and having visited the site.

Johan had promised himself that he would not raise his voice at her even for a second, and that he would hold back from reacting to any hostility she might express, as he anticipated.

"Ilse, I know you're angry with me now, but you'll be happy. Just wait and see. The war isn't going to be short, or easy. Berlin is a strategic city and it's better for you to keep your distance from it. I trust you've found an appropriate arrangement for your son and that he'll be just fine, too."

Ilse couldn't believe her ears. "Johan," she found the courage to berate him, "how will my son be just fine? How? You took his father, his grandfather, and now his mother, so how will he be fine? It's true that I've found an appropriate arrangement for him, but what possible kind of arrangement can be a substitute for a mother? Tell me, Johan, are you even listening to what's coming out of your mouth?"

"Ilse, if I'm telling you that you'll be happy, then you will. Time will tell, all right? Give me a little time to prove it to you."

Ilse kept quiet. Any additional word would be unnecessary, especially the sort of concentrated folly that Johan was spewing. She was glad he hadn't asked about the arrangement she'd found for Manfred. She wouldn't have told him anyway, but at least he hadn't asked.

"Johan, my bladder is about to explode. I have to relieve myself," she said suddenly.

Johan slowed the car and stopped by the side of the road, near some verdant woods. He got out of the car, hurried over to her side and opened the door for her. Beyond the tingle of her full bladder, Ilse felt the bubbling of laughter in her throat. *Ah, he's so gallant with me even when I have to pee*, she snickered, suppressing the giggle. She hid behind one of the thicker trees and knew that Johan was watching over her. *Protecting me from wild beasts or from the wild beast that he himself is?* she thought cynically.

Once she returned to the car, Johan made sure she was sitting comfortably before returning to his place behind the wheel. And the journey continued. Ilse wondered how he wasn't tired from driving for so many hours. When she glanced at him briefly, she saw that he looked precisely as fresh as he had that morning. *A true iron man...* she thought.

She herself was exhausted. After all, she had barely slept from the moment he knocked on her door five days ago and informed her he would be coming to uproot her and tear her away from her son.

The quiet drive made Ilse drowsy, and she preferred to doze off rather than listen to pathetic hogwash about how happy she was going to be, which Johan might continue to spout.

Johan saw that Ilse was closing her eyes and didn't disturb her. She was so beautiful, despite the dark circles under her eyes. He nearly stopped by the side of the road in order to assault her with kisses, but refrained. Oh, it took so much willpower to hold back when he was near her! He was simply mad about her, sometimes feeling like a wild animal next to her—he wanted to hunt her down, but also to spare her, so that he would never run out of her. It really was crazy, much crazier than what took place daily at the camp.

The hushed breath rising from Ilse indicated to him that she had fallen asleep.

◆ ◆ ◆

Hildegard made sure that everything was in its proper place and that the store was thoroughly tidy; she then put on her hat and coat, picked up her handbag, and headed for the door. Evening had fallen and she was on her way to see Ilse. She missed her and the boy, not having seen them for several days. As she was locking up the store, she suddenly sensed someone standing behind her. She tried to turn around and see who was breathing down her neck, when suddenly she felt a stab in her back, followed by another and another. Hildegard collapsed and fell onto the sidewalk, lifeless.

◆ ◆ ◆

Ilse woke up from her sleep in terror. She had had a dream. She had dreamed about an iron gate, barbed-wire fences, and bleeding bodies. She sputtered and Johan offered her some water. He was admirably well equipped, she had to admit: beverages, snacks, a blanket, a pillow—he had thought of everything. *Truly the perfect host*, she thought mockingly as a shiver ran through her. Darkness invaded the car. Evening had begun to fall and they were still driving. Of course—Munich was quite far from Berlin. She looked at Johan and he flashed his most winning smile at her. Suddenly, a dagger seemed to pierce her heart. They were driving to Munich, near the camp. After 10 months, she was back on her way to Munich again. Ten months had passed since the horrible day when she had come knocking on the camp's gates, hoping to find some small measure of humanity in the deplorable place where her beloved husband had lost his life.

"Johan," she suddenly said, "please tell me, how did Abe die, and what... about... his father?"

This time, it was Johan's heart that skipped a beat, although he had expected her to ask, and knew he would have to answer. "Ilse, Abe and his father passed away from typhus," he said, then could not help himself from adding, "Two good doctors who couldn't heal themselves."

Her soul threatened to abandon her completely. Now, nothing else mattered. Both Abe and his father were dead, and here she was sitting beside Johan in his gleaming black car with those two terrible flags in front, driving with him to a residence he had prepared for her to make his dream come true, while her son was left behind in Berlin. By now Manfred had surely read the letter she'd left for him, and her mother had read the one she left for her. She didn't want to think about anything, anything at all. *I won't stay with you for a lifetime, Johan, you can be sure of that*, she thought silently, and continued to stare out the window.

Johan heaved a tiny sigh of relief so that she would not hear it. She hadn't asked him anything else about Abe. She believed that he was dead. That was good. It would spare him several other problems.

It was late evening when they arrived in Munich. Johan led Ilse into the apartment, carrying her suitcase with the same showy gallantry as when he picked it up next to the doorway of her apartment. If the situation hadn't been as tragic as it truly was, she might have smirked again at the sight of his face. He really was pathetic. Where was the tough, ruthless monster who arrested Abe and Isadore, who had opened the door and then rejected her when she wanted his help, who had come to inform her it would be coming to take her away in five days? Where had it gone? He seemed to have resumed being the same Johan he had been when they first met, on the day he was injured and had come to her ward, with a somewhat childish expression of suffering on his face.

Suddenly, the phone in the parlor rang. Johan rushed to answer it. A fleeting smile crossed his face when he received the report of Hildegard's death. Another mission had been accomplished. He hated Hildegard and was terribly angry with her. After all, she had turned against him and stood by Ilse and therefore, he believed, hastened the end of their relationship. In addition, she had consented to her daughter marrying that despicable Jew, and was also grandmother to a Jewish grandson. That traitor! She had betrayed him and the German nation by consorting with Jews herself in that manner. It was truly shameful.

Ilse was now completely isolated from her family. From now on, she would be his and his alone. He would have eliminated the boy—that wretched *mischling*—as well, but he spared him for one simple reason—the boy was a hostage. Johan knew he was the only thing that would preserve Ilse's will to live. After all, her son had been her entire world since her husband left. Johan had to provide Ilse with a good reason to live—to live in the hope that one day she would be reunited with her son. It was true that Abe was still alive but, like many other prisoners, he was actually as good as dead from the moment he was arrested. For the time being, there was no reason to snuff him out. On the contrary. There was no thought that brought Johan more pleasure than the image of Abe as a doomed, long-suffering prisoner, while Ilse was here in the apartment with him. Beyond that, Abe also provided good service at the camp clinic, and it would be a shame to let him go to waste simply due to vindictiveness. His day, too, would come, whether it was at Johan's hand or due to his life of torment at the camp.

The apartment on Weinstrasse was appealing and well-maintained, which surprised Ilse. Elegant, gleaming furniture, stylish décor, flowers, *objets d'art*—it was all there. She didn't remember Johan ever displaying such tidiness or any kind of esthetic touch. He was never physically sloppy or less than well-groomed, but his apartment on Wilhelmstrasse had looked more neglected than stylish, which was why, she recalled, he had not brought her there often, and when he did, he made sure to impose an artificial tidiness upon it that did not look truly orderly. Back then, Johan had always claimed that the apartment had not been a good fit for him. He hadn't liked his place of residence, and therefore didn't invest much in it; she hadn't responded at the time, not wanting to hurt his feelings.

Now, Ilse saw, everything was different. Full harmony reigned with regard to the color scheme and the décor, and every corner of the apartment emitted a fresh breeze of cleanliness. From the corner of her eye, she saw the bedroom—the immense double bed covered with soft spreads and pillows of various sizes, with matching rugs at its feet. There were vases full of flowers on the nightstands. She was overtaken by nausea. She knew she would have to give herself over to Johan, and out of this entire unwilling, coerced affair, she feared this aspect most of all. Even if Abe was no longer alive, the last thing on earth she wanted was to be unfaithful to her husband—and with Johan, of all people. She would have to make a sacrifice in that regard as well. She had become an expert in blocking off her feelings and behaving like a plastic, inanimate doll. Life placed myriad situations in people's paths, teaching them how to deal even with the worst, and Ilse had already experienced many, many extreme situations and successfully coped with them all.

The gentle, fragile Ilse, vulnerable and emotional, had turned some part of her into a block of ice that was now impenetrable. All the human traits within her had also been frozen and stored in the heart of this icy block. At the time, she couldn't think about the moment when she would have to defrost herself and resume being who she had once been, and feared that it would indeed be hard for her to do so. Her soul was so scarred that she knew she would never return to being the person she once was. *There's no way back from this*, she thought, *and nothing that could erase everything I know and everything I have gone through and am still going through.*

Johan made Ilse a dinner consisting of a variety of delicacies. He fussed over her like a devoted mother, going above and beyond to please her and gratify her. Secretly, she mocked him. If she had allowed herself to feel sorry for him, even a little, then she would have revealed human emotions, and under no circumstances did she want to be human with Johan. He was the one who was the epitome of inhumanity in this whole story—why, then, should she display even an iota of human kindness toward him? To please her—oh, what an emotionless, self-centered man... How could she experience any sort of pleasure, knowing that she wouldn't see her son anytime soon? Johan could never satisfy her in any way. He really was utterly obtuse if he thought otherwise.

Ilse pecked sparingly at all the food Johan placed before her. She simply had to eat something if she wanted to maintain her strength. After all, she was in the midst of her own private war. Johan watched her constantly. She merely smiled faintly so as not to provoke him unnecessarily, as she sensed that the scoundrel sitting across from her expected her to savor the meal he prepared and tastefully served her, and perhaps also to compliment him in some way, any way at all.

After the meal, Ilse placed her knife and fork on the plate. She rose from the table and found the bathroom, where she spent a long time. She tried to brainwash herself regarding what was about to take place the moment she got into bed, doing her best to thoroughly disengage from current reality, so that the events wouldn't hurt her at all. It would be an exceptionally hard task, but if she'd managed to make it thus far, she wouldn't break down for that, either. Although it was already late at night, she knew Johan would not succumb to tiredness and would not give up on his plans. She washed herself thoroughly and then put on her nightgown, the warm garment given to her by her mother, who was constantly on her mind as well. Everything, big or small, reminded her of her loved ones, but she pushed these thoughts away from her every time. *I can't think of them too much; otherwise, I'll lose my sanity, and I want to be able to find my way back home*, she persuaded herself.

Meanwhile, Johan was caught up in his own thoughts. After all, his exceptionally well- managed plan had worked out. He found it hard to believe that it was Ilse locked up in the bathroom right there, so close to him, within arm's reach. He had mentally mapped out, time after time, how he would pave the way to winning her affections once more, pushing aside all other thoughts. He still assumed that if he tried his best, he would succeed. After all, she had loved him once. He believed she had fallen in love with him at first sight and admitted that he had single-handedly ruined it all when he applied pressure at inappropriate times, was unnecessarily stubborn, and often hostile and violent as well. He was the main one at fault for the fact that she had drifted away from him, and now he would make things right once more. He had to. If he had initially thought that he could make do with having Ilse living alongside him while she continued to loathe him, so long as she was his, he now realized that he would be unable to stand it. He wanted her to at least like him in some way, as he knew he could never expect her to love him the way he loved her.

He waited for her in bed, patient yet eager. He had yearned for this moment so much and for so long. He swore to himself that he would treat her like the perfect lover, as if she were a fragile doll, with full consideration and gentleness, the sort of behavior to which he was unaccustomed. His work at the camp had considerably coarsened his nature, making his current circumstances very difficult, mostly when he had to fight against what was considered the ultimate sin—sentimentality. And he hadn't needed to do so until the moment he took Ilse away from her son, her home, and her city.

Ilse emerged from the bathroom wearing her long nightgown and approached the bed tentatively. The room was illuminated with soft light. She was exhausted and the only thing she yearned for was to slip into bed, cover herself with the warm blanket and sink into the refuge of sleep. Her knees were weak. Johan pulled the covers back for her and she lay down beside him. He covered her with the fragrant blanket and gazed at her with love. She remained on her back, her arms next to her body and her eyes staring at the ceiling. The intense scent of the flowers on either side of the bed oppressed her. Johan's face was near her own and she had no choice but to look into his eyes. Their metallic gray-blue was softer than ever before. He took her in his arms and began to kiss her gently, fiercely battling his compelling urge to loom over her. Once again, the wild beast was raging within him. Ilse did not resist in any way, which amazed him. He had anticipated difficulties in that regard, and yet here she was, lying in his arms, quiet and peaceful, allowing him to do as he wished with her. Although at first he found this soothing, her total passivity did not truly please him, but he realized he couldn't really expect anything more at that moment. He continued to kiss her and whisper sweet nothings in her ear as his hands roamed over her body with the lightest touch, fluttering more than actually touching. He had longed for this moment so much—had dreamed of it all these long years, until his excitement nearly drove him over the edge. He had never imagined he would react this way. Johan Kirche, stronger than steel, tough, rigid, emotionless, and yes, cruel as well, suddenly found himself drowning in his immense feelings for the woman who lay beside him, letting him to do as he would with her.

"Ilse, my lovely, my one and only, I love you so much, love you so much, do you understand or not?" he whispered to her, and she shifted beneath him when he laid his full weight upon her. He embraced her, and like a man possessed, began to shower her with kisses before gradually entering her. Now, too, he met no resistance. He so wanted to bring her pleasure, even the tiniest bit of it. And if pleasure was an unrealistic expectation, he at least hoped that she wasn't feeling revulsion. The act lasted only a few minutes. Johan could not control himself any longer than that. The anticipation of the moment had been nerve-wracking, and his entire being funneled into his member, ensuring a rapid eruption.

Johan shivered slightly with the intensity of his pleasure and then lay down beside Ilse and hugged her, telling her again and again how much he loved her. He quickly fell asleep, his breathing a soft murmur, while Ilse's eyes continued to be open like two saucers. She continued to lie still, not even trying to break free of his pincer-like grip.

Ilse stared into the dimness of the room, hardly daring to breathe. The deed was over and done with and she didn't feel a thing. Johan hadn"t even hurt her, as she had feared at first. She had felt nothing, physically or emotionally; she had simply been absent during those moments. At last, she began to drift off. She had to surrender to her exhaustion, which had been relentless for several days. If she could only manage to sleep with no dreams of any kind, to sink into a deep slumber that would soothe her tender, exhausted nerves, she might find some relief for her aching soul and from the thoughts constantly racing through her mind, which were the main cause of her fatigue.

◆ ◆ ◆

When they found out about Hildegard's mysterious murder, Sigmund and Gertrude were horrified. The person closest to Manfred, the one intended to mother him during Ilse's absence, had slipped between their fingers. She hadn't even had time to hear about her daughter's departure. At least the poor woman had been spared that terrible grief, they thought, seeking some sort of solace, however minor. And once again, the two were faced with the need to be the bearers of more terrible news to Manfred—this time, the final departure of his grandmother. They chose to gloss over the exact circumstances.

◆ ◆ ◆

Johan was ecstatic. The ultimate conquest of Ilse empowered him. She was finally entirely and totally his. He toyed with the thought that if they had not parted for the reasons they had, they might have stayed together and even gotten married. But this no longer bothered him. Winning her anew, despite the circumstances under which it occurred, was worth it. And taking her somewhat by force gave him a certain pleasure.

∽ Chapter 39 ∾

Johan presented Ilse with new identifying documents, asking her to give him her original papers for safekeeping. The new documents linked her name to his—Ilse Heine-Kirche, and included his address—29 Weinstrasse, Munich. Ilse glanced briefly at the new papers in her hand and didn't react. That morning Johan departed for the camp and she was left on her own in the pretty apartment. Her mind was whirling. She wanted to ask Johan more and more questions, to know as much as possible, as she didn't know how long he would continue to be so kind and patient towards her. After all, she was well acquainted with his monstrous side. *I have to continue to be tolerant with him, and leave him feeling as calm as possible,* she thought, *as this is the only way to preserve the side of him that is less cruel.*

"Johan, why did you actually arrest Abe and Isadore?" Ilse asked that same evening while they were eating their dinner. "After all, we both know that it was a false accusation. Right, Johan? Please tell me the truth. After all, it doesn't really matter now that they're both dead."

Johan looked at her at length, continuing to chew, albeit slowly, as he considered his next words. He had been expecting conversations of that sort.

"Ilse," he finally said, "it's possible that you didn't always know everything. You must understand that each of us has a corner in his heart where there are some personal details that we don't want to share with anyone. Apparently, there were some details you didn't know about your husband and father-in-law. They took on a public role within the Jewish community, but beyond the usual aspects—helping the needy and practicing Jewish traditions and religion—they were also involved in insurgent activity. They had an important role as people of influence, and therefore had a variety of connections. The Gestapo's offices received a tip about them and the danger they posed to the government. They were arrested for good cause, believe me," he said, a tiny muscle twitching in his face.

He was lying. The two doctors had indeed taken on an active role within the community, but they were not involved in resistance activities in any way. Johan knew that he had to lie to Ilse in order to continue accruing credit with her. He had learned from his past mistakes.

Ilse swallowed hard. After all, she hadn't seen Abe very much after he left home, and how could she know certain things if he didn't tell her? She looked at Johan and kept her silence. She didn't want to believe what he was saying, and yet she didn't have any kind of proof that he wasn"t telling the truth.

She then turned to him again. "And why were you so violent that night? Couldn't you have acted a bit more humanely? Violence toward the men is one thing, although I'm not willing to accept that, either, but violence toward me and my son? How could you, Johan? After all, you always claimed that you loved me," she said, playing on his feelings.

Now it was Johan's turn to sputter. He took a sip from his water glass and said, "Ilse, believe me that if I had been alone, without the other officer, I might have been less violent. That is standard behavior among SS personnel. You know that, *nicht wahr*? If I hadn't behaved that way, I might have found myself reprimanded. All necessary information is passed on to the appropriate parties within the organization. There's no room for mercy, especially when it comes to political opponents or other dangerous elements that threaten the administration. The way we treat criminals is what gives us the power to control and deter. Believe me, I really didn't want to hit you or the boy, but I had no choice—and what you said to me really didn't make me feel like holding back. You insulted me in front of others, and that is totally unacceptable. Do you understand?" Once again he found himself justifying behavior that reflected the current regime's ideology.

Although he had used the words "believe me" several times, she found it hard to believe him. She was more inclined to believe that he was merely trying to appease her.

"And why weren't Abe and Isadore released after they were interrogated and punished?" she challenged. "What is the usual sentence for the kind of activities you say they were involved in?"

"It's a life sentence, Ilse, because in the eyes of the government, those who have transgressed with insurgent activity are marked forever. It's all or nothing when it comes to the administration's attitude toward people. Do you remember how many arguments we had about it before we broke up? I supported their approach, and to this day, I live these principles and believe whole-heartedly that they will amend the injustice Germany suffered from various elements, while you never even tried to understand. You were always opposed."

"Johan, forgive me, but how can I support the systematic abuse of innocents? And I'm not only talking about Jews." She couldn't control the urge to let it all out now. "There are many others who suffer because of the Nazi regime's extreme actions, including some of our own people. For example, the camp where you serve as a prisoner commander. I'm sure you encounter unprecedented human suffering daily, and you must agree with me that not everyone there poses a true danger to the government, right? How can you justify everything that's going on there? The high mortality rates, and perhaps the intentional killing of prisoners? After all, it's inconceivable. And what about the constant propaganda campaign against the entire Jewish people? My husband was a wonderful man, who only gave and gave and never harmed anyone or threatened anyone, until what's been happening in the country since

Hitler rose to power might have caused him to get involved in some type of negative activity, as you said. But there are many good people, just like him, and what was their crime?" Ilse had decided that this was precisely the time to challenge him with such troubling issues.

Johan didn't reply, merely gazing at her with admiration mingled with a bit of pity. Any words would be futile. She would never understand what he first understood some time ago, but the last thing he wanted to do was begin arguing with her again. It would be better if she continued thinking as she saw fit and he continued to believe what he had first started to believe a long time ago; it had nothing to do with their relationship. It was true, life at the camp was horrific—for the prisoners, of course—but it didn't affect him personally, not in the slightest. He carried out the role assigned to him as best he could, and there was no room for any emotion. All he wanted at that moment was to simply take her in his arms and love her again and again. He wasn't sated with her at all. How could he be, after the many years for which he had been constantly dreaming of her?

"And one more little question for you, Johan," she persisted, riding the momentum of her previous arguments. "Why were you so cruel to me the evening I came to your apartment and asked about Abe? You didn't show even a tiny bit of compassion for my distress. Do you know the sort of courage I needed to come to you?"

"I really didn't know anything about him," he lied again. "I only met him when I arrived at Dachau." He didn't give even the slightest hint that he also knew about Ilse's arrival at the camp gates, and how she had been turned back empty-handed.

◆ ◆ ◆

Two of the camp hospital's cabins were designated for medical research. Abe was often called in to lend a hand there as well. The term "medical research" had always evoked a sense of admiration within him, and he had greatly appreciated the experimental studies taking place at Charité Hospital. He soon found out that medical research was indeed taking place in those two cabins, but a certain, specific aspect of it was very different from anything he'd previously encountered. The two cabins were labeled as a clinic, since the medical experiments taking place there involved people rather than animals. The experiments focused on the field of infectious diseases and also involved trying out new medications. They were supervised by a medical examiner, while the prisoners served as human guinea pigs.

Abe had a hard time believing what was taking place right in front of his eyes. The prisoners sent to those cabins for medical treatment did indeed receive medical treatment, but this treatment usually left them a lot sicker than they had been before. The horror of those experiments was indeed terrifying, as many prisoners died, or, just as tragically, remained permanently disabled.

For Abe, this was the worst thing imaginable—using the science of medicine to enhance knowledge while also indirectly utilizing it as another means of killing. How was it conceivable that a licensed physician would use people for any sort of medical research without their knowledge? Failing to inform them was bad enough, but doing so while clearly knowing in advance that these experiments put their life in danger? The prisoners were described as "a cheap workforce," whereas in fact they were a totally free workforce, also sometimes used as human lab rats. While the generally abominable conditions led to high rates of illness among the prisoners, mostly due to workplace accidents and infectious diseases, the deaths resulting from the experiments further added to the mortality rates. *This is monstrous cruelty—innocents being gratuitously abused,* Abe thought mournfully, *and in my role as an assistant, I am indirectly aiding and abetting this entire horrific, hellish endeavor.*

❖ ❖ ❖

Ilse spent her days in the apartment. Johan said nothing about it, but they had a silent agreement that she would not venture out on her own, and that she must be discreet. On those rare nights when Johan stayed at the camp, Ilse would spread out on the bed, grateful to be alone, with no nocturnal activity. At those times, her mind was constantly scheming. All her thoughts circled around the quickest and safest way to return to Manfred. For now, although she often thought about it, she knew that the time wasn't right to try and convince Johan to bring her son to her. It would simply be absurd. In her heart of hearts, Ilse understood that Johan wanted to keep her solely to himself. She already knew him quite well, although she was aware of the fact that there was another side to his life, a very dark side from which she wanted to keep her distance; just thinking about it made her break out in a cold sweat. If the boy were to come to her, this would demote Johan to second place, or cast him out completely as far as she was concerned, and she believed he would never agree to that.

But such constant thoughts and planning kept her sane. And when she and Johan were together, Ilse did her best to overcome her intense loneliness. Johan was the last person on earth whose company she craved, but being on her own for many hours, her mind churning frenetically, was even worse sometimes, especially because during the time that he spent with her, he made a massive effort to ensure that she had a good time and treated her with great kindness. He did all he could to make her like her new life, although she concluded that secretly he knew she would never be happy with him, both because of losing her husband and, even worse, because she was being forced to live with him, far away from her son.

And the war continued. The rate of victories convinced Hitler that he could proceed with executing his plans without much resistance from the global community. He was drunk on victory. At last, after all those years of weaving plans, he had managed to carry them out precisely and without a hitch. It was a true affirmation. The German people were also engulfed in a victorious haze, convinced of the virtue of the Führer's intentions. For some time now, most of them had believed that they were indeed the chosen people—that the German nation was healthier, more handsome, and simply better than all the rest. They were the only nation that should rule the world, which could only be attained by war, conquest, and annihilating anyone who stood in their way. Indeed, the years of propaganda, persuasion, indoctrination, education, and enforcing his ideology through intimidation and terror were proving worthwhile, as most people were swept up in Hitler's dream, seeing it as a natural expression of their faith in and support for him.

∽ Chapter 40 ∾

It was the end of October, about three weeks after Ilse first arrived in Munich, and her period was late. Her period was never late. The last time it failed to arrive was when she was pregnant with Manfred. After another week went by, she began to worry. Johan slept with her almost every night, becoming lustier every time. If at first she lay there frozen, disengaging from the entire nightmare; over time, the nightmare decreased. He did all he could not to hurt her or make her uncomfortable, and to be as kind and pleasant as possible, thus easing her mental anguish because, if she was being honest, she wasn't suffering physically. She had resolved to behave as calmly as possible, having started to hope that one day she would manage to convince Johan to allow Manfred to join her. If Johan truly had her best interests at heart, as he was constantly telling her, he might agree eventually—which was the main reason she forced herself to be so patient with him.

Ilse had to find out for certain what was actually going on with her body. What would she do if she really was pregnant? That was the last thing she needed at the moment. She asked Johan to schedule a doctor's appointment for her. "Female troubles," she told him, without elaborating.

"Ilse, I hope everything is okay with you," he told her. "I'm familiar with a well-known women's doctor at Munich University's clinic. It's not far from here. I'll take you immediately once I make an appointment for you, all right?"

"You can make the appointment for me, but you don't need to come. I'll be fine on my own. I promise."

But he didn't want to hear of it. "I'll at least bring you to the hospital entrance."

"Really, Johan, are you afraid I'll run away from you?" she asked with a slight chuckle.

And he smiled but then replied solemnly, "You better not run away..."

Ilse decided to secretly write a letter to Gertrude and share what was happening with her, as well as her suspicion that she was pregnant. She had to tell her. *I'm sure she's been worried about me since the day I left, and who knows what else might happen,* she thought. *Gertrude has to know, she simply has to, and she'll find a way to explain it to my mother.*

The next day Johan informed her that the matter had been taken care of. "You have an appointment on November 8, at 8:15 in the evening. Since there's a convention I have to attend that night, I'll wait for you at the Marienplatz tram station around 9:30 p.m., and we'll go home together."

Ilse was silently grateful for this convention—and she could just imagine what kind of event it was. At least this way, she would be by herself for a crucial part of the outing, without having to worry about Johan's observant eyes, which never left her during the time he spent in her presence.

After Johan had told her how to get to the hospital, Ilse left for the doctor's appointment with a heavy heart. She was certain that she was pregnant. During the last few days, she had felt the familiar signs, ones that had made her so eager and excited the last time, and now filled her with terrible anguish and dread. On her way, she dropped her letter to Gertrude in the mailbox.

The flap of the envelope, which usually contained the return address, was blank. Ilse was wary of including her exact address.

Johan was on his way to the Bürgerbräukeller (beer cellar) on Rosenheimer Street, for the party's annual convention, scheduled for 8:00 p.m. Hitler's opening speech was slotted to begin at 8:10, and Johan planned to leave the site shortly before his planned meeting with Ilse. However, the beer cellar was overflowing with people, all awaiting the arrival of the acclaimed leader. Looking elegant in his uniform, and standing tall as he marched in, surrounded by his entourage, Hitler entered the hall and approached the elevated podium. He stood behind it as the crowd roared and applauded enthusiastically, and began to speak. His speech was passionate and fiery as usual, accompanied by vocal encouragement from the cheering audience.

Around 9:00 p.m., Hitler abruptly cut his address short, announcing that he would have to leave earlier than planned. As he explained that due to the fog in the area, which created hazardous flight conditions, he would have to hurry off to catch the night train to Berlin, Johan took advantage of the opportunity to leave. Hitler bade farewell to the attendees and strode vigorously toward the exit. He and his entourage left the convention hall at 9:15, boarded the armored vehicle awaiting them at the entrance to the beer hall, and quickly took off for the train station. About eight minutes after they left, a huge explosion tore through the packed hall they'd left behind, sowing major panic within.

Johan heard the boom and its echoes coming from the general direction of the beer cellar. Although he was startled, he continued driving toward the spot where he was meeting Ilse. He didn't want to be late.

Following her appointment with the doctor, Ilse left his office in a state of turmoil. She was in the early weeks of her pregnancy. Her head was throbbing and her body was trembling uncontrollably. *There's a tiny Nazi growing in my womb*, she thought, appalled. *The offspring of Johan the Nazi.* Unconsciously, she patted her belly, and when she realized what she had done, she let her hand drop, emitting a tortured moan. She left the hospital grounds, her feet barely carrying her, and walked toward the tram station. When she saw the tram arrive, she speeded up and nearly tripped.

During the ride, Ilse stared out the window; her eyes were glazed, and she saw only a deep darkness. She thought about the baby she would have with Johan, and when she envisioned the tiny, wrinkled face of a baby with blue eyes and light-colored hair, she was overcome by a wave of pity. She no longer knew whom she felt sorrier for—herself or this wretched baby, the product of her mating with a monster.

When she stepped off the tram, after nearly missing the intended stop near Marienplatz, she began to shuffle toward Johan's waving hand. She was about to cross the road. In one brief moment, she would have to face Johan and provide him with an explanation. And what would she say—or rather, what would she *not* say? Her body was flooded with heat and her vision grew somewhat blurry.

Ilse slowly stepped into the street with one foot, then the other. She was confused, and suddenly so cold. The yellow streetlights shining in her eyes clouded her senses and she didn't notice the black armored car hurtling toward her at a dizzying speed.

A moment after she began to cross the road, Ilse was abruptly propelled into the air. She dropped back down and her head crashed violently against the edge of the sidewalk, which she had not had time to leave behind her. It all took place before Johan's horrified eyes; he witnessed every second of what was happening right in front of him. As the armored car sped off, Johan raced to the site of the accident like a man possessed. Ilse, sprawled out in a large puddle of blood, the bottom half of her body on the road and the top half on the sidewalk, looked up at him with lifeless eyes.

◆ ◆ ◆

"Hitler Is Saved," screamed out the newspaper headlines the next morning. "*The Führer, who left the site of the convention at the beer cellar earlier than planned, was spared from an assassi-*

nation attempt that slaughtered eight of the convention attendees, causing panic and destruction."

The assassin, Georg Elser, was caught a short time later and sent to the Dachau concentration camp.

◆ ◆ ◆

Johan had to find out the reason for Ilse's appointment. Although he was somewhat acquainted with the doctor, he still had to respect the normal rules of doctor-patient confidentiality, and therefore presented himself as Frau Ilse Heine-Kirche's husband. Using the calmest voice he was capable of under the circumstances, he said, "*Herr Doktor*, I just wanted to ask if everything is all right with my wife."

The doctor's sympathetic response arrived promptly: "Herr Kirche, first of all, congratulations, and everything is just fine with the lady, as would be expected of a woman in the early stages of pregnancy."

The muscles in Johan's face twitched. His hand began to shake and he managed to hoarsely blurt out, "Thank you, *Herr Doktor*," before the receiver dropped from his hand. Ilse had been pregnant. Pregnant with his child. His child and no one else's. Johan broke down. Tears welled up in the corners of his eyes, something he had not experienced since he was a child. His throat closed up, and along with the feeling of terrible grief, he experienced a sensation that was equally brutal. Rage bubbled within him, causing his right eye to shed a single tear. He thought he would go mad from the intensity of the fury that now shook him.

She committed suicide, he thought, his heart feeling like it had been gripped by pincers. *She wasn't careful on the road because she wanted to end her life. She killed herself intentionally and killed the baby—my baby—along with her.*

Ilse died exactly a month after she came to him.

❖ ❖ ❖

Three days after Ilse's death, Abe noted the one-year anniversary of his arrival at the camp in Dachau. He was summoned to Kommandant Kirche's office. Ever since Abe had found himself frequently assisting at the research clinic and taking part in all that occurred there, his spirits had been particularly low. He walked quickly toward Kirche's office, his emotions in turmoil. He had not seen Johan for several weeks and was grateful for this fact. The last person he wanted to meet with was Johan, with whom every meeting thus far had heralded nothing but bad news.

Johan looked at the specter of Abe contemptuously. Cold rage vibrated inside him, his eyes narrowing into metallic slits. *You*, Johan pronounced silently, *you are responsible for everything that happened. You are to blame for Ilse's death. If she hadn't had a child with you—you filthy Jew—then she would have made sure to keep my child, who was growing in her belly. It's all your fault, and now you'll pay the ultimate price for it.*

"Liebmann," Johan roared in a steely voice, "Ilse was killed three days ago. She was carrying my child—mine, you hear? And she was killed. A car hit her and flung her into oblivion." A small muscle twitched in his rigid face.

Abe stared at Johan and a shudder ran through him. No matter how delusional and unrealistic his words sounded, Abe believed him. This time, he really and truly believed him. He felt that he was about to break down. Until today, he had weathered the travails, the sights, the sounds, the horrors, the suffering, the madness... and even death. Now he felt that he could no longer do it. His knees turned to water and his clenched fists relaxed. His helplessness was absolute. The smell of blood rising from his lab coat made him dizzy and queasy.

Johan continued looking at him the entire time. He opened the drawer of his desk, took out a pistol, and aimed it at Abe's head. Abe never flinched. *I'm better off dead than alive*, he thought.

Johan continued pointing the gun, then blurted out, "Liebmann, your day has come." He pulled the trigger and watched the Jewish prisoner-doctor collapse, a giant blood stain spreading across his splattered lab coat. A mad cackle erupted from Johan's throat as he remembered the night of the massive massacre—the slaughter of the SA's leadership. Once he calmed down, he looked at the bloody body sullying his shiny office floor, and an ironic thought surfaced: *I put him out of his misery with my own two hands—I both punished him and treated him in a considerate, humane manner.*

∽ Chapter 41 ∾

About a month had gone by since Ilse left and Hildegard died. Manfred mourned for his grandmother, but he missed his mother most of all, thinking of her constantly and aching for the moment of her return. Richard became the person closest to him. He could not have been any closer to him even if he were his flesh-and-blood brother. Sigmund and Gertrude instructed Manfred not to tell Richard the actual circumstances surrounding Ilse's departure. They told Richard that Ilse had been sent by her employers to work for some time at a hospital outside Berlin that needed additional help due to the war, and that the two of them had promised her to take care of Manfred until she came back. But as the days went by and Ilse didn't return, Richard sensed that something was wrong and suspected that there was information that was being kept from him. *If they had wanted to, they would have told me*, he decided, thus effectively banishing the thought.

"Manfred, I received a letter from Mama," Gertrude said. "I can't let you read it because it's too personal, sweetie, but I'll tell you what Mama wrote concerning you. I'm sure that you'll get a letter of your own very soon." She hoped that he would accept what she told him without challenging it. Manfred stared at her, his eyes widening in anticipation. Much to her relief, he didn't say anything. For now.

"Manfred, Mama's doing fine. She's feeling well but she's very concerned about you and misses you very much."

"Where is she?" he asked, a slight tremor in his voice. "Did she write that?"

"She didn't, but based on the postmark on the stamp, I assume she's in Munich. She asked me to tell you she's paving the way to returning here as soon as possible," Gertrude added. "That's very encouraging, right? I'm sure she'll manage to do something, Manfred. She won't be able to stay far away from you for too long.

"Gertrude," the boy said faintly, "Mama doesn't know that Oma died. How could she? And when she finds out, she'll go crazy, won't she?"

"First of all, let's wait and see Mama return home safe and sound," Gertrude said, her heart rate accelerating due to the fear that Ilse might be pregnant. "And then we can deal with everything together, just as we've done so far," she concluded, hoping she had instilled the necessary confidence in Manfred. She didn't share her great concern for Ilse with him, or her rapt anticipation of the next letter, in which Ilse promised to keep her posted. She also told Sigmund about the letter, but not about the pregnancy.

"I'll wait patiently for the letter Mama will send me," Manfred said, sadness reflecting in his eyes, "and I really hope she finds a way to cope with everything."

♦ ♦ ♦

Since the war began, the Hitler Youth movement had increasingly emphasized its cadets' military training. Although it was common knowledge that the country's youths willingly volunteered to contribute to the war effort, joining was in fact mandatory for the teenagers, as well as being spurred on by their desire to exhibit masculinity and a spirit of camaraderie—which required everyone to contribute according to their ability. Anyone who failed to join faced punishment, and sometimes elimination as well. There wasn't one boy who wasn't terrified that he'd be publicly condemned or, even worse, snuffed out.

Every day the cadets received an update on the latest developments on the battlefield. The educators constantly sang the praises of the brave warriors, extolling the victories and glorifying the man who was the prime force behind it all—Adolf Hitler, the exalted Führer. The more militant their education became, the more Manfred loathed it. Richard, meanwhile, was proud to be counted among the next generation of soldiers in the German Army. The boys didn't discuss the subject; they knew that their opinions on the matter differed—and it was the only topic on which they didn't agree. *So what*, they thought. *That won't affect our love for one another.*

While Richard anticipated the day they would no longer be cadets and become official members of the organization, Manfred felt increasingly apprehensive. In his distress, he turned to Gertrude. She had showered him with so much love since his mother left that sometimes he felt uncomfortable in Richard's company. It was as if Gertrude liked him more than her own child, although that couldn't have been the case; it was just a sort of feeling.

"Gertrude," Manfred addressed her that evening, "I don't like the youth movement. I don't feel that I belong there, like most of the other kids and teenagers might feel. I've never felt that sense of belonging that Richard, for example, feels. Sometimes I really suffer there."

Gertrude hugged him and was about to respond, but suddenly he added, "You know, I've been thinking about this a lot, and I believe I feel that way because of the Jews, because my father and grandfather are Jewish and I'm half-Jewish too. But not only because of that. I just can't understand anything related to cruelty. You know, Gertrude, the day Mama left, they showed us a film about prisoners in some concentration camp. I can't remember the name of it. Most of the kids were fascinated by it, but it really made me sick. I had a hard time holding back from excusing myself and leaving. I was just afraid they would make fun of me and that I might also be punished for being a sissy. You know, sometimes we're punished for not being strong enough. Did Richard ever tell you?"

Gertrude hardly breathed the whole time the boy talked. Her body prickled with goosebumps.

"Manfred, sweetheart, I understand you. Believe me, Sigmund and I would also be very happy if the material taught at school and the teaching and educational methods at the youth movement were different, the way they were a few years ago... But even we, as adults, don't have any other choice. We have to accept what the administration dictates. You know, honey, adults also get punished if they're not obedient and are considered to be lawbreakers. You understand that, Manfred, don't you? After all, you know where Sigmund works, what his job is, how sensitive everything around him is, and how careful he has to be to keep his feelings to himself, whatever they are." And she stroked his head again and again. She felt such immense love for this bright boy, whose features combined those of his father and his mother.

"Please, Manfred, try to hold back," she added. "Try to maintain some emotional detachment from everything that's going on at the youth movement. I think you're right to think that being Jewish has something to do with your feelings, but you have to understand that we're all really different. What seems good and appealing to one person seems bad and ugly to another, and you don't have to torture yourself because you're revolted by what you're being taught in school and by having to belong to the youth movement. I'm asking you to obey without getting emotionally involved. You'll see that Sigmund will tell you the same thing."

Manfred looked at Gertrude, comprehension in his eyes. Their talk had eased his distress, mostly due to her sympathy. He turned to go when she suddenly said, "Manfred, before you go to your room, I want to tell you something very personal, and I want you to promise me—you absolutely *have* to promise me—that you'll bury it deep in your heart and won't say a word to anyone, especially not to Richard. I'm sharing this with you because you're a very bright boy, and I'm sure that you can keep a secret, and what I'm telling you will help you cope later on."

Manfred sat back down again, keeping still and awaiting what she had to tell him.

"Both Sigmund and I, Manfred, are no fans of the regime, the one heading it, and the ones by his side. Everything that has happened since 1933, when the Nazis rose to power, is in complete contrast to our worldview and our values. In short, my sweetheart, we loathe it, but because of Sigmund's senior position, we have to keep quiet and act as if we stand with everyone else, when deep in our hearts, we don't. We've never had anything against any Jew, or against other people, and we've never understood why such cruelty and violence are directed against all kinds of poor people who have done nothing wrong. Believe me, Manfred, it's as hard for Sigmund and me as it is for you. If you think about it a little more, you'll realize that our situation is quite similar to yours—we're in the same boat. We have no choice but to keep quiet about everything going on around us that we don't understand and can't accept, and also want no part of. It's all simply because we have no other choice." She grew still and looked piercingly into his eyes.

Manfred continued staring at Gertrude and couldn't say a word. He realized that by telling him what she just had, she had entrusted him with one of the deepest secrets of her heart. Her candid admission and the passionate way in which she delivered it made him feel as if he were her peer, her equal. It touched him deeply and greatly enhanced his appreciation for her.

"Gertrude, I've buried your and Sigmund's secret deep inside me," he said, then got up and went to the bedroom, where he waited for Richard to return from visiting one of his friends. Manfred didn't have many friends like Richard did. He didn't have much in common with any of his classmates, and his relationship with them remained one of dutiful courtesy. He sat down at the desk, picked up a piece of paper and a pencil, and began to draw, idly doodling with his right hand while his left hand supported his head, which was heavy with the thoughts speeding through it. He remembered the day his father moved out. He remembered his mother crying. She tried to explain to him that Papa had so much work with Opa, that it was hard for him to drive to Opa's clinic every day, and that was why he was moving in with him for a while. Manfred remembered their brief reunions with his father and grandfather. The sound of words and voices and things they had said echoed in his ears. He so missed those nights when his father had sat by his bedside and told him stories before he went to sleep. He also yearned for his grandfather's company. Isadore would take him out at least once a week for some grandfather-grandson time; he'd loved those outings, which always ended with some surprise or gift. He remembered his grandfather's toughness, alongside his miraculous tenderness and the great love he had for all people.

He also thought about Oma Hildegard, the woman dearest to him after his mother. He had such great admiration for the woman who showered him with so much love and attention. He remembered that once, before his father moved out, he'd asked him, "Papa, maybe Opa Isadore and Oma Hildegard should get married?" Manfred smiled sadly and his eyes filled with tears. He'd been too little to understand back then, as when he saw how harmoniously they all lived together, he'd innocently assumed that his grandfather and grandmother could get married. He had been so naïve. The pure innocence of a five-year-old who still knew nothing about mixed couples, about Jews and Aryans, about antisemitism and racism... nothing about all that disturbing stuff.

Richard came into the room. "Manfred, too bad you didn't come with me. We had a really nice time together, Hartmut and me, and he's always asking me why you don't come. You're really missing out. You know, Manfred, there are some kids who act completely differently at home than they do in class. Come with me one of these days and you'll see."

"Okay, Richard, I'll come with you next time," Manfred acquiesced. He knew it would be best if he kept as busy as possible, rather than spending time on his own too often, so as not to succumb to the painful thoughts that plagued him.

◆ ◆ ◆

Johan fought desperately against the emotional crisis that befell him. He was doubly tormented—over Ilse's death and over the death of the fetus that could have been his child. The loss he felt was so deep that it caused him to encase himself in an armor of rigidity. Gradually, even the traces of human sensitivity that he had experienced during the month he spent with Ilse began to evaporate. Johan immersed himself solely in camp life. If, before, he had looked forward to the weekend, this was no longer the case. He could not forgive Ilse. She could have prevented the accident if only she had been more careful, although he had seen that the car that hit her had been speeding recklessly. He could not forgive her for disappearing from his life just as swiftly as she had re-entered it. He imagined them living happily together, a life that would continue once the war, in which Germany had been amassing grand, showy victories since day one, came to an end. Most of all, he couldn't forgive the Führer for the fact that the car he had taken to the train station was the one that had prematurely ended Ilse's life.

The situation in Dachau got worse from day to day. New prisoners arrived at the camp, and every day more and more of them who succumbed to the torment, suffering, and inhuman conditions joined the ranks of the dead. Johan felt no pity for any of them. Let them all die, as far as he was concerned, especially the Jews. He did his job as best he could, often going beyond the call of duty. He simply excelled at maintaining discipline, both among his subordinates and first and foremost among the prisoners. He became a figure hated by nearly everyone, yet highly favored by the senior Nazi leadership.

And ever since the camp had become his whole world, Johan decided to invest in his work as much as he could. He had quite a few plans, and all he needed was to receive authorization for some of them from his superiors—mainly the inspector of camps—while carrying out other plans on his own. As the camps continued to expand, along with the manufacturing of goods taking place within them, the head office in Berlin took charge of all SS industries. Johan traveled to Berlin about once a month for a meeting at the inspector's office, where he was required to deliver a report. He was often praised for his activity and his dedication to the administration, as the *Obersturmführer* [5] who was his supervisor was a particularly tough, emotionless person who approved of his subordinate's similar inclinations. That winter, the camp and its facilities were being used to reorganize the "Death's Head" unit, and the prisoners were sent to the Buchenwald, Flossenbürg, or Mauthausen camps until the process was completed.

---

5   Senior storm leader, a Nazi paramilitary rank.

∽ Chapter 42 ∾

Gertrude was beginning to worry. It was early February 1940 and more than two months had gone by since Ilse's only letter had arrived. Gertrude's fears were increasing mostly about the pregnancy. She fervently hoped that nothing bad had happened to Ilse. Manfred, too, was beginning to show signs of distress, but was trying not to be a bother. After all, if Gertrude knew something, she would tell him, wouldn't she?

One evening, Sigmund came into the apartment with a heavy heart. Gertrude saw that he was upset and waited for the children to turn to their own pursuits, leaving Sigmund and her alone.

After dinner Gertrude sat next to her husband and looked at him expectantly. Sigmund smiled faintly. He knew that Gertrude had already noticed that he was not his usual self.

"Gertrude," he began, with no preliminaries, "today I found out something sad, very sad." He saw her eyes focus on him, unrelenting.

"Johan Kirche showed up at one of the offices today, when I happened to be there as well. I heard the clerk greet him by name, and that's how I realized who he was. He seemed very distraught and restless when he asked for some documents. These documents were related to the Dachau camp, which made me entirely certain that this was 'our' Johan Kirche. Once he received what he had asked for and left, I heard some whispers about him.

"'He's been in dismal spirits,' the gossips' tongues wagged, 'ever since his beloved was killed, the one he brought to Munich. He simply can't recover. He loved this woman madly, and since she was killed, he's become a much crueler *Kommandant* than he used to be.'"

Gertrude looked at her husband, frozen with horror. Her hand flew to her mouth and she was incapable of making a sound or moving at all.

"Gertrude," Sigmund said faintly, "they were talking about Ilse. It couldn't have been anyone else. I'm sure of it. Apparently something happened to her. I really wanted to ask, but at that moment, I decided not to. Gertrude, I have a bad feeling. I have a feeling that our Ilse was killed." And his eyes filled with tears.

"Sigmund," Gertrude whispered, her voice trembling, "how can we know for sure? We're her son's guardians. We have to find out for his sake. Have you thought about the fact that to this day, we haven't found a way to let her know that her mother died? Can you imagine?"

"I'll do everything I can to find out," Sigmund said. "I still don't know exactly how I'll do it, but I'll find a way. If it really is true and Ilse is no longer alive, then the child is an orphan and we'll have to continue taking care of him for as long as we live. We might even legally adopt him. And it's true, she'll also never know about Hildegard. But until I look into everything, let's keep this to ourselves, Gertrude. We have to be careful. If it's really true, how will we tell him? I can't even think about it."

"Sigmund," Gertrude suddenly came to her senses, "let's wait until we know for sure. In the meantime we'll behave as if nothing has happened."

◆ ◆ ◆

Johan was no longer the Johan of old. If, thanks to Ilse, he had become a more "humane" person, at least in the way he treated her, now the beast in him surged once more, completely eliminating any emotion within him. He directed all his frustrations and bitterness at the camp's prisoners, mostly the

Jews among them. He enjoyed watching their suffering, which seemed to console his own terrible misery. They all had to pay for the death of his beloved and share his bleak life with him. The prisoners were precisely the right people to do so, and they were the ones to unknowingly pay the price.

He felt that he had to share what was so fiercely tormenting him with someone. Sometimes, he thought he would just fall to pieces if he didn't open up. After further deliberation, he decided to visit the person who was closest to him: his mother. Until that day, Johan hadn't mentioned even a single word to her about having brought Ilse to Munich. He believed what he had to tell her would surprise her, but relied on her immense love for him to make her sympathetic to his suffering.

As was her custom, Beatrice greeted Johan with a warm and loving smile and open arms, and as always, rushed to the kitchen to prepare a nice meal for him. And while Johan lustily chewed the familiar, delicious, home-cooked food that he loved, he began to tell his mother about the recent developments. He glossed over some of the more sensitive points that didn't bear repeating, his eyes occasionally growing moist.

Beatrice listened attentively, and other than the simultaneous gaping of her mouth and eyes in horrified amazement in response to what her son was telling her, she didn't move a muscle.

Once Johan's story had come to an end, and he had already wiped his plate clean and handed it to his mother so she could fill it again, Beatrice stood in front of him, took the dish from him, raised her hand, and slapped him across his face as hard as she could.

Johan's hand rose mindlessly to his cheek, and his eyes, which had been tracking the fragments of the dish scattering on the floor, focused on his mother once more. A terrible, instinctual rage began to bubble up inside him. Before he could summon up any words in response, he heard Beatrice's sharp, rigid voice.

"I'm ashamed of you, Johan Kirche! I would never have imagined that my son, the son who came out of my own body, the son I nurtured as best I could and always loved so much, would become such a despicable, cruel creature, with no emotion at all! How could you, Johan? How dare you?" she screamed. "You allowed yourself to abduct that poor woman and tear her away from her child—surely by threatening her in some way—while also claiming you did so out of your great love for her? How could you! And I'm sure that that's what you did, that you threatened her, *nicht wahr*?! And then she was killed as well, the poor woman, right under your nose. Oh, what a terrible tragedy. How horrific." Tears burst from Beatrice's eyes. "I know exactly how she felt," she whispered through the tears. "I lost a little girl once, too..." And her sobbing intensified.

Johan's face had already turned scarlet. His initial rage gradually receded, turning into great embarrassment. The mention of his dead sister pierced his heart like a dagger. He kept his mouth shut and his lips clenched.

And Beatrice continued, her voice now keening: "Is that what they've made you into in that organization, Kommandant Kirche? This is what you've come to? I look at you and I don't know you anymore." She concluded by saying, "I wish you'd never been born at all," and turned her back to him.

Johan was stupefied. He stood up and stormed out of his mother's house. By turning her back on him, she had clearly signaled that she no longer wanted anything to do with him and that she was, in fact, wordlessly demanding that he leave. Johan knew that his pride and the steely toughness to which he was accustomed would not allow him to linger on his mother's doorstep, or to look for some way to appease her, although her reaction had managed to greatly shock him and to evoke some measure of guilt within him.

Once the door slammed behind Johan's back, a heartbroken cry burst forth from Beatrice. She knew she no longer wanted any contact with the son who had transformed a monster. If thus far she hadn't given much thought to what happened to the people who did Hitler's bidding, due to what had just taken place, she realized and admitted that her son, her own flesh and blood, no longer belonged to her—he belonged to Hitler, to his ideology, and to the Nazi Party, with every fiber of his being.

Johan could not stop thinking about his mother's cutting reaction. With the words uttered by his own lips, by wanting to share what he had gone through with her, he had caused her heart to turn against him. He knew he had lost the boundless love of the woman who was so dear to him. Ultimately she couldn't ignore what she saw as the height of cruelty and perceived as her son's lack of humanity and emotion.

And from this, Johan realized, there would be no way back. He had been left on his own, distant from every human being endowed with emotions.

◆ ◆ ◆

Sigmund sought a proper way to find out about Ilse's fate. He resolved to casually question those people he heard gossiping after Johan's visit. He found out that the clerk in the office next to his, who was in charge of all material concerning the camp managers and their performance, knew Johan Kirche more personally. Sigmund decided to find a way to figure out what he knew.

Sigmund was cautious. He didn't want to cast suspicion on himself by asking questions that would come across as too personal, and hoped he would find a way to encourage the clerk—apparently quite a chatty character—to open up.

"Herr Schloss, please tell me, how has Kommandant Kirche been performing lately? I've heard he experienced some personal crisis that has affected him. Has it been affecting his work performance as well?"

Schloss, who was certain that Sigmund's interest in Johan Kirche was purely professional, was happy to provide him with every detail he could. "What can I tell you, Herr Sontag—Johan Kirche has always been an outstanding soldier, both as an SS man and as a *Kommandant* at the Dachau camp. He performs his duties impressively and is held in high regard. But unfortunately, ever since his beloved—the one he took from here in Berlin and brought to Munich—that pretty girl named Elsa or Ilse, I really don't remember—ever since she got killed, he's simply been in a state of crisis. We found out she was killed in a hit-and-run accident at the side of the road. And even worse, there are whispers that she was carrying his child, which devastated him even more. You know, Herr Sontag, these things come out somehow... People always talk... And on top of all that," he added after a brief pause, "his mother passed away suddenly as well. So, if you think about it, we could show some sympathy for him, couldn't we?"

Sigmund couldn"t believe his ears. He was afraid that if his face was reflecting his feelings, Schloss would suspect that something was wrong, and therefore he did all he could to stay calm, although he could feel tremendous pressure building up inside him. So, it actually had happened. Ilse had been killed and, in addition, she had been pregnant. *Gertrude will lose her mind, simply lose her mind...* he thought, horrified.

His eyes constantly appraising Sigmund, Schloss suddenly added, "You know, Herr Sontag, they were also saying that in his rage over the death of the girl, Kirche had such a fit that in order to cool down, he shot and killed a Jewish prisoner-doctor, some Biebmann or Liebmann—who can keep track of all these damn Jewish names?—someone who was assisting at the clinic. It was actually a Jew who was doing some good... Hah!" he snickered. "It happened, if I'm not mistaken, over two months ago."

Sigmund felt that he was on the verge of suffocation and began to cough. He had to react in some way.

Schloss assessed him critically once more. "Is everything all right with you, Sontag?" he asked and Sigmund nodded quickly, tears in his eyes. He coughed once more so as to obscure his real reason for tearing up.

"Herr Schloss, I hope, for the sake of our *Kommandants*, that they don't allow personal matters to affect their daily work. After all, that would be unacceptable," he said once his parched throat was again capable of producing sound. "There is no room for personal affairs, not in the camps or their management, and certainly not in the combat army. This is a period where we must all dedicate ourselves to the Führer's goals and follow him in every possible way, don't you think?" He was on the verge of choking again, having delivered this speech with no pause for breath, even as he felt his guts churning inside.

"Herr Sontag, you are correct. There really is no room to devote ourselves to anything but the administration's goals. I'm certain Johan Kirche would not allow his work to be affected, and that time will heal his wounds. After all, it's just a dead woman; he sees people die every day, and is responsible for some of those deaths himself. Right?" Schloss let out another mocking chuckle. "I'm sure he'll come to his senses soon. All in all, he is an excellent *Kommandant*."

Sigmund turned to go. He barricaded himself in his office and didn't want to talk to anyone. Claiming that he had a bad headache, he headed home an hour earlier than usual.

◆ ◆ ◆

Manfred agreed to join Richard in meeting a friend after school. His mood was low. As the days went by and he heard nothing about his mother or any of his other family members, he felt a sense of foreboding. They were greeted warmly at Hartmut's house; the three friends sat in the children's room, playing, talking, and passing the time enjoyably. Hartmut's father came into the room, his expression radiant, to tell them how the war was progressing. Before too long, he moved on to discuss the Jewish problem, his passionate speech incorporating some strong words.

Manfred's face flushed deeply in response to what he was hearing. While Hartmut and Richard listened attentively and also responded to the father's statements, Manfred retreated into himself and didn't make a sound. He wanted to go home.

Suddenly, Hartmut's father turned to him. "What's wrong, Manfred? Are you not feeling well—or is our conversation not quite to your liking?" he asked in a somewhat barbed tone. Manfred was frightened. He had no intention of saying anything about what was actually going on inside him.

"I actually am feeling a little ill," he said, turning to look at Richard. "Richard, I'm going home. If you want to stay, don't let me stand in your way, okay?"

Richard looked at Manfred with some anger. Now that he had finally come along, he was starting up all his drama again. From day to day, Richard understood him less and less when it came to the war and the Jewish subject. *What's his problem?* he often asked himself, and once, when he secretly shared his concerns with his father, Sigmund replied succinctly, avoiding redundant explanations: "Richard, each of us has his own private thoughts and feelings, which should be respected. Sometimes it's better not to look for answers."

Richard decided to return home with Manfred, as his fleeting anger was soon replaced by pity. *He has every reason in the world to feel emotional after everything that happened with his family,* he thought to himself.

Manfred, who was feeling uneasy, wanted to appease Richard, and on the way home, told him, "Look, Richard, I love you and appreciate you very much. You've been just like a brother to me from the day we were born, and even more ever since I've been living with you, but when it comes to this whole issue, the political one, or whatever they want to call it, I think a little differently and I don't want you to be angry with me. I'm just asking you to understand that not everyone thinks the same, although at school they try to teach us that that's the case."

"Manfred, my father always says we should respect other people's opinions and feelings, even if they're different than ours, and believe me, I'm trying to behave that way. I'm not angry with you—you're my best friend and always will be. It's just that when you don't think or feel like everyone else, try to show it as little as possible. After all, you already know the general state of mind around here, don't you?"

Manfred looked at him and forced a smile. "I'll do my best, Richard. I'm sure you understand that I really don't want anyone looking at me funny, right?"

◆ ◆ ◆

Sigmund came home. Gertrude looked at the clock and then at him. He had gotten back earlier than usual. "Sigmund, is everything all right? I wasn't expecting you for another hour."

Sigmund gazed at her. He walked over and held her tight. "Where are the boys?" he asked, looking around him.

"They're at Hartmut's. They should be back soon. Sigmund, what's wrong? Sigmund?"

Sigmund sighed and dropped heavily into the armchair. "Gertrude, I received definitive information about Ilse today, and by chance, about Abe, too. It's not good news, Gertrude—it's actually as bad as it could get."

Gertrude's eyes opened wide and her pulse began to race. If earlier she had tried to calm herself with the hope that what Sigmund had heard was inaccurate or untrue, she now understood that the previous information was indeed factual; apparently Sigmund had received final confirmation of it.

"Gertrude, our Ilse was killed, I assume, about two months ago. I don't know the exact date. She was involved in a hit-and-run car accident, left on the road, and apparently died immediately." He didn't say a word about the pregnancy.

Gertrude burst into tears. When she hadn't heard anything from Ilse since her last letter, she'd gotten terribly worried, and when Sigmund earlier raised the possibility that harm had befallen Ilse, she expected the worst. But now it was final—as final as could be. Ilse was no longer alive, and it was up to her to tell Manfred. Her mouth remained dry and silent and she merely dabbed at her eyes and nose and edged closer to her husband. *If he only knew that in addition to everything else, poor Ilse might have been pregnant*, she thought to herself, horrified. *What a tragedy. Oh, how terrible!. How dreadful!*

"Gertrude, and that's not all. I also found out that Johan, triggered by frustration over Ilse's death, killed Abe a day or two later. That means that when Johan told Ilse that Abe was already dead, he was simply lying to her."

"Sigmund," Gertrude whispered, "I was sure that Abe had died a long time ago, even before Johan said anything. You didn't say anything; you just stopped talking about him. Could you have known about this the entire time, and just not shared it with me and Ilse, Sigmund?" And she added, without waiting for him to reply, "After all, when Ilse told us that Johan had said Abe was dead, you didn't react, you didn't contradict her. I was sure that you believed her, too."

"I did know something, Gertrude, but not too much, since I didn't want to look like I was too interested at the time and keep on asking questions. In general, I knew that Abe was alive and apparently employed at the camp clinic as a doctor's assistant. Let's not talk about what sort of clinic it is. There's no point discussing it now. In any case, he's not alive any longer and it doesn't really matter when he died. I really did believe Ilse when she told us he was dead. It's hard, Gertrude, it's really hard to hang on to life as a prisoner in a concentration camp. I also had no reason to believe that this wasn't the case, that Johan had lied. After Ilse said that Abe was dead, based on what Johan told her, I didn't even think about looking into it. I believed it. Why shouldn't I believe it? Who just says something like that—and for what reason? And when it was whispered that Johan had killed him, I was absolutely thunderstruck because I couldn't imagine that Johan would lie about it. There's a limit, isn't there? Well, apparently there isn't. The fact is that Johan did everything he could to isolate her. Maybe he also played a part in Hildegard's death. There's no longer any way of knowing. It turns out that Johan is very clever, and when he wants something, he knows how to get it."

"Sigmund," Gertrude said, "I have a feeling that Isadore is no longer alive, either. And then poor Manfred really is an orphan and has been left on his own in this cruel world... and other than us, he simply has no one, no one at all. So far, we haven't even told him that his father is dead. It's so horrible, Sigmund, so horrible. How did all this befall that wonderful, wretched family? And how could one man be responsible for all of it?"

She then broke down and decided to share her secret with him. "Sigmund, there's something important I didn't tell you, which Ilse wrote to me in that letter I got from her about three weeks after she left. She was apparently pregnant, Sigmund, with Johan's child. She promised to sneak off another letter to me once she knew for sure and tell me what she intended to do. And ever since, as you know, we heard nothing from her. So maybe after she found out that she really was pregnant, she committed suicide? But, on the other hand, she would never leave Manfred. Never."

"I don't believe Ilse killed herself, Gertrude. She would never conceive of doing something so irresponsible. She was just killed," Sigmund said, glad he had not brought up the matter of the pregnancy himself.

"We don't even know where he buried her, and we probably never will," Gertrude whispered in pain. "That basic consolation of knowing where a loved one is buried—even that was taken from us and from her child. It's just unbelievable—this whole thing is simply insane. And how will we tell the boy? What will we say to him? Everything's already so hard for him and he's been sitting there, with supreme patience, waiting to hear from her and constantly hoping she'll suddenly show up. His whole world will collapse, Sigmund, when he really takes it in. It's just too cruel."

"Gertrude, everything's been too cruel for a long time now. You have no idea how cruel. I don't tell you a lot of what I know about what's happening in this country because I want to spare you the anguish and the sorrow, but it's unbelievably terrible. And there's one person responsible for all of it—a single person responsible—our 'glorious' Führer. Don't worry, we'll tell Manfred together. This time I won't leave you alone, like when you told him about Ilse leaving—and we'll have no choice but to tell him about his father as well. We've been given an unbearably hard task and we'll do it as best we can. We simply have no choice. We love this boy as if he were our own flesh and blood. He's a charming, wonderful boy, and I'm willing to do anything for him."

Gertrude didn't answer, as she had retreated into melancholy thoughts. How could you tell a child that the father who had been taken from him had lost his life in a concentration camp and that his mother, with whom he was constantly hoping to reunite, had been permanently taken away from him as well?

They decided to wait two or three days in order to process everything that had happened, and to find the right time to tell him all about it—together.

◆ ◆ ◆

Manfred and Richard returned home. They chatted cheerfully, discussing the events of the day. That time, Manfred, too, had had a good time with Hartmut, who was a quiet, pleasant boy, mostly because his father had not interfered. Gertrude was waiting for them with a hot meal, as she did every day, and her eyes caressed Manfred's handsome face with great love.

Her heart was fluttering within her. Sigmund, too, came out to see them, smiled and surreptitiously glanced at Gertrude, distraught; she avoided his eyes.

"Come, children, let's sit down to eat," she said quietly.

During the meal, the children talked about school and about spending time at Hartmut's house. The atmosphere was pleasant, but as the minutes went by, Gertrude and Sigmund felt dread course through them. There was no way to put off the heartbreaking moment of telling Manfred. They had decided earlier that Richard's presence while they shared the news would actually make it easier for them, and for Manfred as well.

"Manfred," Sigmund began once the meal had ended, "we have something very important to tell you. And Richard," he turned to his son, "I'm asking you to be here during the conversation as well."

Both children sat down obediently, as was their habit. Their disciplined approach managed to surprise Sigmund each time anew. *Perhaps, after all, there are also positive aspects to the kind of education they are receiving in school if the children are becoming so obedient and compliant*, he sometimes found himself thinking. After all, he was well aware of what was going on at school and what was taught there, and although some of it seemed wrong to him, when it came to values of obedience and discipline, he had no objections, even if these values were enforced upon the children. He always enjoyed the absolute respect with which the boys treated him and Gertrude. For his own sake, Sigmund tried not to get too involved in the children's school life. If they came to him with stories, he would listen but try not to interfere too much, because if he did, he would certainly have found it hard not to reveal his real opinions. His eyes focused on Manfred and then moved on to Richard. He felt Gertrude direct a penetrating gaze at him. This was the hardest thing he had ever had to do.

"Manfred," he said at last, "Gertrude, Richard and I love you very much—I'm sure you know that. We've always treated you like a son and we'll always continue to treat you that way." He paused briefly, breathing in a tiny sip of air. "Manfred, today I found out something terrible, and believe me, son, it's unbearably hard for me to tell you about it, but I have no choice, you have to hear the truth, and…"

"You're going to tell me Mama is dead, right?" Manfred interjected. "For a long time now, my heart has been heavy, and for a long time now, since we've heard nothing from Mama, I started to suspect that something terrible happened to her. She's dead. Right, Sigmund?"

Sigmund almost swallowed his tongue in his acute distress and Gertrude burst into tears and rushed to embrace the trembling boy. Richard joined her, his eyes darting between his parents while also growing teary.

"Yes, Manfred, Mama is dead… and I'm so sorry to have to tell you this, my boy… your father and grandfather also lost their lives some time ago." Sigmund knew he would not give the poor child any more information on the way his parents died. It was simply too awful, and in any case would add nothing other than more sorrow.

Manfred, who was staring straight ahead as his heart drifted away, sat embraced in Gertrude and Richard's arms. Their tears, raining down on him unreservedly, made him shiver and distracted him from his thoughts. He himself did not shed a tear. Then, after a moment that seemed to last forever, he turned to Gertrude, brushed away her tears with a shaky finger, and whispered, "Don't cry, Mama, everything will eventually be okay." He then turned to Richard and hugged him too.

◆ ◆ ◆

On the day that fate turned Manfred into an orphan, his life was transformed—he discarded any unnecessary sentimentality, even if it was justified, and toughened up his character considerably. Even Richard noticed, and gradually sensed that the Manfred he now knew was no longer the Manfred of old. Richard understood the source of the change, but was less fond of what the change had created. Manfred barely smiled, and when he did, it was a forced smile that disappeared in the blink of an eye. The boy who had become an adult buried himself in books and became a robot of sorts, whose face was opaque. He carried out everything he was asked to do perfectly, albeit somewhat mechanically, just as he was taught to do at school and at the youth movement. He simply excelled at everything.

Chapter 43

Several months had passed since the terrible revelation. Sigmund knew that soon he and Gertrude would begin proceedings to legally adopt Manfred. They were certain that he would not object—quite the contrary.

One day, Manfred asked Sigmund to accompany him to his room. "Sigmund," he said in a strained voice, "please, I want to know exactly how my parents died. I know it's hard for you to talk about it, but I'll feel better if I know. The thoughts racing through my head won't leave me alone and I want to lock it all away in some corner and stop tormenting myself over not knowing—in addition to the torment I've already gone through. I'm asking you, Sigmund, please tell me so I can try to deal with the whole thing once and for all."

A tremor ran through Sigmund. He had had a feeling that this day was coming—the day when he would be asked to say more; now, indeed, it had, and sooner than expected. "Manfred, this really is hard," he said, "but I understand what you're saying and respect your request and I promise I'll tell you everything, since that's what you really want." He paused briefly, and then resumed speaking. "Manfred, Mama was killed in a traffic accident in Munich. A big car that was speeding hit her. I'm sure Johan did all he could to save her, but it was already too late." Sigmund paused again, intending to allow Manfred to react, but he remained silent.

Sigmund continued. "Your father died in Dachau a short time after Mama. He was very ill and didn't survive the deplorable conditions at the camp." It was hard for him to tell the child that Johan had murdered Abe. That would have been simply too much.

"And what about Johan?" Manfred asked. "Did he stay in Munich?"

"Yes," Sigmund replied. "He's a commander at the camp in Dachau." And at that moment, watching Manfred's eyes widen, he regretted volunteering this unnecessary item of information.

"At Dachau?" the boy whispered. "So maybe Johan had some connection to Papa at the camp? Maybe he was cruel to Papa and that's why Papa died?" he challenged. "How can we know, Sigmund? Something like that even makes sense, since I'm sure Johan hated my father for taking Mama away from him."

Sigmund sputtered. How did the boy know this? As far as he could remember, they had never told him about it. He must have overheard them whispering about it at some point and drawn his own conclusions. After all, he was such a clever, perceptive boy.

"Manfred, I tend to believe that there were some encounters between Johan and Papa at the camp, and I know Johan was quite angry with Papa, probably mostly because of the reason you brought up. It's true, son. Before Mama met Papa, she was friendly with Johan, and when she married Papa, Johan saw it as a personal insult—apparently he wanted her for himself." Sigmund had no choice; he had to continue on the path the boy himself had outlined.

"Well, if that's the case, Johan must have done something to Papa," Manfred said sorrowfully. "Papa was a doctor, and he couldn't have just died from an illness like that. Papa was always a strong, healthy person and was very skilled at treating sick people, and definitely himself, too. Please tell me, Sigmund. My heart is telling me Johan had something to do with Papa's death, just like he had something to do with my mother getting up one morning and disappearing, leaving only a goodbye letter behind her."

Tears began to well up in Sigmund's eyes and his turbulent thoughts threatened to take over. He felt as if he were falling apart. After a heavy sigh, followed by a long silence, he blurted out in a stammered whisper, "Manfred, my dear boy, Johan... Johan... he killed... killed Papa." *Oh, this is just horrible*, he mumbled to himself, before continuing: "He killed him... as retaliation for Mama's death. I'm so sorry, Manfred, but you were pressuring me. Now you know everything, and I'm not hiding anything from you." Sigmund shifted uneasily in place. He didn't want to add another word to what he had already revealed.

"And what about Opa?" the boy asked, then answered himself: "He definitely died some time ago, too." And he bowed his head and retreated into his own thoughts, trying to take in what he had just found out after realizing that both his parents had been killed by the same murderer—Johan Kirche. Suddenly he heard Sigmund mumbling. Manfred looked at the man's vacantly staring eyes and for a moment thought he was talking to himself.

"Since Germany is full of all kinds of Johan Kirches, this Johan Kirche is no different from them. Johan Kirche is just a tiny cog in the ferocious war machine, and he behaves exactly as he is expected to behave based on the general frame of mind in Germany... as dictated by his regime and its ideology..."

"Sigmund," Manfred said, his voice hoarse, "the thing that makes me most angry is that my parents died for revenge. That's what I believe."

Sigmund looked at the boy, disengaging from his contemplation, and replied, "I agree with you, son. They really were killed for completely personal reasons—romantic ones—and not for any other cause—not just because Papa was Jewish and not because Mama was married to a Jew or because she was a victim of the war in general. Mama was indeed killed in an accident, but Papa was simply a personal, specific case of murder that was subsumed by all the general murderous onslaught of the war. That's what's truly unforgivable—taking advantage of the situation for personal needs. It's just beyond belief."

❖ ❖ ❖

About a month after the Blitz[6] on London, in October 1940, Manfred and Richard turned 10, and were promoted from cadets to full-blown members of the Hitler Youth movement. Manfred continued to be obedient as well as to maintain the stoicism he enforced on himself, suppressing his true feelings about the movement.

❖ ❖ ❖

Over the next two years, many of the cities in Germany sustained numerous aerial attacks. In November 1941, Sigmund met Richard outside the Ministry of the Interior. They were heading for one of the downtown stores when they suddenly heard an intense, terrifying explosion. Within a short time, the sky was filled with huge black "birds" that dropped a constant barrage of bombs. Berlin trembled, filling with smoky corners. Sigmund and Richard hurried to seek shelter. They covered their ears with their hands in order to ease the deafening noise and ran with their heads bowed. A moment before they managed to reach the entrance to one of the buildings on the street, another bomb landed next to them. Along with several other people, they were thrown up into the air and returned to the ground as seared scraps of flesh that were scattered everywhere.

❖ ❖ ❖

---

6 The Blitz (from the German Blitzkrieg, meaning "lightning attack"), was a German bombing campaign targeting the UK from September 1940 and into 1941. The Germans conducted mass air attacks against British towns, cities, and industrial targets, beginning with raids on London towards the end of the Battle of Britain in 1940.

The camp's commanders greeted Inspektor Gruppenführer[7] Glücks and his entourage, who had arrived for a surprise visit. Johan was having a terrible day—he was in a foul mood after two prisoners under his command had managed to escape the camp's boundaries the night before, and the search for them was still ongoing. The inspector's tough expression reflected great anger when he found out about the incident and identified some failings in the camp's routine procedures.

The heavyset, self-important inspector turned to Johan, and before the other commanders, spat out, "Kommandant Kirche, the next time something like this happens, you'll find yourself on your way there—" and his hand sprang up, his finger pointing toward the chimney of the crematorium at the outskirts of the camp.

Johan's cheeks ignited with a flame that lapped at the tips of his ears; he even lost control of one of his jaw muscles. It was the most humiliating, mortifying incidents he had ever experienced. It was simply horrible: invoking the inspector's wrath, being reprimanded in public, and feeling the sword hovering over his own head.

◆ ◆ ◆

Manfred and Gertrude sat down to their meal silently. For several weeks now, they had been in a state of deep mourning. Out of Gertrude's entire family, Manfred was the last person left by her side in Germany; she had been unable to stay in touch with her brother in the United States due to the war.

Gertrude was alone in the world, and Manfred was alone in the world—two lost souls who clung to one another and took care of one another wordlessly. They were still in shock after Sigmund and Richard lost their lives in the massive British bombardment that resulted in many more casualties.

---

7 A German paramilitary rank meaning "group leader."

Difficult days awaited them. Having no other choice, Gertrude began to contribute to the war effort by finding a job at one of the city's factories. She had to provide for the two of them. She had Manfred and her life nowadays revolved solely around him. *If it weren't for him, I would simply kill myself,* she often thought. After all, she had promised Ilse to watch over her son as if he were her own; she had indeed done so, and knew that she would continue to do so. One thing, however, aggrieved her greatly: that she and Sigmund had not had time to legally adopt Manfred.

♦ ♦ ♦

At the camp, the cruel experiments on human subjects continued, becoming more efficient as they were designated to benefit the army as well. In mid-March of 1942, new experiments focusing on decompression and atmospheric pressure got under way. Their official purpose was to examine the effects of an abrupt drop in pressure or lack of oxygen, of the kind experienced by combat pilots whose planes had been hit, forcing them to parachute from great heights. About 200 prisoners were subjected to these experiments, of whom at least 70 died as a result. Another series of experiments involved freezing, in order to find a quick, effective way to help pilots whose planes had been shot down over the ocean, and suffered from hypothermia after spending a long period of time in the water.

An experimental tuberculosis station was also being run at the camp. A group of prisoners was infected with the disease in order to assess and compare the effects of biochemical cures to conventional ones. At the same time, other experiments were conducted to examine the body's adaptability to drinking seawater, as well as the effects of medication intended to curb bleeding. The suffering of the prisoners who served as subjects in these experiments was unimaginable, and after a barrage of abuse in the name of medicine and science, most of them did not survive. It was ongoing suffering that ultimately resulted in death.

Johan was convinced that these experiments would provide a balm for humanity after the war as well. He believed the leadership was indeed acting to ensure maximum utilization of the camp's human resources.

In the winter, endless transports of prisoners deemed to be unfit left the camp for Wertheim Castle, near Linz, Austria, where they were to be killed by gas. Johan watched the next row of prisoners being gathered and prepared for transport. He spotted the figure of a woman with a round belly protruding from her gaunt body, emerging from behind one of the cabins. The emaciated figure, wearing a kerchief on her head, ran and stumbled toward the marching group, waving her arms like a madwoman and emitting deafening shrieks. Within seconds, several pistols were shooting in her direction and she collapsed. Her mangled belly let out a bloody mass that fluttered faintly and then grew still. A group of prisoners watched the grisly events, mumbling softly.

Johan, too, had witnessed the horror. A brief shudder ran through him. The image of the puddle of blood on which Ilse had been sprawled out after she was killed flashed in front of his eyes. He immediately came to his senses, loudly ordered the acceleration of the group's evacuation, and then hurried off to his office. Closing the door, he made sure to bolt it with both locks. The sight of the eviscerated woman and the red fetus expelled from her had nauseated him. He had never witnessed anything like that before.

He rinsed out his mouth and wiped his face again and again once the contents of his stomach had been thoroughly emptied. That was beyond what the spirit could endure.

The camp's staff was ordered to build another gas chamber in the second crematorium, which had been constructed once it was discovered that the first one—which had only one furnace—was not enough. The extermination machine had been increasingly efficient since the approval of the "Final Solution to the Jewish Problem" at the Wannsee Conference in January 1942, and the prisoners were the ones toiling for days at a time to establish the annihilation operation in which they themselves would lose their lives.

Chapter 44

In the beginning of 1943, the war reached a significant turning point. "General Winter," with its many freezing snowstorms that resulted in numerous fatalities, had a crucial effect on the conquest of Stalingrad. The battle was bloody and heavy in casualties, and Germany could no longer pat itself on the back for its victories. It began to suffer some losses, and worst of all—as far as Hitler was concerned—conclusive defeats. Zealously devoted to his ideology and drunk on previous victories, Hitler absolutely refused to acknowledge the consequences of his actions. The nation began to realize, albeit somewhat belatedly, that it was caught up in a deadly maelstrom resulting from a failure to link actions to results. Hitler's deeds had, for some time, become actual crimes, although they continued to inspire the allegiance of a nation that was in no hurry to relinquish its faith in the leader's cause. And these crimes led to extreme manifestations of human suffering that evoked empathy in some of the people and brutal cruelty in others.

Johan was aware of what was taking place on the battlefield, as well as of the significant regression in executing the army's plans of conquest and expansion. Megalomania and blind faith had been depleted and everything began to collapse like a house of cards. Loss followed loss, and defeat followed defeat, all culminating in a clear-cut reversal of the war's anticipated results, he speculated glumly. His breathing became rapid when he imagined what was probably going on in Hitler's mind. So when all was said and done, the glorified Führer, who had never deigned to consider the option that his plans would not be fully carried out in accordance with his dictates, now faced an alternate truth, a different reality—quite different indeed.

And what about the morning after? Johan's thoughts carried on relentlessly. What if Germany were to suffer a conclusive defeat that would leave it even weaker, more tormented, downtrodden and exploited than before? It was hard for him to allow his thoughts to go there, but he believed that only someone with no grasp on reality would fail to consider it. Also, his views on the Führer and the entire senior leadership holding the reins and spurring on the horses of authority had been turned upside down as well.

◆ ◆ ◆

As time went by, and the warfare spread to include more and more tragic events in its sphere of influence, Manfred felt an increasing resolve to become a doctor. It was true that he would be joining three previous generations of doctors in his family, and that his mother had also chosen a profession that belonged to the world of medicine, but this was not the source of his attraction to such a calling. His greatest aspiration was to help the sick and the needy, just as his father had done. He yearned to cure the world of its ills, craved to bestow life on others, and longed to be appreciated for his kindness and compassion rather than merely for his professionalism. One day he shared his dreams with Gertrude.

"Gertrude, once I finish school, and I really hope this damn war will come to an end at some point, I want to study medicine," he told her, his expression solemn.

"Oh, Manfred, I'm sure you want to continue in your father's footsteps. I really understand that!" she said. He proceeded to explain his motivation, beyond the matter of continuity.

"Manfred," Gertrude said, her voice hard and decisive, "you won't go to medical school here in Germany. After the war, Germany won't be the same Germany anymore. It's been quite a while since our country was what it used to be. I heard a rumor that in the camps, they're making inhumane use of the science of medicine."

"What do you mean—experimenting on *people*?" he asked, adding, "Do you know how many people will stay sick, maybe even seriously sick, afterwards? And that's if they even survive. That's absolutely horrible, Gertrude."

"I can't think about it too much," she replied, "but I tend to believe that those rumors aren't just rumors. Manfred, I truly despise everything that's happening in our country. It's hard to believe that from a nation that was so cultured, orderly, meticulous, and intelligent, we've turned into wild beasts that also devour. If you really want to study medicine, you'll study in America and work there as well. Things here will never be the same."

"America? How, Gertrude? I don't have anyone over there, and besides, I would never leave you. After all, you're my mother now, right? I'd never go to America," he reiterated. "No way!" he added passionately.

"I'll come with you, Manfred. After all, my brother lives in New York. I told you that once, didn't I? My brother is a very nice, warm person. Even before the war broke out, he begged Sigmund and me to come visit him, and even stay. He's never approved of Germany, without even knowing what was about to happen. We'll go to him. I'll always keep taking care of you, and of him, too, if necessary, but you—you'll study medicine only in America," she repeated resolutely.

"Gertrude, Mama," he said, "how would I have the money to study there? It must cost a fortune, definitely for a foreigner like me who suddenly arrives in the United States and wants to study there. Already, I often find myself asking what I am—a German? a Jew? a Christian? maybe even a Nazi? You know, because I'm a member of the youth movement. It's pretty confusing, don't you think?"

"Manfred, what a barrage of words. Wait a minute, my dear.

There are a few more things that you don't know and maybe it's time that I told you. Before your mother left, she gave me a little box with all your documents. Under all those papers is a bundle of money intended for you. I don't know the current worth of that money, but there's no doubt it will still be worth something, at least to get you started. Afterwards, we'll get by. I have faith in myself, in you, and in my brother, too. Don't worry, Manfred. We'll get everything done, and do it together, in order to create a new life. And Manfred? The last thing I want you to think is that you're a Nazi. If it wasn't for that damn organization, which forces everyone to join it, you'd never have taken part in all that. You're half-Jewish, and when it comes to religious faith, you can believe whatever you see fit. There is one God in the world, but unfortunately He hasn't liked his creations very much in the last few years..." She dried her tears with the edge of her sleeve.

Manfred was silent. He had no words left with which to respond. What Gertrude had told him came as a big surprise, but once he understood that she wanted to join him, he decided to consider her words with the same seriousness with which she had spoken them.

◆ ◆ ◆

About four years had gone by since the war first began and, as Johan had anticipated, after the battle of Stalingrad, German victories were increasingly outnumbered by defeats. The army continued to carry out its duties, but the soldiers were plagued by an increasing suspicion that they were in the midst of a death rattle.

Johan found himself living in an ongoing nightmare of sorts, especially once cracks had begun to form in his former faith in the proceedings and, even worse, in the tough, stone-hearted character that he had imposed upon himself. There was nothing he could do about the general state of affairs, but he was no longer in control of the personal aspect, either, and he felt his entire world growing hazy around him. He often tormented himself for his failure to completely eradicate every trace of human sensitivity, even surrendering to such emotion. He chastised himself for killing Abe out of intense weakness and due to the desire for vengeance that bubbled within him. After all, weakness was the complete opposite of emotionless toughness. Weakness was an entirely sentimental concept, one that someone like him should have nothing to do with.

What gnawed at him and tormented him more than anything else was his mother's suicide. After all, he knew precisely who had been most directly responsible for Beatrice's decision to take her own life, and was the only one who knew it. And he felt like a traitor, one who was betraying all of the party's sanctified ideals and rebelling against the leadership's values but was unable to control it. He found it utterly unacceptable.

But the part that frightened him most was his inability to shake off this sentimentality, which had now escaped and extended beyond the limits of the personal. He had begun to suffer as a result of everything he was seeing at the camp. For some time, he could no longer identify with the SS men who exterminated millions of people in the gas chambers as part of their daily routine. Ilse's image was constantly merging with that of the woman whose embryo had been expelled from her body after her belly was torn apart. He could no longer stand the hellish reality of deplorable terror that was currently being inflicted also upon the German nation itself, alongside the screaming, the blood, and the constant carnage. He did understand that they were required to kill and exterminate, but why abuse those sentenced to death to such an extent, and for so long? Something had gone wrong here, and too many people were blindly following the raging madness.

Johan's mind then began to fill with burning questions. Wasn't gratuitous abuse in complete contrast to the need to carry out what was required of them in a meticulous manner and within an allotted time, while prioritizing the main goal? How was the Nazis' Spartan restraint being expressed? How was the mission of mass extermination related to whiling away time by prolonging suffering? And the medical experiments—some of which had become quite questionable—and the turning of women into prostitutes, and the systematic torture...What part did they all play in the whole matter of extermination? After all, there was a cost to maintaining all those camps, although the human resources were free. Why didn't they simply eliminate those intended to be eliminated, and call it good? Johan no longer believed in the idea of the cheap workforce, which was in fact working for free. What still remained to be developed and built in and around the camps, after so many years of maintenance and expansion, when the cheap workforce toiling for free looked the way it did?

◆ ◆ ◆

As the military losses became increasingly significant, more and more manpower was recruited to join the ranks of the fighters. The young men from the youth movement had been serving as an additional source of military personnel for some time now. If at first the youths summoned to perform tasks for the army were 16 to 18 years old and were stationed near their homes, as Germany's defeats continued, the age of the young men being sent to the front began to drop. On their way to their missions, these child-adolescents often fell victim to bombs, and were killed.

After each bombing, Manfred and his friends were also instructed to pitch in around the various neighborhoods. They were to clear the ruins and identify which houses had been hit. They knocked on the doors of residences that had been spared, looking for unoccupied rooms where they could house citizens who had become homeless. The residents who refused to share their homes with the new tenants were reported to the police and could soon expect a visit from the Gestapo.

Manfred was happy to help citizens who had been hurt, but he hated snitching. He had already heard about the fate of the citizens visited by the Gestapo. All of the city's residents were suffering greatly. People often returned home to find their residences replaced by a pile of rubble. The city was gradually being destroyed, falling apart as its inhabitants succumbed to despair.

When Manfred was forced to participate in youth movement activities, Gertrude was anxious and frightened. *What if something were to happen to him?* she worried again and again. She had heard of quite a few teenagers who had been sent on some mission or other by the government in order to support the war effort, and had lost their lives. There was nothing she could do about it, other than to pray for the poor boy.

And Manfred continued to comply and to carry out his role, but did so with a very heavy heart, as he had no faith at all in the movement, its commanders, their commanders, and everything related to running a war that he had perceived for some time to be an abject failure. When he headed out on such an activity and looked at the red armband with the black swastika that he was forced to wear on his sleeve, he thought that if it weren't for this band, he would certainly have been required to wear a yellow badge on his chest, or else he would have found himself in a concentration camp, or even worse—in a death camp... Most of all, he was increasingly worried about Gertrude. He had noticed that lately, part of what she said consisted of confused mumbling. He also observed that occasionally she blurted out incomprehensible words that were directed only at herself.

PART SIX

⇜ Chapter 45 ⇝

In mid-winter of 1944, the ever-growing piles of corpses at the camp created a dismal atmosphere of decay. A sickening stench from the bodies rose in waves, and even the damp, wintery weather couldn't mask the odor of death.

Such brutal sights had been leaving their mark on Johan for a while. Sometimes he even felt more dead than alive. How much longer would it be possible to keep living amidst such horrors, witnessing systematic brutality toward such a huge accumulation of people whose entire crime consisted, in fact, of not being pure Aryans? Already the conditions of war had completely unsettled people, leaving them increasingly distraught, and being constantly exposed to images such as these made it even harder on them.

As Johan was further sucked into the routine of camp life, which revolved mostly around agony, cruelty, and death, he became increasingly revolted by what he saw around him, wanting to disengage from this mad world. After all, since it would be illogical to believe that it was possible to annihilate all the Jews in the world in this manner, he found himself thinking again and again. Surely some Jew would always remain in some godforsaken corner and would re-establish the entire race. If at first he was fully confident that this was indeed the way to eradicate Jews and Judaism, he no longer thought so.

The venture had become an uninhibited murder machine that extinguished people with no distinctions or mercy... including babies.

These thoughts made him shudder, reminding him yet again of how appalled he had been when Ilse's death also killed the fetus in her womb—the one that was to become his own child. Again and again, he envisioned his infant sister, whose death had caused his father to lose his mind. Johan could find no peace. He began to experience actual nightmares due to the war and in particular due to where he found himself spending most of his time. He rarely left his office, and continued to carry out his role in his habitual way, but with great effort and little personal involvement. He sought emotional detachment from everything going on around him, as he felt that he was on the verge of insanity. Johan was frightened. He had never before experienced such fear.

The German Army continued to accrue casualties alongside ever-increasing defeats on all fronts. And as the soldiers risked their lives on the battlefield, Hitler was conducting a desperate battle against the failing generals and the military losses. No one wanted to think about Germany being defeated after all its victories, and losing everything it had managed to attain thus far. It was simply inconceivable.

Johan no longer cared about anything. In his current state, he didn't want to be involved in any shape or form in what was happening around him. All he dreamed about was being in some isolated corner at the end of the world, far, far away from the hell he was in. All of the values he had been educated on, from the day he first joined the Nazi Party and the SS organization, had lost their effect on him some time ago. He only wanted to be a person like any other once more, one who was not burdened by such heavy Nazi obligation. He yearned to be a sane person living a sane life among other sane people—if there were still such people to be found. This surreal war, which had been steered in directions that were completely different from those of a conventional war for months, no longer amazed him. Not only did he fail to be impressed, fascinated, and thrilled by this monstrous display of power—he found it utterly terrifying.

And the part that stood out most for him, and which he found equally frightening, was that from day to day, he would find himself increasingly wondering about his own cruelty, which, for all those years, he had allowed to take control of him with a loving bear hug while he increasingly tended to love it back.

I have to get out of here, Johan told himself every day. *I can smell the very bad end of a war we're not going to win, an end that will definitely not leave any of us who are orchestrating it unscathed. We will have to pay the price for the terrible things we've done— no doubt about it. Someone will certainly want to get even with all of us one day, and I don't want to be among those who will be denounced. I have to disappear, even if it's deep into the ground or to some godforsaken jungle where there are real animals, and not these two-legged beasts that can't be defined as human anymore.*

Johan began to concoct a secret escape plan, knowing precisely who would help him. He wouldn't be the first to come up with such a plan—of that he was certain—nor would he be the first to carry it out.

Chapter 46

In the early spring of 1944, John Church, wearing a faded sailor's uniform, disembarked from a freighter in New York Harbor. A frayed satchel dangled from his shoulder, containing essential necessities, as well as his pistol, from which he refused to part. In his pocket he held the most important thing of all—his new documents, including one priceless item: a new passport bearing his new identity. He was now
Name: John Church
Place of birth: Great Britain
Year of birth: 1900 (aging him by three whole years)
His perturbed expression encountered a city dense with a variety of buildings and long streets; it was a foreign city, lacking in warmth, which did not seem to quite welcome the face that he presented to it. His metallic blue eyes no longer gleamed as they once had. John Church felt and looked somewhat older than he was, stooping in a way that did not befit the tall frame he had always proudly displayed.

It was early in the morning, and a light spring drizzle was falling. The cool air eased John's feeling of suffocation, while the dim light deepened his sense of alienation.

Now I'm all alone in the world, he thought, *solitary and far from everything I've known thus far—which is a good thing—but I'm also so far away from my homeland, which I once loved so much.*

He took a slip of paper with worn-down edges out of his pocket, and headed for the address scribbled on it. At least someone was waiting for him, someone who would help him acclimate to this foreign city. There was some solace in this, another service provided by those who had paved his escape route.

The man waiting for John in the one-room apartment explained everything he would need to know in fluent German. "This is your new home, Church," he told him, "and we've also arranged an initial job for you. Two days from now, you'll start working as a janitor at the public school in the nearby neighborhood. I've heard that you're an expert at maintaining order." And the man winked knowingly, evoking obvious discomfort in John.

John bowed his head. He hoped that in the new world in which he had just arrived, no one would know much about him or about his past. After all, the whole point of escaping was to allow him to run away both from who he had been as well as to start an entirely different life. Much to his relief, the man talking to him was signaling his intention to leave.

"I'm leaving you my phone number, Church. If you need anything, call. I wish you luck in your new placement." And with that, he turned to go.

John was left on his own. He looked around him. A studio apartment in an old, grayish building, in a grayish neighborhood, and with gray, leaky weather. A minimum of essential furniture, and prominent disorder. He sighed. He so loved sublime order, and it had been quite a while since he last experienced any sort of order—definitely nothing sublime. He decided that after a brief rest he would go down to the street and get to know his new surroundings. Most importantly, he was a free man in a free country, with a new identity that, to the best of his knowledge, had saved his life.

◆ ◆ ◆

Berlin, the breathtaking capital, glittery and meticulously maintained, had for some time been extinguished, having been transformed into a wide array of stones of all sizes. Most of its buildings survived only as dark shadows, and the streets were strewn with piles of rubble and remainders of every conceivable edifice. It was a horrific sight: one big cemetery in a state of blood-curdling chaos. And the people scurrying here and there among the ruins and the gaping craters also seemed like frenetic shadows.

Twelve-year-old children from the Hitler Youth movement were now beginning to join the ranks of the *Volkssturm*.[8] This was a manifestation of the regime's state of despair, as it was forced to resort to such measures. The children didn't have a choice other than to comply. Now that the battle over the city had begun, the members of the youth movement played a central role in providing Germany's last line of defense, often mingling with combat soldiers.

Once Gertrude heard about this, she decided that Manfred would no longer risk his life by being conscripted into military activity, so she hid him in the building's basement. "Manfred, you'll stay here in the basement with me. With all that mess out there, no one will notice that you've suddenly disappeared. After all, the end is near, Manfred, I can feel it in my bones, and I won't let you be taken away from me," she said. "They've taken enough, enough," she cried out and began to sob.

And Manfred obeyed, but this time it was Gertrude whose orders he followed. He feared for Gertrude's sanity more than he feared for himself if he were to be caught hiding like a pathetic chicken.

The basement was cramped and dark, yet still gave a feeling of protection. Like everyone around them, Gertrude and Manfred had to fight for every piece of bread and every glass of water, and they were frightened each time bombs were dropped on the city, shaking it to its core. Life was subsumed in an ongoing nightmare, tinged with the terrifying fear of what was to come, above all the dread that Manfred might be taken away. Every little rustle filled Gertrude with panic,

---

8   The Volkssturm was a national militia established by Nazi Germany in September 1944, during the last months of World War II. It was staffed by teenage boys and older men who were not serving in any military unit.

and every time it happened, she would run to him and try to hide him under her dress, trembling as a result of her frazzled nerves. Manfred's heart went out to her. He loved this woman so much, and sometimes he felt more attached to her than he ever had been to his mother.

One thing was now clear to everyone: victory over Germany was imminent.

"If I once had immense love for my homeland," Gertrude lamented for the umpteenth time, "now that I know what it has become, and what it has turned its citizens into, I deeply regret not listening to my brother a long time ago and leaving when he did. Apparently, my brother was a lot more realistic, or had a special prophetic instinct when he anticipated the worst even years ago. If we had followed him, Sigmund and Richard would still be alive today, and I wouldn't find myself in this terrible state." And she sobbed, her weeping becoming heartbreaking. "Look at us, Manfred, just like mice—hiding in dark cellars, unable to bathe, unable to change our clothes. Oh, it's disgusting, it's so terrible..."

"Gertrude, if you lived in America, who would take care of me?" Manfred asked with childish solemnity that also conveyed a trace of a smile. He stroked her hair, no longer soft and perfumed, trying to encourage her with a bit of humor.

Gertrude looked at this charming young man, for whom her love surged from day to day. "You're all that I have left here, Manfred. It's only for you that I keep clinging, tooth and nail, to sanity, as well as to the hope that it will all be over soon. And once it *is* over, Manfred, we'll pack a little suitcase for ourselves, take the wooden box Mama left you, leave everything else behind and take off. After all, what will still be here to leave behind? A city that's been completely destroyed and a house tottering on one leg?"

"This city's also full of bad memories, Gertrude. Not a day goes by when I don't think of my parents, and often about my grandmother and grandfather, too, and I also constantly remember Sigmund and Richard. It's all terribly sad. This war has caused so much damage and pain to everyone."

"Damage?" Gertrude said. "This is a true, horrible catastrophe that will be talked about for many years to come. All of this country's resources were invested in the war. The entire nation has been conscripted—if not to the army, then to the war apparatus in general. After all, you and all the boys from the youth movement were conscripted, too. There's no doubt that funneling all the funds to the war, the army, and the combat soldiers, inevitably comes at everyone's expense. And what about everything that was destroyed? Do you know how long it will take to restore all this ruin and rebuild everything again? It doesn't matter how new everything will be once more, maybe even prettier. None of the capital's citizens will be able to forget the dreadful destruction caused by the war, and the casualties, the wounded, and the disabled that it left behind."

Chapter 47

At the end of April 1945, word spread that Hitler had committed suicide in his bunker—the same bunker that had sheltered him for many days, but not forever. It happened precisely 10 days after the Führer's 56th birthday. He had realized that the death of his grand dream was also his own death sentence.

The catastrophic Second World War, with the colossal amount of casualties and bereavement it had caused, came to an end in May, after more than five and a half years of violent upheavals. The scope of the tragedy that humanity had experienced before the war came to an end was inconceivable, and it was said that anyone who had not experienced it first-hand would never be able to truly grasp what it had wrought and brought about.

John's work as a school custodian allowed him to focus on action, rather than on thought. He would linger on school grounds even after the last of the students had disappeared beyond the big gate. There was nothing special waiting for him at home, in the tiny, oppressive apartment that was so different from the one he had cultivated back in Munich.

John had never felt so lonely, but life far away from his ruined, blood-soaked homeland made up for it. Despite Germany's abject defeat in the war and the death of its questionable heroes, John felt no sorrow—neither over the defeat nor over the elimination of the Nazi regime and its leaders. He read that the Dachau concentration camp had been liberated by the Seventh United States Army. According to the news, 40 SS men who were among the camp's staff were tried by an American court and 36 of them were sentenced to death.

John envisioned himself being executed along with the others, all of those others who had once been close to him—operating alongside him or under his command—and whom he had left behind when he fled. He shuddered. He was lucky that he was far, far away from it all and was merely reading about it in the newspaper. For some time he had been feeling increasingly American, especially now that he had a reasonably satisfactory command of the English language.

John didn't make any friends; he wasn't even interested. The fear that someone might wonder about him and maybe expose his real identity haunted him. *It will take quite a bit longer before I'm over this fear*, he often thought. The only thing concerning his homeland that he couldn't help but think about was Ilse. There wasn't a single night when her lovely face did not peer at him as he daydreamed. There wasn't a single night when he didn't remember her extraordinary sweetness before closing his eyes, or when he felt a lump in his throat as he recalled losing her again only a short time after she became his again, as well as recalling who was responsible for her death, albeit accidently. And he had not only lost her, but also what had been growing inside her. He was then always taunted by the question of whether Ilse's death had indeed been an accident, or whether she had taken her own life.

When he first felt the stirring of revulsion while he was working at the camp, he had often resented Hitler for killing his Ilse, right in front of his eyes, without the car even bothering to stop for a moment to check what it had hit. At the moment that he saw the Führer's black armored car toss Ilse into the air and speed away as if nothing had happened, the first crack had formed in his blind admiration for the Führer; although he constantly tried to seal the crack, it broke open again and again. At the same time, he would envision the horrific sights of the camp, which made him sick to his stomach. Although he'd embarked on a new life, the memory of his previous life kept its hold on him.

In November, an international military tribunal of prosecution teams from the United States, the Soviet Union, Britain, and France convened in the city of Nuremburg, Germany, in order to prosecute war criminals. In the very city where the laws concerning race and purity of blood were first publicized, John thought, those responsible for enacting those laws, as well as committing additional, terrible crimes against humanity, would now be judged. He was familiar with all the venerated leaders who would stand trial. After all, he had anticipated that the day would come when the world would bring to justice all those who had carried out the mission of horror and extermination, and so he escaped early, as others had probably managed to do as well.

John pored over the main charges against the defendants:

1. *Conspiring to wage aggressive war while violating international treaties.*
2. *Waging aggressive war, or "crimes against peace."*
3. *Committing war crimes, mostly in the treatment of prisoners of war.*
4. *Crimes against humanity: murder, annihilation, deportation, enslavement.*

That's what it says on paper, John thought, *but I, I was a part of this industry of war and carnage. I was there in this procession of crimes against humanity. I took part in the daily murders and annihilation, out of blind faith in the proceedings.*

"Six organizations will be tried," he continued reading, "*so that once the members of these organizations stand trial, they may be convicted solely on the basis of their membership in the organization. These are the organizations: the SS, the Gestapo, the political leadership of the Nazi Party, the SA, the Reich Cabinet, the General Staff, and the High Command of the German Unified Armed Forces.*"

John sputtered in alarm. The SS was at the top of the list

of organizations they wanted to convict. If he had stayed in Germany, today he would be accused of war crimes like all the others who had already claimed repeatedly that they were *not* responsible for what had happened, that they were just carrying out the orders they received from their superiors.

John himself was an escaped Nazi war criminal—he had no choice but to admit it. He had followed the orders given to him and continued to follow them even as the orders grew increasingly horrifying and caused so much carnage. Ultimately, he was no better than the ones who had escaped like pathetic chickens, some of whom had been hunted down like animals, and were now on trial—the same ones who surrendered to authority, and perhaps were unwilling to admit it. Even if he himself had changed his life and his approach, and did all he could to transform himself, there would be no clemency for what he had caused and what he had taken part of during the war.

◆ ◆ ◆

The 1946 school year began. John was fixing a shelf in the teacher's lounge that came loose. He heard the rustle of paper behind his shoulder. When he turned his head, he found himself freezing in place. A beautiful woman with golden hair that was stylishly cut was sitting in one of the chairs. Her pale, long-fingered hands were briskly leafing through the stack of papers she held. She looked up and fleetingly smiled at him. John broke out in a cold sweat. He tried to regain control of himself and returned her smile. She was the spitting image of Ilse Heine; only her chest was fuller and her eyes were brown.

"You must be Mr. Church, the custodian," she addressed him. "I'm Elizabeth Lustig, the new history teacher. It's nice to meet you." She stood up and offered him her hand.

John approached her with a tentative step, grasped her extended hand and shook it. "Nice to meet you, too," he said.

"I wish you the best of luck. Usually teenagers don't really like to study history, *nicht wahr?*" He quickly caught himself and switched to English, "Isn't that so?"

Elizabeth was perceptive, and immediately asked, "*Sprechen sie Deutsch?*" ("*Do you speak German?*")

John had no choice but to stammer, "Yes, a little, I learned from my mother, who was born in Germany." He then thought of another coincidence—the new teacher's name was also the name of the hospital where he had first met Ilse.

Elizabeth moved on to discuss teaching history. The conversation between them flowed until the bell rang and she turned to go.

"It was nice to make your acquaintance, Mr. Church," she said. "I believe our paths will cross frequently from now on." His meticulous appearance had greatly impressed her.

"No doubt about it," he replied. "I enjoyed talking to you, too." And he immediately turned back to the loose shelf, tightened its screw with a somewhat unsteady hand and returned to his other routine tasks.

John couldn't stop thinking about Elizabeth. Although she appeared to be much younger than he was, after a few days he mustered up the courage to ask her out and she agreed. In order to act preemptively and prevent any possibility of the conversation inevitably drifting into matters of the past, he decided to put a stop to this before it ever began.

"Elizabeth," he told her, "I'm willing to talk to you about any topic in the world, but there's one thing I really don't want to discuss—my past. My past is too painful, and I have no desire to recall it. I hope you can understand. All you do have to know is that I was born in... England in, uhm... 1900, and that I came to the States before the damn war broke out and to New York about... two years ago. I'm an only child and lost both my parents at... um, a relatively young age... several years after the end of the First World War." He did his best to speak quickly and fluently so as not to make any mistakes, wanting to avoid any dangerous slips of the tongue. It was the second time he found himself forced to lie to a woman he liked about his true identity...

"Of course I have no interest in asking any questions that will sound nosy and free any genies from bottles, John," Elizabeth said. "And I'm entirely on the same page—I don't want anything to do with my unhappy past, and all you do have to know," she adopted his phrasing, "is that both my parents were born in Germany and left it after the end of the First World War. I, an only child just like you, was born here in New York in 1918. And finally, I broke up with a very violent husband who almost killed me, and all I want is to live my life quietly, work as a teacher, and, at some point, have a family of my own, far away from everyone who caused me pain. And just like you, John, I've lost both my parents."

"So we have quite a few things in common, Elizabeth," John said. "We're both only children and orphans with a difficult past and Germanic origins, although we were both born far from Germany..."

∽ Chapter 48 ∾

In the summer of 1947, Gertrude and Manfred each packed a suitcase, remembering to tuck in the wooden box Ilse had deposited with Gertrude. They boarded a ship, waved goodbye to a homeland they no longer loved, and turned expectantly toward America—the new country to which they were heading. They were both gaunt, their faces showing evidence of many years of suffering.

"I'll be so excited to see my brother again," Gertrude said, her tone optimistic. "After all, he's my last remaining blood relative."

"The first thing I want to do when we get there," Manfred said, "is to change my name. That will be one part of my new beginning in America."

"Oh, Manfred, Manfred, your name, especially your last name, has already caused so much trouble for you," Gertrude sighed. "When you were first born, you were called Manfred Heine-Liebmann, and then you became Manfred Heine, for well-known and painful reasons. Later on, Sigmund considered legally adopting you and changing your name to Manfred Sontag, but he never got the opportunity to do it." And she shed a tear, as she did every time she mentioned the name of the husband who had been stolen from her by the war. "And now," she continued, sniffling, "you're the one who wants a name change. What will your new name be?"

"I've given it a lot of thought," Manfred said, his forehead creasing solemnly. "I want a name that will remind me of both my parents and commemorate them and their origins. It's a first name derived from the name 'Manfred,' which was the name of my mother's father, whom I never knew, unfortunately, and a last name that combines both my parents' names: Manny Heimann."

◆ ◆ ◆

John and Elizabeth's relationship, which was constantly deepening, blossomed into love. As they had initially promised each other, they didn't mention their pasts in any way, and focused solely on the future. John had learned his lesson and no longer discussed problematic or controversial topics more than once. He was not that preoccupied with his opinions on various issues. All he wanted was to nurture his relationship with Elizabeth, whom he had grown to love and cherish, and mostly to find the subjects on which they agreed. The future was much more important and was the focus of their conversations. After several months, he proposed to her, and she accepted.

"And you don't mind that I'm older than you by 15 years?" he chuckled, slightly embarrassed.

"No, John," Elizabeth replied confidently, "I don't mind that you're older than me by... hold on there... not 15 years, but 18, isn't it?"

John's heart skipped a beat.

She giggled and then added earnestly, "That's really not what's important. So long as we have a loving, warm, wonderful relationship, and so much in common, I don't care about your chronological age. I was married to a man who was about my own age, and what did I get out of it? I served as his punching bag, so he could take out all his frustrations on me, with plenty of cruelty." Suddenly, her face darkened.

John rushed to embrace her. "Elizabeth, have you forgotten that we promised not to talk about the past? Well, then, let's promise not to think back on it, either. Okay?" And she nodded silently, a smile illuminating her face, while he continued to torment himself for his slip of the tongue regarding their age difference.

Pooling their resources, they moved into an appealing, roomy apartment together.

No one could have been a kinder and more generous husband than John. He loved Elizabeth almost as much as he had loved Ilse, but this time it was without the madness that had mingled with his obsessive love for the first object of his affections. He spoiled Elizabeth, indulging her every whim and thanking the Almighty, whoever He might be, for providing him with this woman who had allowed his heart to open up to new love. He quit his job as a school custodian and with Elizabeth's help, opened up a little neighborhood store that sold school supplies.

John's heart soared when Elizabeth told him she was pregnant. His eyes filled with tears and he swallowed the lump in his throat. He could already have had been father to an eight-year-old...

John and Elizabeth Church's first child, a son, was born in the spring of 1948 and Elizabeth let John name him.

"We'll call him Herman," John said, looking somewhat contemplative. "A little memento from our parents' old, distant homeland."

And Elizabeth smiled and nodded in affirmation.

◆ ◆ ◆

When Manny Heimann was in his early twenties, he was accepted to The New York University College of Medicine. He and Gertrude were still living in her brother's spacious house. Her brother clung to them and refused to let them move out.

Manny dove into his studies with great interest and dedication, investing all his energy in his schoolwork. And when the time came to begin his internship in the hospital's various wards alongside his theoretical studies, his fascination and devotion to his new profession reached new heights. His frequent presence in the oncology ward allowed him to meet many patients, some of whom were on their deathbeds. There was nothing he found harder to watch than those emaciated patients, the light in their eyes extinguished, some of them bald, as they drifted down the hospital corridors like pajama-clad ghosts, or lay in their beds, totally exhausted. *What a terrible disease*, he thought every time. *One that squeezes every bit of strength out of the human body, deforms it, irreversibly wounds the spirit and causes great misery to the families as well.*

Manny delved into many of those sad cases and even formed a personal bond with some of the patients. He found out that quite a few of them were Holocaust survivors, which sparked a suspicion in him.

"Dr. Rosenberg," he asked the head of the department, "could it be that the cancer patients—or more accurately, some of them who survived the Holocaust—got sick as a result of medical experiment performed on them during the war in the camps? Or could they possibly have come down with the disease as a result of the terrible years they experienced?"

"Mr. Heimann," the chief physician replied, "that's really an interesting question, and several studies have already looked into it. One of the studies found that Holocaust survivors do face an increased risk of cancer, for example. The main cause is related to the dietary deprivation they suffered. And those who survived that hell and then got sick find it difficult to recover. Even worse, children who experienced the war years are also at higher risk of getting cancer."

"Dr. Rosenberg, I was a young boy during the war," Manny said. "I didn't suffer from food deprivation for long, it's true, but I did suffer from many other things—mostly mental anguish."

Dr. Rosenberg assessed the handsome young man and then said, "Mr. Heimann, that's the reason I chose this profession," saying no more on the subject. After a moment, he added, "It's also been found that the frequency of cancers of all kinds is higher among male Holocaust survivors than among female ones."

"What are the more common varieties of cancer?" Manny asked, becoming increasingly interested.

"Colon cancer and breast cancer are the most common, but lung cancer plagues them mercilessly as well," Dr. Rosenberg specified.

"It's probably mostly related to living in the ghettos and the camps under conditions of severe overcrowding, deprivation, unhealthy hygienic and environmental circumstances, ongoing hunger culminating in malnourishment, cold, exhaustion, and mental stress as well, which I'm sure should not be underestimated," Manny said, his hair standing on end. After all, he was intimately acquainted with all this, and from Dr. Rosenberg's subtle hint, realized that he was as well…

"It's a bit surprising," Dr. Rosenberg continued, "that the survivors managed to get through the horrors, but can't cope with the disease, much less overcome it. It's heartbreaking, but most of them pass away."

"I'm convinced, Dr. Rosenberg, that the twisted medical experiments conducted on people in the camps play a role in the incidence of many illnesses, including the high rates of cancer," Manny opined.

"I'm sure there's something to that," Dr. Rosenberg concluded, then apologized, adding, "Heimann, I'll be happy to continue discussing this topic with you some other time. I've got to rush off to an urgent meeting."

◆ ◆ ◆

Little Herman evoked intense emotions in his father. John loved his son in a way he had never loved any living soul before. He loved him more than he loved himself, devoted himself to raising him, and was thoroughly knowledgeable about every single matter that concerned the boy.

"John, sometimes I feel like you're the boy's mother, rather than me," Elizabeth often said with a smile. "You've really become a sort of *'Yiddishe Momme,'* as they say." When confronted with his startled expression, she added, "Oh, come on, John, it's a pretty common expression. It's hard to even translate it." And she laughed, having no idea that her husband's eyes had widened not because he failed to understand the expression, but for a completely different reason...

It was a sunny Sunday morning, and John took Herman to the playground. He sat on a bench and watched his son, who was thoroughly enjoying the swing in which he was nestled. Suddenly, just a few steps away, John saw a father slap his young son's face. Shaken, he couldn't hold back and he addressed the father. "Excuse me, sir," he said rigidly. "How can you raise your hand to someone so helpless, who also happens to be such a little boy?"

The disconcerted father looked at him, then looked down wordlessly.

How can you abuse a little boy, John thought sadly. And then a violent shiver ran through him. *How could you murder so many children... little children, so many of them babies who had done no wrong? I'm willing to die for my son.* Once again, his whole body shuddered. More than a decade ago, he had—with his own two hands—separated a mother from her son. He had—with his own cruelty—forced her to sacrifice herself for the welfare of her child. And she had. Not only had she sacrificed herself, but she had also fallen victim to his own unjustifiable abuse... The more he thought about it, the more he realized that he would never forgive himself for that. He had indeed crossed a line as thick as a bright scarlet rope.

◆ ◆ ◆

The many hours Manny spent on the oncology ward, and the extensive knowledge he acquired on the subject, partly due to his personal interest in the disease, shaped his final decision regarding an area of specialization. He chose oncology and began a residency at the hospital's oncology ward, spending part of his time hunched over his books, preparing for his medical licensing examination.

PART SEVEN

Chapter 49

John had just turned 60. He'd begun suffering from frequent headaches, which assailed him mostly during the morning hours after he woke up and then eased up over the course of the day. John attributed them to unrestful sleep due to insomnia. Throughout the last year, he had begun to once again be plagued by nightmares, after a number of more tranquil years he had experienced since the day he met Elizabeth. Almost every night he woke up drenched in sweat, still gripped by the brutal images from his most recent dream. Once again, he was a commander at the camp, and every time he saw himself standing at the center of a circle, surrounded by piles of corpses with gaping eyes and mouths emitting toothless laughter. *What happened to bring it all back?* he asked himself again and again.

Even Elizabeth awoke often, feeling his restless shifting in bed.

"John, what's going on? What's bothering you?"

He always answered, "Just a silly dream, Elizabeth. Go back to sleep. Don't bother yourself on my account."

And she would kiss his head, wish him a good night, curl up in his arms, and doze off.

Now, in addition to his headaches, he also started to suffer from nausea. It wasn't too bad and even disappeared on its own, but John, who had been as healthy as an ox for most of his life, was concerned. One night he woke up again, but this time due to a particularly stabbing headache. He rushed to the bathroom. *Only a proper stream of cold water on my head will help*, he thought. As he enjoyed the refreshing cascade of water, he massaged his achy scalp when suddenly his fingers found a strange bump behind his right ear. Touching it didn't cause pain, but the very presence of the lump was a novelty to him— one that stirred up some anxiety. He got out of the shower and realized that although the headache had eased, the lump remained where it was.

John decided not to share the issue with Elizabeth for the time being; he didn't want to worry her. When it came to questions of health and illness, Elizabeth was somewhat hysterical... Like every '*Yiddishe Momma*,' he silently chuckled, as he often did when recalling the expression Elizabeth herself sometimes used.

There was no choice but to discreetly schedule a doctor's appointment.

John headed off to see Dr. Rogers, their family doctor, who was extremely affable and pleasant, as well as highly professional and reliable. After the doctor palpated every part of John's body at length, he gave him several forms for more tests. "No way of knowing yet, John, buddy," he told him. "Once we get all the results back, we can diagnose you and move on from there."

John was summoned to Dr. Rogers's clinic a few days later. "Your blood tests were abnormal, John," Rogers said, poring over the material before him. "And your cranial x-ray also clearly indicates that you have a tumor. The tumor's not good, John. I'm sorry to have to tell you this," the doctor continued, looking directly into John's eyes, "but... you have a malignant cranial tumor."

Dr. Rogers waited for a short time in order to give the patient time to take in the bleak news. Then he said, "John, I have a colleague, an oncologist named Dr. Heimann. He's an exceptional doctor in his field and I highly recommend that you make an appointment with him at the hospital where he works and sees patients. Take all these test results with you as well as my personal referral and medical evaluation, and go see him. He'll know exactly what has to be done."

After a brief silent interlude, John asked, "Doctor, I'd like to know. Am I going to die?"

"I can't provide an exact assessment at this point, John. Dr. Heimann is the one who will give you clearer answers."

"Dr. Heimann… he doesn't happen to be Jewish, does he, Dr. Rogers?" John queried, the question suddenly popping up in his head, as if out of nowhere. The years he had spent under the influence of the Nazi ideology and its colossal hatred of Jews had definitely left their mark on him in some ways that he couldn't entirely shake off.

Dr. Rogers looked at John critically, raising an eyebrow and causing him some discomfort. "No," he finally said. "He's not Jewish or else he's half-Jewish or entirely Jewish. Come on, John. What difference does it make?" he asked, some impatience in his tone. "The main thing is that he's an expert in oncology who can help you."

❖ ❖ ❖

John was on his way to Dr. Manny Heimann's office, a cardboard file containing medical documents tucked under his arm. He had barely managed to hide his inner turmoil from Elizabeth from the moment the test results arrived and he found out that a malignant tumor was growing inside his head. He knew that he would eventually have to share the news with her, but for now he wanted to cope with the matter on his own. When he looked at his watch and saw that he was late for the appointment, scheduled for 5:00 p.m., he quickened his steps. He arrived at the door to Dr. Heimann's office, knocked, and was immediately called to come in. John found himself facing a young, handsome doctor with delicate features, sporting a thick mane of dark hair, wearing a white, unbuttoned lab coat, with his stethoscope's earpieces peeking out of its pocket. *He looks quite unkempt,* John thought to himself, *but also projects a pleasant aura, I must admit.*

After conducting a comprehensive physical examination and leafing through the medical documents, Dr. Heimann asked John to sit down across from him. "Mr. Church," he began, with some hoarseness he tried to fight by clearing his throat. "Pardon me," he said, and then continued. "You do indeed have a malignant brain tumor. I'll be honest with you: It's not an ideal spot for the cancer to settle, although regardless of the spot, the last thing a doctor wants is to find a cancerous tumor. I'll go over all the treatment options with you, and after consulting a neurosurgeon, I can decide what sort of treatment would be best for you."

John's eyes remained fixed on the doctor. Such a young man, and already exhibiting so much confidence. He found it admirable.

"Look, Mr. Church," the doctor explained, "surgery is the usual treatment for most brain tumors, but some growths cannot be removed with surgery, and it appears as if your tumor is the kind that would be dangerous to remove due to its location. If that's the case, we can only do a biopsy so a pathologist can examine tissue from the tumor and determine its composition. This will help me reach a decision regarding the best treatment."

Manny saw a deep flush spread across Church's face. The patient was deeply frightened—of that he was sure. Sympathizing, he continued, "The high-intensity x-rays we refer to as 'radiation treatment' can harm the cancerous cells and keep them from developing. Using radiation, we can also destroy malignant cells that can't be removed through surgery. A special device pinpoints the location of the tumor, and then high-energy rays are sent from various directions around the skull to target the tumor directly. That way, a high dose of radiation reaches the tumor without harming healthy tissue. And then, the final treatment is chemotherapy, a pharmaceutical treatment intended to destroy the cancer cells, usually administered through direct injection into the vein. This treatment is given in cycles; in other words, a cycle of treatment, followed by a cycle of recuperation and another cycle of treatment followed by recovery, for as long as it takes. You won't have to be hospitalized for this, unless there's no other choice. I want you to know, Mr. Church, that we will perform every possible treatment to bring about a cure, but again, I want to be entirely honest with you—the chances are 50-50, as the expression goes, and we'll know more the further we get into the treatment."

Manny looked into Church's eyes, which had become two metallic slits, and noticed that a muscle in his face was quivering. Once again, the scarlet birthmark in the shape of a distorted heart was revealed to him, and his deep suspicion regarding his patient's true identity threatened his composure. Usually, he was full of empathy for patients when they heard news that was far from hopeful, but this time the patient's tortured face could not evoke the proper compassion within him. Manny felt that he was talking to him in a professional, attentive manner, while also speaking mechanically, without an iota of emotion.

"*Herr Doktor,* uhm... Dr. Heimann," Church stammered, "I asked Dr. Rogers this question and he said only you could answer it. How much time do I have left? I know that in most cases, brain cancer is fatal, *nicht wahr?* Um... isn't that so?"

The emerging foreign accent and the occasional word in German further convinced Manny of Church's original identity and he was intensely eager for the meeting to come to an end. He felt that he was on the verge of truly losing control.

"Herr Church, uhm... Mr. Church," Manny could not refrain from saying, "we can't know for certain for now. As I've told you, we'll only be able to tell after treatment. Please come see me in two days. In the meantime, I'll consult with my colleague about you, as I explained earlier, and then I can provide you with all the paperwork you need to begin treatment here at the hospital. I'll personally supervise all the proceedings."

"The doctor speaks German?" John asked mechanically as he heard Dr. Heimann pronounce the word *"herr."*

Manny directed a meaningful look at Church and replied, "Yes, a little. It's my mother tongue," saying no more.

"Oh, mine as well," John said, distracted, then rose and extended his hand. "I'm sure I'm in good hands, doctor, and I thank you for your patience. See you in two days."

Manny was left alone in the room. The sigh rising from his chest was so heavy that he had to hold on to the sides of the desk with an intensity that made his knuckles go white. A moment ago, the Angel of Death himself had been sitting across from him, the one who was now confronting his own death, the one who had taken so many lives, including those of the people dearest to him.

Manny was now certain, beyond any doubt, that John Church was indeed the one and only Johan Kirche. Even the name he had chosen for himself resembled his real name: "Johan" had become "John," and "Kirche," which meant "church" in German, was now "Church." *How sophisticated—new growth without cutting down the roots. Ah...* Manny chuckled to himself. *While I changed my name to commemorate both my parents and blur the painful memories somewhat, that damned Nazi changed his name and without a doubt created a false identity for himself out of necessity, forced to bury who he really was.*

Out of all the people in the world, it has to be the demonic killer who turned my entire world upside down when I was eight years old who's now knocking on my door and seeking medical assistance from me!

It was simply inconceivable. *It really is a small world*, Manny thought, *so small that it can't hide, in all its nooks and crannies, the villains who live in it.* He was experiencing such overwhelming emotional turmoil that he needed to retreat into himself and just think, remembering all that he and his family had endured and marveling once again at all the surreal wonders of the world. Luckily, Church was his last patient that day.

Manny knew that for the time being, he wouldn't share what was happening with anyone at all—including Gertrude, who might have been the only other person to be truly affected by these astonishing developments.

❖ ❖ ❖

Two days later, Church returned to Dr. Heimann's office. The doctor handed him all the paperwork he would need to begin treatment. "Mr. Church, as I've already told you, we'll treat you here in the oncology department. After consulting the neurosurgeon, we decided together that following a biopsy of the tumor, we'll begin chemotherapy, and reconsider once we've completed the first cycle of treatment. Mr. Church, I should prepare you for the fact that chemotherapy usually induces some side effects. This is inevitable. After all, the body is injected with a variety of chemicals that might cause nausea, general weakness, some weight loss due to a lack of appetite, as well as, unfortunately, hair loss. But after the treatment, things generally return to normal," he concluded encouragingly.

Unconsciously, John ran his hand through his thick mane. He could already envision himself—a bald man, emaciated, with an extinguished look. He was absolutely astounded.

"Mr. Church," the doctor continued, interrupting his thoughts, "please go to the main office and take care of the paperwork for the ward. I'll handle the medical proceedings and, of course, be directly in touch with you."

John left the doctor's office with a heavy heart. How long could he put off telling Elizabeth, as well as Herman, about his condition? He felt that lately, Elizabeth's eyes had been appraising him, as if she expected some sort of announcement from him. She suspected something but didn't nag, which he greatly appreciated. As far as he was concerned, he would prefer not to say anything to anyone, especially not to her and his son. But as his body was expected to change in the near future, he would simply have no choice. He just didn't know how he would deal with her reaction to what he was about to tell her. After all, for years now, he had had a hard time coping with any sort of excessive emotion.

◆ ◆ ◆

Manny knew that he was going to do all he could even for John Church, his new patient. Church would benefit from all his medical skills, but, in contrast to his usual empathy toward his ailing patients, his sensitivity regarding John Church would be negligible indeed. After all, if he weren't a doctor, he would consider killing him. He had every right to kill the person responsible for killing his family... to avenge his parents, his grandfather and grandmother, and all the Jews who were lost, as well as the non-Jews who had suffered. In Manny's eyes, John Church, who to him would forever remain Johan Kirche, would always represent the epitome of evil and cruelty, even if in the second half of his life he appeared to be a completely different person, a dedicated family man, a loving husband, and a devoted father.

It would be so easy to bring about this patient's death, Manny thought. *Injecting another substance into the chemotherapy IV would do the trick, oh so quietly... and peacefully...* Manny was shocked by his own thoughts. *But I'm sinking to the level of the Nazi murderers if I can even contemplate something so horrific—using my medical knowledge in order to intentionally kill someone. It's not my job to take another's life, even if my reason is justified—even highly justified.*

After all, he won't live for much longer anyway, Manny told himself repeatedly. *The hand of justice will settle the score with that killer. It's not only wretched Holocaust survivors who get cancer. The strong, the tough, and the healthy who caused the Holocaust and are responsible for so much death are not eternally invulnerable, nor are they immune to this cruel disease.*

⚜ Chapter 50 ⚜

John was among a group of four cancer patients receiving similar treatment by intravenous injection. And like any gathering revolving around a shared subject, a conversation developed between the patients, and it didn't deal solely with the accursed disease. Each of them brought up topics as they saw fit, but ultimately they always resumed discussing the purpose of their visits to the oncology ward.

A new patient joined the group. He was around John's age and looked particularly tormented. He was seeking someone to lend an ear and found that person in John, of all people. Soon John's new friend also began to share the story of his life with him.

"I'm certain, my friend," Joseph Mandelbaum said to John, "that the years I spent in Auschwitz brought this curse upon me. I also know that with all due respect to the treatment, my body won't be able to stand it. For years now, I've been as vulnerable as a newborn baby, and the cancer, which apparently sensed it, came and settled on me like a *vilde chaye*, like... like some vicious animal."

John once again recalled the old Johan, and his face paled. Just the mention of those years and the horror they entailed, along with the German-Yiddish words, was enough to bring up a maelstrom of turbulent emotions within him. He remained silent, waiting to see where the story was heading.

"All those horrific medical experiments we went through back there in Auschwitz—it's a miracle we even survived. But we weren't left unharmed. *Sie sehen?* Oh, I'm sorry, you see? It's already been 18 years since the war ended, and there are still new casualties. I know plenty of Holocaust survivors who never recovered from everything they went through back then, and are still dealing with the physical damage and the emotional damage."

Johan felt as if he was about to throw up. He no longer knew if he felt sick because of the physical injection or because of the conversation with Mandelbaum. He bowed his head.

"I'm sorry to burden you like that," Mandelbaum said. "I see you're having a hard time with the treatment. I'm also starting to feel nauseous."

Johan was silent. He closed his eyes, unable to escape the images running through his head, which now felt like such a heavy burden. He knew exactly what Mandelbaum was talking about. After all, two of the cabins at Dachau also served for medical experiments masquerading as a clinic. Such a variety of experiments that maybe even the doctors themselves no longer truly knew the point of—all on behalf of the Germany Army. The pitiful prisoners had become true human lab rats. He remembered how many of the prisoners passed away in great suffering as a result of all that experimental horror, and believed that those who survived were probably permanently disabled.

The last thing John wanted to think about now was that terrible time. He never wanted to think of it, but this was currently more true than ever. He tended to agree with Mandelbaum, as he was certain that many of the survivors who had undergone such experimental abuse were indeed still paying the price in sickness and suffering.

◆ ◆ ◆

Every time Manny was in contact with John throughout the treatment, he was more firmly convinced that he was simply concealing information about a Nazi war criminal who was walking around free, living an ordinary life just like anyone else. He felt a fierce desire to reveal his true identity to John, but every time he managed to tuck it away in some hidden corner. After all, Manny found himself thinking again and again, *What would be the point?* So John would know, and perhaps react, and perhaps try to escape, although in his current condition, that would be quite stupid. Manny decided that only one thing would help him continue coping with the situation—sharing it with Gertrude.

"Gertrude, I have to, simply have to share something with you," he told her that evening, an extremely tense expression on his face. "I've debated for quite a while whether to tell you or not, and I've finally decided I just can't keep it to myself any longer."

Gertrude examined Manny's face, her eyes reflecting her curiosity. She kept quiet, waiting patiently for him to continue.

"Gertrude, a few weeks ago, a man of 60 or so, suffering from a malignant cranial tumor, came to my office, calling himself John Church. When I examined him, I noticed a birthmark in the shape of a distorted heart on the left side of his neck. The color of his eyes was distinct, too—blue-gray. He has prominent cheekbones and a dimple in his chin."

He saw Gertrude's eyes gape in amazement. "Gertrude, he suddenly blurted out '*nicht wahr*,' and then quickly added 'isn't that right,' and when I addressed him as 'Herr Church,' he asked if I speak German and added that it was his mother tongue."

Gertrude began to shiver. She still hadn't said a word. She felt incapable of doing so.

"Manny, that's impossible," she finally blurted out. "Simply impossible. Don't tell me it's Johan Kirche—anything but that."

"It's him, Gertrude, there's no doubt about it. Doesn't the name 'John Church' somehow remind you of the name 'Johan Kirche'? As if he's replaced his German name with its English translation. I remember that when I was a kid I told you I would never ever forget Johan Kirche's face—remember? Back then, the last thing I could ever imagine was that one day my father's murderer and the person responsible for my mother's death would be my patient. The world is so strange sometimes, Gertrude, so strange and amazing. And now I have to treat his cancer—after all, he's my patient."

"And what about him, does he know who you are?" Gertrude whispered. "Did you tell him?"

"No way. I don't want to tell him, either. What would I get out of it? Nothing. Today he's a married man, Gertrude, and he has a 15-year-old son, just like I was when that damn war ended. He's started a proper family here in America—which I'm sure he entered using forged documents. He managed to escape under everyone's nose and leave his entire past behind him. He—the monster that cut short the lives of entire families—started a family of his own, while I always say that I don't want a family of my own, due to the terrible fear that they'll suffer some kind of harm at some point. It seems like this nightmare will haunt me my whole life."

"Manny, since you've already told me all this because you had to share it with me, I want to share something with you too," Gertrude said. "Manny, Sigmund and I—in light of everything that happened—often thought that Johan Kirche was involved in your grandmother's murder, too. All of the events happened in such quick succession, and were so insane, that we couldn't help but think that." She saw Manny's face change colors. She didn't regret telling him since, despite her understanding of the professional medical code of ethics that was so important to Manny, she found it hard to accept the fact that he was treating Johan Kirche with the same dedication that he gave to all his other patients.

Manny was silent. If Johan had indeed been involved in his grandmother's death, it was simply too much. He then recovered a bit and quietly asked, "What could Johan possibly have had against my grandmother? A poor, elderly woman—how could she have harmed him?"

"Apparently he didn't want her to stand in his way. He didn't want anyone to stand in his way. I know that in some regards, Johan was angry at Oma for welcoming your Jewish father with open arms rather than actively encouraging Ilse to go back to him. That's what your mother told me at the time."

"You two were really close, you and Mama. Right, Gertrude? She must have found a kindred spirit in you, someone that she could tell almost everything."

"I'm sorry, Manny, I needed some closure regarding all of that. It simply seemed crazy to me that you, out of all the doctors in the world, would be treating that evil Nazi. Apparently he really did manage to escape from Germany in time, and if it weren't for you and your sharp eye, no one would know who John Church really was. And you're right. I've never loved any other friend the way I loved your mother."

"You know, I could have easily killed him, Gertrude," Manny said, his voice growing hoarse. "I could have, although obviously I'd never do anything like that. I don't want to be considered a criminal, least of all by myself. I believe that Johan Kirche was sent to me in particular so that I can put myself to the test, and it's a very hard test, I have to admit."

Gertrude merely nodded. It was very difficult for her to hear what Manny was telling her.

"You know, Gertrude," he suddenly added, "I often think about the radical change that Johan has gone through—suddenly transforming from a monster into someone pleasant, gentle, polite, and human. That extreme gap between who he used to be and who he became keeps eating away at me, and beyond that, constantly troubling me. I'm so curious to know when the fracture took place that pushed Johan out of his morass of cruelty and sub-humanity, and caused him to change the way he did. It could be the basis for a medical study," he chuckled while his face remained solemn. "I'm sure plenty of psychologists and psychiatrists would love to delve into the depths of his mind in order to understand the brain function of a man who, at a certain period in his life, was a cruel beast and afterwards shed that skin and resumed being human. I wonder at what point a person realizes he's involved in perpetrating an atrocity. What is he willing to forgive himself for, and at what point, if ever, does he start to draw a line in the sand that he can't cross?"

"Manny, I'm not a doctor, not a psychologist or a psychiatrist," Gertrude said, "but I'm certain that the Nazis' evil was pathological. They were sick in the head, all of them, with no exceptions, if they could take part in that criminal apparatus of Hitler's regime."

"Evil might not have a pathology, but sometimes it does have a government. Do you know, Gertrude, that most of the Nazi leaders were said to be exemplary family men? How can you process something like that? On the one hand, they were good husbands and devoted fathers, but on the other, they indiscriminately and ruthlessly slaughtered men, women, and children.None of the explanations posited by studies that try to get to the root of the matter can help me even begin to understand it," Manny said.

"They all joined forces," Gertrude continued, "and were obedient to a fault, perfectly meticulous and organized, as well as extremely creative, blatantly impudent, touting their own virtue, and together they brought devastation to millions throughout the world. It's true, Manny, no study will ever allow the human mind to grasp it, and beyond that, as you said, to even begin to understand it."

"I completely agree with you," Manny replied, "and now that we're talking about it," he solemnly added, "I'm starting to feel as if I'm concealing information about an escaped Nazi criminal by keeping all this to myself instead of exposing him to the proper authorities."

✧ Chapter 51 ✧

When John's hair fell out and his body grew increasingly gaunt, he was forced to tell Elizabeth and Herman about his disease. And, as he had expected, their grief was terrible, their heartbreak nearly unbearable. John felt that he didn't have much time left. Cancer had already wreaked havoc in him, despite the treatment. It was a tenacious cancer, apparently not truly intimidated by the chemical substances seeking to destroy it.

The settling of scores with the Nazi monster came to John in the form of cancer. It had reached him as well, although he was far from his German homeland. And he decided to enact his own ending to the terminal process. He didn't want to keep on suffering, knowing that more torturous and many more painful days still awaited him. When he sneaked a glance in the mirror and saw his own reflection, he was horrified every single time. In its current form, his figure truly resembled those people from back then. Now he looked just like them—the bruised, tormented prisoners of the camp—and he was suffering, maybe suffering even more than they had...

♦ ♦ ♦

Manny was on his way to meet an Israeli Mossad agent in order to provide him with information about an escaped Nazi war criminal. Although he knew Johan Kirche's time was running out, he decided to report him. He simply felt it was his duty to do so. Even if Church died right in their hands, the important thing was that the Mossad's records would reflect that another

Nazi criminal had been captured, although the hand of fate had caught up with him first...

◆ ◆ ◆

John opened the drawer of the dresser in his bedroom. His hand fumbled frantically for the gun. Suddenly, his fingers encountered a small, velvety object resting next to the weapon. He retrieved the gun, followed by the plush object. Before his eyes lay a blue jewelry box, its weave frayed. He stroked it and examined it from all directions, his curiosity growing. He had never seen it before. His fingers grasped the top of the box and pried it wide open. Inside, on a soft, golden surface, lay a small gold Star of David pendant. His hand trembling, John picked up the delicate piece of jewelry, which glittered in front of his eyes. The golden interior of the box displayed an engraving in small blue letters:

"*To our dear Elizabeth on her Bat Mitzvah, with love from Mother and Father, 1930.*"

John's scrawny legs trembled. He had to sit down on the edge of the bed. His eyes bounced between the small blue letters and the symbolic pendant again and again. He returned the Star of David to its place, closed the velvety box and put it on the bed. His legs faltering, he stood up again, picked up the gun and thrust its metal barrel into his mouth.

A moment before he pulled the trigger, he remembered the first time he had shot people to death—the Night of the Long Knives—and envisioned the scattered body parts and the bloodstains splattered all over the wall.

THE END